TENPENNY ZEN

a novel of sex, cults, and an
interdimensional henge contraption

Rune Skelley

You always did know who I was talking to.

The Divided Man Series

Book One: Miss Brandymoon's Device
Book Two: Tenpenny Zen
Book Three: Elsewhere's Twin

CONTENTS

Chapter One

NICE TOWN

Control subject EE may be exhibiting the traits we hoped to see in Group Sigma. Work continues toward establishing a reliable set of tests and measures for subject EE, but several measures are already in place, including surveillance gear in the school and the house.
        Project Lullaby archives, 1962

JUNE 1973

Strapped down on her back on a black slab, Ester Elizabeth Finch felt like the dead frog from last year's biology class. At least this year she'd be taking chemistry. Plus she'd turn 18 in November and her dad could no longer drag her to this asinine research program.

At first today seemed like the same familiar nonsense. Friendly but vaguely creepy men in white coats wanting her to guess what playing cards they held, make the marble roll, tell them what color light was shining on her hand within a box. Hypnotizing her and interviewing her about weird stuff she didn't know while a lie-detector ran off its record of the answers she made up.

But then they wanted to give her a physical. A complete physical.

They apologized that no female nurses had clearance to examine her. When the doctor left, she couldn't find her clothes. She was still wearing the stupid hospital gown.

Next they told her they needed a scan. It was a very sensitive machine. Any little movement would mess it up, so they needed to strap her down. They attached electrodes to her temples and forehead. It had now been over 15 minutes since any of them said a word to her. About half a dozen very creepy men in white coats drifted around the chamber, looking at the consoles and conferring excitedly, green-faced in the glow of their data screens. Ester caught isolated fragments of their speech.

"…resolution is awful compared to x-rays, but it images soft tissue…"

"Did you calibrate this scope?"

"…dripping serotonin today?"

"No. The synthetic."

"…got it on-scale now. Jesus."

"Hold off on that drip. We're not…"

"…that can't be right…"

"But the instruments agree. It must be."

"Dial back another couple pegs. The synth has quite a kick."

One of the men pushed an IV stand over to Ester's left, and dabbed her arm with a cold swab before inserting the needle. He twisted the valve to start the drip, tossed a heartless little grin down at her, and strode off.

All the chatter ceased abruptly as a line of tiny green spiders began streaming down the IV tube and into Ester's veins. Her chest constricted. She couldn't scream.

The arachnids scurried to her brain and started flipping switches, turning on all the lights, cranking the volume up to max.

Regaining partial control of her breathing, Ester told herself the spiders were a hallucination. She rolled her eyes to the clear bag at the top of the stand. No bugs inside it.

They kept coming anyway. Columns of them converged through the air, meeting at the IV stand and flowing into her. She traced them to their source, saw them emerging from the foreheads of the researchers and from the equipment. Everything in this place seethed with them.

The men sat motionless, unblinking eyes riveted to their monitors. Ester craned her head for a better view. She discovered she could sit up and lurched off the slab. No one said anything or glanced in her direction. Looking back, she saw herself strapped down with her mouth agape and green eyes bulging. Her pupils were pinholes.

She backed up a step. Spiders continued to swarm the body there on the slab, unaware she had left.

Had the drugs killed her? Ester doubted it. This must be an out-of-body experience. No need to worry about the hallucinatory army spiders until she went back.

She turned away. Smooth panels of brushed steel confronted her, and she spun around to find herself inside an elevator, albeit one with no controls or music. Facing the doors, she fidgeted until they slid apart.

In the room she entered, a small knot of Top Brass crowded around a television screen. She edged up behind them to see what they were watching, although the television itself was more intriguing than the program. Dark blond hair covered the top and sides, having been combed back to reveal the oval screen where missiles and tanks paraded through Red Square.

Ester tried to put her hands in her pockets, but the flimsy gown had none. She tugged on the hem of the barely adequate garment, holding it closed in the back. As she shifted her weight from foot to foot, the channel changed several times in pace to her swaying motion. Sometimes a map would come up, with toy submarines and planes bearing hammer-and-sickle pennants. Sometimes it was hallways, where uniformed people drifted in gray silence. Sometimes random explosions.

Ester watched for a few moments. She snuck around behind the weird television and looked into her own blank eyes again.

She gasped, choked, coughed, and couldn't wipe her mouth with the back of her hand because she was strapped down. Blurry darkness brightened and cleared. The spiders were gone.

Two of the white-coats popped up, one peeling back her eyelid with his thumb to blind her with a penlight, the other squeezing her forearm and staring at his watch. The rest of them laughed and praised their experiment's success.

They turned her loose and returned her clothing without asking how she felt. Her father asked, but she didn't say anything. The drive home was silent. Ester wondered how much he knew.

***   ***   ***

14 MONTHS LATER - AUGUST 1974

This is a nice town, Ester thought. If I stay here any length of time, I'll have to get some shoes.

She looked at her grimy, grass-stained feet and blinked several times. When, exactly, had she ceased wearing shoes? Sometime east of Denver, but west of St. Louis. There'd been something about 'no more shoes 'til we bathe in the cool, clean Atlantic.' Who had she made that particular pact with? The three girls in the mint green VW Beetle certainly had an endless supply of drugs and a predilection for nudity. Ester almost thought she could remember the one with the long brown braids tossing sandals and tennis shoes one by one out the window as they sped across the prairies. A zen twist on Johnny Appleseed.

"As some of you know, Feather has left. She and baby Journey will join Drum in Nova Scotia. They welcome any of us who wish to visit or move in with them. This leaves an empty room at Beacon and Ember's house..."

This guy talking was obviously in charge of the unusual tribe Ester now found herself in the middle of. Easily ten years older than anyone else, he had a gruff, commanding voice at odds with his appearance. He wore all black and looked like a misunderstood intellectual loner, not a hippie leader. Though he did have the hair. His dark beard and mustache were full and streaked with gray, blending into his shoulder-length hair. He continued talking about people Ester didn't know, so she didn't pay much attention. She plucked a strand of grass and wrapped it around her finger, watching as the skin went white. She picked three more strands and began to braid them as she surreptitiously glanced at the hippies around her.

They were all riveted on their leader.

It was more than a little paranoid to assume any of these people were working for the military, searching for her, acting as spies for Nixon, or now Ford. First of all, aside from their leader, they didn't seem terribly bright. Second, they were all smoking dope. Right now. So even if they were spies, they weren't very alert. Probably dropouts from the local university.

She felt uncomfortable when anyone paid too much attention to her. Ester noticed for the first time just how dirty her clothes were. The hem of her long, calico skirt was nearly black, her blouse the color of a coffee stain. Nothing in her pillowcase was any cleaner.

Trying to blend in with the counterculture could be taken too far. Using henna to make herself a redhead, calling herself Liz, and wearing Indian-print skirts and batik dresses gave her a new persona designed to make herself invisible to her father and his military cohorts. But that didn't mean she had to be a slob. Time to clean up. It had been over a year since she'd run away from home and the unacceptable experimentation, and she'd not seen any signs of pursuit. Besides, she was 18 now. They couldn't do anything to her without her consent, right?

Ester suddenly wanted a shower.

Maybe after dinner she'd find an unoccupied bathroom in the enormous old, green boarding house this commune was squatting in. It needed new paint, but the windows were all intact. Chances were good they had running water.

"I've heard from the landlord," the leader said. Maybe they weren't squatters after all. "He tells me he has decided to sell the property."

The small, laid-back crowd around Ester moaned and the speaker raised his hands to calm them.

"He already has a buyer." The speaker paused, and his electric blue eyes skittered over them. His gaze rested on Ester for several seconds before resuming its fitful travels. Brr. "That buyer is us."

Excited buzzing erupted all around Ester while she reassessed her impressions of this crowd and their enigmatic leader. The man strode back and forth on the grass in front of the 20 or so hippies, and Ester noticed that he went barefoot like everyone else.

He continued, "After dinner we can discuss the details."

Finally! Ester thought. To the food! It was the compelling factor in her decision to come to this place with her new acquaintance who called himself Beacon. Free food.

"But before we eat," the man continued.

Oh, damn. A prayer right?

"Beacon has brought us a new friend this evening."

Oh damn!

All eyes turned expectantly to Beacon and Ester. Beacon grinned and stood, his ample belly blocking Ester from many inquiring eyes.

"Hey guys. This is Liz. She's new in town and she looked hungry. You all know how good my vegetarian chili is," he patted his stomach to appreciative chuckles, "so I brought her along tonight."

He sat and motioned for Ester to stand, which she did reluctantly, after dropping a small handful of grass braids. What did they expect her to say?

"Hi."

Various murmured greetings came from the upturned, smiling faces.

She smoothed her hands over her hair, tucking the stray locks behind her ears.

"Like Beacon said, I'm Liz," Ester said. "I just sort of blew into town. I've been traveling for a while and thought Webster might be a good place to take a break, do my laundry."

Her audience found that humorous enough.

"Well, Liz-Who-Just-Blew-Into-Town," said the leader, "I'm Severin

Tenpenny. On behalf of the Threshold Elsewhere Following, I welcome you."

*** *** ***

Alone under the slanting rafters of the attic, Severin turned his mind to the new friend Beacon brought along to dinner. A beautiful young lady, and far older than her years. Petite but not frail. Liz, she called herself. She said she just arrived in Webster, and it was easy to believe. The road clung to her, called to her.

Everything else about her was a mystery.

She must stay, that much Severin knew.

The attic was Severin's domain. He spent much of his time up here, alone, seeking answers to the questions no one else thought to ask. Today those questions would be about Liz, and the answers would come to him from the Elsewhere.

The portal stood in one murky corner of the attic. It looked like an old door propped atop two sawhorses and draped with a dust sheet.

In actuality his table was so much more.

Severin regarded the immaculate white linen. Beneath it he could discover objects useful in unraveling whatever question he faced at the moment. He found them by touch, like a tangible form of automatic writing. These items came from deeper in the universe than matter and energy. From the Elsewhere, a place where thought and meaning were palpable.

The treasures were only his for a short time before they slipped away, returning to the Elsewhere, so as a gesture of respect he always placed them back under the sheet before they expired.

Thinking about Liz, he raised the edge of the sheet with his right hand and extended his left underneath. A mild tingle, a slight warmth always caressed his palm as he quested. Soon, on the rough surface of the old door, he encountered a smooth, flexible object. He closed his fingers around it and drew it out.

A length of plastic tubing trailed behind, the end slithering out to swing almost to the floor. It was an IV bag. Severin studied it and the military decorations and insignia it contained. Frowning, he memorized details about the tiny ribbons so he might look up their significance, which branch of the service would issue them, what rank they might indicate. Nodding to himself, he laid the bag back on the table and fed the tube under the sheet as well, taking care not to stick himself on the needle.

As he patted the empty spot under the sheet where he'd set the bag, he detected an unusual smoothness under his fingertips and slid out a playing card. One side was blank, while the other bore a red bull's-eye. He smiled at this and replaced it. That he hadn't managed to pull the whole set, including the star, the X, and the three wavy lines, disappointed him.

A picture of Liz's past began to form in his mind.

Severin reached under the sheet again. This time he couldn't make any guess as to what his hand brushed against, and even as he picked it up he didn't understand it. Something unevenly shaped, wrapped in a poorly fitting cover.

He could readily identify the ladies' leather glove once he pulled it out where he could see it, and inside was something round. It rattled. Severin dropped the sheet so he could manipulate his curious find with both hands. Coaxing the leather and the fur lining aside he revealed a silvery circle showing a pattern of small holes. He held its rim with thumb and forefinger, tugging the glove's middle finger with the other hand to slip it off. A salt shaker. The glass body held one die. Severin shook it a few times to see what numbers would come up. Twos, fours, and sixes were all he could get. *Make that one loaded die.*

Severin chuckled humorlessly. Mockery from the Elsewhere? What could all this symbolize about Liz? Shaking his head, he wrapped the salt shaker in the glove and consigned the bundle back to his table. As he lowered the sheet, it fell smooth and flat across the door without a trace that any other object had ever been present under it.

After six years in the attic, Severin still didn't know all the secrets of his table. It had been here before him, along with uncounted boxes of abandoned junk. It was in fact the thing that drew him to the house. Responding to its mysterious pull, he encountered a disordered rabble of hippies squatting in their dilapidated mansion and scratching a pitiful existence out of the dirt in the back yard. They made him welcome and he took up residence on the unfinished top floor in order to study the portal. He'd planned to stay just long enough to work out how to move it to a less squalid locale, but concluded the house sat at a mystical junction. Anyplace else the table would be merely two sawhorses, an old door, and a sheet.

Thus he found himself linked to the house and therefore its occupants. Soon they got in the habit of asking his opinion or approval for every insignificant thing, distractions he greatly resented. It turned out to be for the best, because they listened to him when, eight months into his tenure, the house was in danger of being condemned. To save his font of otherworldly knowledge, he had to help them save their home.

The episode cemented him as their leader, something he never wanted. But he'd quickly learned to find the small pleasures in having followers, how to be the type of inscrutable paternal force these poor nature-children yearned to obey.

Now another adept had been drawn to this house.

A glance out the window confirmed she was in the garden, helping with the weeding as he'd seen her do yesterday. Admirable that she lent her back to their work so willingly. She moved among the Following so comfortably it was hard to believe she'd only been at the bungalow with Beacon and Ember for two days. Unless you understood that she had no intention of staying, her ease that of a polite guest.

He watched her excuse herself from the agriculture detail and head toward the house. It was time for their appointment. Such punctuality didn't fit the hippie persona she tried to project.

Severin walked over to his hammock and settled into it lotus-style, shut his eyes, and contemplated Liz. Such a mystery. Severin smiled, envisioning her progress toward their meeting. Liz would wash up and ask the way to the attic. Then ascend the main staircase, her footsteps like a cat's, tentative and light. Severin could see her delicate frame poised for flight even as curiosity propelled her onward and upward toward his lair. At the third floor she would have to locate the smaller stairs leading to the attic, hidden behind one of several doors. Severin heard her open it. She was padding up his stairs in total silence. The fifth step, the eighth, the tenth, peering into the room...

"Hello," Severin said, opening his eyes. Liz stood on the top step and regarded him sidelong, seemingly unsure what to do with her hands. She took in the attic's contents, flicking her eyes toward the shadowy corners and never quite looking directly at Severin. He smiled slightly with the left side of his mouth at the thought of how he must appear to her, levitating cross-legged between the two naked bulbs that struggled to illuminate his domain — a dark, ragged Buddha casting two shadows.

"Come in, please." He disengaged one foot from his meditative posture and exited the hammock with practiced grace. As Liz nodded and stepped fully into the room, Severin strolled to a nook in the exposed wooden framing where several bottles and a few clean glasses resided. "Some wine?"

Striking a more confident note, she made eye contact to say, "Sure, thanks."

"You don't have to worry. I'm not up to anything."

"Who's worried?" she smirked.

More leopard than house cat, perhaps, Severin mused.

"Have a seat." He handed her a glass of red. "And tell me why you think it is I asked you here."

Liz placed her drink on an ottoman, and dragged a beanbag nearer before settling into it sidesaddle. "You want me to join up," she stated flatly, placing her right elbow on the ottoman and resting her chin on her knuckles. She hadn't taken a sip of the wine.

Severin tipped his glass, took a healthy swallow. "Yes. Why?"

Liz's brow furrowed. "You want everybody to join up, don't you?"

"Not at all."

She watched him take another sip, weighing her words. "Well, just the hippies then." She glanced down, looked back up, and spoke more rapidly. "And I'm very grateful for the food and shelter. I don't want you to think I'm a freeloader, I came—"

"I saw. Thank you. But we do not ask anything as payment for our kindness."

"Just my brain, I suppose," she muttered, looking toward the opposite end of the attic. Severin knew, without glancing away, what she was studying. His table was a deceptively uninteresting piece of furniture. He had expected Liz to be drawn to it.

Severin came over and sat on the floor next to her. He set down his drink and steepled his fingers, staring hard at her face. She didn't back down, but tension showed in her neck and arms. He smiled with the corner of his mouth again, resuming their conversation. "Actually, your brain appeals to me quite a lot. More so because nobody controls it except you. Your eyes are open."

She returned his stare more fiercely. "They have to be, you know?" Those bright green eyes darted down, and she began smoothing her skirt, examining its folds and the embroidered hem.

A subtle vertigo crept through Severin, emanating from Liz. When she looked back at Severin, her fingers kept plucking at the material and weaving it between themselves. Severin felt as if the room were suspended from an enormous rubber band.

"Sorry," she continued, "I'm no good at taking compliments."

Severin forced his breathing to stay controlled, glanced at his wine to see if it felt the motion. "On the contrary. I think you esteem them precisely their worth."

The young lady wasn't really shaking the house, she was shaking the Elsewhere. Severin could feel the fluctuations because of his own innate affinity. She had to be wedged in the Threshold, half in the ordinary world and half Elsewhere. How could such a thing happen? The implications swarmed Severin's imagination. A living, breathing connection between worlds! The table was a parlor trick by comparison.

Liz's fingers quieted as she took the tiniest sip of her wine, then spoke into the glass. "So why do you want me to join?" The room's pulsations ceased at the same moment as her fidgeting.

She had no idea. Her power was mysterious to him, a complete secret from herself. If she didn't stay, he'd never get the chance to learn how her link to the Elsewhere operated, but that was hardly what she needed to hear right now. Severin smiled with both sides of his mouth, but it dropped as he drew a breath to speak. "Your name isn't Elizabeth." He studied her response. Her eyes locked onto his over the rim of her glass, drilling into him while she tipped the wine back to flow over her lips.

She lowered the glass to her lap. A potential weapon, kept readily at hand. "Why do you say that?"

He sipped his wine before answering. "Because it's true. I pride myself on my honesty."

"What is my name, then?"

He tossed off the remainder of the drink and stood. "I can't tell you today." She was curious, good.

"And you can't tell me why you want me to join your followers, either."

Severin chuckled. "They aren't my followers. We're the Threshold Elsewhere Following. And I could tell you, but I want to hear you tell me instead, if you can." The subtle challenge in his voice drew a raised eyebrow.

She placed her glass on the ottoman. "Because my name isn't Elizabeth?"

"Partly."

"Because I have no place else to go?"

"That is why we took you in, and why you are free to stay on. But we want you to truly join the Following."

Liz shut her eyes and drew her knees up to her chest. Her bare toes pattered on the ancient floorboards, running for their lives as she mulled something uncomfortable. Severin watched her nostrils flare, felt energy splashing over him with each tap of her feet. Her eyes snapped open and she planted her feet. Ripples faded rapidly as she announced, "I could tell you why you want me to join, but that's what you want. Me telling you my story. That's your game, isn't it?"

It was Severin's turn to weigh words. "Fair enough." He replaced his glass on the improvised shelf before continuing. "You ran away, not realizing you were going toward anything, just running away, as far as possible."

Liz drawled, "Help, I'm being held prisoner in a fortune cookie factory..."

"You changed your name so they wouldn't find you — doctors, scientists," he went on. She lowered her head. No sarcastic comeback.

Severin said urgently, "I want to help you, because you can help me." Trembling, she stared at his feet. He crouched and touched her shoulder, and she turned her red face to him.

"It'll start making sense. Isn't that reason enough?"

She straightened, pulling away from his hand. "I don't know how you know—"

"I'll show you."

"—but it's one less reason to trust you. I'm leaving."

"Don't."

Liz stood, glaring down at him. He rose, and despite the few inches height advantage he possessed it seemed she towered as she demanded, "Do you work for them? Or did my father send you?"

"You came to us."

"Then how do you know this stuff?"

"You needed to be convinced, and now you're freaking out. It'll pass."

"No it won't!"

"Stay one more night. I'll show you tomorrow."

"Show me now." She shook. Wine spilled from her half-empty glass.

"Tomorrow. Then I'll be able to tell you your name and you'll be able to see what I must show you. For that to happen, you must make a choice. You must choose to remain, at least for another day. You must choose to see."

Severin knew she wanted to protest that she chose to see now, dammit. She wanted to threaten to leave. Running away was no big deal to her. Severin waited, while the equally powerful desires to say different things held her speechless long enough to realize nobody was making her stay. That it didn't make sense to think Severin and the Following were part of a plot. That she was curious, house cat or leopard, and she wanted to stay long enough to see what he had in store for her tomorrow.

She tossed off the remainder of her wine, handed the glass roughly to Severin, and stormed down the stairs without a word.

***   ***   ***

Ester suspected that Beacon's vegetarian lasagna contained at least one herb not found in every kitchen. Beacon's wife, Ember, poured cheap red wine from the second bottle of the evening into their glasses and sat at the tiny round table again.

"Severin wants to tie me up," Ester said, looking from her hostess to her host and back again.

Beacon said, "He tied me up."

"He ties everyone up," added Ember. "It's just ceremony."

"To Severin!" shouted Beacon, raising his glass.

"To Severin," Ember echoed.

Ester raised her glass and took a swallow, but wasn't comfortable enough to invoke Severin's name.

The hippies beamed at her. Ester tried to be somber, but giggled.

"Didn't he explain about the energies?" asked Beacon.

Ester shook her head.

Beacon sat back in his rickety kitchen chair and took on a professorial air. He crossed his hands over the great expanse of his belly and stared pointedly at Ester. Then he cracked up.

"When Severin's going to name someone, he calls upon energies and forces we can't see," he explained once his belly stopped jiggling. "You need to be tied to the chair so you don't disturb them."

"Why can't he just tell you to sit still?"

"If you let him tie you down, it shows that you trust him," said Ember. "It's symbolic."

"But also, there's the drugs," said Beacon. "When you're tripping you don't always know what's going on."

"What drug?"

Beacon smiled sheepishly. "Whatever he's got on hand, I'm afraid. Like Em said, it's symbolic."

Ester was trepidatious. "Needle drugs?"

Beacon looked horrified. "No, no. Pot. Sometimes it's mushrooms. Sometimes acid. I think he used peyote once or twice, but that tends to get messy." He mimed someone throwing up.

Both women laughed.

"So, he does this to everyone? Then gives you your Threshold name?"

Beacon nodded. Ester thought about that. Trusting Severin wasn't something she felt ready to do yet, but she didn't want to make a big deal about it with these two. They were warm, generous people who had opened their home to her. The way things usually worked, their bungalow served as an introduction to the Threshold Elsewhere way of life. People in need of refuge could crash here for a few days and either continue on their merry way, or make the move over to Threshold House. Ester had been a guest for a little over a week, about twice as long as the average person stayed.

If smoking a joint with Severin would appease everyone and buy her a little more time to rest and hide while deciding where to run to next, so be it. Even if she would be tied to a chair. Beacon's cooking was worth a little inconvenience, and talking to Ember was comforting. The two of them together were like the mother she had never known.

Ember got up and pulled a deck of cards out of a kitchen drawer. Beacon cleared the table, except for the wine. Every night after dinner, the couple played cards for an hour or so. Ester usually left them alone and went out, or to her bedroom, but tonight it was raining and she still didn't have any shoes. She had no place she wanted to go, and the cowboys and Indians on the wallpaper in her room were creeping her out.

Ember asked, "Liz, do you wanna play?"

"I don't know any grown-up card games," she admitted.

Her hosts chuckled.

"Well, what do you know?"

"Crazy 8s?"

Beacon dealt the cards.

*** *** ***

Severin sat at the long table in the Threshold House dining hall and listened with great interest to Beacon.

"She got all the suits right. It was amazing!"

Bell, Cricket and Leviathan looked glassily amazed, but Severin knew it didn't take much to stun them. The miracle of a lit match often held Bell's attention.

Beacon continued, "Once Em noticed what Liz was doing, we stopped actually playing and had her guess them."

"Groovy," said Cricket, trying hard to concentrate.

"She seemed nervous at first, kept tapping her foot like a bunny and drumming her fingers, but we gave her more wine and she relaxed a little. After that, I suggested she predict the values of the cards. We went almost the whole way through the deck before she got too freaked out. Em even shuffled a couple times in the middle. Liz was right about three quarters of the time. But, man, the nervous energy just poured off her. She couldn't sit still."

Severin was impressed. Liz would be a valuable asset to the Following if she would ever let her guard down enough to join. He was eager to investigate her talents himself, and to see what his table would tell him if she assisted in the questing.

*** *** ***

Ester gazed across the small circular table at Severin. He looked like a poorly groomed wizard, with his long, aquiline nose, heavy brow over penetrating blue eyes, and the standard bushy hair and thick beard. The only source of light in the cavernous basement of Threshold House was a lava lamp. Its blood-and-amber illumination gave him a demonic aspect. His eyes were on her, his hands busy with a small knife dancing mushrooms into slivers. He chuckled.

"I realize," he said airily, "custom dictates that the medium be the one who gets tied up. I prefer it this way."

"Custom also recommends a crystal ball," she replied, with a glance at the lamp.

When she'd first seen the basement, Ester was taken aback. The single wooden chair and table looked ominous in the center of the otherwise empty room. The spareness gave the room, though enormous, the feel of a jail cell.

Ester tugged on the cords fastening her wrists and ankles to the chair. She did not feel fear, just certainty that something unpleasant would happen soon.

Severin lit a tall candle. He loaded a tablespoon from the pile of fungus fragments and held the bowl over the candle flame. The bits of mushroom wilted quickly, bubbling out a thin brown ichor. Severin kept the spoon in the flame while he positioned the tip of a syringe needle in the liquid, steadying its barrel against his wrist while he drew back the plunger with thumb and forefinger.

When Severin stood up with the needle, Ester's calm shriveled as quickly as the mushrooms. He moved beside her and rolled the hot glass of the loaded syringe across her bare forearm. She stopped breathing. She fought to remember why she needed to do this, but couldn't. Her muscles contracted, the restraints cutting into her skin and her veins standing out.

"Ohh," Severin sighed and fingered the prominent blood vessels. Ester's vision darkened.

The needle's entry was a white-hot jolt, the hit like lava pouring up her arm, flowing across her chest. Her heart gulped the fire in. The next beat sent a plume into her mind, a euphoric burst of insight that brought salamanders slithering out of every surface. She stared into the lava lamp, all fear forgotten.

"Now," Severin intoned, "we both get a glimpse into the shadows."

But there were no shadows. Ester had become a searing flare that saturated the deepest recesses of the room. Her gaze flowed over and around everything, seeing all sides at once. Severin raised his hand before his eyes, squinting. He was the exception, the only thing in the room casting a shadow. His mouth moved but his words were lost, drowned out by the light.

Ester raised her hands, the ropes and the wooden chair stretching and sagging like hot cheese. She stood and extended her right hand, smearing together her surroundings like finger paint. Turning her head, she watched the results as she traced an oval with her left index finger. The magic fire Severin injected made her finger white hot. With it she cut a loophole in reality.

Ester stepped through the flaming hoop, floating weightless on the other side. No horizon, no walls, just a warm ocean of green tie-dye fire. The aether swarmed with almost audible conversations, babble in a thousand languages she could understand but not identify.

Vague shapes floated through her peripheral vision, making her uneasy. Ester hugged herself and rubbed her bare arms, relishing the tactile sensation when everything around her was intangible. The motion agitated her surroundings, stirring up large thick bubbles. Ester peered inside them as they bobbed past.

The first one held cold dark water beneath a shroud of mist, home to teasing glimpses of a serpentine neck.

Three stars within the next bubble made a triangle of blue sea and sky. Airplanes and ships dissolved in its subtropical splendor, transformed into spinning disks that zipped heavenward.

Another held a forest of enormous fir trees, where soft pools of shadow loped elusively away leaving ponderous footprints.

Ester's gaze followed the rising bubbles up to a great wheel of stars, with archetypes sketched dot-to-dot. Most prominent was a pair of human figures, between a bull and a crab. The wheel slowly turned, but not about its center. The two figures clutched at something immobile, and their struggle became the point of rotation.

Like a hellish Escher-esque metamorphosis, the stars transitioned into an irregular scattering of holes. From each one leered a nose cone, the pronged countenance of Mutual Assured Destruction. Sudden inferno, a forest of towering atomic mushrooms, shimmered at the periphery. A dream of self-incineration, held at bay by a veil so thin Ester was terrified some innocent gesture would rend it.

The gossamer partition between existence and nuclear oblivion undulated with a regular rhythm that Ester matched up to the nervous drumming of her own fingers on her crossed arms. Terrified, she froze. The screen settled.

She wanted to leave before anything got broken. Before she drew any direct notice. Something here was awakening, becoming aware of her intrusion.

A feeling of belonging squeezed Ester, a feeling of family. It made her uncomfortable, made her want to duck out of the embrace. She was swimming in overfamiliarity.

The fiery green waves rolling around her began to roil and the dome of an enormous bubble breached the surface, filled with a chaotic amalgam of lightning and cloud.

Like an iceberg, the bubble capsized. Rococo engraving took the place of lightning, a pulsating filigree shot through with Latin words. The sloping side of a pyramid came into view, slowly righting itself. Ester knew it would be topped with an all-seeing eye. It was the secret military echelon, her father's cabal. If it saw her, she wouldn't be safe in Webster, or anywhere.

Ester turned to escape through the portal. She stopped. Would she be leading the eye to her hiding place?

A memory of the Army's spiders invading her sent a shudder

through her body, awakening every nervous tic she worked so hard to suppress. Her hands fluttered at her sides, sending covert messages in the sign language of her subconscious. Her toes tapped restlessly as she shifted her weight from foot to foot and back again, her impulses torn between flight and fight. Neither fight nor flight would serve her this time. She needed a third option, and quickly. The blunted tip of the pyramid broke the surface and the evil eye of providence was imminent.

Lightning quick Ester's fingers flew to her temples and drummed, hoping to jar loose a usable idea.

Camouflage.

Along with that one word, a wave of energy pulsed from Ester's terrified mind. Her hair bristled with it, and her hands dropped and grappled with each other at waist height. Each strand of her henna-red hair seemed suddenly alive, and at every tip swam a small many-legged creature.

Spiders.

Her hair was alive with thousands of spiders.

Whatever illicit chemical manipulation Severin had wrought on her today was mixing badly with the pharmaceuticals injected by the military doctors all those months ago to give her the mother of all bad trips.

Ester's scream came out a wheeze.

Her mane floated in an ever-expanding halo, the spiders spinning out more and more of it. With dizzying speed they wove an iridescent screen before her that reflected the colors around it, concealing Ester and the portal back to her life of wary freedom.

The enormous pyramid righted itself fully, its radiant eye blazing.

Grateful for the cover, but repulsed by its agents, Ester shook her head. The ghostly green spiders and their filaments detached from her hair and drifted away, carried toward the wheel of constellations. Through their web she saw the pyramid in its entirety, the eye staring calmly and seeing nothing as it coasted past.

Ester took a shuddering breath and backed away, through the hoop and into consensus reality.

She saw the basement room, herself tied to the chair, and Severin pacing, looking vexed. Crimson, his mouth snarling, he stalked up to the chair and shook her.

Ester swept back into her body. She moaned and struggled to focus, tried to reach up to rub her temples before reencountering her bonds.

Severin stood up straight. The color of his face cooled and froze to a ghastly white. He took a deep breath and asked, "What did you see?"

Ester swallowed, then cleared her throat. Such a simple question, but how to answer? The details wouldn't make any sense, and she lacked the strength for that much explaining. In a faint, hoarse voice she said, "Legends, myths, and nuclear annihilation." *Plus the bureau of supernatural affairs canvassing the area.* "It was," she cleared her throat again, "it was frightening. I didn't belong there."

Severin smiled and stood up. Turning away, he said, "I thought I'd overdone it. I'll have to use a smaller serving next time." He walked up the stairs to the kitchen, abandoning her in the shadows.

Ester worked her right hand free, squirming it around the arm of the chair into a position that gave her not quite enough slack and forcing it at the expense of some skin. She undid the other knots.

Severin came back with a mug, which he presented to Ester without commenting on her escape. Water. She drank deeply. It worked miracles on her throat.

"Next time, you can do that without me."

Severin quirked a corner of his mouth. "That which doesn't kill you makes you stronger."

Ester stood. "What exactly made me stronger this time?"

"South American fungus. The natives chew it, but I wondered if the effects would come on faster, more intensely, by injecting it. I think so." He looked wistful. "Apparently drop off a lot faster too. Didn't expect that."

Ester's head was not entirely free of backwards messages. It was impossible to know if her perceptions of time were reliable, but she thought only five minutes had passed. She did feel pretty certain of the severity of her physical reaction to the mushrooms. Probably lucky to be breathing, let alone standing. She bypassed the stairs leading up to the kitchen and headed for the door to the outside, the dirt floor cool under her bare feet.

"Where do you think you're going?" Severin had somehow gotten ahead of her. "You must collect yourself." He reached for her.

"Yeah, put my zen back in place." Ester dodged his offered hand and sank to the floor where she pressed her back against a sequoia-sized column for support while keeping her eyes on Severin. He studied her, not blinking.

"What?" Ester demanded.

"I'm just concerned, Willow. I want to be sure you're all right."

Ester blinked slowly. "What? What did you call me?"

Severin almost smiled, his face tightening a bit and his eyes glinting. "Willow: graceful and strong. I couldn't let you dash off without your name. I said I would give it to you, and I'm a man of my word."

"So you keep saying." Standing unsteadily, she moved again toward the exterior door. She pulled it open and looked up the half-flight of cement stairs into the late-afternoon glare.

"You need to not be on your own."

Ester turned back to him, but her pupils had overreacted to the waning daylight and Severin was a voice in the gloom. The only thing she could see clearly was the lava lamp. She moved instinctively toward its warm light.

Severin spoke as he climbed the creaking wooden stairs to the kitchen. "Tomorrow we'll find your destiny."

Ester squinted and could just make out his blurry shape. "Destiny?"

"Couldn't look for it until we knew your name. You'll find the experience fascinating."

"I'm leaving. I'm leaving!" Ester shouted.

Severin's calm voice said, "See you tomorrow," and he exited into the kitchen and shut the door behind him, leaving her alone in the basement despite his alleged concern.

Ester looked down at her left hand which rested on the warm lava lamp. She unplugged it from its extension cord and went outside. Severin would need to make do in the future without his crystal ball.

Chapter Two

THE ATTIC

*General, I assure you Project Lullaby can and will deliver results
even in the absence of subject EE. A new direction was called for
in any case, as it has become clear we will not be able to induce
the desired traits through transfusions or related techniques. The
sophistication of current medical knowledge is inadequate to our
ambitions. However, scientific advances on the horizon promise to
make possible the fabrication of devices to emulate subject EE's
distinctive electromagnetic signature.*
Project Lullaby archives, 1974

The sunlight faded quickly as Ester put distance between herself and
Severin. She carried the glass capsule of the lava lamp in her left hand,
its base tucked under her arm. Gravel and broken glass littered the
shoulder of the road. Ester picked her way gingerly around the worst of
it, striking out in hopes of hitching a ride. Away, far away.

Should have worn shoes.

The early fall weather had been kind, so far, but she was pushing her
luck.

A car slowed and pulled over ahead of her. Two-door, mostly
primer gray, with a big black dog sticking its head out the passenger
window. Ester approached that side cautiously. The dog whimpered and
sniffed at her. The driver leaned over and pushed the animal out of the
way. All Ester could tell was that he had a nice smile and longish dark
hair, then the dog was back, trying to lick her face.

"Komodo, get down," the driver laughed.

Ester stood unsure by the window. Should she hit the road tonight,
with no shoes and no supplies except a lava lamp? The driver's door

opened and he stood up.

"Hi," he said. "I'm Brad. Where you headed?"

Ester looked Brad over carefully before replying. He was on the tall side, and slim. Clean-shaven. A few years older than herself, maybe 25. He was dressed nicely for several years ago, and smiling at her. He had a very nice smile indeed, and was cute besides.

"The Bleu House," she lied. It was downtown, close enough to the bungalow. She'd go back there to sleep, find some shoes, and leave town tomorrow.

Brad gave her an appraising look before he nodded, no doubt wondering what a little barefoot hippie girl hoped to do at such a swanky bar. He wrestled the dog into the back seat and Ester got in.

The car eased back into traffic. Ester sat quietly, the lamp in her lap, staring out the windshield at the deepening twilight.

"So, I'm Brad Tanner and that's Komodo," said Brad, gesturing into the back. He turned toward her and flashed a winning grin.

Ester smiled back. "Apparently I'm Willow," she said and paused. She needed a last name other than Finch. A flock of finches is a charm, so, "Willow Charm."

Brad glanced at the road and back at her, extending his hand. "Charmed, I'm sure," he said, and winked. Ester smiled again and took his hand. Her breath caught at the first contact with his skin and her nipples were suddenly on alert, poking against the thin fabric of her celadon sundress. Lightning-indigo images of primal passion flashed through her mind and left a haunting afterimage on the inside of her eyeballs. Ester swallowed hard and stared into Brad's ethereal, smoky gray eyes. When he finally looked back at the road, Ester fancied it took an effort.

Those mushrooms really pack a wallop.

She still held his hand, stroking the back of it with her thumb. Feeling self-conscious, she let go and cleared her throat.

"Who's your friend?" Brad asked. Ester's confusion must have shown because Brad pointed, adding, "Your lamp."

Lost in her internal Kama Sutra she had forgotten all about the lamp. She blinked at it in her lap several times. Did it have a name? "I'll ask it," she mumbled.

"Everything okay?" Brad asked.

She nodded dreamily.

Brad chuckled. "What are you on?"

Ester's gaze slid over her arm and the telltale bruise forming there. "I'm not sure," she answered honestly. Her eyes crept back to Brad's face. Tan. Strong jaw. A small scar on his chin. Lazily hooded eyes. Unruly hair the color of strong coffee brushing his collar. A small smile on his lips.

"Are you meeting friends?"

"Hmmm?" Ester shook her head to clear it. She could listen to his clear, mellow voice all night.

"At the Bleu House. Friends?"

"Oh. Yeah." Sitting up straighter, she looked out the windshield again. Cars were turning on their headlights and the glare dazzled her.

"Will they keep you out of trouble or get you into more?"

Ester didn't know how to answer. She found it difficult to prevaricate under these conditions, whatever these conditions were.

"Willow?" He said her new name and she was christened. Happily. It sounded right coming from Brad. Natural. *I am a graceful, slender dryad and my name is Willow.*

"Willow?" Now he sounded worried.

Closing her eyes cut off the hypnotic rush of oncoming headlights. Brad's hand on her bare shoulder spread warmth through her. He shook her gently and she opened her eyes, looking at him.

"I'm fine," she managed. "I thought I was down, but I guess I was wrong. It's fading. Really."

Brad looked relieved. "You said you were a dryad."

"Was that out loud?"

"'Fraid so. Look, we're almost there. I'd feel really bad dropping you off in this condition."

I was fine.

"Let me buy you a cup of coffee at the Shamrock and keep an eye on you, just for my peace of mind. You do drink coffee?"

Willow nodded.

Brad parked and they left Komodo wagging his tail forlornly in the driver's seat. A group of boisterous students surged out the double glass doors as they approached the Shamrock Diner, and Brad put his arm around Willow's shoulders to guide her through. Inside they sat at the counter. Willow assembled the lava lamp and Brad flagged down the waitress.

They sat quietly while she poured. Brad turned to Willow, his face serious.

"I don't think they'll let you into the Bleu House without ID."

"I'm 18," Willow said defensively. "I have ID," Because she was short and slight, everyone assumed she was 15.

Brad smiled warmly. "You don't seem to have it with you, that's all I'm saying."

Willow blew on her coffee and took a sip. She saw Brad in the mirror behind the milkshake machine, studying her.

"You don't want to tell me where you're going, that's fine. Just tell me: do you have a place to stay?" He looked at her sidelong while he raised his mug.

His concern seemed genuine. Willow smiled. "Yes."

"Oh well. I was gonna let you stay with me." He finished his coffee and signaled for another.

Willow's stomach fluttered. Was it from the caffeine, the 'shrooms, or Brad? Her hands kept trying to creep over to touch him.

They sat together for the next half-hour. Brad kept Willow talking until convinced of her sobriety. Except for the heady rush each time they touched, she felt fine. She wanted him, but thought she should wait until she was certain her heightened responses could be attributed to him alone, and not Severin's mysterious South American fungus.

Outside she thanked him and stretched up on tiptoe to kiss his cheek, but he turned at the last moment and her lips met his. Sparks ricocheted through her mind and down her spine, permeating her flesh and making her tingle all over.

"Wow," Brad said. "Static." He rubbed his lips and ran his hand through his hair.

Willow rocked back on her heels and stared into his face. That couldn't have been the mushrooms.

They both tried to talk at the same time and both stopped, laughing. "You first," said Brad.

Willow hesitated. "Could we get together some time?"

Brad smiled. "I was going to ask you the same thing."

*** *** ***

Willow approached the huge Threshold House with some hesitation. It loomed over the other old houses on the outskirts of town.

She paused at the street, tugging a lock of henna-red hair and contemplating flight, leaving Webster and taking her chances in the next town down the line. Keeping on the run. If she stayed here, there would be no avoiding the Following or its leader.

But maybe there'd be no avoiding Brad either.

She stepped onto the broad front porch.

Severin greeted Willow at the front door. Evidently he owned only black clothes. "Hello. Please come right up."

Willow followed him to the foot of the grand, open staircase in the center of the building. It led as far as the third floor, and from there a door off the landing revealed the far less imposing flight to the attic. They didn't speak on the journey up, and Willow made herself let go of her hair when she discovered it twined around her fingers.

The other people in the House looked happy but busy. Most of them acknowledged Willow with warm smiles. There were probably worse places to go into hiding.

Severin turned on the attic lights. Willow squinted into the recesses of the room, surveying the floor-to-ceiling stacks of crates and trunks and cardboard boxes. It looked just the same as it had on her previous visit. It seemed he was in no rush to unpack. Severin moved off toward the most remote zone, which held a large flat object under a white sheet.

Willow glided up to him and looked at the sheet. It would look more complete with some china, silver, and crystal. Perhaps a couple of candlesticks.

Severin interrupted her musings. "This table gives me access to secrets. It shows me things. It will show you, too. Today it will show you your destiny."

Willow looked at the unexceptional table and back at Severin. After several awkward seconds of silence she said, "Okay."

Severin chuckled. "I'll show you how it works." He pulled up the front edge of the sheet with his right hand and reached under it with his left. Without looking under the fabric, he probed and explored for a few moments before withdrawing his left hand and showing Willow an ebony figurine of an owl. He replaced the item, lowered the sheet, and smoothed it back into place.

"Now you do it," he said.

Willow stepped closer to the table and swept her hand over the sheet. It covered a hard, uniform surface. Tapping out an intricate rhythm with her thumbs, she tried to figure out the trick. She rolled her eyes toward Severin and found him smiling. Looking back at the table, she reached down and raised the sheet's edge with her right hand and placed her left underneath.

Her fingers instantly fell upon an object. Hard, flat and round, about four or five inches across. Definitely not thin enough to have been hidden by the sheet. Willow let go of it and the sheet and stepped back, compulsively wiping her hands on her cutoffs.

"Take it out and look at it. It's meant for you."

Willow looked at the spot where she touched the strange thing. The sheet lay flat. Nothing under it. Except Severin went first, and probably planted something for her to discover. It must be some kind of trick. She crouched and looked at the underside, which was smooth varnished wood. No obvious sliding panels or hinges. Standing, she brushed the cover again, and felt no telltale edges or bumps beneath. With a deep breath, she raised the hem and reached under, and again unerringly found the mysterious item. Willow brought it out from under the sheet.

A pill pack. Birth-control pills. She quirked her eyebrow at Severin and asked, "Is this my destiny? What are we looking at here?"

"I don't know yet. Open it."

Willow obliged, and stared with furrowed brow at the pack's contents. It looked like the innards of a transistor radio, with all the wiry bits arranged along the circular shape like the pills should have been. She turned it toward Severin, counting on him for a wise interpretation. He smiled sardonically and rubbed his chin.

Willow scowled. "Of course everything is funny to you."

"The mysteries of the Universe are for our amusement. Would you prefer that I show a different reaction?" Severin's jaw went slack, his blue eyes bulged out, and he quivered with inexpressible horror. He smirked and gave Willow a sly look.

"Fine," she said. "Am I supposed to supply my own interpretation?"

"By all means. I would love to hear it."

"Then you'll correct me."

"If necessary."

Biting back her opinion of Severin's arrogance, Willow stared at the object in her hand. She opened it and closed it a few times, and turned it over. She sighed.

"The Pill means no babies. That's too obvious. And besides there are no pills. This thing could be an electronic birth-control device, but I doubt it. Anything like that would be too literal."

Severin nodded. "The obvious and literal meanings of things are lies."

"Okay," Willow said. "It also reminds me of a radio, at least the insides. It could be meant for communication. How would that relate to my 'destiny'?"

"Perhaps your destiny is trying to contact you."

"Perhaps. And maybe it's all supposed to mean something different.

You said all this superficial stuff is false. I'd be jumping to conclusions if I went with my first impressions. Right?"

"You make it sound like I want you to doubt yourself."

Willow shrugged. "I didn't say that."

Severin said through a hard smile, "Are you ready to hear what it means?"

"I want to figure it out. Give me a minute. When is a pack of electric birth-control pills not a pack of electric birth-control pills? When it's a contraceptive walkie-talkie... No. That's not zen enough. What this is," Willow paused and flashed Severin a grin, "is symbolic. It stands for something else. Like tarot cards. And it's meant for me, so how would I use these symbols? Whatever I would say with it, that's what it means. Right?"

Willow thought she detected a slight nod, but he said nothing. She took that as a sign she was getting warmer. While she considered, she opened and closed the pack several times, ran the tip of her finger over the electronics, slapped the whole thing in her palm.

She resumed, "Freedom. That's what the Pill really is. And it's made of the thing that will give me that freedom, which apparently is..." her expression fell. "Transistors."

Severin pursed his lips and nodded. "You got it."

"I was afraid you'd say that."

He directed her to place the pack under the sheet, where it disappeared.

"You don't yet have the knowledge to see how it fits together. By extension, you lack the knowledge of how to attain freedom. That is the first step: knowledge."

This was, by Severin's standards, amazingly direct and helpful information. Willow listened attentively.

"Tomorrow," Severin wrapped up, "we'll get you enrolled at Buckminster. Electrical Engineering. For now, your destiny is to be a freshman."

***   ***   ***

Severin guided Willow up to the next available window at the registrar. Buckminster U's recent steps toward becoming an easy-going, liberal educational institution for the people were about to be put to the test.

"This is my niece, Willow. She needs to register for fall semester."

The middle-aged woman behind the counter gave them a flat look. Severin glanced at Willow who looked horribly embarrassed, like she was about to apologize for lying before she even said a thing.

"Okay," the counter lady smirked. Severin caught himself in the process of shooting her a look, and turned it into what he hoped she'd take for a kind of nervous pride in his niece's achievements. GLADYS, her name plate stated.

Gladys slid a pen and a small stack of forms across the counter. "Fill these out, so we can have you take the placement test. I'll need to see some identification."

"Oh, right," Willow said, fishing in her small borrowed purse for the driver's license they'd picked up on the way here. She pulled it out with shaking fingers and almost dropped it, then put it on the counter in front of Gladys with a darting motion. Gladys lowered her chin to blink at Willow over her glasses, and picked up the license. She frowned.

Severin held his breath. The key to passing off a fake ID was confidence, and Willow was falling apart. She snatched up the pen and put it back, twice, looking from Gladys to Severin. Picking up the sheaf of forms, she tapped the pages against the counter to square them up. Severin could feel rippling energy like heat shimmers pouring out from Willow, making his pulse quicken and his vision swim. Gladys hadn't looked at the ID, but stared at Willow, still frowning.

Willow directed her attention to the forms, seeking to escape Gladys's awkward scrutiny. Rather than entering any information, though, Willow rolled the pen in her fingers and tugged on a lock of hair. Shortly, she began tapping the pen on the counter, sending a telegram to the Elsewhere, seeming to Severin to be trying to get them caught. He decided he would have to abort this mission, make up some excuse about not expecting so much paperwork. Clear out before they made so much of a scene they could never show their faces here again.

"This is fine," Gladys announced, and returned the license to Willow. Severin was positive she never even glanced at it, and saw that the woman's expression now showed a distinct, almost maternal warmth. Willow paused her mystic Morse code, and the subtle funhouse-mirror distortions overlaying the whole tableau snapped back to rigid ordinariness.

Willow sighed and started filling in the form. Her anxiety lifted, she tucked the strands of hair behind her ear. She held the pen still. Severin smiled, relieved that Willow's assortment of nervous tics had taken a break. Gladys now frowned at him, the warmth all but gone. Severin made the connection then. Without Willow's fidgeting to warp probability, the long odds against them reasserted themselves. He kept smiling, thinking it might be helpful to their cause if he looked a bit stupid, and considered his next move. Happily ignorant of their again perilous footing, Willow printed neatly in the spaces provided.

"Let me see if you have this right," Severin blurted. He took Willow's incomplete form and ran his finger down it slowly, counting under his breath and darting glances at Willow. She smiled an embarrassed smile at Gladys and looked over at Severin, bouncing slightly on the balls of her feet.

Her soft bouncing made the room a trampoline. Severin feigned puzzlement over something halfway down the form, and Willow twisted the pen back and forth in her fingers. Gladys blinked and said, "Here, honey. Let me take a look at what you've filled in. These things can be so confusing."

With a grunt, Severin relinquished the page to Gladys, who quickly determined that all was in order. Willow smiled gratefully, and Severin narrowed his eyes at her. As Gladys took it upon herself to do Willow's paperwork, Willow tugged on her hair again and rubbed her right foot up and down on her left calf.

Severin couldn't fully appreciate the waves Willow sent out, because he had to wear a stern expression to keep her nervous. Once they had the necessary voucher they set off for the third floor, where an entrance exam would commence in fifteen minutes. In the elevator, Severin finally permitted himself a grin.

***   ***   ***

In the bungalow, Willow sat cross-legged on the hardwood floor, facing the corner. Buckminster U showed uncommon dedication to the ideal of inclusiveness hyped in its brochures. Yesterday, using only a bad fake ID, she registered as a provisional student named Willow Charm. This morning, she attended her first college classes.

An EE text lay open in her lap and she was ostensibly studying. Her fingers drummed on the floorboards and she glanced at the wall clock every few minutes. She'd had to move away from the window so she would quit watching for Brad. They'd arranged their first date for this afternoon.

Beacon and Ember were over at Threshold House and weren't coming home until tonight. Everything in the bungalow was quiet. Willow didn't like it. She looked at the clock again, stretched, and cracked her back. Rolling onto her stomach, she laid the book open in front of her, facing into the room now.

I'll give him half an hour, then I'm going for a beer.

Ember's big calico cat, Gaia, wandered into the room and bumped Willow's shoulder repeatedly with her head. When this did not produce the desired food, Gaia turned to present her derriere. Willow shoved the cat off her book and froze. Through the screen door she saw a pair of desert boots. Following them up past pegged black cords and a dark green V-neck tee, she found Brad. He stood on the stoop, leaning against the door frame and smiling. How long had he been watching her? He raised his right hand and wiggled his fingers in a small wave.

Willow hastily stood and brushed the floor dust from her cutoffs and gauzy white peasant blouse. Brad pulled the screen door open and stepped inside. "Hi," he said. "Remember me?"

Willow felt embarrassed, her unease compounded by Brad's

seeming lack of any. He could at least act sheepish. She didn't know what to say.

Brad stooped and picked up her textbook, making a face when he saw the topic.

"Is this yours?" He sounded incredulous.

"Yes. Girls can be engineers too, you know."

"Oh, yeah, I know." Brad cocked an eyebrow, unfazed by her defensiveness. "Isn't it boring though?"

Willow took the book from him and put it on the industrial spool they used as a coffee table. Now that he was here, she didn't know what to do. She was eager to find out if she would respond to him physically like the other day, but didn't want to just jump on him. The silence grew awkward.

Brad took in the small room in a glance. Willow followed his gaze. What would he think of her home? It was greatly lacking in furniture, with only a musty brown-checked sofa and the spool table, lately accented by the red and black lava lamp. There were a few cushions on the floor and lots and lots of plants. Her bedroom was even worse. She suddenly wished she'd told him to meet her somewhere else.

His smile never wavered. "It must be nice to have more than one room," he said. "How many people live here?"

"Two besides me." Maybe he wasn't having second thoughts.

"Wow, that's great. I've got a room. This nice old lady, Mrs Lehrer, rents out all her spare bedrooms to a bunch of us ungrateful grad students. She even feeds us, when we're around. But I'd gladly give up that luxury just to have my own bathroom." He looked wistful for a moment but couldn't keep a straight face. "So are the other two your parents?" It sounded like an innocent question, but his wink gave him away.

"No," Willow laughed. "I told you I'm 18."

"Doesn't mean you don't live at home. Are either one or both your old man?" He ran his hand through his dark tangle of hair.

"Oh, please! No. They're a couple."

"How nice for them. So," he looked at her texts on the table, "you wanna ditch the books and go have some fun?"

***

Brad had a bottle of red wine and a picnic basket in his car. During the drive he told her about being in the MBA program and that he would be graduating in the spring. She told him about her newly discovered ambition to be an electrical engineer and nothing about Severin or his group.

They arrived at a state forest and parked on the side of the road. After a short uphill hike through dense evergreens they came to a large outcropping of rock which Brad easily scaled. Willow handed up the basket and started her climb. Being nearly a foot shorter than Brad, she had trouble. He reached down and clasped her hand. Prickly warmth radiated up her arm and through her body — not as intense as the reaction the first time they'd touched, but close. With Brad's help, Willow soon stood atop the rocks. Unaccountably out of breath and slightly dizzy, she stood for a moment with her eyes closed.

"We're almost there," Brad said and took her hand again. He carried the basket and led her down a rocky path that descended quickly, nearly overgrown with ferns and small animals. They emerged into the late afternoon sunlight on the shore of a clear lake. A peaceful scene. No breeze to ripple the lake's glassy surface. The shore had a ribbon of beach that was more gravel than sand. A cluster of large mossy rocks trailed into the water off to Willow's left. A few birds made noises in the trees and an occasional squirrel chittered. She and Brad were the only people around.

"I figured a self-proclaimed dryad would enjoy this sort of setting," Brad said as he spread out a large plaid blanket in the shade of a massive oak.

Willow blushed and rolled her eyes.

"The only places I could think of with lots of willows were too swampy for a picnic."

"This is lovely," Willow said and sat on the blanket. She took off her sandals and turned her face up to the sun.

Brad unpacked the picnic basket and opened the wine. "Oh, shit. I forgot glasses."

Willow took the bottle from him and sipped. "We can share," she said.

The meal consisted of French bread, red grapes, Gouda cheese, and the wine. They passed the bottle back and forth, its mouth carrying a lingering trace of Brad's essence to Willow. By the time they finished off the bottle, they were mellow and happy. Willow packed away their trash and Brad wandered into the woods. When he returned, he presented her with a bouquet of late wildflowers and threaded a daisy into her mahogany hair.

"You're beautiful, just like a wood nymph," he said.

Willow hugged him to hide her blush and a rush of lust overcame her. She held him tightly and marveled at the feel of his hands as they pressed against her back. His heartbeat soothed and excited her at the same time. His lips brushed the top of her head. Her knees were weak. This was too intense.

She broke away from the embrace, Brad letting go reluctantly. Smiling, she scampered to the lake and waded in. The cool water brought clarity to her thoughts. There was definitely something happening with Brad that could not be attributed to magic mushrooms. He was an odd duck in his out-of-fashion clothes, but fun and kind and possessed of an animal allure she found irresistible. Why not go for it? She waded deeper into the water, getting her shorts wet. She dove under.

When she came up, her white top was sheer and clinging. Brad sat on the shore, watching her.

"Come on in," she called. "The water's divine."

He pulled off his boots and socks and made a show of sticking a toe in to test the temperature. Willow stood in the waist-deep water and watched as Brad stripped off his shirt, pants and briefs. His body was lean and tan, and he was unselfconscious in his nudity. Stepping into the water, he quickly closed the distance between them. As he approached, Willow stood her ground and stared shamelessly.

"Why don't you hang your clothes up so they can dry?" he said.

Willow splashed him and waded toward shore, pulling her blouse over her head as she went. She tossed it onto the grass and added her shorts and panties to the pile. When she turned back to the lake, Brad was farther out, treading water and looking at her. As she moved out to join him, he slipped under the surface and bobbed up seconds later in a new location.

"Wanna play Marco Polo?" he asked.

What Willow wanted to do was touch him, feel his flesh, taste his skin, smell him. But she didn't say that. She said, "Do you?"

Brad disappeared under the water again and resurfaced directly behind her. He slid his arms around her waist and turned her to face him. "No," he said and bent to kiss her.

The feel of his lips and tongue and teeth, their wet bellies pressed together, his right hand in the small of her back, his left holding her head. There was nothing else. Willow melted into his embrace, her hands exploring his back and shoulders, her feet no longer touching the bottom. He lifted her and held her tightly. Wherever their skin met, Willow felt bursts of radiance and an undercurrent of aching pleasure. The kiss lasted hours, at least, and left Willow breathless and spent. Brad looked similarly shell-shocked.

As the sun began to set the air took on a seasonal briskness. Willow's skin sent conflicting messages, cold and hot and shivering. Goosebumps stood up on her arms, and her nipples were like pebbles. All she wanted was to kiss Brad again. He cradled her cheek in his hand and stared into her eyes, the gray of his own deep and full of promise.

"You're shivering," Brad said. He led her to the shore and wrapped her in the picnic blanket. He gathered wood and started a small fire with his lighter. By the time the flames caught, the sun dipped behind the trees and everything took on an eerie purple cast. The fire crackled comfortingly and quickly took the chill off, but made the shadows in the trees deeper. Willow remembered elements of her mushroom trip and became uneasy at the thought of what could be lurking.

Once he had the fire blazing, Brad got under the blanket with Willow. His naked flesh felt warm and smooth. His nearness soothed her. His scent stirred something deep inside her. She was almost accustomed to the sparks they threw. With his arm around her they sat together watching the flames. Their silence felt comfortable now, as if they'd always known each other. This closeness, this connection, erased any doubts Willow felt about hiding in Webster.

The moon and stars came out and the night creatures with them. The woods were much louder now than during the day. Willow snuggled closer to Brad and rested her head on his shoulder.

"I don't want to go back through the woods in the dark," she said, looking up into his velvety eyes.

"Okay." Brad sounded serene. "We can sleep here."

"Can we do something else first?" Her voice sounded throaty and lusty, even to her own ears.

"Whatever you want," he said, and winked.

Willow moved to Brad's lap and kissed him. His hands traced intricate designs along her spine and buttocks and hips, leaving luminescent trails of desire. She kneaded his chest and arms and felt him grow firm under her. Brad lifted her gently to the ground. She looked up at the waning moon, smiling. Brad kissed her mouth and neck, her small breasts, her nipples, her belly, her hips, stroking her with his gentle hands. He made love to her slowly under the stars. Closing her eyes, Willow relished their unique shared electrochemistry.

An eternity later, and blissfully happy, Willow slept, anointed with Brad's scent and wrapped in the picnic blanket with him, her unease about the shadow-shrouded forest forgotten.

*** *** ***

Brad Tanner hoped like hell Willow really was 18. He studied her now as he had the previous afternoon before she'd noticed him in the doorway. Her delicate, feline features looked practically girlish in sleep.

He brushed a tangle of red hair off her cheek and she murmured. Brad softly kissed her lips and pulled her slight body closer. She was almost short, under five and a half feet, with narrow hips flaring slightly from her waist. Her breasts were small and perky. Probably didn't own a bra. She was also incredibly fun and spontaneous. He'd definitely need to spend more time with her.

Willow radiated heat against him like a furnace, but the dawn air showed his breath. Their small fire had burned out overnight and he wanted to rebuild it before she woke. Braving the cold, Brad extricated himself from the blanket and Willow's embrace. He pulled his pants on before venturing into the forest to gather firewood.

The clearing's feeble bluish-gray light wasn't brave enough to follow Brad into the trees. Under the canopy it was still nighttime. All around him the forest pressed in, ominous and silent. The cold air was still, and he found himself holding his breath. He exhaled and began feeling around for kindling and larger branches.

On his way back to the lake, Brad became disoriented.

Soon there'll be more light and I'll be fine, he thought.

Turning in a slow circle and scanning the trees, Brad waited impatiently. After ten minutes, he thought there should surely be more light, but there wasn't. Striving to keep his cool, Brad spun around again, then again. Dizzy, he put out a hand to steady himself, dropping the wood. He blinked several times and bent to gather it again.

He hadn't noticed before, but he stood, crouched now actually, in the center of a ring of mushrooms. His stomach growled, but unfortunately the fungus didn't look at all edible. The 'shrooms were each about three inches tall and bright, waxy green. Very beautiful, but most likely very toxic. Brad stared at them and reached out, but froze before he made contact. He'd heard something, like a sharp intake of breath, behind him. Brad turned and looked over his left shoulder.

A girl sat about ten feet away, leaning her back against the mossy, lichen-covered trunk of a large tree. Brad thought it was Willow for only a moment. This girl looked shorter and even younger, but was incredibly pregnant. Brad stood. She stared at him with sad, arsenic green eyes that practically glowed. Water dripped from her sleeveless gray smock and the blond hair hanging limp around her pale faerie face and narrow shoulders. Her mouth moved but no sound came out. She clutched her swollen abdomen with gaunt hands. Pain crumpled her face, and she pulled her knees up, digging her bare feet into the deep green moss.

"Hey! Do you need help?" Brad stepped toward her and she shimmered, losing color. She vanished. He stumbled to where she had been sitting, but found no sign of her.

"Hello?" he called. "Miss? Are you okay?"

No reply. In the strengthening light Brad knew he would see her if she was nearby. He concluded it had been his imagination, perhaps augmented by hunger. Where the girl had seemed to be sitting was a blackberry bramble which still protected some berries, even this late in the season. Brad shivered and said a silent thanks to the ghost girl for drawing his attention to the bush.

Wanting to surprise Willow, Brad gathered the branches he'd dropped and easily found his way back to the lake. He got the fire started again and laid her damp clothes by it to dry, then took the picnic basket and picked all the berries he could find. There weren't many, but probably enough, supplemented with the chunk of leftover bread, for an adequate breakfast.

After feeding the fire and warming himself, Brad stripped and climbed back under the blanket next to Willow. The feel of her smooth, cool skin aroused him and he woke her with a lingering kiss.

"Good morning, Willow," he whispered.

She smiled sensuously and said, "Good morning, Brad." Her pale jade eyes were wide and trusting. They stirred in him the desire to protect her. They stirred other desires as well and he showered her torso with kisses, relishing the taste and scent and texture of her. He felt virile and alive on a whole new level.

After they enjoyed another romp, Willow noticed the fire.

"When did you get more firewood?"

"Before you woke up. It was pretty cold and I wanted you to be comfortable."

"Thank you," she said and kissed him.

"I also picked some blackberries for breakfast."

She raised her eyebrows in appreciation.

"And," he paused for dramatic effect. "I saw a ghost."

Willow looked incredulous. Brad opened the basket, proffering the berries. Willow took a handful and popped a few in her mouth. Finally she said, "A ghost?"

Brad ran his hand through his hair. "Yeah. It was a girl."

"Oh, really? Was she pretty?"

He considered for a moment before answering. "Hard to say. I think so. For a second I thought it was you. But she was shorter, and had light hair." He ate some berries. "She looked about 14, but she was hugely pregnant."

"A pregnant ghost?"

"It's what I saw. She looked very sad and it seemed like she was trying to tell me something, but she wasn't making any noise."

"Maybe you were dreaming?" She ate more berries.

"No. I was already out in the woods. And after she dissolved, I found the berries where she'd been sitting."

Willow stopped eating and looked at her stained fingers.

"You're kidding right?"

Brad shook his head.

"I'm eating a breakfast provided by a pregnant teenage ghost?" She sounded somewhat horrified. Brad suddenly saw her point and felt slightly repelled himself.

"Well, it sounds bad when you say it."

They looked at each other and burst out laughing.

"We'll need to go soon," Brad said with marked reluctance. "I've got a class to teach at 11:00."

"They're almost gone," Willow said, peering into the basket. "Let's just finish them so we don't make her angry."

Chapter Three

Cigarette Fog

At birth, (3-20-35) Brian Shaw was given the name Prophet. His parents died before he was two and he was raised, along with many others, by Paul Shaw and his multiple wives.
from *Brainwashed*, by Julie Rome ©1998 Futhark Press

The stars were all already dead, they just didn't know it. That made them ghosts, in a sense, so their haunting of Melissa Thomas could be seen as 'normal.' If you had an open mind and a broad definition of normal.

The stars were her most consistent tormentors. In order to rob them of their unique power, Melissa had intended to declare astronomy as her major upon entering Buckminster University for her freshman year. Know thine enemy.

So far, life in Webster was working out. There were all the new patterns to deal with, but she got the bottom bunk in her dorm room and would at least be spared the nocturnal beseechings of the acoustically speckled ceiling tiles. Her room was exceedingly small, and Patty, her roommate, exceedingly loud. But so far Patty hadn't noticed Melissa was a freak.

That part of the 'clean break' plan was going well. Sure, she'd only been here for three days, but no one at all knew.

She'd waited to buy her new school wardrobe until she saw what everyone else was wearing. Hemlines were a little higher here, for one thing. She blended right in today wearing her patchwork jumper in autumnal colors, mustard-yellow blouse, and sandals. The long-practiced smile helped, too, as long as she kept it plastered on her face.

Melissa knew she would need to find an escape, a quiet place with no distracting patterns.

The fucking patterns! At home, she knew what would most likely trigger an insight, but not here. The pipes in her dorm were noisy, knocking and sighing every time anyone flushed a toilet or took a shower, and they wanted to be sure she knew one thing: All signs point to accounting. Accounting!? Why the hell would she want to go into accounting? All those columns of numbers, ripe with meaning. They might tell her anything. But, accounting it was.

Melissa knew she couldn't duck fate, and dutifully signed up. Accounting 150, English 50, AmHist 100, Astronomy 102. The minimum credits she could take and be full time. She got everything, first try. Predetermination. Or, she picked all the most boring classes Buckminster University offered.

That had been the last of the good news. The dining hall food was as bad as expected, Mom had been weepy on the phone, and this morning she got lost on campus and missed her first class — the deified accounting.

The map was more hindrance than help, detailing an outbreak of food poisoning at an orthopedic footwear sales convention. Melissa had shoved the map into her purse and fled to a bathroom until she could calm down and plaster her smile on again. She'd checked her reflection carefully in the mirror amidst an influx of ETAs for flights at Gatwick airport in London and was satisfied with what she saw. Her dark blond hair remained neat in her new short flip, thanks to the liberal use of hairspray and a brown headband — flight 394 from Oslo, ETA 2:12 — all trace of tears gone from her dark green eyes, mascara intact and unsmudged — flight 563 from New York, ETA 3:45 — no ugly red blotches on her pale complexion, just a few freckles — touch up the blush and powder the nose — flight 781 from Athens, ETA 2:50 — bland, lipsticked, close-lipped smile in the lower quarter of her pixie face. These people would *not* know she was a freak. Anyone could get lost on such a big campus.

When she finally asked for directions and found Josephson Building, her class was long over.

English was dry, but thankfully free of both poetry and biblical study. Those two types of texts were swarming with portents and Melissa avoided them. The history class was likewise dull, but covered mostly information she already knew from high school. She shouldn't need to study too many time lines. Astronomy met tomorrow. That meant the only thing left for today was to find the accounting teaching assistants' office and get the syllabus for the class she'd missed. Then she could go somewhere quiet, close her eyes and just be.

The accounting department's offices occupied Tavish Building, a five-story neoclassical edifice not far from Melissa's dorm. The banal architecture told her only that the alumni who endowed Buckminster's financial colleges expected to see their money transformed into proper temples of higher education. A breeze stirred the leaves of the ivy clinging to the facade, and by their fluttering she knew that someone named Marvin Wegler would hang himself in two days to escape allegations (true ones) of pedophilia. Melissa sighed and mounted the steps.

In the foyer she located the building directory and searched it for her instructor's name. Fighting against the distracting realization that by rearranging all the little white plastic letters, one could spell out six vulgar limericks and have two 'a's and a 't' left over, she found Sam Masterson listed in 438. That, came the unwelcome knowledge, was the number of unpaid parking tickets outstanding against members of the Buckminster Broncos football team.

Melissa climbed to the fourth floor and reminded herself to keep doing the smile as she cast her gaze madly about for a safe zone. Bulletin boards, the floor tiles, the light fixtures, the frosted glass of the office doors, everything flung patterns and hidden meanings at her. She discovered the baseboard was sufficiently bland that she could stare at it and walk down the hall without running into things.

Melissa reached the door to 438. The grain of the wood reminded her of a topographic map. It showed her where the Civil Air Patrol would finally discover the wreckage of a Piper Cub that vanished two years ago.

She pictured the office, with bookshelves and curios and memoranda and who knew what else that would assault her with pointless messages. Drawing a deep breath, she opened the door.

It was much different. First off, it was spacious, and sunny. She'd assumed Mr Masterson would have his own office, but from the eight separate desks in the room she surmised such was not the case. While it did contain an abundance of accounting artifacts, nothing, so far, emitted irritating insights.

The sole inhabitant of the room looked up when she entered. He wasn't at the desk with the Masterson nameplate. He said, "Hi there."

The heavenly quiet in this room, the complete immunity from portents, signs and omens, overwhelmed Melissa. Small talk was far too intense, and she blushed. Realizing it brought a rush of embarrassment that she knew only made her face even redder.

The man said, "I think I'm part of Buckminster's research into the properties of grad students under high compression. They're putting two more in here next week. Who're you looking for?"

His nameplate said TANNER. He was only moderately ungroomed and wore a winning smile. Melissa tried to speak, but the simple purity of things as themselves was too novel. Dazzled, she wondered why this room was different. If she tried too hard to see what it meant, would she break the spell? Was this why she had been impelled to enroll in accounting? If she didn't answer Mr Tanner's question, would he think her idiotic?

She pointed to Sam Masterson's desk, feeling a new hot wave of crimson flood her face.

"Did you miss class?"

Melissa nodded weakly, her smile no longer a labor. She breathed deeply and closed her eyes for a few seconds. When she opened them, Mr Tanner was pushing his chair back to stand, and still smiling at her.

"Don't be so worried," he said. "Sam's pretty easy going. Just don't skip any more classes."

Melissa shook her head, not yet trusting herself to speak. She wanted him to keep talking. His voice told her nothing beyond the words he spoke. Rapture.

As Mr Tanner stood, a loud scuffling sound came from under his desk and an exuberant black dog appeared. It bounded around the desk, spotted Melissa and sat abruptly, staring at her in what she took to be a not altogether friendly manner.

"Komodo, stay!"

The dog slowly turned to Mr Tanner and began to pant.

"Good boy." Mr Tanner patted the dog's head and ruffled its ears before crossing to Mr Masterson's desk. He moved several papers around before picking one up and glancing at it. The dog eyed Melissa.

"Here you go." He handed her the paper. Melissa stared at it, uncomprehending.

"It's the syllabus," he explained. "When Sam asks, tell him Brad and Komodo took care of you." He winked.

Melissa felt her face flushing again and feared her smile now verged on the imbecilic. The pure beauty of this room, the ordinariness of everything, bewildered her but she didn't want to leave. To leave would be to invite the rushing return of meaning. She needed to stay in this haven, even if just for a little bit longer.

Mustering her wits, she managed to say, "Thank you, Mr Tanner."

He looked at her and laughed. Her smile didn't falter, but her heart plummeted.

I was a fool to ever think I could mix unnoticed with normal people.

"I'm Brad. When I go to work in a bank I'll be Mr Tanner."

He sat on the corner of Sam Masterson's desk, absently petting the dog. He wanted her to call him Brad. Perhaps he was just being nice. Maybe this was one of those 'laughing *with* you' situations.

Melissa finished pretending to scan the syllabus and folded it neatly in half. She opened her hideous but en vogue macramé shoulder bag and with great deliberateness retrieved her notebook. Taking her time, she slid the folded paper into one of the pockets. While she stalled, she studied Mr Tanner. Brad. He was making strange faces at the dog and speaking some sort of doggy baby talk. He didn't seem to be paying any attention to her. Just as well. But how could she plausibly extend her time in this wonderful room?

"Is Mr Masterson coming back today?" she managed to ask, thinking she'd wait as long as necessary.

"No. I'm the last one out. I got in a little late and had some work to catch up on." He looked sheepishly at the dog. "Komodo was looking neglected, so I had to bring him with me. You're lucky you found anyone here. The office is usually deserted after 4:00." He looked up at the clock above the door. "And, since it's now 4:30, I've done my time and am free to enjoy happy hour at Nero's." He went to his desk and cleared it. "I'll walk you out."

Melissa swallowed hard to contain her disappointment. "Sure."

The dog scurried out into the hall ahead of them as Melissa steeled herself for a renewed onslaught. She stepped out and everything remained quiet. Brad locked the office door and whistled for the dog. Together, the three of them walked to the stairs.

Melissa kept waiting for hell to return with each step she took away from the door, but all was serene. Brad made small talk about life in the accounting department and Melissa made noncommittal sounds at the appropriate times.

This dread was worse, even, than the messages themselves.

Students packed the lobby, all crowding into a large lecture hall. Their babble was loud, but wonderfully innocuous.

Maybe I'm cured! Melissa thought, but immediately regretted it. No point in getting her hopes up.

Brad held the door for her and they stepped outside. The clouds in the sky were just clouds. The sidewalk just a sidewalk. Down three steps and everything was still normal. Despite her best efforts, hope sprang in Melissa's chest and rocketed to her head. She felt giddy. She walked blindly beside Brad and the dog until they reached a walkway she recognized. It led to her dorm. Melissa decided to hurry back to it and see what it was like as itself.

Impulsively she stretched up and kissed Brad on the cheek.

"Thanks for being so nice to a bewildered freshman," she said.

He looked amused. "See ya."

Melissa turned and started toward her dorm. Her pace slowed. Birds chirped, and she could hear traffic noise drifting in over the quad, and a familiar oppressive sensation dripped down her scalp as she became aware of an undercurrent of meaning in those random sounds. An insistent little message just for her, that lapels would get wider before the trend ran its course.

Grimacing, she looked up. White clouds in a sapphire sky like islands of cotton in cobalt waters, but she saw the grade-point averages of various strangers, mostly sophomores. She tried to screw the smile back in place, but her lower lip curled over and tears streamed down her cheeks. She ran for the entryway. Just outside the building she stopped, on the verge of passing out, hyperventilating.

She commanded herself to take slower breaths, and tried to think. It was coming back, the useless data, rivers of things she didn't want to know. The peace had been too good to last, the bitter shock more potent after a few sweet minutes of relief.

Tavish! Things would get better as soon as she started to get near Tavish Building.

Smoothing her hair and wiping her face, Melissa began to walk sedately back along her recent route. She kept her composure even though every impression captured by her senses came burdened with extra information. Her world had been like this for years. She put the smile back on and berated herself for even noticing the patterns anymore.

Why did I never learn to tune them out?

The smile wavered. She had tried, and failed, repeatedly. The knowledge that these messages were all true did nothing to alleviate her torment. She wasn't crazy. The smile disintegrated in her acidic thoughts. Melissa found it difficult to even smirk about the irony. It wasn't like she would ever tell a soul — no one could help her anyway — but if she did, they would only think her sane if she 'admitted' that she was mad.

Ascending the stairs in Tavish Building, Melissa concluded that this wasn't working. The patterns were trying to make up for lost time. Stone-faced, she stalked down the corridor and reached 438. It was locked. Of course. Brad locked it. She knocked, blinking away the vision of a child who would be crippled by meningitis later that year. No answer.

Hoping to pick up whatever vibrations lurked behind it, Melissa pressed herself against the door. She was desperate to get back into that magical room. Whimpering, she knelt and tried to look under the door, tried to inhale the room's essence. It did no good. She jumped to her feet and brushed off her skirt and blouse before anyone could see her.

Melissa pounded on the door. She kicked it. She slammed her fist into the frosted glass which rattled alarmingly. Melissa stopped short. Would shattering the glass to gain entry break the spell? She couldn't risk it.

Melissa collapsed in despair, sobbing into her hands. Several minutes later she regained control and went to the bathroom to clean up. She glared at her reflection in the mirror until it smiled back at her the way she had practiced.

Tomorrow she would come back here first thing in the morning and find an excuse to spend the rest of her life in that mystical, quiet office.

On her way out through the lobby, Melissa passed the office directory. Instead of the dirty limericks, random words jumped out at her: fiddle, burn, Rome, happy, hour. Melissa scowled at her own clumsiness for letting things like this catch her eye. Most of those words weren't really present, of course, not such that normal people would notice anyway. Just two of them appeared verbatim: 'happy,' because someone wanted to suck up to the dean by wishing him well on his birthday, and 'hour,' because of a line about office schedules.

Melissa turned away, but kept fuming about the distraction long enough to find a meaning in it that actually made her laugh. What she sought was not in the office.

It was at Nero's.

***

Brad's dog was sitting with the doorman, ignoring the customers and chewing on a yellow plastic squeaky porcupine. She wasn't too late.

Melissa adjusted her ochre linen skirt and her smile, and handed her ID to the doorman.

He didn't believe she was 18. Melissa ignored him while he scrutinized her license, wishing he'd hurry up. Her reprieve waited inside and she itched to get close to him again.

Finally convinced that she was, indeed, Melissa Thomas, and, in fact, old enough to drink, the doorman returned her ID and let her in.

Nero's was a dank, poorly lit basement bar. It stank of stale cigarette smoke and the urine-like odor of cheap beer. The ceiling hung low over the bare concrete floor. Lovely. The only way to move through the throng was to squeeze through in the wake of a waitress. Loud bass-heavy blues poured from wall-mounted speakers, forcing everyone to shout.

Melissa couldn't yet find Brad in the crowd but the aether was clear, even if the air was not. A blessed calm came over her and she bought herself a richly deserved beer. With her back to the wall, she scanned the room for Brad.

Everyone in this damn bar looked the same. All scruffy student-types. What the hell had Brad been wearing, anyway?

Melissa closed her eyes and tried to sense him, to detect the tranquil center. No luck. He apparently didn't give off serenity rays. One advantage to the bar being so crowded was that nobody could move around much. She decided to start in one corner and check every face until she found him. Five minutes later, she wondered if she would have the patience to see it through.

Ah, there he was, playing pool over near the restrooms. He held a cue stick in one hand and a beer in the other, a cigarette in his mouth. Melissa watched as he clumsily shifted things around to free up a hand and move the cigarette. He laughed smoke, nearly spilling beer on his shoes. Melissa did not find herself filled with confidence, but he was the reason she was meant to enroll in accounting. With beer in hand, she began the tortuous, serpentine crossing of the overcrowded room.

Brad's companion racked up the balls for another game as Melissa got near. What this situation called for was a subtle way to start a conversation so she didn't look desperate, and Melissa had no experience in this area. The tension made her have to pee.

After Brad broke and didn't sink any balls, she stepped up and touched his elbow. He turned and looked at her with a total lack of recognition. She widened her smile and berated herself for changing her clothes and respraying her hair without the headband.

"I'm Melissa," she shouted.

"Hi," he shouted back. Still no bells.

"Masterson's no-show," she prodded and saw a dim light dawn behind his weird gray eyes.

"Oh, yeah. Hey." He smiled and started to turn back to the pool table.

"Could you watch my drink for me?" she shouted again.

He looked back at her, confused as ever.

Melissa gestured toward the bathroom. "Watch my drink?"

"Oh yeah, sure." He took her beer and set it on the edge of the table. Melissa hurried into the bathroom.

***

Brad's friend was not Sam Masterson, as Melissa feared, but a fellow rooming-house tenant. Oscar was not a very good pool player, but an excellent drinker. Melissa suspected the latter played a part in the former. Brad, on the other hand, displayed moderate talent for both.

Melissa watched them finish another game and asked if she could have a turn. The boys were genial about letting her join in and even offered helpful tips, though it was Oscar, not Brad, who put his arms around her to help her with her stroke. Melissa saw why men liked this game so much. Normally such physicality would have made her skin scrawl messages of dubious interest in its bumps, but for once she was enjoying herself.

Brad could take some grooming cues from Oscar, whose sandy hair was neatly clipped in the back. Even at this hour he bore the scent of after-shave. For the next game, Oscar proposed that he and Melissa work as a team, to offset Brad's distinct and unfair advantage of having actual skill. Oscar insisted that Melissa should break, and spent nearly a minute helping her position her right hand on the felt.

"I just realized you're left-handed," Brad said as Melissa lined up to take the shot.

She smiled at him. "So I am, thanks. I've been wondering."

Oscar laughed. "Let's kick his ass."

All the coaching must have paid off, because Melissa sank two balls off the break, earning her a peck on the cheek. From Oscar. She blushed, then saw Brad concentrating on the game. He hadn't seen the kiss, because he wasn't even looking at her. Melissa set up for her next shot and pointedly waved off Oscar's further offers of advice. She missed on purpose.

Brad put in three shots before Oscar's turn, and Melissa complimented his steady hand. While Oscar picked out a shot, she stood next to Brad, inching closer until he shifted his weight away from her. Oscar missed, and she wished Brad good luck. She only made one shot the rest of the game, accidentally.

The three of them split a pitcher right as happy hour ended. Oscar finished most of it. He left once the beer ran out. Melissa timed her drink so she would finish when Brad did and they walked out together.

So far, so good. Being with Brad was keeping the unwanted information at bay. Now, she just needed to stay with him forever.

Before rushing into anything permanent though, Melissa decided she would put Brad to the test. If he could keep the stars silent, she would know he was her destiny.

It was dusk, still too early. Melissa asked Brad if he wanted to get something to eat. She'd become almost comfortable with her new role as social butterfly and the invitation sounded casual.

He balked because of the stupid dog.

"Komodo's not allowed in restaurants."

Melissa felt a scream building in her stomach. She thought quickly. "Doesn't Reggie's have outdoor seating?"

Brad cocked his head for a second and smiled. "You're right." He winked and they were off.

Melissa always thought she could use Health Inspector as a fallback career. How novel to read a menu and not know the complete molecular structure of every pesticide and fertilizer used in the food's production, be privy to the details of the line cooks' love lives, or be treated to details from the insurance actuarial tables for both fast food and sit-down dining establishments.

Brad ordered a Rueben platter and gave all the french fries to the dog. Melissa chose a club sandwich and decided to make points by giving him her fries too. She had the distinct impression that Komodo didn't like her. That would have been fine under normal circumstances, but Melissa didn't think Brad would consider dating her without the creature's approval.

Brad prattled on about people she could expect to meet around the department. She used the time to study him and commit him to memory. His dark brown hair was on more than casual terms with his collar. His skin was tanned, and a small smile perpetually lingered on his mouth. This all implied irresponsibility and a carefree attitude that Melissa both despised and envied. He made eye contact a lot, which unnerved her. His eyes were the color of smoke which creeped her out, and she was unused to close inspection. She kept her expression blandly happy. It wasn't too hard, because she thoroughly enjoyed the respite Brad afforded, if not Brad himself.

He must be some sort of weirdo, she decided. Not only was he being nice to her, but his clothes were all wrong. Black, slim-legged jeans, pointy-toed boots, a burgundy v-neck tee. Melissa didn't usually pay attention to men's fashion, so it took a while for her to figure out what was odd about them. They were from 1968. Modish. On the threadbare side. He must be 24 or 25. Hadn't he bought anything new since he started college?

Melissa ate as slowly as she could without being ridiculous, and as she finished it was finally getting dark. The stars were silent so far. Melissa's heart raced. What next?

"I'm a little nervous about walking alone on campus," she said. "You know, after dark."

"We'll walk you, won't we Komodo?" Brad said. The dog leapt to its feet and pranced in a circle. Melissa supposed that meant 'yes.'

"Which dorm are you in?" he asked.

Melissa had to think for a minute. She couldn't very well say, 'The big ugly one that feels like an African famine and an oil crisis.'

"Irving Hall," she said when she remembered.

When they arrived, it was 7:45 by Melissa's watch.

"I have 15 minutes before curfew. Wanna go up to the roof and look at the stars?"

"We can see them from down here," was his cautious reply.

"Komodo wants to go, doncha boy?" she said to the dog, imitating the overly enthusiastic tone Brad used with him. The creature thumped his tail and perked his ears.

Brad was amused. "Well, I wouldn't want to disappoint 'Modo." He led her around to the side of the building and effortlessly scaled the wall to the fire escape. When he lowered the stairs, Komodo bounded up and Melissa followed.

"He's done this before," she said.

Brad shrugged and started up the metal steps.

"I'd forgotten about curfew. They didn't have it at my dorm," he said.

"That's 'cause you're a boy."

"Eight's early isn't it?"

"It's later on weekends. Ten I think."

"Party, party, party."

They reached the roof. Brad lifted Komodo over the ledge and helped Melissa. She looked around. The stars were bright and silent. The moon was half-full, or was it half-empty? Melissa laughed.

"What's funny?" Brad asked.

Melissa shrugged. He was the one. The doldrums in her sea of meaning. She'd found the man she would marry and he was unimpressive. Perhaps she needed him because while she noticed too much, he noticed nothing. Whatever. Time to stake her claim.

As he slouched against the wall of the elevator housing, she stepped up, took a deep breath and kissed him. The kiss should be passionate, even if she felt no real passion. Brad responded meekly at first, but then with feeling. Or maybe he was faking it, too. Melissa had no real way of knowing. She'd done this once before, of course, but had been distracted by tides of visions.

The physical sensations were fairly enjoyable and by the time they were ready for intercourse, Melissa could detect traces of desire in herself. The sex act was lackluster, but a lot of that could be blamed on the setting. The rough, cold roof, the staring dog, plus the added pressure of needing to be done in time to make curfew. Brad seemed content enough, at least. It would be good if it didn't take much of that to keep him happy.

*** *** ***

Smoke seeped from Brad's nostrils and formed a thin haze before his eyes. By tightly controlling his exhalation and not moving, letting the cigarette dangle in the corner of his mouth, his whole head became enshrouded in a comforting fog. His eyes were gray, the same as the smoke, and Brad fancied that the tenuous cloud extended his own vision. It gave him perspective. His brain was also gray, or so they said, so the halo was also his mind, expanding and allowing him to think more clearly.

He lay on the low stone wall that surrounded the campus green, one hand across his chest, the other dangling to the sidewalk below. The stones were also gray, but they did not feel like his eyes or his mind.

Brad felt his lungs achingly empty, and cautiously switched from exhale to inhale. This was the most dangerous time. He could not gasp air in because that would disturb his fog, but if he waited too long before adding to it, it would vanish. He wished it could go on for hours, this clarifying ritual, but it never lasted longer than a single cigarette.

Through the smoke and the edges of the tree beside him, Brad saw the stars. Melissa liked the stars. She wanted to share them with him. Before, they seemed distant and constant. Now, he wasn't sure. Some people believed in the Zodiac. Melissa was probably one of them. Not Brad. He would never believe that his future could be told by what was written in the stars.

If he expanded his vision and his mind enough, perhaps he could know his future.

Exhaling again with excruciating slowness, Brad watched the smoke swirl and coalesce, begin to dissipate. An intricate dance meant only for him. He felt a sudden certainty that Willow would appreciate the beauty and serenity of it, but also a reluctance to share it. What would Melissa think? Would she understand the finding of meaning in something so ephemeral? Probably not. She seemed very practical. He was struck with a longing to see each of them again. Each so young and vulnerable. They both needed him.

He chuckled, thinking what a dirty old man he'd become, and broke the spell. The cloud disappeared. Sighing, Brad turned his head and saw Komodo sitting patiently in the grass.

"Life is certainly getting interesting," he said, and stood.

They walked briskly in the direction of home, Komodo at Brad's side. Brad continued his internal audit and the dog kept looking up at him expectantly.

"What? I'm just thinking."

Komodo cocked his head.

"Don't act so surprised. You know I don't usually have such good luck with girls. Women." Brad looked sheepishly at the dog. "No, girls. I seem to be having my mid-life crisis."

A loud group of male students passed them in the opposite direction. They all wore polyester sport-coats in various shades of brown and orange. Brad snickered to himself and looked down at his own outfit.

"It must be the clothes."

Thanks to Melissa's influence, he was off his customary route home from Nero's, and felt uncomfortable. The whole campus was familiar ground in daylight, but things were far more sinister in darkness.

Brad paused to take in his surroundings. North of the library, nearing the edge of campus. This area lacked the old-world orderliness found in more southerly parts of the university's grounds. Construction had been hemmed in by residential streets, giving the impression that the labs and theaters were deposited in a jumble by a receding tide. Even the trees were different, oaks and maples with limbs like twisted hands instead of the graceful arching boughs of elms in careful rows.

"C'mon, 'Modo," he said softly.

Passing around the fountain in the courtyard between the music building and the Proscenium Theatre, Brad flinched at the tall ragged shapes that caught his peripheral vision. He chastised himself for being afraid of abstract sculpture, even if it was ugly.

Komodo pricked up his ears and trotted alertly to the opposite side of the large dry fountain. The shadows of the ugly sculpture created pools of moonlight, and the animal stopped in a circular one.

"Hey, dog. Let's go," Brad called. Komodo sniffed the ground for a moment, turned around on his axis three times, and laid down. He stared at something in or near the fountain, the way dogs are supposed to watch the front door while Master is out. Brad snapped his fingers, he whistled, but Komodo seemed suddenly deaf.

Sighing, Brad walked over to his dog. "What's got into you? Let's go home, buddy. This place is spoo—"

Brad stood frozen. The pregnant ghost girl lay against the verdigris-stained liner of the fountain. He worried more about knowing what to do if she was real this time than about dealing with a ghost. As in their first meeting, she was trying to tell him something but made no sound. Brad shook his head, and he mouthed the word, "Sorry," on the logic that she couldn't hear him either.

She seemed to be in great pain. Brad wondered if she was about to have her ghost baby. With a grimace she drew her knees up, and Brad moved closer, instinctively wanting to help. She vanished, and left him leaning on the green tiled side of the fountain.

Komodo yawned, the characteristic canine whine utterly inappropriate to the somber mood.

Chapter Four

TABLES TURNED

You, we, all of us of the Following, stand nearer than most to the future. To the Threshold. But we can draw even closer.

It is nearness to Nature that lets us approach the Threshold, and as we better our understanding of Nature we will someday reach, and cross, that Threshold. So, hereafter we must remember not to exclude anything as we contemplate the meaning of Nature. We must include the gifts of science, for these works of mankind illuminate small and distant reaches of our Universe that we would otherwise never know.

This is why it is important to expand our contemplation, that we may thereby expand our understanding. We mustn't forget the truth as we learn new ideas. Embrace all of Nature, as Nature is itself all-embracing.

The first major change here at the House is that we're getting cable...

TEF after-dinner announcement by Severin Tenpenny

"Shh!"

Willow looked up from her comparative lit text. Everyone else at the table was glaring at her. Belatedly she noticed her new mechanical pencil tapping on the cover of a closed book and stopped her hand.

"Sorry."

The others bent their heads back to their studies.

After stretching her arms and neck, Willow closed her eyes to rest them for a few moments. Thoughts of Brad crept in and chased all scholarly notions away. He would be meeting her here in the library after his last class of the morning and they would have lunch together before he spent his afternoon in his office coaching struggling accounting undergrads and she spent hers discussing the fall of Troy and wishing she were a struggling accounting undergrad.

Having someone in her life again after months of solo journeying felt reassuring. And it wasn't just Brad. Beacon and Ember, too, were good, gentle friends. When she ran away from her father and the military program, she told herself that she didn't need to rely on anyone. That she could take care of herself. While she had proven she could be self-reliant, she now found she enjoyed and needed connections to other people. It was too early to say she loved Brad, but it certainly felt like she did.

Her impulsive decision to stop running and hide in Webster was, so far, working out. It had been almost a month and she had seen no signs anyone was looking for her, but she did keep her eyes open. She had to. Severin and his Following couldn't be expected to protect her, and neither could Brad. Especially when she couldn't tell him what he would be protecting her from.

That was her one regret: she couldn't be honest with him.

Luckily, he didn't ask questions about her past. The way she didn't ask questions about what he did with his time when they weren't together. When they were together, they were totally together and that's what mattered.

"Shh!"

With a start, Willow realized she was arrhythmically bumping the wooden table leg with her sandaled foot. She stopped, blushing.

She had obviously tortured these people enough, and gathered her books into her tie-dyed canvas shoulder bag.

"Lay off the caffeine," a black girl in an aqua jumper suggested, none too nicely.

"Speed, you mean," sniggered a thick-necked guy in a denim shirt, leaning back in his chair with his copy of *Being and Nothingness*.

The whole table laughed.

Willow stood and adjusted the strap of her bag, berating herself for not being able to control her fidgeting, even after all these years.

As she tossed her long hair out of her face and walked to the glass exit door, she heard a loud thud. She turned and saw Mr Denim Shirt sprawled on the beige speckled linoleum floor, having leaned too far back in his chair.

Suppressing a smile and feeling unaccountably guilty, Willow hurried through the lobby and spotted Brad outside on the wide granite front steps, finishing a cigarette. He saw her through the window and smiled, sending a thrill through her heart.

Yes, hiding out in Webster is definitely the right decision.

Pushing through the mass of students loitering around the pretty blond library aide, Willow exited into the cool fall air and Brad's eager embrace.

***   ***   ***

Real mussels and barnacles encrusted the wooden pilings flanking the entrance to the coffeehouse. The door itself boasted numerous heavy rivets and a large wheel rather than a conventional knob. It looked able to repel the largest waves likely to ever break over Beech Street. The place had been a seafood restaurant until a year ago, and the new owners apparently liked the original decor.

Brad stopped outside the Foghorn and pretended to check his reflection in the window while he scanned inside the shop for any sign of Melissa. He knew he'd agreed to meet her at a coffeehouse, and this one was a likely candidate. It could also be Cafe Mocha two blocks away, and there was an outside chance she'd mentioned Sumatra's, the priciest, but they'd already been there once and that seemed to rule it out.

He didn't see her, which could be either good or bad. Good if it meant he was on time, bad if it meant he was in the wrong place. He went in.

This would be the first actual date they'd arranged. All the other times they went out started as simple coincidences. She would suddenly come out of a shop and bump into him, or appear in line waiting to be seated at the same restaurant. Brad enjoyed talking to her, and he didn't want to be rude, so he humored her whenever she invited herself to join him.

The last time that happened she'd said they had to stop running into each other, and clarified that she wanted to meet him at a coffeehouse, possibly this one, the next evening.

Five minutes later, Melissa opened the door and darted inside. Brad waved, but she didn't look his way. She stood still for a moment, then the tension eased from her face and she smiled a contented, eyes-half-shut smile. She glanced around, spotted Brad, and shook her head as she trotted over.

"I was supposed to be at Cafe Mocha, wasn't I?" Brad asked.

"It's okay," Melissa said as she patted his hand. "I tracked you down."

They ordered cappuccinos and discussed where to have dinner. Melissa knew the local eateries well for a freshman.

"Are you from around here, originally? Most freshmen think downtown Webster is only the row of shops facing campus."

"No," she said. "I just have a good memory for details."

"That'll come in handy as an accounting major."

Melissa smiled broadly. Brad couldn't figure out why it startled him. He took a sip of his coffee and she kept beaming at him. He cleared his throat, and at last she glanced down at her drink, still grinning. Teeth, Brad realized. This wasn't the same smile she wore all the time.

"Wow," she finally said, "I was unsure about majoring in accounting. Now I'm not. All the sudden, since you said that." Her smile settled into the familiar shape, lips pressed together, but her eyes sparkled.

Brad gulped. To cover it he said, "Ahh, we were trying to pick a restaurant. I'm getting hungry now."

"Me too," Melissa said. "We could just go for pizza."

"That'd be great."

"We can do something more romantic another time."

"Okay." Now Brad smiled, knowing she would think he was calculating the best balance of candlelight and moonlight and where to obtain it, but he thought pizza sounded far more appealing. "The Oboe's not too far to walk."

They strolled in the mild evening. Melissa told Brad, "Pizza was always this rare treat growing up. There were only two places to go for it, and my mother has never really approved. I'm still getting used to living in a sea of it."

"College town," Brad agreed. "My mom liked to get a break from making dinner. Dad would bring home a pizza once or twice a week."

"Oh, Daddy loves the stuff. He'd eat it for every meal if Mother would permit it."

"She sounds a little strict."

"A little. But that's not such a bad thing."

"I should let you know," Brad confided, "I sometimes don't do so great with too many rules. You didn't inherit her strict streak, did you?"

"Not likely, because I'm adopted. I think that's more the sort of thing one learns, anyway. So it probably rubbed off. You'll just have to learn how to behave."

They reached Original Brick Oven, known as the Oboe, and got one of the tiny tables near the jukebox.

"Adopted? Wow. Did your parents, your adoptive parents I mean, did they tell you or did you have to figure it out?"

"They told me. I must have been really little because it's something I've always known. I can't remember them first telling me, but we've talked about it a lot. Mother especially wanted me to know."

"Didn't that make you curious about your real mother?"

Melissa folded her arms over her chest. "My 'real' mother? I grew up with my real mother. The person who gave birth to me, you mean?"

Brad hid behind his menu. He heard Melissa's fingernails drumming on the table in a steady, almost martial cadence.

"No." A disgusted, weary sigh was smeared through Melissa's words. "I've never been all that curious about her. She almost certainly did me a favor by giving me up, so I guess that's all I feel the need to know." There was silence for several seconds. "Brad, put down your damn menu."

Brad obeyed, and tried to look Melissa in the eye. It worked for a second, then he had to lower his gaze. "I see," he offered. "Shall we just get slices, or split a pie? I'm hungry."

"You mentioned."

"The whole pie then?"

"Sure."

A waiter stepped up to the table moments later, and Melissa handled the entire order, smiling a becoming smile and speaking for Brad in a way that made him feel like a toddler. Their waiter smiled back, no doubt gunning for a nice tip, and Melissa didn't face Brad again until the waiter went around a corner into the kitchen.

When she did look his way, Brad felt she was looking through him. He sat perfectly still, because his only other option was squirming. It didn't seem fair that she got mad at him over an insensitive remark, given that he had no practice with adopted people. Do they like to be called adoptees, or is that rude? His overpowering urge to say something to fix it all met an equally paralyzing terror that anything he uttered would dig him in deeper. She scrutinized something taped to the inside of his skull, disappointed by both the penmanship and the composition.

Brad knew the typical tactics in this scenario. Crack a joke, or compliment her hair. He also knew Melissa would see through it. Maybe that would be all right, if she could tell he was sorry.

"I've been thinking," Melissa finally began, and Brad slouched. First he went to the wrong place, then he insulted her mother. He could guess what she'd been thinking about.

She went on, saying, "About our trip up to the roof. I think about it sometimes. Don't you?"

*** *** ***

Brad stood quietly at the front door, watching Willow work. She sat on the floor, as usual, fiddling with her slide-rule and occasionally writing something in her notebook. She probably knew he was watching — it had become his habit ever since their first date. He liked seeing her unguarded. It confirmed that the face he saw was real. She was genuine. Willow Charm. Not anything else.

Standing on her front porch like this heightened his desire. He wanted to touch her, and reached out. His fingers bumped the glass and it rattled. Willow didn't look up, but Brad saw her smile as she continued her homework. He drummed his fingers on the window, but she still ignored him, her smile growing wider.

Brad opened the door and entered the house. Willow's head didn't move, but the gentle flutter of her lashes told him she peeked. He closed the door and stood watching her again. She kept changing the settings on her slide-rule, but no longer wrote anything down or consulted her text.

She won. The desire to touch her overwhelmed the desire to make her look. Brad sat behind her on the sofa and placed his hands on her shoulders. Willow leaned back between his knees and finally looked at him.

"Oh, Brad. When did you get here?"

He kissed her.

"Hitting the books again, I see."

"They started it, officer. Honest."

"I'm afraid I have to take you downtown, young lady."

Willow blinked.

"To a nice restaurant that just opened. It's called the Vagabond. I hear it's very... nice. But not so nice that they would turn away nice people like ourselves. Isn't that nice?"

Willow chuckled and nodded. She stood up facing away from the couch, and Brad set his hands on her waist. Her hips rocked a few times, and his hands guided her into a swiveling motion. With her hands on his, she asked, "Isn't that nice?"

Brad pulled her into his lap and wrapped her up in a big embrace.

"Very, very, nice," he said into her hair. He laid out across the couch, pulling Willow on top of him. They kissed deeply, wanting each other more than air, not letting up until they both gasped.

Willow sat up, straddling Brad, and peeled off her peasant blouse.

"What if someone comes to the door?" Brad asked, rolling her nipple between his finger and thumb.

"I'll make you answer it," Willow replied, leaning down to where Brad could kiss her breasts. While he did that, he caressed her thighs and undid both their pants. Another soul kiss, while they shed their jeans like snake skins, rubbing them against one another in a tangled but elegant dance.

Willow tumbled them off the sofa, and let Brad cradle her as he landed on top. They poised for a long moment, eyes locked, before he entered her.

*** *** ***

Willow savored the dregs of her vanilla malt, coaxing the final rivulet into her mouth with the extra-long spoon from Brad's root beer float. How long had it been since she'd tasted anything so delicious? She couldn't even remember.

"You want another one?" Brad asked.

Smiling behind closed eyes, Willow sighed and shook her head. "You'll spoil me. I won't be able to eat lentil soup ever again."

"Would that be such a loss?" He took her right hand and kissed the knuckles.

Willow felt so content, so calm. She always did when she was with Brad. He was a balm, a soothing potion that quieted her usual nervous energy. Something about him silenced all of her accustomed tics and fidgeting. He was her inner peace.

She squeezed his hand.

Preceded by the smell of malt vinegar, their waiter approached bearing two platters of fish and chips. Willow's stomach growled at the sight of all the grease. After living with the hippies for so long, her body craved something unhealthy. "Can I get some ketchup, please?"

Brad broke his fillets in half to let the steam escape in fragrantly fishy clouds and toyed with a fry. "My mom called yesterday to harass me about coming home for Thanksgiving. Thanksgiving! It's not even October."

"Wow," Willow concurred and chewed on a bite of fish. The waiter deposited the ketchup pot and left.

"Does your mom do stuff like that?" Brad asked while dunking his fry in the ketchup.

"My mom's dead. So, no."

Fry halfway to his mouth, Brad froze and looked like he'd just killed her mother himself, accidentally. "Oh jeez Wil, I'm sorry!"

"Don't worry about it." She smiled and guided the fry into his mouth like she was feeding a child. "She died when I was born. I never knew her, so I don't miss her."

Brad chewed hesitantly, as if afraid that by enjoying his food he would be showing disrespect for her motherless state. To compensate, Willow gulped down two ketchup-smothered fries and took an enormous bite of battered fish.

"It must have been rough growing up without a mother," Brad said. "You're probably really close with your dad."

The wad of fish in her mouth swam straight at her esophagus, trying to choke her. With much effort, she swallowed and shook her head. "Not really." Hopefully that would be enough to get him on to the next topic.

"Oh. So your brothers and sisters took care of you?"

Is Brad pumping me for information? She took another nibble of dinner and studied him. He looked as guileless as ever, slurping up his rapidly deflating float. Most likely he was just curious. How should she answer? It would be unwise to give out too much accurate information about herself, even to Brad. She didn't feel up to inventing an entire sibling or two, and frankly she didn't know anything about normal family relationships anyway. Anything she would say was bound to sound peculiar to someone with a normal upbringing. The key was to stick close to the truth.

"Only child," she said.

Brad looked like he felt sorry for her, which made the lies all the more distasteful. She dove into them before she had a change of heart. "My dad's a cop." Almost true. "Very authoritarian." That was the truth, but she didn't like talking about Ted Finch at all. It brought back memories of both a fairly happy girlhood and an extremely troubling finale to her time with him.

Brad nodded like he understood everything, not just what she'd said aloud. But he said, "So will you be going home for Thanksgiving?"

"Didn't we cover this? No. I will not. He's too far away." *In more ways than one.* Ester Finch would not be going home ever again. Willow went through the mechanics of eating until she noticed Brad staring at her with furrowed brow. "What?"

"What do vegetarians eat on Thanksgiving?"

A laugh of relief escaped her and she smiled. "I hope it's not tofu-loaf."

***   ***   ***

Brad wrapped his arms around Melissa's torso, enfolding her and caressing her naked buttocks. She lay on top of him, tracing the cords of his throat with a fingertip, rocking her hips slightly. Brad bit his lip and she smiled devilishly.

She whispered, "See? I told you this would be nicer than the roof."

Brad nodded. He didn't trust his voice, knowing Mrs Lehrer lurked somewhere in the house and would evict him immediately if she caught them. It was in the lease.

Brad glanced at the clock and Melissa pouted. She shifted her weight, now grinding more than rocking. Brad mouthed, "Curfew," but hoped she'd continue to resist the idea of leaving.

She didn't. With a perfunctory kiss, she dismounted and began gathering her clothes.

Brad sat up and reached for his pants. "I can walk you home," he whispered.

Melissa stood with her back to him, fastening her bra. At his offer, she looked over her shoulder smiling, and mouthed, "Thank you!"

They finished dressing, stifling their giggles at every inopportune noise or bump. Brad checked the hallway to make sure the coast was clear. He saw Mrs Lehrer in the kitchen, busy over the sink, so they got away clean.

The entire way to her dorm they held hands. At first Melissa was practically skipping, but she settled down along the walk. At the entrance to Irving Hall they stood nose-to-nose, Brad's head bowed and hers upturned, for several silent moments.

"Good night," Brad said.

"Can I see you tomorrow?" Melissa asked.

Brad kissed the top of her head. "I don't know. I have classes and meetings. I'll give you a call." The dejected look on her face squeezed Brad's chest. "Maybe," he offered in a hopeful voice. She blinked away tears and stepped back, nodding. "I'll call, for sure. At least I'll call."

This news brightened Melissa's expression a little, and she crushed him in her embrace. Brad was shocked at her speed, and the sheer strength with which she clung to him, the sharp pain in his ribs. He hoped she'd be done before he passed out.

Finally she let go, and took a few backwards steps toward the door so she could wave at him. He smiled, and her teeth flickered for an instant before she spun and marched into her dorm without looking back.

Brad stuck his hands in his pockets and set out for home.

He whistled. Melissa's reluctance to be away from him was a powerful compliment.

Thinking back over their brief acquaintance, Brad couldn't find any single magical moment when his feelings for her appeared. But he looked forward to calling her, maybe even sneaking off to spend time with her tomorrow.

*** *** ***

Komodo's cold wet nose burrowed under the blankets and

encountered Brad's shoulder. Brad unclosed his eyes and saw the dog smiling and wagging his tail, ready for his morning trip outside.

A glance at the bedside clock told Brad it was 7:15. He would need to hurry or he would be late for his first class. He patted Komodo's head.

"You're a good alarm clock."

"What time is it?" Willow asked from deep inside the warm blanket nest they shared.

"Quarter past."

"Quarter past what?" she asked as she rolled over and snuggled up against him.

"Seven." He kissed the top of her head.

"Eight o'clock classes should be abolished."

Her smooth, warm skin fleetingly brushed across him as she climbed out of bed.

"Morning, 'Modo," she said and scampered to the bathroom.

The balance sheet in Brad's mind ran through the same calculations it did every time he spent the night at the bungalow with Willow, weighing the pros and cons of trying to coax her back into bed. As usually happened, he concluded that he shouldn't. While both of them would like nothing better than to spend the morning lazing around naked together, they both had responsibilities. That Willow took her studies so seriously was one of the things he liked best about her, and she never complained about occasionally taking a back seat to his own academic commitments. With graduation only a semester and a half away, he needed to focus. Knowing she was naked in the next room didn't make that easy, though.

Brad heaved himself out of bed and pulled his pants on. After supervising Komodo's brief sojourn in the back yard, Brad joined Willow in the shower.

"If you take Komodo home before class you won't have time for breakfast," Willow said as she rinsed her long hair. "Why don't you leave him here today? Ember will be home most of the time, so he won't be lonely."

Soaping his armpits, Brad agreed. "I don't think I can get away with taking him to class too many more times. Having him at my office doesn't cause too much trouble, but I can't leave him there when I'm out."

They switched places so Brad could rinse. Since this was not a leg-shaving day, Willow was done, and began to wring the water out of her hair. Brad speeded up his ministrations. He wanted to be ready to give her a ride to campus.

As she toweled herself dry, Willow said, "'Modo's welcome here anytime. I think he gets bored when he's alone."

"Don't we all?"

*** *** ***

Melissa risked a glance at the clock. 4:16 a.m., which was zero hours, 182 days, and four years until some kind of scary event with an island and three miles.

She returned her attention to the desk. Clean white typing paper was carefully arranged to cover as much of it as possible, and she could keep her grip so long as she sat motionless and stared at the blank pages. Their featurelessness wasn't as good as Brad's influence, but any port in a storm.

Patty had figured out Melissa was a freak. She hadn't said anything about it, but now Patty was never in the room at the same time as Melissa. When she wasn't sleeping at her boyfriend's, or with other guys, she was at another girl's place, and never came in except while Melissa was at class or with Brad.

Melissa hadn't said anything either, but the smile and the idle chit chat became pointless and so she dropped the pretense. And she called Patty a faithless slut, which while somewhat rude was also true. So, correction, Melissa had said something. In effect she'd said, 'I'll show you what a freak I am!' Normal people, even if they know their roommates are sluts, don't throw it in their faces.

The strain since meeting Brad had gotten unbearable. Before that she never had any perspective, no basis for comparison.

It seemed for every moment of relief she enjoyed, some hideous pressure would build to make her suffering that much deeper upon their separation. She hadn't slept in days.

So, Patty the shallow slut could be forgiven. If the mildewed grout in the third shower stall from the left could be believed, and Melissa had no doubt that it could, the number of unwed mothers in the United States would continue to rise. Patty, forever forgetting her birth control pills, would probably soon be one of them. Why should she have to put up with a freaky roommate too?

It didn't matter if Melissa terrified Patty. Solitude was desirable, if Brad wasn't an option. But she couldn't let Brad see she was a freak. Never. The fact that the visions melted away with him near made it doable, but the lack of sleep would start so show soon.

His fucking landlady was the problem. She'd evict him if they got caught. The night, when she could be in paradise, became Melissa's darkest hell. Challenging this state of affairs made sense, intellectually. Brad would find another place. For that matter, if she got kicked out of the dorms it wouldn't be the end of the world. But the risk, the chance that he'd blame her for the upheaval, was paralyzing.

Her mind spun horrifying abandonment scenarios if she contemplated anything assertive. She wanted to make him understand how trapped she felt, how he compressed her world. He didn't mean for it to happen, but still she wanted to scream sometimes.

Things were fine out to about 100 feet, and went to hell by unpredictable degrees beyond that. He didn't have to stay in the same room. In the same building usually sufficed, once she'd been near him for a few minutes to get stabilized. Melissa resented the awkward length of her leash. Having Brad as a next-door neighbor would be almost good enough. Almost. She'd have to tail him all over town every day of her life, and move whenever he did. Eventually she'd get arrested and go mad in prison.

By now it was probably 4:18. *Stare at the white. Not at the edges of the sheets, not at the subtle shadows thrown by the reading lamp. Stare.*

Why did it have to be Brad? There was nothing wrong with him that couldn't be fixed, he was even handsome underneath the scruffiness, but Melissa couldn't get any tingle at the thought of him. She looked but she couldn't see what made him special.

Other women could. Brad turned heads continually, although he seemed to be as oblivious to that as to everything else. Thank god. They'd had nine dates now, and he'd been equally distracted throughout each of them. He was very nice, he paid for dinner, but she had to make all the moves. She threw herself at him, and even then it wasn't a sure thing.

Melissa sniffed, and the sharp noise brought her a dense mass of numbers representing relative humidity as a function of altitude, in thirty-inch increments, above all the parking meters in Seattle at noon the previous Tuesday. She rubbed her nose and fought against tears. Brad couldn't see what made her special, either. He didn't even realize he was supposed to be looking.

A grimace stretched Melissa's lips. All she had to do was show him what made her special! Just confide in him about being a freak, because what could be more special than that? Tears splashed on her clean white paper as a croaking, mirthless laugh freed itself from her chest.

What she needed was a tool, an implement to work on Brad with. A means of manipulating him without confrontation. It wouldn't have to be anything subtle. Hell, too subtle and he'd miss it altogether.

He had her trapped, so she had to turn the tables.

*** *** ***

"Okay, but that doesn't really answer my question," said Cloud, her voice losing its accustomed purr and gaining a rougher texture. She stood in the doorway, blocking Willow's escape from the small living room. Willow couldn't decide if it was a conscious move or not.

Cloud wasn't someone Willow spent much time with, but it was impossible not to notice her. She had lustrous strawberry-blond hair, flawless porcelain skin, and sepia cat eyes. And in spite of the fact that she'd had her baby, Dragonfly Bay, less than a month ago, she wore hip-huggers and a halter-top, and her stomach was flat.

She came straight to the bungalow after the feast at Threshold House, distraught over Severin's big announcement, which Ember and Beacon were still coming to grips with themselves. They tried gamely to help her understand, while Willow looked on from the sofa, braiding and unbraiding a lock of her own hair.

"All I'm saying is we need to keep an open mind," Ember said.

"And I'm saying that Love is Truth, and I love nature. Not... not *that*."

"But—"

"They're not!" Cloud growled. "They're not the same at all."

Ember looked to Beacon and Willow for help.

The announcement was big for a few reasons. First, it was novel to have any announcement per se. Severin often spoke to the group at a meal, rolling ideas around or giving a news brief for House activities, but this was more formal. Even bigger, the announcement amounted to a declaration of the TEF's beliefs. It verged on dogma, and as such the group had never dealt with its like before. Biggest of all, the details of this new doctrine seemed at odds with the simplistic nature worship the Following had always practiced. Severin laid it out clearly that there were certain things that were vital, they were 'of the Threshold,' and several he named were scientific and technological marvels. This caused a ripple of dissent to sweep through the crowd. He'd adjourned, leaving everyone to cope without further clarification.

Cloud wasn't coping well. "What do you say, Wil?"

Oh hell. She didn't care one way or the other, didn't see why the others in the Following let Severin dictate their beliefs.

Letting go of the braid, she watched it slowly unwind itself and tried for something noncommittal. "I don't know yet. Maybe with something this big, it's best to sleep on it."

Willow could tell by Cloud's expression that she wasn't going for it. From the corner of her eye she saw Beacon mouth, "Nice try."

Willow sighed.

Cloud folded her arms. "You believe all this new crap?"

"I told you." Willow didn't want to alienate anyone, especially those she lived with. She smoothed her hair. "I need time to think about it."

"Not me."

"You plan to leave?" Willow asked. "Over this?"

Cloud looked uncertain for a moment but, though her golden-brown eyes were sad, she said with conviction, "Can you imagine a better reason?"

Willow felt Cloud should be free to choose. Maybe she would choose badly, but her freedom was more important. Willow wanted to say so, but Beacon and Ember were horrified at the prospect that Cloud might leave. They sat together on a large floor pillow, holding hands and radiating acceptance and solidarity. The details of Severin's announcement mattered little to them. The mission was to keep Cloud. Willow didn't want to fail them, even if it meant advancing Severin's agenda.

Another sigh escaped, and Willow spoke quickly before Cloud could interject. "Which part bothers you the most? It was a lot to take in, but maybe not all of it was awful."

Cloud glared down at her hands, counting off the offensive parts of Severin's speech on her long fingers as she stalked toward Willow and sat on the edge of the spool table. "The stuff about computers, and the space program, and television, but mainly when he told us we've been wrong about the things we worship. He made all our beliefs into a lie."

"He just added some things. He said, 'We mustn't forget the truth as we learn new ideas.' He didn't say we were wrong."

"We mustn't forget, we just don't believe it anymore," Cloud said. Willow was amazed by Cloud's sudden perceptiveness, her usual childlike air abandoned. "The things he added are wrong! They wipe out the old truth!"

"You think it's impossible to believe both, the old and the new?"

"Of course! You're just taking his side." Cloud narrowed her eyes.

"You don't care."

Willow noticed Beacon and Ember's heads turning back and forth as they followed the argument. It dawned on her that Severin's mishandling of such a momentous announcement was calculated. A test for her, an experiment to see what she would do. He would doubtless hear a complete transcript later.

"Then why would I argue about it?" Willow asked, seeking to counter Cloud's assertion. "Why take his side? Why take any side, if I don't care about you, or about the Following?"

"I don't know. You tell me."

"I'll tell you what I think it means. It kind of makes sense to me, but you can decide for yourself." Willow took a theatrical breath before continuing. "Now, people are basically good. Right?"

"Uh-huh." Cloud nodded.

"Why is that?"

"Because we're part of nature. Animals."

"Right. So the things we build, the inventions—"

Cloud shook her head.

"—are extensions of nature." Willow continued, before Cloud could verbalize her objections. "All science is, is a way to measure nature and figure it out. It's connected." She brought her palms together and touched the tip of her nose with the tips of her thumbs. "If you think about it a certain way, everything there is comes from nature. Science is nature refined."

"Things like science pull us out of nature," Cloud corrected. "Rockets — trying to escape our Mother on rocket ships. And computers are dangerous! Science will push us away from the truth until it kills us all."

The week before, a group that included both Willow and Cloud went to a campus showing of *2001 — A Space Odyssey*, and Cloud had been subdued for the next couple of days.

"Computers aren't like that, Cloud. They don't work that way. Besides, I don't think the evil computer was the main message of the movie."

"Then what was the main message?"

"That science and technology have become part of us. That it's a natural part of our growth. That there are places we can never reach without them."

"You're wrong. You're being seduced by the clever little tricks they're teaching you at Buckminster."

"And my classes are full of people who think I'm being brainwashed by the weirdoes I live with. They don't understand, and they don't want to."

Willow saw the hurt look in Cloud's eyes, could picture the stunned faces of Beacon and Ember, but what was said was said. She unknotted her fingers and reached out to take Cloud's hand. Cloud left it limp, which hurt Willow in a way pulling it back would not have.

When she spoke, Cloud's voice seemed more serene, resigned. "I can't live in two worlds, Willow. Sooner or later, you'll have to make a choice, too. I can't stay anymore."

Willow was struck between the eyes by the zen notion that by her current lifestyle, she followed two paths. That there could be an inevitable decision point. She wanted to drop the discussion to go meditate on the paradox, but she was on a mission. Not for Severin, but for Beacon and Ember. She opted to raise a practical concern. "Where will you go?"

"I can camp out."

"With Dragonfly? He's only two weeks old. It's autumn."

Cloud was stubborn. "I love—"

"Nature, we all do. That hasn't changed."

"Severin doesn't love it. He loves power." Cloud thrust out her chin to emphasize the irrefutability of the claim. Willow realized that until tonight Cloud had never considered this. She just didn't know how these things work. Persuading her might be only too simple.

"Right. He does love power. Do you?"

"No!"

"That's why he's the leader. Not because he's always right."

Cloud shook her pale copper hair. "You think we should follow him, even if we think he's wrong?"

Willow couldn't help picturing her father's likely response to this, a question that to him would be nonsensical. The led don't pass judgment on their leader. They don't contemplate right or wrong: they follow.

Willow simply nodded. "He loves us, too."

Cloud's eyes welled up, and she bobbed her head in emphatic agreement.

A group hug engulfed Willow, and she didn't have to look anybody in the eye.

***   ***   ***

Komodo lay on the floor beside Willow with his head in her lap. She scratched him behind the ears. Brad liked to watch her do little things like that. Unguarded things. He liked being with her, here in her bedroom with its funny cowboys and Indians wallpaper and scuffed floor. It was tiny, and unfurnished except for several homemade candles and the twin mattress on the floor, but that was all they needed. They could talk for hours in that bed, cuddling together under the electric blanket he'd bought for her. He finished making the bed and joined her on the sheepskin rug.

She glanced at him and said casually, "'Modo thinks I'm pregnant."

"Are you?"

"I'm pretty sure."

Brad hugged Willow and kissed the top of her head. The news elated him. He marveled at how being in love could make something so complicated feel so simple.

"We'll get you in for a test so we can be sure."

"Ye gods, no! I just finished midterms. No more tests, please."

"Don't worry, babe. I grade on a curve."

Willow smiled ecstatically and kissed him. Brad pulled her into his lap and Komodo whimpered.

Willow reached down and patted the dog's head while kissing Brad.

Komodo settled down, but Brad thought he still looked concerned.

"You'll make a fine babysitter, 'Modo," Brad reassured.

Well, that settled the relationship dilemma. Time to break things off with Mel. He'd try to let her down easy, but knew she'd take it hard. She was sweet and hadn't done anything wrong except fall for him. He hated being in the position to be the bad guy, hated the idea of hurting her, which was how he'd gotten in this deep in the first place. It was hard to say no to Melissa.

Once he'd cleared that account, he would be free to make plans with Wil. Brad wondered if she would want to marry him, whether she believed in that sort of thing. A quick count of the months told him the baby would come in May or June. That lined up well with graduation. Viridian Bank wanted to hire him once he earned his degree. They were quite happy with the job he'd done as an intern.

The future looked good, if a bit rushed.

*** *** ***

Sifting through the trash at the bungalow was undignified, but Severin couldn't delegate it to anyone else. At least there was little to no decomposing food waste mixed in, thanks to Beacon's zeal for composting.

Most expeditions yielded one or two crumpled, discolored pages of sketches and doodles, which he carefully smoothed and stored in a folio. Willow's drawings were poems in a lost language of tangled diagrams. He knew next to nothing about their technical significance, but more than Willow herself about their real meaning. She drew maps of the unmappable Elsewhere.

Unfortunately he didn't yet know how to use them.

Tonight, after pulling a few mysterious treasures from Willow's trash, he decided to see what he might pull from his table. Interpreting those finds would come naturally, and might even cast light on the cast-off drawings.

Or not.

Severin paced. Four objects rested on the sheet covering his table. A feather, sleek and black, coexisting uneasily with the pristine white fabric. A brilliant green chrysalis. Obstetric forceps. Several turns of soldering wire, light gray in color.

If viable, the chrysalis was the first living thing he'd ever retrieved. The feather was unusual, too. Rarely did natural objects come to him in this manner. The other two were more typical. That all of these items emerged in rapid succession indicated a connection between the people or things they symbolized.

The forceps told him there was to be a birth. The soldering wire tied something in all this to Willow, to the path he had chosen for her. He smiled for a moment, but admonished himself not to jump at the first interpretation.

Severin stopped before the table and regarded the small collection. He touched each object in turn, absorbing whatever residual vibrations they carried from the place that sent them. The feather seemed defiant, with a strong connection to him. Something personal. He would return to it for deeper consideration. As his fingers touched the forceps he noted their construction. Two identical pieces of metal, joined and set in opposition. Apart from suggesting Willow's studies, the solder only hinted at a holding or binding of some kind. The chrysalis could be a harbinger of change. That struck a note with him, but it wasn't satisfactory. It held still more meaning. He picked it up.

The color of the butterfly-to-be shamed emerald. It was phosphorescent. What kind of creature would it turn out as? The potentiality, the stasis, aroused Severin. Mysteries held power, and he held a mystery in his hand. An unanswered question. The delayed resolution would build up a charge, and the longer the wait, the more vibrant the wings that would eventually burst from the shell.

He went back to the feather. Shimmering. Surreal. Proud. The answer to an unasked question. Something missing that hadn't been missed. Severin's connection with it carried a sense of authorship.

Powerful mysteries, with Severin as their author. He liked where this was going.

Holding the feather in his right hand, he picked up the forceps in his left. A current passed through him from one to the other — he wasn't sure of its direction. He was sure he was going to be a father.

His smile tentatively returned, and he put down the feather to pick up the soldering wire. A milder energy pulse traveled between it and the forceps, and he grinned. Willow was to be a mother.

Sometimes the first interpretation is the right one, after all.

He reverently replaced the objects, one by one, under the sheet, and smoothed it. He passed his hand over the sheet again. Again. Severin thought of Willow, feeling the cool texture on his palm, applying more of his weight. Thinking about how sturdy the table might be.

Severin straightened up and frowned. Carrying out such an undisciplined daydream would be foolhardy. His table was a conduit into places where primordial forces flowed, not all of them known to him.

Besides, the hammock was certainly more comfortable.

Either way, it would be an immense improvement over digging through her garbage cans.

He caught himself whistling and laughed. The mental image of Willow with a pregnant belly thrilled him. She would be like a chrysalis. Although she wouldn't produce any winged offspring, not literally, any child of hers would do great things. The months of buildup would be ecstasy. Such energies would swirl around her! They would overflow, a continual fountain of power during her entire gestation.

Severin decided it was something of a pity it would only last for nine months.

Chapter Five

GREEN LIGHT

*At 39, Brian Shaw was a bachelor, unless you believe the evidence
which suggests a teenage marriage and his status as a widower. In
any case, on February 3, 1974 he married Molly Oliver, a church
secretary 19 years his junior. (See marriage license, Appendix F,
and wedding photo in the supplements.)*
    from *Brainwashed*, by Julie Rome ©1998 Futhark Press

OCTOBER 1974

Gale Napier stared into the glossy black surface of her scrying pool.
A light, acrid mist curled up, but otherwise all was still. No insights this
morning. Gale emptied two sugar packets and a creamer into the mug,
but didn't stir. The white cloud of not-milk roiled portentously, but told
her nothing. Shrugging, Gale stirred her coffee and sipped.

The only other customer in the restaurant was the old man at the
other end of the counter, engrossed in conversation with the career
waitress. Gale had been following him for a week and knew he would
soon leave and buy a newspaper before walking to his office, two blocks
away. This morning for the first time she followed him into the
restaurant. She wanted to hear what he and the waitress talked about,
but to sit any closer would arouse suspicion. From the little she
overheard, they were discussing the waitress's mother's health. Nothing
important.

After finishing her coffee, Gale left some change on the counter and
went outside. It would look less like she was following him if she left
before he did. She wanted to surprise him when she confronted him,

and what better place than in his own office?

Gale walked up the street, head down, not looking around. She stopped at the entrance to a nondescript two-story office building. Dr Gladstone's office was on the second floor, with windows over the rear parking lot.

The receptionist was not at her desk. Gale opened the door to the exam rooms quickly, as if she had business there. Noises came from a large supply closet. As Gale passed, she caught a glimpse of a well-groomed woman reaching for something on a high shelf. She heard the front door open again as she spotted a room with cheap paneling and an overflowing desk. The doctor's office.

Funny, thought Gale, to think of doctors as having actual offices. She entered and looked around.

Behind the desk, the only window afforded a view of a utility pole for those unlucky enough to be called in here for a conference. For such unluckies there were also two pea green vinyl chairs facing the desk. Gale nudged the door partially shut and sat in one. The desk was a fine example of metal and formica construction. It held a pile of charts and files, a telephone, an empty ashtray, and a plastic model of a kidney. All around the room were wall-mounted shelves brimming with texts and more models. Gale was vaguely disturbed by the absence of a diploma.

With shaking fingers, Gale opened her purse. She checked her gaunt, elfin face in her compact. She smoothed her pale hair and tried a hesitant smile. All neat. She set her purse on the floor by her feet and waited, sweaty hands limp on the lap of her russet polyester pantsuit. She dressed carefully today, in order to impress upon the doctor her maturity. The only mistake, she now noticed, was that her raffia purse didn't match her low brown heels. Hoping Dr Gladstone wouldn't notice the faux pas, Gale picked up her bag and hung it over the back of her chair.

Less than five minutes passed before she heard Dr Gladstone's phlegmy voice greeting the office staff, and his heavy steps in the hallway. Gale heard him say, "Buzz me when Mrs Grunwald gets here," then he was in the office with her.

He closed the door and hung his beige overcoat on a hook on the back. He turned and saw her. Gale took the time while he got over his initial surprise to study him. A dumpy man with deep-set brown eyes and heavy brow, as well as the patronizing habit of clasping his hands behind his back and rocking on his heels. She could smell his after-shave across the room, the same overpowering medicinal stuff he'd worn back then. It was definitely the same Dr Clarence Gladstone. She gave him a minute to see if he would recognize her.

"Good morning, Miss. You'll need to speak with my receptionist about arranging an appointment."

He didn't remember. Of course not. Hers wasn't the only life he'd ruined. He looked sallow and sickly. The whole office did, with the greenish cast of the air right before a thunderstorm.

Gale took a steadying breath.

"I only have one question, Dr Gladstone, then I'll go."

He looked faintly puzzled, but waited.

"Where is my daughter?" Gale kept her features impassive, but her pulse was frantic.

She hoped Dr Gladstone would hear the undercurrent of desperation in her voice and understand the gravity of the situation. He didn't.

"Who is your daughter? Wouldn't she be in school today?"

Gale smiled bitterly. Dr Gladstone moved to his chair, shrugged into his white coat, and sat.

The coat with the stethoscope protruding from the pocket like a skeletal jack-in-the-box, his name embroidered in blue — Gale's stomach clenched. She felt unprotected and at his mercy again.

Blinking away the memory, she said, "My daughter is almost 19. I haven't seen her since she was one day old. I was 14 when you took her away from me." Gale was pleased with her even tone. "I want to see her."

Now Dr Gladstone showed interest. He studied her face, trying to pull a name from the distant past.

"You were at Renaissance Center," he stated, any trace of humor or goodwill gone.

"Yes," Gale said too stiffly. Where else would she have known him? The greenness of the air intensified, and Gale glared at the overhead lights. The doctor took no notice.

"I'm afraid I can't help you." He gestured toward the door.

Gale didn't move. She tried so hard to project a mature image. Having known her as a teenager he was incapable of seeing her any other way. That wasn't fair.

"That's it?" She had to make him see she was serious. "You don't even take the time to learn my name?" This wasn't how she rehearsed it. Her eyebrows were, she realized, bobbing all over her forehead. She counted to five as Gladstone spoke.

"Very well." He leaned forward, placing his elbows on his desk. "There's something memorable about your eyes. An odd shade of green, like apples. And so full of hate. You have no need to hate us. We lived up to our name. You and your child each had a new beginning."

"Whether we wanted it or not." She couldn't keep the acid bite from her words.

"Don't be ridiculous. You said yourself you were 14. How would you have supported a child?" He sat back. "I honestly don't understand this attitude. Most of the girls were happy enough to be rid of their mistakes and given a clean start, but there was always the stubborn minority who insisted we were the problem."

He was trying to deflect her. He was hiding something. "Who took all the babies? Where were they sent?" Gale settled back in her seat, having all but lunged onto the desk.

"Now, now. I'm meant to be figuring out which little tramp you are." Gladstone was unperturbed. "There were so many. What was your last name?"

Why wouldn't he give her a straight answer? She couldn't let him see the extent of her desperation. She wasn't a child now. She had to be mature, indifferent, like all adults. With her eyes closed, Gale took two quick breaths. When she opened her eyes again, she felt calmer, and the lights looked normal.

"Napier," she said.

"Napier." He steepled his fingers. "Oh, yes! Gertrude. Gretchen. Gale. Gale Napier."

He remembered. That meant he could give her what she needed. She smiled again, slightly.

Gladstone continued, "You were the little idiot who refused all medical care on religious grounds. Wouldn't even let us listen for a heartbeat." He sat up straight, fingering the stethoscope, and stared at her. "And, as I recall, when your time came you ran away and gave birth in a field or a barn or some such. No medical care for you, oh no. But as soon as you heard how loud a newborn can squall, you came right back to the Center, didn't you?"

Gale remembered her return to Renaissance Center. November was no time to be outside in the rain, barefoot especially. Shivering and soaking wet, she'd cradled her tiny Kelly. Kelly who was supposed to buy her freedom.

Kelly who had been such a surprise.

Gladstone kept trying to distract her, but it wasn't going to work. Gale threw another angry glance up at the damn lights which were suddenly green-tinged again. She glared at the doctor. "Where is she?"

"How should I know? The mothers were my thankless responsibility, not the babies. We were sponsored by a government agency. They took charge of the infants. I have no idea what they did with them."

"Who would know?" Gale practically shouted. Losing her temper wasn't going to do any good.

"Not me. And that's all I'll tell you. Leave now. I have patients to see."

Gale kept her hands in her lap, the nails of her left hand digging into her palm, the whitened knuckles concealed under her right hand. "I want my daughter." Why couldn't he see she was serious?

"She's an adult now, but you're still young. Have another."

Gale lurched to her feet, glaring at Gladstone's face through a virescent tunnel. After several deep breaths, she began unsteady steps toward the door. She needed to think and then come see this man again. Now that she knew what she was up against, she would prepare her argument. Contain her rage. Make him see.

"That limp, you got it during the birth didn't you?"

Gale froze. Most people didn't notice the limp.

"I remember now. You pinched a nerve. You see, you did need us after all."

Gale turned back to face the old man. He looked smug.

"I didn't need you then," she corrected, "but I n—"

A whirl of green light coalesced behind her eyes and shot down to her heels. Gale sank to her knees. *Not again!* Tears ran down her cheeks. This was utterly unacceptable. She would not belittle herself in front of this man.

She had only experienced the whirling light once before, and attributed it to the hormonal hurricane of labor. It drove her from the relative security of Renaissance Center to give birth alone in a boxcar. Nothing so lowly as a barn. She'd been told that she herself was found in a train car as a newborn, so it seemed fitting.

Dr Gladstone stood and approached her, a look of contempt on his face, which he tried to pass off as concern.

Gale's head tipped back and she looked up at Dr Gladstone. Her tear-blurred sight showed him taller, younger, his eyes now gray and lost. She clung to him with her gaze, desperate. The green whirl coiled in anticipation.

"Please," she croaked, "help me find my baby."

"Miss Napier," he reached for her hands to help her stand. "I urge you—"

He touched her and the green light sprang. It rocketed up from the soles of her feet, turned her loins to tingling water, sent her pulse racing and, with a crackle-zap of static, leapt from her fingertips to the doctor. His eyes went wide and he bit his tongue. He toppled onto her.

When she was 14 and in labor, the green feeling built with each contraction. She felt cornered in the Center. She hadn't wanted anyone to know the baby was coming, had tried to keep her secret. The nurse, no fool, recognized what was happening. When she approached Gale to put her on a gurney, Gale felt the bolt of infernal internal lightning ricocheting inside her. She'd thought it was the next awful stage of labor, but when the nurse touched her, the energy shot out in a green flash. The nurse collapsed, hitting the bed on her way to the floor where she lay unmoving. Immediately, the monstrous green energy began collecting inside Gale again.

Wearing only a thin sweater over her shapeless dress, Gale made her way down the hallway between labor pains. The green screen around her senses strengthened with each contraction. She only wanted the horrible ordeal to be over, but the green wouldn't let her rest.

The afternoon was breezy, but the rain didn't start until dusk. By then the cramps had become almost nonstop. When her time came she was alone.

Now she was alone in the office.

Several minutes passed before Gale could move. She lay awkwardly on the floor with the immobile, unbreathing bulk of Dr Gladstone pinning her, engulfed in the stench of his after-shave. He was not a large man, but Gale was petite and her limbs felt heavy and asleep. His body, tense at first, slowly relaxed and pressed down on her more thoroughly. The tension seemed to flow out of the doctor and into her, reenergizing her with pins and needles. When her muscles finally responded, Gale shoved and wiggled and whimpered until she got free.

Gladstone was my only lead! Gale wanted to gut herself and be rid of the horrible swirl of light before it ruined anything else. She needed to get out of this building, this town, before she was discovered.

She stood and brushed off her slacks. After tying a kerchief over her head and putting on her sunglasses, Gale left the doctor's office as quickly as she could without running.

*** *** ***

Afternoons by herself in the bungalow were some of Willow's favorite times. Ember and Beacon were good friends, but she needed some time alone. To study, for one thing. And of course, so Brad could come and interrupt her.

The knock came right on cue. Willow wondered why he wasn't letting himself in, but went to the door. She pulled it open to find Severin standing in the chill afternoon. She was so startled she just blinked at him.

He stepped inside with a sardonic look, and said, "Hello."

"Hello, Severin. What brings you over here?"

As he took off his coat, Severin replied, "I wanted to find out how things are going with you. Your studies, and Beacon and Ember. I always hear wonderful things about you from them, but I thought it might be best if I came over once in a while."

"Well, make yourself at home," Willow said. She expected him to say something like, "I am at home," but he just dropped his coat on the floor and sat on the spool next to the lava lamp Willow had claimed from his basement.

Komodo wandered into the room. He placed himself between Willow and her guest and tilted his head to the side as if waiting for Severin to explain himself.

"Normally, the arrangement with the bungalow is temporary. Its purpose is to provide a transition into the Following, and people either move into the House or depart our company within a week. I thought you understood."

"What does that have to do with my studies?" Willow asked.

"Now, don't get defensive. I just want you to think about that. Think about moving into the House. I think it would be a good idea."

"I don't think now's a good time." Noticing her hand rapidly clicking her mechanical pencil, she stopped.

"Soon, though."

Willow gave no response, which seemed to be Severin's signal to move to the next topic.

"Classes are going well." He wasn't asking.

"Sure."

"You thought there would be more challenges. You expected to struggle."

"Oh, there are some tough spots. I wouldn't say there's no challenge."

Severin's voice deepened. "You expected to fail."

Willow surprised herself by not being able to utter an objection.

Severin filled in the lull. "The sign you are following was only a start. Only part of the message. I want you to come back to the attic. And I seriously want you to move to the House."

"I have enough things going on that I don't think that's such a good idea." She put the pencil down on her notebook and stuffed her hands in her pockets.

Severin shifted his weight. He folded his arms and looked off to the side.

"I have some news, actually." Willow had hoped she wouldn't have to tell Severin. "Ember knows, but I asked her not to tell anyone else yet. I guess now is a good time to tell you, since you're here." She told herself to quit stalling.

Severin regarded her, his eyes tired and his mouth in a tense frown.

"I'm pregnant." The news sounded exciting to her own ears. "I'm pregnant!"

Severin's eyes no longer looked tired, but he didn't say anything.

Komodo thumped his tail on the floor.

"It feels good to make it official. I was dreading telling everyone, but I was going nuts trying to decide how and when. Anyway, that's the main reason I don't think moving is a good idea right now, and especially not starting another quest."

With sudden brightness in his voice that didn't match his gaze, Severin asked, "Who's the lucky father?"

"My boyfriend, Brad."

Severin stood and went to his coat, put it on. "Pass along my congratulations. I understand about the timing." He smiled, looking through Willow for a moment. "I suppose this tops anything you'd find with the table, anyway. You went and started a new quest without me."

"I'm not sure where it's going to lead me, honestly."

"Don't neglect your classwork. This doesn't change anything."

Willow again withheld her response. Severin stared at her, his mood unreadable. "This is wonderful news," he stated. He left without saying good-bye.

*** *** ***

Severin paced the rough attic floor, testing the edge of the knife with his thumb.

He spared a glance at the table, still too angry to go near it. He hadn't yet forgiven it for making a fool of him, although he knew he'd provided all of the foolishness himself. The clues it gave about Willow's pregnancy seemed calculated to mislead him.

He'd brought a large blade from the kitchen, but studiously restrained himself from hacking at rafters and beams. Such scarification of his sanctum would compromise his authority. He needed some other target for his frustration, a victim that would not tell of his abuse.

Nearly two-thirds of the cavernous attic level was taken up with floor-to-ceiling stacks of trunks, wooden crates, and cardboard boxes. Severin had never before taken an interest in what abandoned treasures of past occupants surrounded him.

The first box he moved held an assortment of glass vases and figurines, tempting to his vandalous mood. But the one beneath held books, musty leather-bound tomes that would be far less noisy in their throes. He lifted one out, hefting it, thinking of tearing paper, slicing the tooled leather into strips.

He opened it and examined a few brittle pages. It was old, printed in 1873, doubtless worth money to a collector. How many years of its century had passed pointlessly in this box? He held a minor tragedy in his hands, with a whole box more at his feet.

The point of the kitchen knife easily passed through a few dozen pages, even with only moderate force applied. The ancient paper disintegrated in ragged furrows as the blade dragged through it. In a matter of minutes Severin reduced the bulk of the volume to confetti, all contained by the pages' intact outer edges. He firmly shut the unblemished leather cover, compressing the ruined leaves within, and slid the defiled book back into line with the others before replacing the boxes as he'd found them. The image of someone's face, decades from now, as elation upon finding the valuable book turned to horror at its senseless desecration, satisfied Severin deeply.

Still angry, but now in full command of his impulses, Severin set aside the knife and approached his table. He took hold of the sheet and rolled the smooth white fabric between his thumb and fingers. Only a thin sheet separating him from the Elsewhere, such a flimsy lid for a portal to such unimaginable power. A woman as slight as Willow, he could easily seize and fling under the sheet so quickly there wouldn't be time to scream. She remained wary of him, but if he asked her to come see what the table indicated about the child, he felt confident that she'd approach it with him. It was something she'd done before. Then his left arm wraps around her waist, and he lifts and bears her forward, not even a violent action but graceful, almost tender. His right hand is free to manage the edge of the sheet, to cover her up. The sheet lays smooth across the table, as always.

Severin let the material slide from his grasp, frowning. Such a juvenile revenge fantasy was embarrassing. It was as reckless as it was impractical. He had no confirmation that the table would even accept a foreign object, deliver it to the Elsewhere. The items he pulled from under the sheet never lasted more than a matter of minutes, so even if she did pass through, it seemed unlikely she'd remain disposed of.

No, he didn't really want to be rid of her. He wanted to have her nearer, especially during her pregnancy. Gritting his teeth, he recalled the insistent little humming he'd felt from the moment she opened the door at the bungalow, his dismay when she told him the news, how he'd understood only then that he felt the earliest tingle of the very energies he so looked forward to. It was the faintest hint of what was to come, and he'd dismissed it out of vanity, out of his erroneous certainty that the job of fertilizing her womb was his, that it might even happen during that particular visit.

Now she had it in her head that a move would be too stressful. Clearly an excuse. After all, she owned few possessions and it was a distance of only a few blocks. Hardly a traumatic relocation. She was thinking ahead to having the infant about, and deemed the sedate atmosphere of the bungalow a better environment than the teeming House.

But that distance of a few blocks was too far, robbing him of contact with Willow's gestational aura. If Beacon and Ember could be influenced to express their displeasure at the idea of a squalling newborn in their home, Willow would be left with no place else to turn. She'd have to come to the House. Severin smiled ruefully. Beacon and Ember not welcoming an infant was absurd. Willow would see through the scheme and pull away all the more.

Severin went back to the box of books to choose another victim.

He would simply have to get used to the idea that this opportunity was not meant for him, and bide his time until the next one.

Chapter Six

WAITING ROOM

Divided Seed shall a Divided Child Beget
who shall grow into a Divided Man
from *New Revelations* by Reverend Brian Shaw, unpublished

JUNE 1, 1975

They'd been gone a long time, or so it seemed. Brad, having no basis for comparison, didn't really know how long it should take to cut a hole in a woman's stomach.

The doctor had said, "Mrs Tanner has a rather narrow mid-pelvis, Mr Tanner. The best way to proceed from here is a caesarean."

Brad had never noticed anything wrong with Mrs Tanner's pelvis, but deferred to the doctor's presumed expertise, even though it bothered him a stranger knew things about his wife's private parts that he himself had been unaware of.

He lit another cigarette and tried not to pace.

He failed.

As his boots scuffed monotonously back and forth in the waiting room, his head swirled with conflict. Brad looked up at the clock and again talked himself out of making a run to see Willow.

Although he didn't know for a fact that Willow was also in labor, he felt sure of it. And she was having a home birth. No doctors around to decide on the best way to proceed if she also had a narrow mid-pelvis. He needed very much to go to her, but was trapped in this windowless, pale-green room with its monolithic coffee machine and its brown vinyl furniture.

Since marrying Melissa, it had gotten harder to be with Willow. It was something he subconsciously knew would happen, but hadn't accepted, and he still wasn't adjusted. He missed Willow desperately.

Mel had happily announced her pregnancy the very day Brad planned to break things off with her. Once she'd told him, there'd been no easy way out. He didn't want to hurt her, didn't want to hurt either of them. They were both having his baby. He couldn't stand the idea of letting either woman down. Melissa hit him hard with "of course you'll do the right thing," and of course he did, at least where she was concerned. In a matter of days they were in front of the Justice of the Peace.

But he didn't feel married. He didn't even have a wedding ring, since at the time they could only afford one. The busy semester left no time to find a home together. Mel stayed in the dorm and he kept his room with Mrs Lehrer. Melissa hated the situation, but accepted it. She wanted to spend all her time with him, which made sense since she was his wife, but it made things awkward with Willow.

In fact he'd almost stood Willow up on her birthday. Melissa made it hard to make excuses, until he'd promised to do something special for her own birthday the next day. With Melissa thus appeased, Brad got to be with Willow for the entire day, and night. He took Mel out to dinner the next evening and enjoyed himself until he figured out she was mad at him for not having a big surprise planned.

Brad sighed.

Once the semester break arrived he and Melissa got a small apartment, and that ended things with Wil.

In his quest to not be anybody's bad guy he'd wound up hurting the woman he loved. He tried to explain that things didn't have to change between them, but Willow didn't see it that way. Her views on love and marriage were, perhaps, not as counterculture as the company she kept.

Now he was out of school, the proud owner of a shiny MBA, and employed as a junior loan officer at Viridian Bank. Now that they could have afforded a second wedding band, Mel never mentioned it. He and

Mel were great financially, and he was putting money away to help Willow, too. She and the baby would be taken care of.

He slumped onto one of the shit-colored chairs and tried to wreath his head in smoke. The trick usually worked better indoors, but apparently the hospital's air circulation system was of the take-no-prisoners persuasion. *Ah well.* Rumination sans fumigation.

Melissa had a hard time connecting with most people. Maybe that was why she demanded so much of his time. After all, even married people were allowed to leave the house, right? She was often a bit too attached, but at the same time she made him feel like the center of the universe.

Of course her clinginess made it cumbersome to see Willow. Brad winced at the thought of how much worse it would get once Mel knew about Wil. He had been rehearsing how to tell her, because he knew he would have to. "Mel, honey, there's someone else. But don't worry. She's not some fling I've taken up with since our wedding. I've been seeing her all along. Actually, she was there first."

More rehearsal would be needed, of course.

The situation couldn't be viewed as cheating. These women were going to have his children. He loved them both. It's not like he went out picking up one-night-stands in bars. He was monogamous with both of them.

Binogamy. The term brought a small smile, which died quickly.

He was still seeing Willow. He saw her walking to her classes, or walking Komodo, and sometimes he saw her through a window. She didn't show any sign that she noticed his spying, but Brad figured she must have. He needed to know she was okay, and although it hurt he would wait until she was ready to talk to him again. 'Modo would take good care of her.

Wil and Brad and Mel and Brad. Only there was just one Brad. It was like keeping two sets of books, Brad thought, and smirked. Embezzlement of affections. The bemusement transformed into depression, and Brad decided he didn't want to think of it like that.

He thought about his children, whom he would soon be meeting. That was also both happy and sad thinking, because he could see that the awkward state of affairs with their mothers would impact the kids too. He would simply insist that he be allowed to be a good father to both. After all, it wasn't fair to anybody any other way.

It was never going to be perfect. It was going to feel strained, forever. What made him do this?

They did it, not him. Wil and Mel.

Crazy, delusional, to think two such beautiful girls would get stuck on him. Beautiful but quite unalike, each from a different world. Middle-class Melissa's hair was chin-length and blond. She had bangs, wore makeup. Free-spirit Willow's hair hung loose well past her shoulders and she colored it a deep red. She never styled it, never wore any makeup. They dressed differently, too. Melissa was fashion conscious, Willow wasn't. Underneath their clothes Willow was slimmer, verging on skinny.

Crazy too how there were odd things alike about them. They were both left-handed. Both had green eyes. They were the same height, shared the same graceful profile. In fact, they could pass for sisters. Take away Wil's henna, give her a haircut and something to worry about, and she and Mel would look identical.

They were the same age, almost exactly, with birthdays only a day apart.

Wil never knew her mom, Mel was adopted…

"Mr Tanner? Did I wake you?"

The cigarette might have done more than burn a small hole in the vinyl seat if the doctor hadn't interrupted then.

"No, no, I'm fine." Brad stood shakily.

"Congratulations, Mr Tanner. It's a boy! Mrs Tanner's going to be fine."

Brad barely comprehended anything the doctor said. He was preoccupied by something else. "Uh, sure. Yeah."

The doctor chuckled. "Have a seat, or we'll soon have another patient on our hands. You look white as a sheet. Do you have any names picked out?"

"Mel wants to call him Kyle."

"Swell. Hey, catch your bearings and get some coffee."

The doctor left.

Brad sat with open, unseeing eyes.

Twins. Willow and Melissa are twins.

***   ***   ***

A thousand and thirteen fire-tongued salamanders licked Melissa's gut, her nipples were raw where they nursed while she slept, and the baby of the lady in the next bed would go to prison for murder at 24.

Where the hell is Brad?

A nurse saw that she was awake and smiled at her. The cafeteria would be all out of egg-salad sandwiches by the time the nurse got there for lunch, and she would need to eat tuna salad, which she didn't like nearly as much because of an incident involving her ex-husband.

"You had a boy, Mrs Tanner. Would you like to meet him?"

Melissa nodded. It was what was expected.

The nurse walked out into the hall, her crepe-soled shoes whispering.

There would be an accident at an appliance assembly plant in Mexico tonight. At 4:28 a.m. Melissa didn't know if that meant her time or local time.

Why did I have to have a caesarean? Not that she had been looking forward to a vaginal delivery, but at least she could have gone home sooner. Now she was trapped in the hospital, without Brad's stabilizing presence, for two weeks. She'd be insane by the time they let her out, and all her planning and misery would have been in vain. Plus she'd have *two* parasites to take care of. What horrible messages would she find in dirty diapers? Melissa shuddered.

She lifted the blanket and looked at the gauze bandage on her belly. Blood seeped through in places, informing her that tapioca was the most popular flavor of pudding in Raleigh, North Carolina.

The nurse wheeled a bassinet into the room and the barrage of trivia stopped. Melissa looked past the nurse, expecting to see Brad, but he wasn't there. She looked at the tiny bundle the nurse was picking up, and warmth spread through her. The baby. It was the baby. He was doing it.

He works.

He was in her arms, sleeping, with his fist in his mouth. Melissa didn't know what to think. How did he compare to other newborns? He was bald and somewhat pudgy. At least his head wasn't all misshapen, since he hadn't squeezed out through her narrow mid-pelvis. The important thing was, he worked.

Melissa glanced at the little blue sign on the side of the bassinet.

I'm a boy! My name is Kyle Robert Tanner!

Kyle? Was that one of the ones they discussed?

*** *** ***

"Fin? Is that short for something?"

"No."

Her tone was flat, and short answers were never a good sign. Brad decided to try for humor. "You didn't let Severin name him, did you?"

"Don't be rude, Brad."

He was losing ground. "Wil, please don't be mad." This was the first he'd seen her in weeks. He wanted to be with her and his son. Their son. "He's beautiful."

"Yes." She snuggled deeper into the corner of the sofa, holding the baby to her breast.

"I'm sorry. It's just not the kind of name I expected. It's..." he struggled for a nice way to say 'weird.'

"Fin Chester," she challenged. "His name is Fin Chester. Tanner."

Chester? Brad bit back another inappropriate comment. "Tanner?" he asked finally. "You gave him my name?"

"He's your son."

"Thank you." Brad was touched. He might not be completely shut out.

"Is Fin a family name? Or Chester? Oh jeez Wil, please tell me your dad's not named Chester Charm."

She laughed. A little. "Yes and no. No, my dad's name isn't Chester Charm. Yes, Fin Chester is, in a way, a family name." She glanced down to the baby again.

"When was he born?"

"Last night. Early evening."

He wanted to tell her about Kyle being born at that same time, but feared it would drive the wedge between them deeper. Mel and Kyle didn't seem like safe topics. "Did everything go okay?"

"Yes. Ember and Cloud helped me." Her eyes fluttered up to him, then back to Fin. "I wish you could have been here," she whispered.

Tears stung Brad's eyes. "Me too." He shifted down the couch and touched her shoulder. She looked up and their eyes met. Many minutes later she looked away. Brad closed his eyes and tried to contain his emotions. Willow placed the baby in his arms. He looked down and saw his son — Fin — staring up at him with enormous green eyes. The same color as Kyle's.

"How's Melissa?" Willow asked.

Brad's heart thudded like he'd been caught at something. What should he say? Certainly not that he thought she and his wife were twins separated at birth.

Now that he knew, he saw more similarities. A certain tone of voice, a certain bearing, a certain walk. There were differences, of course, but it was no wonder he was attracted to them both.

"Brad?"

"She's fine."

Willow looked at him expectantly. She wanted details? Wasn't this hard enough? Couldn't they pretend Mel didn't exist?

"She had the baby yesterday." He could see Willow stiffen and Fin made a small noise. "A boy. We named him Kyle. She had a caesarean. They'll stay in the hospital for about two weeks."

"Congratulations. I suppose."

Brad spoke before he could reconsider. "I know I'm not your favorite person right now, Wil, but could I please stay here while she's in the hospital? I could help you take care of Fin."

Willow stood and walked into the kitchen. Brad knew that no amount of pleading would influence her decision.

He held his son and tried to get to know him.

*** *** ***

"We were sponsored by a government agency," Dr Gladstone told her before he died. Many programs were run by the Department of Health, Education and Welfare in the 1950s, but Gale didn't think that's what the doctor meant. He was evasive about it. A government agency, but which one?

She'd been through all the public adoption records, and every restricted and confidential source she could access through her job, and found no mention of Renaissance Center.

"It's not like I wanted to talk to Gladstone because he was such a dear old man. He was my only lead!" The events of that wretched October morning in Dr Gladstone's office haunted Gale, lurking in the shadows of her memory and coloring her world a pale, unhealthy green. In the half year since she'd lost control of whatever unearthly force struck through her, Gale's life shrank. It had been limited to begin with, but now it was fully stunted. Her fury with herself for failing to contain the green lightning, and her overwhelming sense of despair at the loss of her only lead, drove her few acquaintances away.

Everyone except her girls. Gale would never allow herself to raise her voice in anger or cry in front of them. That would never do.

Kelly and Grace smiled sweetly.

Gale dabbed her eyes with a tissue and smiled back.

"And now I've got nothing again. There weren't any other doctors." Gale lifted Grace onto her lap and fingered her long golden hair. "Well, there were, but I didn't meet any of them." She picked up a soft-bristled silver brush and began to smooth Grace's hair.

"The nurses were just called 'Nurse,'" she continued. "So that doesn't help. I honestly don't know what to do now."

Grace's downy hair shone in the soft lamplight. Gale brushed it absently as she gave voice to her tribulations. She knew Grace couldn't really hear her, nor could Kelly. That's what made the dolls such good listeners. Real people quickly grew tired of Gale's repetitious conversations.

"Last summer I found the building. It's a drug rehabilitation center now. No one there knew anything about us."

She dressed Grace in her pink flannelette pajamas and laid her on the white quilt on the floor. Now it was Kelly's turn with the brush.

"I've been through all the records at the courthouse. You know that's why I got the job there in the first place, but it hasn't done any good. I just don't have enough information. Your daddy was such a private man." She sighed. "I can respect that about him, of course, because who wants their personal business being whispered all over town? I do wish he'd had the time to be more forthcoming with me, to at least tell me his last name."

A small tangle in Kelly's hair required several minutes of careful teasing to remove. Gale gave it all of her concentration.

"Tomorrow's Sunday again, girls. I've decided to attend services in French River Township. Isn't that a pretty name? They have eight churches and I should be able to check them all in one day. Maybe by tomorrow noon, I'll have found your daddy."

After dressing Kelly for bed, Gale carried the twin dolls into her bedroom and tucked them into their white bassinet together. Their glassy green eyes rolled shut when they were on their backs, and she kissed them each on the forehead.

Sitting on the edge of her bed, Gale closed her own eyes and whispered a story to her lost babies.

*** *** ***

The sofa or the floor. That's where Brad expected to sleep, assuming Willow agreed at all. But when he returned from a rather perfunctory visit with Melissa and Kyle, she invited him to sleep on the mattress with her and the baby.

Willow fell asleep immediately. Fin was already out, nestled between his parents.

Brad propped himself up on his elbow and watched them in the moonlight. Now that Fin was here, it seemed he and Willow might reconcile. Melissa, meanwhile, didn't have much need of him now that she had Kyle. Their meeting at the hospital was awkward, with Melissa deflecting his attempts to hold his son. She didn't have anything to say to him, besides how glad she was to have a room right beside the nursery. Then she made a big point of how tired she felt, and how he probably needed his rest, too. She practically kicked him out.

Fin started to cry. Willow groggily sat up against the wall and began to feed him. She looked at Brad and smiled.

*** *** ***

The streetlight outside shone through the roller-blind in the drafty old window, providing enough light for Willow to study Brad's face and the naked adoration it held. It was clear that he loved her. She smiled. She loved him, too. To have him nearby again made her feel safer and more confident about the future. Lowering her eyes, she reveled in the sight of her son. Their son. If only they could be together as a family.

That couldn't happen.

Willow swallowed a lump of sorrow and fought off her tears. She knew she couldn't demand that he leave Melissa and his other child. It was inhumane, and she had no right to make demands of Brad when her entire life was a lie.

Brad didn't even know her real name. He never could. With her deceptions so deep, she had no right to feel entitled to honesty in others. Not even her lover. Allowing Brad back into her life without making any demands of him would be her punishment for lying to him.

There was no way they could be together anyway. They couldn't marry, not legally. True, she could use the same fake identification she'd used to enroll at Buckminster to get a marriage license, but it would be a big risk. It wasn't something she could get Brad tangled up in. Being in the banking profession, he couldn't afford to be associated with any sort of scandal. What would happen if they did marry, and she was discovered? What would Brad say when the military police or the CIA marched in and reclaimed their property?

Not for the first time, a cold blade of fear traced her spine. *Fin can never fall into their hands. Never.* She would always be ready to run at a moment's notice.

Brad reached through the darkness and stroked Fin's downy hair. He sat up and kissed Willow on the cheek. She swallowed hard.

No permanent entanglements.

Chapter Seven

THE SLAB

The critical virtue among members of a family is trust. Mutual reliance is the essence of the family, or the tribe, the flock. Survival is a function of the trust that binds these natural units.
Disloyalty — betrayal — is a sin against Nature.
TEF after-dinner announcement by Severin Tenpenny

JUNE 1976

The hammock's gentle motion had almost ceased. All that remained of the candle was a misshapen lump that had gone dark an hour earlier. The night was clear, with a new moon, leaving the attic virtually lightless.

Severin's eyes glittered with gathered starlight and concentration, his mind focused on a puzzle. Trying pieces of Willow in every possible arrangement. Putting that picture in order was the key to even greater things.

From Willow's first days with them, Severin sensed a deep power within her, something that drew him. Something kindred to himself. He hoped to bring that submerged treasure to the surface. He watched her, studied her, but at times she was indistinct in his mind. Sometimes even when he looked right at her, which maddened him.

She often took her meals at the bungalow, even when Beacon and Ember came to Threshold House. Tonight she dined with the Following, brought along her yearling son. New moon, perhaps newness of her bond with them. She spoke of her schooling, and spent much time catching up with friends.

Her conversation with Severin had been quite weighty, her resentment gone. She was close to understanding the Following's evolution, and his need to rely on her to help others understand it too.

He'd held back his impulse to ask about her discarded drawings, unwilling to reveal his scavenges and sour the mood. Or share the profits.

Twice now he'd successfully converted her trash into patents, one of which had been licensed to an aerospace company in California. Using the drawings as a TEF entrance exam meant Severin could harness aspiring scientists' eager young minds while weeding out those unable to adapt to ideas from the Elsewhere.

There was a beautiful symmetry between the applicants and the drawings, because both were salvaged from the trash heap. Buckminster treated a certain type of intellect poorly, turning them into misfit loners ripe for recruitment.

The present arrangement suited Severin, for now, but eventually Willow should become a knowing participant in the process. Eventually.

Willow, who saw things Severin longed to see, who was naturally attuned to the Elsewhere. She'd succeeded effortlessly with the table. By walking into the room, she commanded forces he struggled for decades to comprehend.

Smiling, Severin caressed the smooth, warm skin of a thigh.

It had been too long since they could speak easily with one another. Her mind hungered for a peer, someone to pace it. To challenge it. The engineering curriculum was a mere game, her classmates far too shallow for her.

After dinner, there had been long and deep discussion. Fin's bedtime came and went, and Ember gathered the slumbering child, winked at Willow, and departed. Willow remained, scarcely pausing in their discourse.

She'd even accepted wine when he'd poured.

The woman entwined with him in the hammock trailed her fingers through his beard. "Again?" came Cloud's voice. With a throaty, purring chuckle, she slid atop him and kissed him on the mouth.

When she paused to breathe, Severin said, "Yes, again."

The hammock's motion in the darkness became less gentle.

Bringing Willow back to the attic, Severin thought, is a very good idea.

*** *** ***

6 MONTHS LATER - DECEMBER 1976

Brad leaned against an elm tree and finished his cigarette in winter's first heavy snowfall, watching shadows move behind the curtains in Willow's bungalow. First thing, he would bring Fin outside and they would build a snowman before it got completely dark. That would give them some time together and it would give Willow a break. Brad scooped a handful of snow and tested it. Sticky and wet. Perfect for packing. He tossed the snowball from hand to hand and knocked on the door.

Willow opened it with Fin at her side. Komodo jammed his nose between them, then bounded into the snow. Brad crouched down and presented the snowball to Fin who took it warily, smiling. Willow called the dog back inside. Brad tousled Fin's hair and patted Komodo. He stood and kissed Willow. The familiar tingle traveled through him as he held her close, snow melting in his hair and trickling down to kiss her too. She reached out and pushed the door closed.

"Momma!" Fin said, and Willow disengaged from Brad. "Momma!" Fin held the snowball tightly, a look of great concern on his face.

"Let me see that, Fin." Willow took the melting thing away. Fin looked relieved and studied it while she held it. They walked into the kitchen with it while Brad took off his jacket and boots. He could hear Beacon and Ember being impressed by Fin's treasure.

Willow returned alone, smiling mischievously. She stretched up to kiss Brad again, and slid her hand under his turtleneck. Her fingers were frosty. She giggled as he flinched away.

"You have to be good if you want Santa to bring you a present," Brad told her.

Willow's eyes grew wide. "Is he watching right now?" she asked.

Brad nodded.

"Then we'd better give him a good show." She slipped past him and down the hall into her bedroom. Brad followed and locked the door.

Willow was quickly naked. She helped him strip and they embraced, sharing heat in the chilly room. They were soon on the bed, pressed together and breathing heavily. Her skin was smooth and taut. Her green eyes caught the light and kept it, almost glowing. Her mahogany hair was pinned beneath her.

Brad touched her body with his hands and with his mouth. Each contact produced a current. Her hands were in his hair, gripping and releasing. She smelled of cinnamon. Her breath on his neck and chest was too exquisite, so Brad kissed her.

It lasted for half an hour and was over far too quickly. He could never get enough of her, missed the time when they could luxuriate in each other.

Willow's breathing slowed and the dreamy look faded from her face. Right on schedule, Fin began rattling the doorknob.

*** *** ***

Willow heard the shower and waited a minute longer for Brad to get in. Once assured of ten minutes' privacy, she picked up his pants from the floor and took his wallet out of the pocket.

Fin smiled at her from where he sat on the mattress, drool covering his chin. She smiled back and opened the wallet.

Brad had charge cards and a lot of cash. Willow found what she wanted easily: photographs. Only two, but they were enough. The first showed a woman with chin-length, dark blond hair and a nice smile, holding a baby. Melissa. She was pretty. Somehow familiar. Willow studied her, trying to decide if they'd ever passed on the street.

The next photo held more interest. Brad and a little boy. Kyle. Willow stared at him. He looked remarkably like Fin. Most 18-month-olds looked similar, but this was almost eerie. Their eyes were the same green, their hair the same brown. They had the same number of teeth, in the same spots, which gave them the same smile. Brad wore the same disconnected look he always had around Fin.

This had been a mistake. Knowing something about Brad's other family, seeing them, was supposed to be better than wondering, but it only drove home her second-class status. Her eyes stung.

She wanted more, much more, than she could ever have, from Brad or from anyone. It got harder to believe as the months passed, but she was still a fugitive. She had to stay vigilant and wary, ready to flee. The doctors and generals who haunted her childhood could never be allowed to know Fin existed, could never be permitted to make him a guinea pig in their experiments. If this half-relationship was the price for her son's future, Willow would pay it, even if it wasn't fair to anyone. Fin had to be protected.

Willow glanced at her son. He was bouncing on his knees and talking to the horses on the wallpaper, one of his favorite activities.

After putting the wallet back in Brad's pocket, Willow scooped Fin up and tickled him to distract herself from her melancholy mood. They were still giggling when Brad came back.

While Brad dressed, Fin entertained them with a song he'd made up. He'd been singing it a lot lately, but Willow had yet to figure out what it was about. Something to do with Komodo and macaroni, she thought. The melody roughly followed that of *I Went to the Animal Fair*, but it featured an extended chorus of quacking in the middle. He granted them an encore performance on the way out to the living room.

Brad slipped into his shearling jacket and bent to pet Komodo. Willow carried Fin over for good-bye hugs, which went better than last week.

After Fin was back on the floor, Brad pulled Willow to him. She hugged him and aimed a kiss at his cheek, but he outmaneuvered her, as usual, and the peck became a shivery, searing soul kiss. Goosebumps sprang up on her belly and thighs and she couldn't pull away from him.

"Soup's on," came Beacon's voice from the kitchen.

Brad broke the embrace and kissed her forehead.

"See you next week," he said. "I'll take Fin for ice cream."

Willow nodded. "He needs to spend time with you."

"Love you, Wil."

"Love you, too, Brad."

*** *** ***

15 MONTHS LATER - MARCH 1978

"I've made up my mind, and this time you won't talk me out of it," said Cloud. "I'm leaving." She looked defiantly at Willow from her position in the doorway.

Willow put her textbook down on the spool table and sat up. It had been years since Cloud made her previous last stand. It was back before Willow had even known she was pregnant with Fin, and he was two and a half now. She couldn't think of any recent events or announcements that would have upset Cloud's applecart this way. Granted, she didn't participate much in Following activities these days, but Ember or Beacon would have said something.

"Well?" Cloud demanded.

"I'm surprised," Willow said.

"I'm going, and I'm taking Dragonfly. And Bridge."

"Dragonfly's your son. Of course he'll go with you. But why? And why Bridge?"

"He's a good man."

"Okay. But, I still don't understand."

Cloud looked exasperated. She almost spoke several times before collapsing on the sofa beside Willow.

"Could I have a glass of water, please?" she asked.

"Sure." Willow went into the small kitchen and got Cloud's drink. When she returned to the living room, Cloud seemed calmer. She smoothed her long, green hippie skirt around her drawn-up legs and stared at the bubbling lava lamp. She took the glass and sipped. Willow sat and waited, wondering if Cloud would explain.

She finally said. "You told me he loved us. You said I should stay, even though he was wrong."

"Severin?" Willow asked. "Has he made a new announcement?"

"You know damn well he hasn't. He always makes sure you're there to soothe everyone's sensibilities afterward."

"Keep it down please, Cloud. Fin's napping."

"Aren't you going to defend yourself?"

"Against what? You're not saying anything about me. You seem to think Severin is somehow my fault. He's not."

Cloud looked at Willow. Her golden eyes were cold.

"Who's Fin's father? Really."

"Brad. You know that."

"Is he, really?" Cloud searched Willow's eyes.

"Are you asking biologically? Or spiritually? Or in some weird Following sense?"

"Who's his father?"

"I know it's popular around here to think of the children as being everyone's, but Fin isn't. Fin is mine and Brad's. He binds us."

"Severin didn't tell you to say that?"

"No." Willow didn't know where Cloud was going with this, but she knew it was serious.

"When you first joined the Following, everyone could tell you were Severin's favorite. He talked about you all the time. He made exceptions for you. After you started school he changed the Threshold to include technology. I thought he did it to keep you."

"I hope not. I never cared what Severin believed."

"You talked me into staying! You said that even though he was flawed, he loved us! You stayed. It's your fault *I* stayed. It's your fault I fell for him. It's your fault I'm pregnant."

Willow shuddered. Cloud slept with *Severin*?

"Once I told him, Severin made me sleep with Bridge, so that Bridge will be this baby's father." She placed her hand on her stomach.

"Oh, Cloud, no..."

"Severin's not the man I thought he was. The man I loved would never tell me to do that."

"But—"

"If I force Severin to admit he's the father, he'll have a claim on me. And on the baby. I can't let that happen. I see now how wrong I was. Bridge is a good man. If he thinks he's the father, he'll marry me. He'll be a good father."

"But you can't—"

"I can, and you won't say anything. It's your fault I'm in this mess. If you keep your mouth shut, you can help me get out."

On her way out the door, Cloud looked back at Willow and said, "I thought maybe he'd done this to you, too. Then I wouldn't feel so stupid."

***   ***   ***

"No."

Ember tried to smile and frown at the same time. She shook her head. "That's not one of the choices."

Willow hadn't looked up from her reading. "What I mean is, 'No, I will not justify that pompous, egotistical little shit's personal agenda by reinterpreting it through rose-colored Threshold glasses.' Not this time. Ask him to explain it."

"This one's not so big, Wil. I think it's something he's taught us already, but I can't remember how it adds up."

"Then it probably doesn't."

Ember sulked. She went to the kitchen, and Willow heard dishes clinking and cupboards opening and closing. Willow's eyes were fixed on a paragraph about temperature and electrical resistance while in the kitchen Ember shifted things around with her hands to keep her mind from dwelling on Willow's gruffness.

Willow folded her legs underneath her, then shifted her weight, then stretched out her legs across the floor again, trying to banish her discomfort. She knew she had made the right decision. Even though it would hurt her friends, she couldn't stay. She just didn't know how to make it all hurt the least.

Willow plunged ahead into the paragraph, recognizing and instantly forgetting each word.

Perhaps this would be easier for all concerned if she told them about the Cloud business. Except she would be violating Cloud's trust, much as Severin had. She'd be kidding herself to think he would let her ruin him. It would be her word against his. Some, like Beacon and Ember, would want to believe her. Want to.

If Willow tried to maintain a facade of normalcy her friends would see through it, would know something was eating at her. Now Severin had put her on the spot again, and normalcy dictated that she indulge him, that she compromise her principles at least one last time. And she just so recently rediscovered them.

Willow reread the same paragraph.

It was foolish to expect anything to make this easier. It would be hard, no matter what, but she couldn't let herself remain in Severin's trap. It had been years since she toyed with supernatural forces, but he kept pressuring her. Just being around him put her at risk of irreparable harm. Worse, it could transfigure her in Severin's image. She had to take steps, renounce all the freaky supernatural weirdness.

Ember wandered to Willow's room, trying to 'accidentally' wake Fin from his nap.

"Please let him sleep a while longer, Em."

It was for the best.

*** *** ***

"I'll need you to be on time. And it has to be Thursday."

"No problem."

"Brad, don't play games," Willow responded.

He kept smiling. "I said, 'No problem.'"

Willow resumed eating her pancakes. Brad sipped coffee, and Fin lined up sugar packets in a mosaic on the tray of his high chair. The only other people in Denny's were employees.

Brad stretched, and said, "Are you stiffing your roommates with the rent?"

"You know I don't pay rent. None of us do."

"Nice. So why the cover-of-darkness routine? For that matter, why are you leaving?"

"I have my reasons." Willow wolfed down the last few bites and drained her milk glass. Brad's gaze hadn't wavered since he'd asked his questions. "Look, I love Em, and Beacon, but they don't know I'm moving. I don't want them to know. Okay?"

"Fair enough." But his eyes didn't seem to think so.

"So, you're sure about Thursday?"

"Positive. They snore, don't they?"

Willow glanced over at Fin, who was regarding Brad disdainfully. She smiled. "Yeah, that's the reason. Snoring. Poor Fin can't sleep."

"You'll have to learn how to cook. I know you'll miss their food."

Willow rolled her eyes. She'd hoped Brad would look at this as a chance to be her hero, would try to make it easier. Instead, he had questions. Brad never had questions!

He slurped the dregs of his coffee and gave Fin a nervous smile and a wink. Fin smiled, but Brad turned back toward Willow and didn't see it. Willow resisted the urge to ask him for the third time if he would be there Thursday.

Brad twisted his head almost all the way around, trying to determine what pressing business kept the waitress from getting him a warmup. Without looking at Willow, he asked, "How does Severin feel about this?"

Willow was speechless. Brad finally uncontorted himself and looked at her mildly. She drew in a breath and shrugged.

"He doesn't know either, does he?" Brad tried to sip from his empty mug, frowned.

Willow shook her head, and said, her voice brittle, "But you do. I hope it won't be a problem."

Brad smiled. "I never talk to the man. Relax."

"So why did you ask about him? How do you think he would feel about it? I mean, shit, Brad!"

Brad set aside the mug and reached out to Willow. His eyes danced, and her hands scurried across the table to join his. Before she could remember she was mad, the tingle flooded across her fingers, and Brad clearly felt it too. "Not a word he'll have from me. And I shall be ready to lend my manliness, which could leap a tall building, I'll have you know, to whatever secret mission you need it for on Thursday."

Willow smiled, as much from the twinkle in Brad's eyes as from his corny speech. He meant it. He would be her hero after all.

***   ***   ***

Beacon was pale, and appeared to be losing weight. Ember's eyes were red, her face drawn. Both of them were uncharacteristically quiet, and neither one would look Severin in the eye. It had been two weeks since Willow's last visit to the House.

Severin toyed with the idea of calling Beacon over for some chit-chat. Talk about cooking. About blending herbs. Ask him if he still hoped to see universal vegetarianism in his lifetime. Make a point of not asking about Willow.

Such a game with Ember would be unworkable. She was too far gone.

Severin patted his lips with a napkin and smiled around the dining hall. It felt insincere to him, but went over well enough with the others.

Hindsight. Clarity.

He had not anticipated Willow's departure, and yet did not feel surprise. Chagrin, anger, and betrayal, yes. The fault lay with Beacon and Ember, overlooking their duty to move Willow along to the House. They'd let themselves become attached, too blind to see that the attachment didn't flow back to them as she edged away. They failed because they underestimated Willow, a mistake Severin would never permit himself.

Willow's abandonment was not publicly known. That would at least grant him the chance to control how the news came out, to frame it as part of his overall plan. A nigh-inscrutable plan, which called for him to make special allowances for one who often undermined his authority. A plan that operated by funding the education of a traitor. In point of fact, royalties on her numerous unwitting inventions covered her tuition several times over, but it would be better not to advertise any of that.

Too bad Willow wouldn't be available to field questions this time.

It would be counterproductive to give chase. He could find her, but then what? Her return wouldn't be voluntary. Several ways to subdue her came to mind, all undignified. Cornering this stray, taunting her with the impossibility of escape before holding her by the neck. This image lingered in Severin's mind. It would be most satisfactory to correct Willow's misapprehension that she could outwit him.

Unfortunately, detaining a fully grown human being long-term raised a host of inconveniences for the jailer, such as sanitation, and seclusion. A distasteful undertaking, and it would leave him with what? A broken Willow. Useless.

He would have to be patient, keep an eye on her movements. She wouldn't go far, if he refrained from scaring her off with any rash pursuit.

Severin stood and tossed his napkin onto his plate, covering the untouched meal. He departed the room, forcing himself not to march, not to stalk or stomp. His hands would not desist in clenching into fists, his jaw had set like concrete. Once in the hallway, alone, he opened his stride toward the grand staircase. He took the steps in twos all the way up, his pulse racing but his breathing steady.

At the table he snatched up the edge of the sheet and froze, gritting his teeth. Thoughts of hunting Willow down raced like wildfire, consuming all else. Severin flexed the fingers of his left hand, reaching out onto the table. Strong warmth breathed over his palm, something that never happened before. Willow's face filled his mind, her features placid and pale, and he shuddered at the quickening of power, Willow's mysterious power, flooding through him like a river surging over a cliff. It could all be in his reach. His palm seared.

He reached deeper, far past where he had taken all his previous treasures. Willow floated ahead of him, peaceful and enigmatic, beckoning or defying him to reach deeper yet. The heat against his hand spoke of white coals.

Severin pushed ahead with a grunt and his palm struck a rough, flat surface. It was cool, a shock after such intense heat, momentarily indistinguishable from a blistering burn. Severin drew a rattling breath and considered how to proceed. The material could be metal or stone. The object's width exceeded the span of his fingers, with no contours to be grasped. What would happen if he broke contact, to explore the shape and find a way of taking hold of it? He felt sure he would lose it if he tried to reposition his hand.

Not that he could break away. The unspeakable weight of the object flowed into his skin. The bones in his hand groaned.

Severin pulled, applying more force. His hand didn't move, but he sensed a grudging kind of inertia in his prize. Sweat rolled down his forehead as he strained his entire body against the enormous mass. Its crushing weight invaded his arm. He couldn't gain an inch, but the impression of sluggish momentum grew. The resistance seemed to diminish as the force clamping his hand to the object multiplied. He heard a popping sound, distantly aware it came from his back, but he kept pulling.

He could picture his left hand mashed out thin enough to see through. His back and legs burned with fatigue. Suddenly the huge thing he'd found became weightless, like a sunken wreck pumped full of air, tearing loose from the muck and rising inexorably to the surface.

The pressure on his hand and arm disappeared, flushed out by burning agony as sensation returned. Now the mysterious object pressed up against his palm. Its bulk was more alarming each moment as it gathered speed. Severin stared in horror, awaiting the certain destruction of his table, possibly the entire House.

The floor kicked. Stacks of boxes toppled, and a throaty rumble shook the walls. Glass shattered on a lower floor, and voices cried out.

Severin yanked his hand free and stared at it for a few seconds, fascinated by the complete lack of injury. He laughed.

Dust rained around him. Downstairs, he could hear panic or something close. He dashed down the steps, all the way down, ignoring everyone he passed.

At the top of the basement stairs he pulled the door shut behind him and descended slowly in total darkness. At the bottom he crept along the wall, through the corner and over to the outside door. He found and tugged on the ceiling fixture's pull-string.

In the precise center of the sprawling dirt-floored space jutted a large wedge of gray stone that had not been there before. One corner protruded to knee height, from which the sides sloped to disappear into the floor. The upper surface showed for almost eight feet, subtly concave like a druidic altar worn by heavy use. Scales of lichen and tufts of bristly moss clung to the sides like barnacles deposited by the ethereal ocean of the Elsewhere. The sheer immensity and age of the thing, coupled with the evidence of long-ago human use, put Severin in mind of Stonehenge. He thought longingly of its likely circle of towering brothers, still submerged and awaiting his efforts to birth them into being.

The floor around it appeared undisturbed, and the slab itself was free of dirt, as if it hadn't erupted from the packed earth moments earlier, born from the depths by his own intervention.

Severin rubbed his hand.

*** *** ***

Fin scampered into the bathroom where Willow was busy scrubbing a stranger's bathtub. He carried a sponge and a spray bottle of water. He had taken off his shirt, and his brown hair was plastered to his head in unruly clumps, nearly covering his bottle-green eyes. Time for a trim, next time he was napping. Water dripped off his chin as he smiled at her.

"Mommy, I was dirty." He banged the lid of the toilet closed and climbed up onto it, where he sat and sprayed a stream of water at his chubby bare feet.

Willow chuckled at the sight of him. "Were you really?"

Fin nodded, splattering more water.

"It does look like you could use a bath," Willow agreed.

"No. I cleaned me." He demonstrated by spraying his head and belly and scrubbing them with his sponge, giggling madly all the while.

"Well, when you're done there, do you think you could clean the counter in the kitchen?"

"No. I clean Dodo." He ran out of the bathroom, calling the dog's name.

Willow laughed, glad Komodo was safely behind closed doors downstairs. Her smile faded as she looked at the sponge in her own hand. Only two more days to clean the remaining three apartments.

She thought herself lucky when she found this gig. Apartment Manager. No rent. Two bedrooms. $100 a month salary. She was supposed to keep an eye on things for the owner, make repairs, and take care of the lawn. No big deal. Up until now, the job had been easy.

Now, as the semester ended at Buckminster and all the leases were up, it was her job to get the empty apartments ready for the next tenants.

The end of the semester also meant she would need to drop out of school. Without Severin paying her tuition, she couldn't afford to continue. Brad offered to pay, of course, but she declined. It was one thing to take money for things Fin needed, but she didn't want to rely on Brad that way for her own benefit. She had to be self-reliant for the inevitable day when she would need to go on the run again. It would be that much harder if she were spoiled.

Besides, without school taking up her days she would be able to spend more time with Fin, who ran back into the bathroom naked, waving his spray bottle menacingly and making machine-gun noises.

Willow decided the bathtub was clean enough.

***   ***   ***

5 MONTHS LATER - OCTOBER 3, 1978

"I'm not a midwife," Willow said into the phone.

"But you've had a baby," said Ember. "And she was there for you."

"Doesn't Cloud already know how to do this? She had a baby before."

"Willow, you're not being rational," said Ember. "She wants support. Wouldn't you want friends supporting you if you were having another baby?"

"I'd want the father supporting me." *Shit.* Willow swung the phone around in small circles by the cord, making a face and weighing her options. It had been delicate work to maintain her friendship with Ember and Beacon after moving out. They tried to be supportive, although they didn't understand her reasons for leaving. Did Cloud still blame Willow for her situation? Should she clean up after Severin this one last time?

Fin looked up from his Legos. His eyebrows went up and Willow abruptly stopped abusing the phone.

That's just the sort of behavior I need him imitating.

"Wil?" Ember's voice was faint. Willow put the phone back to her ear.

"I'm thinking."

"Well, think fast. Her first labor wasn't long, and this one will probably be shorter."

Remembering her own labor, Willow made up her mind to help Cloud. If it turned out that all Cloud wanted her for was abuse, she would leave.

"What about Fin?"

Ember had been expecting that. "Beacon will watch him. At your place, if you want."

Willow sighed. "All right. Let's go have a baby."

***

Willow stood at the stove, sterilizing a sheet in boiling water. Cloud had gone back to calling herself Linda, and Bridge was Casey. Together they were the Martins. They lived in a tiny two-bedroom apartment in a converted house, much like Willow's own. Casey worked as a contractor and planned to adopt four-year-old Dragonfly Bay as soon as they saved enough money. The strides they had taken into the normal world impressed Willow.

So far, Cloud was handling herself well. She looked tired and uncomfortable, yet beautiful and calm. Bridge was a wreck. His scraggly blond ponytail accentuated his receding hairline and his dark brown eyes had deep circles under them. He couldn't sit, or stand, still.

"I can't wait to meet my child!"

He kept saying things like that.

It annoyed Willow, and she'd only been there for half an hour. As the water bubbled in the big soup pot, she tapped the metal tongs against the rim, trying to dredge up enough Morse code to spell "Oh lord won't you buy me a Mercedes Benz," but she kept forgetting the Morse and slipping into the rhythm of the words instead. Who knew what zen message she was really sending.

"Well, this isn't going to get any more sterile." Willow hung the sheet on a line over the radiator and made herself go back into the labor room.

Nude, Cloud squatted in the center of the bed with Ember and Bridge supporting her. Dragonfly followed Willow in, looking bored.

"Cloud, Beacon's watching Fin. Do you want him to watch Dragonfly, too?" Ember asked.

"No. I want him to see his brother or sister born. I want this to be a family time." She closed her eyes and took a few deep breaths before continuing. "When he was born, he was my only family. Now I have him and I have a husband. I want this baby to know it has a mother and a father and a brother. Right from the start." She closed her eyes and groaned.

***

"It's a girl!" said Ember. "Look at all that black hair!"

Willow winced. Cloud was a strawberry blond, Bridge plain-old blond. Dragonfly was blond.

The baby girl gave a thin wail. Bridge glanced from her to Cloud, puzzled.

"Dragonfly had dark hair when he was born, too," Cloud said quickly. "Remember, Em?"

Ember nodded as she handed the baby to Willow.

Willow's emotions overran her as she held the baby for Cloud, Bridge and Dragonfly to see, while Ember cut the cord. Joy. Heartache. Fragility. Strength. This little girl embodied endless possibilities, the magic of a new life. She could complete this fledgling family.

"What's her name?" she asked.

"Brook Bramble," said Cloud.

Willow handed Cloud's daughter to her. Baby Brook opened her eyes. They were electric blue, not the muddy blue of most newborns.

Bridge recoiled.

"Hey, Bridge, let's get you some air." Willow steered him out of the tiny bedroom.

"Casey. Not Bridge. I'm Casey."

"I'm sorry. I keep forgetting." She got him a glass of water and made him sit on a kitchen chair.

"You saw it too. It's not my baby." He set the glass on the table without taking a sip.

"I think that's something you should talk to Cloud, er, Linda about."

"Oh, believe me, I will."

"Casey. Please wait until you have some privacy."

He sat fuming, then nodded.

Willow went back into the bedroom and helped Ember with the placenta and cleaning up. She said, "Now that Dragonfly's met his sister, I'll take him to my place. He can play with Fin and spend the night. That way you can rest."

Cloud nodded absently, staring at her new daughter.

Willow kissed Brook's tiny fingers, gave Cloud a light hug and whispered, "Good luck."

Chapter Eight

TANNENBAUM PARK

*Even through my extensive research, I have been unable to
determine where Brian Shaw spent the first year following his
graduation from the seminary in 1954.*
    from *Brainwashed*, by Julie Rome ©1998 Futhark Press

SPRING 1979

"Look at these woods! Kyle, you wanna go build a fort?"

"He certainly does not," Melissa interjected. "Never mind the
woods, Brad. Nobody is going to be living in the woods." Brad winked
at Kyle, and Melissa glared. Did Brad honestly think their son was going
to play in those woods, right now? Maybe the realtor would go too, and
build a fort of her own? "Kyle, come here. We need to see if this house
has a good bedroom for you."

Brad jammed his hands into his jacket pockets and stared out the
rear sliding door at his precious woods, as Kyle ran over to take
Melissa's hand.

The neighborhood was good, quite good, and the lot offered
considerable privacy, due mainly to all the mature trees. The woods
could be a plus, but now Brad had given Kyle this fool notion of
running amok and it would be a constant fight to keep him out of them.

As they ascended the stairs, Melissa kept a tight grip on Kyle's small
hand. The wallpaper would have to come down. Diagonal stripes of
varying weights, navy, white, and silver. Enough to induce visions in
anyone. Or vomiting.

The architecture, however, was clean and modern, a nice open layout. Practical. No extraneous molding details or other gingerbread, inside or out, except the shutters flanking all the windows. A nod to tradition. A message to visitors that good, solidly normal people dwelled within. Whatever house they bought would need shutters.

Compared to the last five places they'd looked at, this one at least had the potential to be livable. The Victorian was out of the question, and the one with the enormous frowzy flowerbeds, and just all of them. Too much of what the realty profession called charm. But not this one. Here the problems were all superficial, like the wallpaper.

Kyle pulled free at the top of the steps and darted left into the first room. By the time Melissa turned the corner, he was at the far end, trying to elbow himself up onto the railing overlooking the family room.

"Kyle, get down!" Melissa shouted, cringing that the outburst would be heard throughout the house. Kyle continued to climb, trying to get his knee over the rail. Melissa strode across the room, the master bedroom, she noted, and plucked him off the bannister.

"My room!" Kyle exclaimed.

"No, this is Mommy and Daddy's room. Well, if we live here it will be. It's nobody's room right now."

"I saw it first."

"No, Kyle. This is not a room for children. See, you could fall down."

"Jump!"

Melissa carried Kyle back to the hallway, where Brad and Jeanne, the realtor, were cresting the stairs.

"Everyone all right?" Jeanne asked. Brad smirked behind her. Melissa flushed. She deposited Kyle on the aqua carpet, but kept a firm grip on his arm. He tried to yank loose but couldn't this time.

"Kyle wonders where his room would be," Melissa said.

Jeanne stooped down to the boy's level, and cooed, "You turned the wrong way. There's a nice big room over there. Come on!" Melissa tightened her grip as the woman flashed a grin at her son. Kyle whined and tried to squirm away again, as Melissa maneuvered herself between him and the interloper.

"Thanks," she said tightly. "Why don't you show Brad the master suite while Kyle and I investigate this 'nice big room.'" Brad shrugged and drifted into the master bedroom, followed by the realtor. Melissa stalked to the end of the hall and pivoted right, bringing Kyle stumbling in her wake.

Like the whole house, this room was empty. Kyle worked futilely at freeing his arm while Melissa looked at the walls. The room was almost as big as the master. Nice view across the street. It would be worthy.

"What do you think, Kyle? Would you like to have this room?"

Kyle shook his head, attempting to pry his mother's fingers away from his sleeve.

"You haven't even looked. If I let go, will you stay in here with me and look at the room?"

Kyle nodded, worrying at Melissa's grip on his arm.

She released him, and intercepted his dash for the door by stepping in front of it. "Now, let's talk about this room. What do you like about it?" She didn't want to direct his attention to the window, not after his stunt in the other room, but there wasn't much else of note. Kyle sullenly turned around, looking at the floor. "Try to picture all your things in here. There's enough room for your bed, and your dresser, and all your toys. There's plenty of room, don't you think?"

"There's room for more toys," Kyle drawled.

"Yes," Melissa smiled. "There's room for more toys."

*** *** ***

2 YEARS LATER - JULY 1981

"I wouldn't call if it wasn't important," the voice on the phone said. It sounded like Wil, but in their ongoing six-year romance Willow had never once called him. It could also be Mel. That was one of the problems with being intimately involved with twins.

"Brad?"

"This is Brad," he confirmed.

"It's Willow. I'm not trying to make trouble for you," she explained.

"I know. What's up?"

"Are you... is she standing right there so you'll have to talk in code?"

"No."

"That's good. Look, Beacon fell off a ladder and broke his wrist and I need to help Ember get him to the hospital."

"Sure. Do you need a car?"

"No. I need a babysitter."

Oh boy.

"Brad? This is hugely important. He's in a lot of pain."

"I know. I'll have to meet you at the park. Mel's out today and I've got Kyle."

"Oh shit."

"It'll work, babe. We'll leave now. I'll be at Tannenbaum Park in ten minutes. Just..."

"I'll be subtle." She hung up.

Well, at least Fin won't give anything away by being overly affectionate with me.

With Kyle in the back seat, Brad sped to the park. He wanted to make sure Kyle was off playing before Fin and Willow arrived. This would be awkward, but nothing compared to the result if Kyle saw something unusual and later told Melissa.

This was the first time Melissa had ever left him alone with Kyle. Could that be true? It sure sounded strange, but it felt right. The first time Mel ever left Kyle with him was the same day Wil called him for the first time ever.

Twins.

Brad parked and scanned the playground before opening his door. He didn't see Willow.

"Hey, Tiger," he said to Kyle, "how fast do you think you can run to the jungle gym?"

"Faster than you."

Brad opened his door and pulled the seat forward, releasing Kyle who sprang out and sprinted away across the grass. Brad locked the Volvo and sauntered over to a bench in the shade.

The park was crowded with families, and kids from at least one day care center on a field trip. That would help. If it was just him and his sons, Brad wouldn't have been able to hide.

He glanced down Walnut Street and saw Willow hurrying Fin along. Her hair fell to the middle of her back and shone like a burnished sunset, the color so vibrant he knew she had given herself another henna treatment. Probably yesterday. When he buried his face in it, it would smell like fresh-cut grass. As if she knew she was summer personified, she wore a filmy green sundress that fluttered in the slight breeze, exposing her thighs. Brad was helpless. She saw him too, but didn't signal. After making sure he knew Kyle's whereabouts, Brad walked over to meet her.

"Hi, Tiger," he said to Fin.

Fin stared coldly at him. "My name is Fin Chester Tanner. But you can call me Fin and I'll still know who you're talking to."

Brad chuckled. "Okay, Fin."

Willow caught Fin's gaze and said, "I'm going to help Beacon now. Brad's going to keep an eye on you."

Fin looked at his sneakers.

"You just go play with the other kids," she continued. "I'll be back as soon as I can."

Fin looked up at her and nodded. He walked off toward the sandbox.

Brad touched Willow's bare elbow. She jumped.

"Don't I get a hug?" he asked.

"That would be stupid." She kissed her fingertips and squeezed his hand. "I'll be back as soon as I can."

*** *** ***

Her smile was cracking. How long would they make her sit and wait? Melissa checked her watch. Five minutes, and a woman in Toledo had been listening to *Endless Love* non-stop for three hours.

Closing her eyes, Melissa thought about Kyle. She tried to block the sensory overload with his face, but it didn't work. His eyes told her about the imminent popularity of something called 'rap.' The curve of his nose showed her that no one in this building was a Scorpio.

Melissa opened her eyes. As she shifted her weight on the exam table, the paper liner crinkled, and she knew that Lady Diana, who as of that morning became Princess Diana, would have two sons, a divorce, and a fatal car crash. Melissa gritted her teeth.

With a small tap on the door the doctor walked in, looking at her file. Melissa thought she would be more comfortable seeing a female gynecologist, but now she wasn't sure. The woman looked inexperienced, and reams of statistics rolled off her.

"Hello, Melissa. It says here you're trying to get pregnant. How long have you been trying?"

"My son is six."

"You've been trying since he was born?"

"We never use birth control, but I've only been really trying for about a year."

"Well, slide right down to the edge, put your feet in the stirrups, and let's take a look."

It was the most humiliating experience of Melissa's life. The woman even offered to get a mirror so Melissa could see her own cervix. Melissa had less than no interest in what she might learn from it, and declined. She was losing her grip, and desperate to get back to the stabilizing influence of Kyle. Hell, even Brad would do.

And of course, it was all her own fault. Her stupid 'narrow mid-pelvis.' Her stupid uterus. Scarring from the caesarean caused implantation difficulties.

Her situation wasn't hopeless. A zygote might implant in a non-traumatized area. The doctor offered to run some tests, but Melissa couldn't be in the office any longer. She threw on her clothes and hurried out.

Melissa pulled into her driveway and pushed the button to open the garage door.

Where was Brad's stupid little sports car?

Screaming for Kyle, Melissa ran into the house. When she calmed herself enough to listen, she got no reply.

They were gone.

She whirled around, searching for some clue to where Brad took her son. A Dachshund would win the Westminster Kennel Club dog show. The air traffic controllers were going to strike. Cats would invade Broadway.

Melissa bolted to the kitchen and drew a glass of water. She took four sleeping pills from the bottle behind the toaster oven and swallowed them. It was 1:20. Twenty was the number of the day on Sesame Street.

Melissa collapsed on the sofa in the living room and was dragged down into a deep green sleep.

*** *** ***

As the afternoon wore on, Brad sat in the shade, smoking, watching his sons, and occasionally chatting with other parents. His bench grew crowded as it got hotter and more adults left the hard business of playing to the kids. A constant ebb and flow of children surrounded them, eventually washing up Fin.

"What time is it?" he asked.

Brad checked his watch. "4:43."

"She's been gone a long time."

Brad nodded. He was about to say something fatherly and reassuring when he noticed Kyle approaching. Before Kyle had a chance to call him Dad, Brad said, "Fin, this is Kyle. Do you guys know each other?" He knew they didn't.

Fin shook his head. So did Kyle.

"Maybe you like some of the same games."

He suspected they didn't. His sons weren't much alike, aside from looks. To his horror, Kyle said, "You wanna play in the fountain?" and Fin agreed. Before he could think of a way to separate them, they ran off.

It was wonderful and horrible at the same time. The boys were brothers and should get to know each other, but they certainly shouldn't get to know that they were brothers. Not today anyway.

So far Willow hadn't told Fin he had a half-brother, or that Brad had a wife. She hadn't told Beacon or Ember either. Mel certainly didn't know about Wil or Fin. He still meant to tell her. There just never seemed to be a good time. And even Willow didn't know the whole story, didn't know his wife was her twin sister.

Fin and Kyle waded into the fountain with their shoes on. Their mothers would not be pleased, but there was no way to tell them to stop without revealing his paternal connection to them both.

"Boys will be boys," he muttered.

The longer it went without Melissa knowing about Willow and Fin, the more difficult the potential bean-spilling became. It felt like if there had ever been a good time to come clean, it flew past years ago, leaving Brad in an increasingly untenable position. In hindsight Brad saw that he should have told both women back when both announced their pregnancies. That would have been painful enough. Add to it six years of good intentions, and, well, he didn't even want to think about it. The status quo wasn't fair to anyone, but Brad couldn't stomach the idea of the hurt feelings and tears and anguish that would inevitably accompany his admission. He didn't want to be anybody's bad guy.

Willow's cool fingers brushed his shoulder and neck and she sat beside him.

"Where's Fin?" she asked.

"In the fountain."

She nodded when she spotted him. "And Kyle?"

Brad sighed. "Also in the fountain."

Willow jerked and stared at him.

"They're getting along," he said.

Willow shook her head.

"How's Beacon?"

"They have him in a cast for at least three months. I guess it's a pretty bad break."

Brad noticed Kyle approaching again, but not Fin. To cover, he put on his banker voice and said, "Interest rates are generally over 15%, but it depends on how many points you want to pay."

Willow looked confused.

"Dad, I'm hungry. Mom always has a snack in her purse."

Brad looked around himself. "Sorry, Kyle, I forgot my purse."

Kyle laughed.

"We'll leave in a minute."

"Kyle," Willow said.

Brad tensed.

"I'm Fin's mom."

"Oh."

Brad jumped in, "If you go tell Fin it's time for him to go, I'll buy you ice cream on the way home."

"Cool!" Kyle ran off in search of Fin.

"He's blonder than I expected," Willow said.

"You gonna be home tonight?" After giving Mel the entire afternoon off, Brad knew she wouldn't begrudge him an evening out.

Willow shrugged. She wasn't wearing a bra. "I have some homework to catch up on, but I'll probably be done at a reasonable hour."

Brad knew that by 'homework' she meant some kind of moonlighting for an engineering company. Even without a completed degree, she got assignments from them. If she would let him pay her tuition, she could complete her schooling and her opportunities would really open up. Brad continued to be amazed at how clever and resourceful she was, and to be frustrated by her prideful stubbornness.

Fifteen minutes later, Kyle came running up, his shoes caked with wet sand. "I told him, Dad. He was in the sandbox in a big deep hole. That's why it took me so long to find him. Can we get the ice cream now?"

Brad stood. "Race you to the car."

Kyle took off. Brad bent and kissed the top of Wil's head, breathing deeply. Fresh cut grass and sunshine. He saw Fin trudging their way, looking angry.

Willow sighed.

"Love you, Wil."

"Love you, too, Brad."

She started toward Fin as Brad jogged to the car and his triumphant son.

"I won!" Kyle shouted.

*** *** ***

Melissa caught herself staring at Kyle. He drank his juice, one green eye tracking her over the rim of his cup. She smiled, warmly she hoped, and turned back to loading the dishwasher.

Her attention was not on the dishes, though. She was thinking about the torture she'd undergone last year, when Kyle went to kindergarten. Only half days, yet it had been a nightmare. She couldn't survive with him in school all day long and Brad at work. Summer was flying past, August nearly over.

Maybe it would be okay, with enough sleeping pills.

Melissa dropped a plate, which clattered against the others already loaded. Kyle laughed. She took a steadying breath before righting the plate in the rack, and shut the machine.

She could volunteer at the school. They always wanted people to supervise at lunchtime and such. Lunch ladies. Melissa knew Kyle was looking at her, so she smiled again. Inwardly, she doubted lunch lady was a better fate than being abandoned. For that matter, the kitchen help weren't expected to loiter during the rest of the school day. The idea was both impractical and unappealing.

What, then? Pills? Tough it out?

She had looked into a different possibility, something called 'home schooling.'

Evidently, just anyone could decide her child wasn't going to school, and take over his education personally. Melissa felt the urge to scoff. If a child couldn't get through school, isolationist measures wouldn't help. Besides, rising above the inadequacies of the school system was a rite of passage. Survival of the fittest. If you side-stepped that, how would anyone know how to judge you? Her research indicated people who chose home schooling tended toward religious fanaticism, fundamentalism at least. Not normal people.

Normal people didn't become addicted to powerful sedatives, either.

It would mean Kyle wouldn't have to go away, and she wouldn't have to drown in supernatural messages. His education wouldn't suffer. She was confident she was at least as intelligent as any grade-school teacher, and certainly more concerned about Kyle's future success.

She wiped Kyle's juice mustache and smiled at him some more, her beautiful boy. He smiled back at her. She thought about the man he would one day become. He was handsome and precocious, sure to be very popular.

Of course, if nobody knew him he wouldn't get the chance for popularity. Keeping him out of school would be wrong. It would be clipping his wings.

The other angle on her dilemma was Brad. She only needed one or the other around the house, but if Brad stopped going to work, there wouldn't be a house for long.

Melissa wished there was another way.

***

The only conversation during dinner consisted of Kyle explaining the nuances of *Tom and Jerry*. This explanation had been running continuously for over thirty minutes, and his central thesis seemed to be that Tom was going to get Jerry some day. That would be the funniest one ever.

Melissa watched Brad eat meatloaf and string beans. Her own food sat almost untouched. She wanted to announce that she'd made an important decision about Kyle's education, but couldn't do so with Kyle sitting right there. Guilt knotted her stomach. She told herself he was too young to be consulted about the matter anyway, but it didn't make her feel better. The silence between the adults didn't appear to be bothering anyone other than Melissa, but it was driving her mad. When she was about to snap at Kyle to shut up and eat his dinner, Brad spoke around a mouthful of baked potato.

"I'm not looking forward to the next couple of months at the bank."

Melissa looked back at Brad. He took a sip of wine and another heroic forkful of potato.

"Why's that, Brad?"

He chewed before replying. Kyle's monologue went on unabated, complete with sound effects.

"Well, Nicole's husband got some kind of fantastic job and they have to relocate. To Idaho."

Melissa struggled in vain to remember who Nicole was.

"So," Brad concluded, "I'm going to need a new secretary. There'll be a couple weeks when I won't have one at all, and a new one always takes a month and a half to figure out the routine. But Nicole's excited about her husband's new job, although I think she wishes it wasn't in Boise."

Melissa took a bite of meatloaf. She sipped her wine. Kyle said, "Pauvre, pauvre, pooshie-cat."

"I guess they'll be running an ad in the paper? For a secretary?" Melissa skewered a bean with her fork.

"I suppose."

"Hmm. The people who apply probably all have a lot of secretarial training."

"That would be nice. No, they lie about their typing speed and it goes downhill from there. Really, a basic understanding of the banking industry would be more helpful."

"Like someone who's worked in other banks."

"Sure. Or someone with a degree in a related field."

"So a degree is a requirement." Melissa ate a forkful of meatloaf while Brad answered.

"Not at all. I was just thinking about all the wasted time with a green secretary, and it never comes down to shorthand or anything like that. It's knowing how to prioritize, and knowing the lingo. Until they get a feel for what's important they waste a lot of time on filing things, and mess up phone messages."

Melissa swirled her wine. She said, "I guess it could be confusing if you don't know the difference between a credit line and a credit rating." She watched Brad through the glass as she took a sip. He was nodding and chewing, then his eyes widened and he swallowed hastily.

"Melissa! I have a fantastic idea!"

*** *** ***

Sitting on the edge of her bed, Gale closed her eyes and whispered a story to her lost babies.

"Once there was a young maiden, all alone in the world. She was an orphan, abandoned on a passenger train when she was born, four days before Christmas. No one knew where she came from or who her family might be, but they all knew she was special. So special that nobody was allowed to adopt her and take her home. No one was good enough to be part of her family and the maiden was very lonely, until one day a handsome young man appeared."

His name was Brian.

"The man was 19 years old and had beautiful eyes. Deep mossy green in the center around the pupil, blending into golden brown around the edge. His hair was a rich chestnut brown. He always dressed in clean white shirts and crisply ironed black pants, and the maiden thought he was unbearably handsome. He taught Sunday school to the maiden and the other orphans. The maiden listened carefully to what he said because she loved his voice and his accent, which wasn't quite southern."

If she'd only been able to trace his accent, she might have known where to look for him.

"On the maiden's 14th birthday, the handsome man married her in secret. The man, now her husband, explained very carefully that no one could ever know or they would be separated, and the maiden listened.

"The maiden's husband took her to a secluded hideaway where they could be together as husband and wife."

Gale's breath came rapidly as she recalled her time in the cave with Brian — the cold air on her naked skin, the urgent kisses, his warm, forceful hands, the sharp, sweet pain between her legs, the ecstasy.

Clearing her throat, Gale continued, "For months they met in secret and the maiden's husband taught her many ways to show her love. But of all the ways, the best was to keep their secret, which the maiden did. She never breathed a word, even when it became clear that she would have a baby.

"Her keepers were furious and sent her away, separating the maiden from her beloved. The maiden escaped just before the child was born and was rewarded with not one baby, but two. Two perfect baby girls with bright green eyes. The first baby, the one she would keep, she named Grace. The second baby she named Kelly. Kelly would be offered to the maiden's tormentors, in exchange for the maiden's freedom. The exhausted maiden hid Kelly, then went to her husband and gave him Grace. Their reunion was joyous, but brief. Little did the maiden know she would never see them again."

Pausing, Gale called up the image of Brian that last time she'd seen him. It was late at night, and raining. He was so surprised to see her, he didn't know what to say. Oh, how she wanted to stay with him forever, but it was impossible. The authorities at Renaissance Center would be searching for her and she couldn't take the chance of them finding her with Brian. After one last hug she left him, and beautiful little Grace, and went back into the stormy night.

"Upon the maiden's return to her captors, the greedy nurses took baby Kelly. The maiden never saw her again either. By the time she returned to the orphanage, her husband and Baby Grace were gone. Remembering her promise of secrecy to her husband, the maiden asked no questions about him. It was the only way she had left to show her love. The maiden waited in vain for almost four years for their return. When she was allowed to leave the orphanage for good, she began searching for her lost family, and has searched for them ever since. I wish I could say they all lived happily ever after."

The story was more complicated, but they'd been over it so many times already. Gale was sure even the dolls were sick of hearing it by now. Suffice it to say she only ever knew his first name: Brian. Even that she had never once been able to utter, or even write. An unnatural compulsion always prevented her. Brian had impressed upon her the importance of secrecy, and she had never been able to disobey. Miss Kent told her he'd left because of a family emergency, which meant he thought of them as a family. Brian probably thought she abandoned him.

Of course it was ridiculous to think that for the last twenty-five years he had been living somewhere with their daughter, waiting for her. Still, that's what her heart and half her mind believed. That their separation was her fault. If she had just remembered one vital clue she would have known where to find them.

Gale shook her head and walked out of the room, switching off the lights on her way.

Chapter Nine

FIVE MINUTES

General, recent advances in electronics and materials science have persuaded us that it is time to revive the project. A subcontractor has placed a bid that, while high, demonstrates proficiency well beyond that of their competitors. They claim they can construct miniature devices that emulate subject EE's distinctive electromagnetic signature, and thereby allow a wearer to emulate her talents. It is entirely feasible, but it won't be cheap.
        Project Lullaby archives, 1987

APRIL 1985

"I know you didn't hear his announcement, Wil, but..." Ember stopped, unable to go on.

"But you want me to explain it anyway? Em, that's not fair. I stopped explaining Severin a long time ago."

"This time..." Beacon struggled. "This time he changed our name."

"What? You're not Beacon anymore? That's ridiculous. Don't listen to him."

"No. We're not the Following anymore." It sounded like that was even harder for Beacon than changing his own name would have been.

Willow went to the stove and poured the boiling water into their mugs, releasing the peppermint smell of the tea. She took too long finding spoons, allowing herself a moment of thought. This was more than the standard Severin angst, and she wasn't sure how to handle it. Perhaps he wanted to see if she would still do his dirty work. Assuming he still gave a damn about her. Since she'd left the Following, he continued to make announcements and proclamations, steadily steering the group toward technology, but he never tried to contact her.

Carrying the mugs to the table, she asked, "So what are you called now?"

Ember looked grim.

Beacon said, "The Technological Evolution Front."

Willow laughed in spite of herself. Ember and Beacon forced tiny smiles onto their faces.

"Technological Evolution Front? That sounds ridiculous! It sounds paramilitary. What the hell is he thinking?"

"That's what we're wondering," Ember said. "He keeps saying science is purified nature, but I just don't feel that, Willow."

Willow shook her head and held Ember's hand. Poor Em. This was going to be hard.

"You guys aren't so much into the technology, are you?"

They both shook their heads.

"Maybe it's time to say goodbye to Severin."

The two of them looked at each other uncertainly. Willow decided to keep quiet and let them reach their own conclusions. She sipped her tea. Severin might be surprised to learn she wasn't going to help him this time.

"That would mean leaving the TEF," Beacon reasoned.

"Well," Ember huffed, "it's not our TEF anymore, is it?"

They were starting to accept the idea now. Willow had rarely seen Ember angry, but she was getting there.

"We couldn't stay in the bungalow," Ember said. Beacon shook his head.

Damn. It made sense now. The damn bungalow.

Their neighborhood was recently rezoned to allow apartment buildings. Severin wanted to sell the bungalow. To do that, he had to get rid of Beacon and Ember. What better way to do that than to completely change the rules on them. They clung to the TEF for years longer than any of the other early members. He must have realized this was the quickest way to see the back of them.

And she had aided and abetted.

Damn.

Before Willow could think of anything to say to counter Severin's schemes, Beacon grabbed Ember's hands and said excitedly, "Green Earth!"

"Oh, Beacon! You're right!"

"Green Earth?" Willow asked.

Ember rushed to explain that the Green Earth collective ran an organic farm and a stall at the farmer's market. They had the best fresh herbs, simply the best. Beacon had already talked to them about selling his hemp clothing and Ember's beads.

"The farm is expanding, and they're looking for helping hands for the growing season," Em concluded. "We can talk to them about joining."

Willow fumed over inadvertently furthering Severin's agenda, but was pleased to see Ember and Beacon excited. For too long now they had subjected themselves to Severin's whims, and if he was now discarding them, it was precisely what they needed in order to be happy. It didn't even look like they would need much of a mourning period, not if things worked out with Green Earth.

Time to be selfish.

"Where is the farm?" she asked.

"It's just on this side of Gambler's Mills," Beacon said.

About five miles from downtown Webster. Not bad at all. A bus even ran there. Beacon and Ember could keep baby-sitting Fin after school on Tuesdays. Not that it was really baby-sitting anymore, since he was 10, but it gave her and Brad couple time without Fin scowling at them. Anyway, Fin loved his time with their old friends, listening to their records, playing cards, and drinking way too much Mountain Dew. He was even learning how to cook vegetarian food.

*** *** ***

Gale poured the coffee into her lime-colored mug and waited a moment for the surface to still. When she peered in she saw only blackness, but it always started that way. After several seconds, the center of the circle of liquid cleared, all its color drawing outward to the edges. The center became her window. Into what, she wasn't certain. She thought about Brian and glimpsed light glinting on something golden. Standard stuff when she thought of him. She took it as a sign he was healthy.

Next she thought about Grace, and got an image of new shingles. That could mean Grace was getting a new roof. Or had gotten a new roof. Or wanted a new roof. Or needed a new roof. Or worked at a hardware store. The shingles were grayish-blue with a staggered, random tab pattern. They made Grace uncomfortable.

All Gale had to do was locate the one 30-year-old woman in North America who was not thrilled about new shingles. Piece of cake. Thistle cake.

When nothing else came about Grace, Gale switched over to Kelly. Scouring powder and a resigned feeling.

Well that's helpful.

She was always reluctant when it came to Kelly, always saved her for last. They were twins, but Gale felt a stronger affinity for Grace because she had been given to Brian. Kelly was the fortunate accident that allowed Gale to throw the Renaissance Center staff off her trail, for all the good it did.

She hadn't known she was having twins. No one did. As part of her compulsion to protect the secret she shared with Brian she refused to let the doctors touch her. It would be like admitting something, to let them confirm the obvious. To this day only she knew there were two babies. Except for the babies themselves. They wouldn't consciously remember their months spent together, but on some level they must know.

Gale raised her mug to sip, and saw a fleeting image of gray eyes as she tipped it. Cold coffee slopped over the sides and the image vanished.

*** *** ***

Ember's laughter bounced around the room — some of it tiny bubbles that ricocheted off the walls in crazy zigzags, and some larger, like slow spongy beach balls that toured the room in arcing bounds. It was 57 million different colors, and Willow could count them all.

Willow knew, somewhere that wasn't really there right now, that Beacon's special lasagna recipe contained certain herbal enhancements. And there was a lot of wine. Or lots of empty bottles, in any case. This was the last hurrah for the bungalow. Tomorrow, Ember and Beacon were moving to Green Earth Farm.

Beacon himself was snoring, which presented gyrating coils and hovering cubes to Willow's augmented perceptions.

"Do it again!" Ember begged. Blue hexagons faded.

Willow laughed, but was brought up short by the zen realization that her mirth was invisible.

"Please?" Ember urged. Green octagons this time.

"Okay, just a minute," Willow replied, sitting up straight on the beanbag chair. She leaned forward to the rough wooden spool, to the lava lamp. She put her hands on the hot glass. What should it be this time? Another butterfly, or maybe a bunny? Ember would laugh again if Willow made a bunny. But what did Willow want to do?

There were no other lights on in the bungalow. Willow's fingers grew into immense shadows, engulfing all four walls except for narrow slivers of golden light that escaped between. Willow thought about the light, thought of it as alive. The slender bands of illumination projecting onto the walls began to migrate. The bright bars moved and combined and multiplied, bearing no relation to the way she held her hands. Willow used them to create a picture of a tree with graceful sweeping fronds, her namesake.

Ember breathed a soft, "Wow!"

Willow stared at the image she had called up, appreciating it. Suddenly she remembered her skin was pressed against the hot lamp. It felt like a bottled volcano.

The tree's color plunged to infernal red and Willow yanked her hands off the fixture with a yelp. She looked at them, found no damage. Her mind cleared.

Such was evidently not the case with her friends. Beacon's snoring halted for a few seconds at Willow's brief exclamation, while Ember giggled.

"I think I should go now. Check up on Fin. He doesn't stay over with friends very often and I worry. Thanks for dinner."

Ember gave no indication of having heard. On an impulse, Willow unplugged the lamp. It was only an inanimate object, but such an elemental part in her life here in Webster it felt almost like a friend. It was her trophy from a wizard's dungeon, and was with her when she met Brad. But tonight's mischief had been foolhardy, precisely the sort of activity she'd been trying to escape when she moved out of the bungalow seven years ago. She changed her mind about taking it with her and stashed it with the macramé wall hangings and old bathroom drapes in one of the moving boxes stacked by the door.

"Good night, Vesuvius," she said as she crept out of the house.

*** *** ***

3 YEARS LATER - 1988

Jay Marshall could hear his mother telling him to stand up straight. Since she was 400 miles away, he didn't listen. Hands jammed in his pockets, he slogged along the sidewalk toward microbiological engineering.

He was early, not that it mattered. He didn't have anything better he should be doing, or worse for that matter. He might as well go sit in an empty classroom. Or keep wandering around campus in the gray drizzle, because ultimately his BioE grade wouldn't matter much anyway. He couldn't imagine anyone taking an interest in a dropout's grades.

Now he heard his father talking about the basketball scholarship. Jay's head drooped until his chin rested on his chest. Being the tallest kid at Flyspeck High just made him tall enough for everyone there to get it into their heads he would be great at basketball. Buckminster University already had at least five students taller than Jay, and at least a hundred with actual athletic talent. But Dad had faith, and didn't like to be disputed. So Jay went to tryouts, and the coaches let him hang around at practice for his freshman year. But that was last year.

Dad was so damn sure there would be a scholarship. Jay couldn't apply for student aid without parental cosignature, so effectively he couldn't apply. His tuition was paid through fall term, but his rent was three months behind. He just hoped to ride it out until finals without getting tossed into the street.

He'd reached Kuznachik Building. The front steps were an amphitheater, holding a damp but gleeful audience for the tragedy of Rodney, the Kuznachik Preacher. Being in the back row presented no problem for Jay, as Buckminster's five taller students were absent from the scene. He'd eventually need to use an alternate entrance, but this would be better than brooding alone in a classroom.

Rodney wore a pale yellow windbreaker with the hood pulled up against the chill November precipitation. He didn't look much older than the undergrads in his congregation. He tended to tilt his face upwards when he spoke.

"And you whores should know you shall be punished with meticulous justice for each of your sins, and you will know misery to repay your lust tenfold."

A smattering of "Fuck you" phased Rodney less than the rain. Most of the assembled sinners wore disbelieving grins.

"A temptress, flaunting her flesh to corrupt others, that's what you are. And you. All you women, you're demonic and accursed in His sight."

Some laughter, lots of people shaking their heads. Unamused coeds looking daggers at the preacher. Rodney's customary misogyny was turned up a few pegs today, but Jay wasn't finding anything funny in it, either.

"Religion is such a small part of that guy's problems, I can't begin to express it."

Jay nodded, glancing at the person who'd made this observation. He expected to see an army surplus jacket and stringy hair, but the speaker wore a clean pea green sweater, neatly buttoned, and held a yellow umbrella over his crew cut.

"I'm Beach," he said. "Here, you hold the umbrella over both of us. I think that will work best."

Jay accepted the umbrella uncertainly, unable to reconcile a simple show of hospitality with a possible veiled overture for something tawdry. Sharing an umbrella was pretty personal. Now that he held it, he couldn't very well deprive its owner of shelter.

Beach quirked one side of his mouth and turned to walk back the way Jay had just come. Jay lurched after him automatically, and they traveled almost half a block before he blurted out, "I have a class in, like, ten minutes. Thanks, but I need to go back and find my way around that mob."

Beach stopped and turned, but wouldn't accept the umbrella.

"You can miss one class. In point of fact, you could teach that class. Mr Marshall, I have a much better idea than rotting away in Kuznachik."

Jay knew he should put down the umbrella, or keep it, and head for class.

"Are you in my class?" No, Beach wouldn't blend into the herd. Jay had never seen him before. "How do you know my name?"

"My organization takes an interest in talented students. Come on, let's have a cup of coffee and I'll tell you about the TEF."

Jay smirked, which embarrassed him but didn't seem to bother Beach. "I'm sorry, but it sounds like you're trying to pick me up. That's, well, flattering I suppose..."

Beach nodded, then hurried to clarify, "I can see what you mean, but no, I'm not asking you out. Look, I know about your financial problems. You could be evicted any day. I also know about your exceptional academic record."

Jay snorted. His grades were not superb. If his professors weren't such morons, things could be different. Not that it mattered, he reminded himself.

"Let me put it another way. I know that your GPA doesn't tell the real story. You're an extremely clever person, Mr Marshall, who needs some help. The TEF wants to help you."

Jay pretended to chew on this decision for almost a minute, because it seemed like he ought to, but the surreal conversation pulled into focus how badly he wanted to blow off class, maybe forever. Plus, hot coffee sounded divine. He nodded and the two of them ambled off. Jay appraised Beach's dapper wardrobe once more, trying to figure him out.

"So, TEF. Is that a fraternity?"

***   ***   ***

Brad wasn't ready to go home.

It had been a hell of a day and he was bone-tired, but he felt a powerful need to be away from other people. Specifically his families.

Melissa was in an impish mood at the office, and talked him into calling it a day at lunchtime. Over three hours of together time before Kyle came home from school. Mel didn't let any of it go to waste.

It had been a physically pleasant though tiring afternoon. Except that something felt strange. Melissa was chatty and almost, well, businesslike. She brought up subjects like the inconceivable promotion of Harold to branch manager, or things Kyle's teachers said, all mood killers. Even so, she insisted on an encore.

Sex with Melissa seldom involved any talking at all. She'd shush him, whether he asked if she liked something or moaned his own pleasure. The oddest part about today had been the daylight. Normally she was pretty strict about scheduling their love in darkness.

They barely got themselves dressed before Kyle came home. At that point, she stated unequivocally that she needed to go over fractions with the boy, so Brad should stay out of the way. Brad decided to take a quick shower. He said he would go for a drive and she murmured something he didn't quite hear, so he left.

He went to see Willow. She called her former roommates and asked them if Fin could do his homework over there.

Next came another three-hour session of carnal pleasure. This time, Brad was the distracted one. The physical similarities between Melissa and Willow were glaring, accentuated by the back-to-back encounters. Fortunately, Willow decided to claim the driver's seat, sparing Brad the need to focus, and giving his already taxed body a break. Moreover, it eliminated any impression of Melissa.

Eventually she told him it was time for Fin to come home for supper, and he dressed hurriedly in advance of his son's arrival, again. Brad asked him about his day. Fin stared at him for several seconds, and said, "It was fine, Brad."

Oh well, Brad thought, rhymes with dad. Close enough.

Now he stood on a street corner, ostensibly trying to decide which restaurant would give him the quickest service but actually adrift in a vague haze of dissatisfaction. It bothered him that Melissa never asked him where he drove to, that she didn't think to check the odometer. He didn't want to fight with her, but it hurt that his routine absences didn't warrant more concern.

It was getting dark. Brad didn't have an appetite, so he struck off in a random direction. He lit a cigarette, only dimly aware he was doing it and would therefore have to quit all over again. Walking east, he passed two bars and a church on every block. Revelers lined up outside all the bars, and packs of them roamed in between. No offsetting behavior corresponded to the churches, no hordes of worshippers lining up on Thursday night to be sure of good seats come Sunday. It always seemed to Brad that the supply of churches in Webster was out of all proportion to the demand.

He paused at the curb before a side street and dropped his cigarette butt on a manhole cover to mash it out with his toe. He blew a last plume of smoke as he looked around. Another block or two in this direction would put him on the outskirts. Beyond the outskirts lay the boondocks.

Brad pivoted as he considered doubling back in the direction of his car. Turned again, more slowly, and thought about cutting over a block for a change of scene. There weren't enough restaurants along that route. He turned east again to face the boondocks. Maybe there was someplace he subconsciously wanted to reach, miles out on the road. Well, that being the case his subconscious would have to nudge him as he drove. He completed one final revolution on the manhole, facing west toward his car and several half-decent eateries. His appetite had returned.

She stood next to a dark green van. Smartly dressed in a brown pantsuit, clutching a raffia handbag, dry, and not pregnant. Had she not dropped to her knees as Brad spotted her, he never would have recognized Ghost Girl.

Brad stopped. "Hi, again. Didn't expect to see you along such a busy street. Everything going all right?" He noticed the rivers on her cheeks, and glanced away. "Yeah, me too. Things are a bit of a mess. I'm not sure what's going to happen."

She hadn't moved, wasn't trying to speak. Brad wondered if she might be drunk. This was different from any of the other times he'd encountered her. Ever since the first time he'd seen her in the woods, she'd appeared at almost regular intervals, two or three times a year, always when he was alone. Up until now she'd always looked the same and gone through the same routine. Seeing her older was a relief, because it implied she hadn't died in childbirth, as he always suspected. It did raise plenty of other questions, though.

The silence felt awkward, even with a ghost. No one else was around to hear him, so he filled it by unburdening himself. "I have this situation. I can't understand how it got started. I have two houses, and no home. I don't belong anywhere. And, I have a wonderful, terrible secret."

Ghost Girl stayed put. She always was a good listener.

"I want to tell them, more than anything. I want to bring us all together, but that would never work. They wouldn't believe me anyway. I can't always believe it. Then I watch them again, and I know it's true. So different, and so much alike."

A traffic signal changed at the end of the block, its green stare reflected on the side of the green van behind her. Her eyes cleared and caught his, held him. Her left hand rose tentatively, and Brad extended his right, wondering how close he would get this time before she disappeared. He felt a charge building over his skin. Her lips moved at last, and though she made no sound Brad made out the words, "...my baby."

Brad's hand reached hers, and as she flinched he heard a tiny, sharp noise and his right arm went numb. She vanished.

∗∗∗   ∗∗∗   ∗∗∗

Willow brushed a few stray hairs out of her eyes as she leaned on her elbow to ponder her current freelance assignment, fanned out on the small bureau she used for a desk. The wayward lock fell across her forehead again, and she jutted her lower lip to direct a puff of breath upward. The hair settled back into place.

Willow blew her hair out of her face several more times.

When she got paid for this assignment she'd be able to afford the electric guitar Fin had his eye on. The secondhand acoustic served him well enough, but as a teenager he now hungered for more noise-making ability. With maximum decibels on the line, it was fitting that her employer was Industrial Harmonics, a minor player in the military/ industrial complex. Her old friends from the Following would be dismayed to learn of her involvement in anything so corporate, let alone government financed, but the pay was a nice supplement to her apartment manager salary. Besides, apart from Ember and Beacon she hadn't seen or spoken to anyone from the Following in years. For all she knew they all worked in advertising or politics.

Her advisor from Buckminster, on the other hand, kept in touch when she'd been unable to continue her education, and a few years later he'd taken a job with Industrial Harmonics. Through his position there he slid some work her way, under the table at first. Very hush-hush. Over the past five or six years, her situation had grown more legitimate, and these days they treated her more or less like any other freelance contractor. Which meant she still didn't get health benefits. Maybe she should go back to school and get hired as a staff engineer. Except, without a past, she couldn't get a security clearance.

Willow sighed, and focused her attention on the papers. The project was typical of what Industrial Harmonics sent her lately, something bungled by their in-house engineering staff. In this case, they went so far out of the way to cobble something out of off-the-shelf components that, rather than reducing costs, they doubled the board's size, and failed to arrive at anything that actually worked. Time for Willow to breathe life into their ugly little monster. Which was pointless, because the intended application required something unobtrusive and portable, two qualities most conspicuously absent from this design.

Such unremitting foolishness in the halls of Industrial Harmonics kept her employed, but nevertheless it was difficult to imagine how one firm had tracked down all the least competent engineers on the planet.

The real fault probably lay with management, a group Willow didn't have to deal with. That could be the entirety of her unfair advantage: the lack of supervision.

Along with the drawings came a list of performance specifications, all unrealistic. Extreme audio sensitivity, with no external microphone. Huge transmission range, but no external antenna. Send and receive capability across just about the whole electromagnetic spectrum, with wicked strong encryption. Miserly power consumption. Virtually zero heat generation. Willow doubted it was achievable, even with unlimited materials research. Maybe that accounted for the pigheaded reliance on stock chips. Why struggle with a fool's errand, when you can get it off your desk faster by fucking it up?

That wasn't a viable option for Willow. Her pay was a bounty awarded for success.

Again smoothing back her hair, Willow selected a sharp pencil from the cup against the mirror and placed a legal pad in her lap. She planned to purge her mind of the dead-end design they sent by roughing in the simplest possible sketch that would encompass all the required features.

Stacking all the drawings, she laid the sheet with the performance specs on top to hide them. As she reviewed the ridiculous list, she took the troublesome strand of hair and twirled it between her thumb and index finger. The pencil danced in her left hand, sometimes waltzing and sometimes tangoing. Willow let herself doodle while she tried to seriously consider the science-fiction expectations. Maybe she'd wind up with an abstract masterpiece, and sell it to replace the income she'd lose when she gave up trying to bend the laws of physics for her unappreciative client.

Her hair fell in her eyes again. She'd let go of it at some point in order to drum her fingers on the bureau. Stretching, she looked down at her doodle.

For a few seconds it didn't even register as something she had drawn. Instead of the scratchy strokes she thought she'd been making she saw smooth, uniform lines. The dominant shape, a perfect circle, contained an intricate tapestry of components and connections. Some standard symbols appeared here and there, a diode or a transistor, but mostly the components bore strange glyphs that left Willow guessing at their meaning. Nothing was labeled, there was no indication of scale.

Willow smirked. *Is this my abstract masterpiece?*

Assuming that this diagram represented a device to do all the things on the list, and choosing as her starting point an area relatively free of alien notations, Willow traced out the whole thing in her head. It was deeper than she'd first realized, because it cunningly allowed almost every part to serve multiple purposes. The layout was like a Möbius strip, several times over. Soon she inferred key properties of some of the mystery components. They hadn't been invented, as far as she knew, but they didn't strike her as impossible to construct.

The truth smiled up at her from the paper. She beheld blueprints for the impossible. What she'd taken for a hopeless job, accomplished handily.

Tiny hairs stood up on the back of her neck. It was exactly this kind of freaky weirdness she was supposedly done with, but apparently it wasn't done with her.

Shutting her eyes, she drew a slow breath to extricate her mind from the arabesques of the design.

***   ***   ***

Jay Marshall. He supposed he'd never completely get over the conditioned response of looking up when someone said those syllables, but his TEF name would be more important, would symbolize his deeper nature. It would be true in a way that his old name simply couldn't. Anthro 101 touched on rites of passage, how they define one's place in the tribe, and at the time Jay dismissed their possible relevance to modern life. To his life.

In just a week, Jay had come to feel a greater need for belonging at the Technological Evolution Front than he'd ever known. Everyone was so smart, so focused. Such a thrilling, happy urgency about their work. Work years ahead of its time, even the little bit they'd shown him so far. The opportunity to rewrite all the rules sang to him, and Jay would risk any jagged rocks to reach it.

There had been a test, or something, the first day. Probably a hazing ritual.

Beach set him up at a desk and left him alone there with nothing but a calculator, a fresh pad of graph paper, a mechanical pencil, and a manilla folder. The folder contained a single sheet of creased and tattered paper covered with crudely sketched circuit diagrams. Jay took his best guess at which of these bizarre drawings was the right one, and began a transcription to the graph paper. Partway through cleaning it up he discovered that it made no sense.

It was nothing so simple as crossed wires. It was demented. It reminded Jay of how Escher could trick you into seeing a world made up of contradictions. There was nothing to fix.

So what was he supposed to do?

Acting on sudden inspiration, he borrowed sections from another of the sketches on the paper. Their crazinesses canceled each other out, and he ended up with something odd but not irrational. Only after completing the new drawing did he really make an attempt to figure out if it would do anything useful, and was pleased to discover that he'd drawn some type of control system. He started writing a detailed description of how he would use the device, but only had enough time to scrawl 'robot cruise control' because Beach came back for him.

Although he was sure he'd blown it, he was accepted by his new tribe. Yesterday Beach and Smoke accompanied him to his tiny apartment to help collect his belongings. Someone had already squared things with the landlord, freeing him to move into the House, as the TEF's imposing headquarters was known.

Now he would meet the leader, Severin Tenpenny, who would bestow his TEF name and make it official.

Jay Marshall sat alone in the dining hall, waiting to become someone new.

Severin emerged from the basement, startling Jay. It wasn't the arrival he'd expected, nor did Severin's shaggy appearance match the image Jay had formed. The rank and file of the TEF all wore green cardigans, and Jay already had one of his own. They gave a professional, clean-cut first impression, and Jay had assumed the leader would wear a stylish suit and the most expensive wristwatch in the county.

"Hello, Jay. Pleased to finally meet you." Severin extended his hand, and Jay shook it. Despite his initial surprise, Jay found the man commanding. His sharp blue eyes and rumbling voice gave a magnitude of presence greater than any suit or Rolex could convey.

"It's a great honor to be here," Jay said. "I already feel like I'm in your debt, Sir."

Severin smiled slightly and nodded. "We are grateful to have you among us. You excelled on your test, I must tell you. There is quite a market for a simple, robust design like yours. Don't give the rent money another thought. Now, on to important business." He walked to the sink and ran water into a mug, dropped in a small pouch, and set it up in the microwave. "Your name."

Jay tried to sit still. He tried not to be Jay, to erase that so the new identity could be written.

Severin waited for the beverage to get hot, then set it before Jay. He fetched a small honey jar and a spoon before taking a seat himself.

"Thank you," Jay said. He sniffed the tea, not finding it appealing.

Severin's eyes glinted and he chuckled. Jay now felt genuinely nervous. This was an interview he had to ace. He added a generous amount of honey to his tea and stirred it, cringing at each clink and scrape of the spoon in the quiet room.

"In the old days," Severin said, "the naming ceremony had a strong mystical component. I used to tie people up." Jay nodded. This too amused Severin, for a moment. "Finding your true name is a skill I have refined over the years, and I no longer require as much paraphernalia. You need simply drink the tea, as a symbol of your trust in me, and I will read your name from the aether."

Jay nodded again. He took a sip, discovered it was not overly hot or as foul as it smelled, and drank deeper.

Severin smiled again and said, "We ran out of Kool-Aid."

Jay swallowed, the pungent mouthful of liquid acquiring corners in his throat.

"It's herbal tea, admittedly a rather rough brew. Laced with a touch of phenobarbital. Oh, and honey. You added some honey."

Jay nodded. The warmth and softness around the edges was a nice feature of the dining hall. He took another swallow of the spiked tea, to ace the interview.

Severin nodded, regarded Jay from a few slightly different angles.

Jay took another sip. Any moment now, he would be a new person. Then he would go take a nap.

"Welcome, Marsh, to the Technological Evolution Front." With that, Severin clapped him on the shoulder and left the room.

Marsh floated in a mist of soft, warm disappointment. He wasn't a new person. Marsh was what he'd been to his classmates since tenth grade. He tried to see the deeper truth in what just happened, but couldn't shake the knowledge that he did not get a cool TEF name.

Marsh drank the rest of his tea.

*** *** ***

Five minutes could really crawl. It was longer than the package called for, but Willow didn't want to misread the results. She had already watered her jade plant, African violet, and two ferns, wiped the faux butcher-block counter and the stove, and drunk a small glass of orange juice. Two minutes to go.

Eyes closed, Willow exhaled and shrugged some of the tension from her shoulders. She counted to sixty before opening her eyes.

One minute. She began to walk slowly through the kitchen, straightening salt shaker, napkin caddy, dish towel, fridge magnets. In the hallway she adjusted the curtain ties and the area rug. The bathroom door stood open in front of her.

There it sat, on the sink, an innocuous-looking square of white plastic on which her fortune was written. Plus for positive, minus for negative. What could be simpler?

Plus.

Willow nodded. No real surprise. She stashed the pregnancy test and its packaging in the bottom of the bathroom wastebasket, under used tissues and floss, but wasn't satisfied. She pulled the liner from the basket, tossed it into the larger kitchen can, pulled that liner as well and took the whole lot out to the dumpster.

Back inside, she stood shakily in the kitchen with her left hand resting on her belly and drank a large glass of milk for the baby.

Baby.

How would she tell Brad? Or, for that matter, Fin?

Willow could only imagine Fin's reaction to having a baby around. He would be 14 by the time it was born. Would he be more embarrassed or pissed off? The pregnancy would certainly shine a light on the nature of her ongoing relationship with Brad, a subject of which Fin had only a murky understanding and next to no approval.

A small fluttering tickled her insides, and Willow felt her abdomen twitch under her hand. That meant she was a couple months along. She smiled. In spite of the difficulties a pregnancy presented, Willow was excited.

A half-hour later she was leaning against the counter, pondering and daydreaming when Fin walked in.

"What's for lunch, Mom? I'm starved. I didn't get breakfast, and I've got soccer for gym this afternoon. Bill always makes us run a lap before we start to play." He opened the refrigerator and moved things around.

Willow pulled herself from her reverie and ruffled his dark hair. It was getting quite long, but he wouldn't get it cut again until spring. He liked to winterize, as he called it.

"Why don't we go out today?" she asked. One of the nicest features of Fin's alternative high school was the open campus. While some parents might worry about their children getting into trouble when they should be safely locked inside for the day, Willow took advantage of the freedom by having lunch with her son several times a week. Usually they ate sandwiches or soup or macaroni and cheese at home, but not today.

Today called for a celebration, even if Fin would not be privy to the reason.

Chapter Ten

THIS TIME

Based on current projections, we should take possession of the first group of infant test subjects by the end of November. I don't need to remind you, General, how ticklish this is. The medical and clerical staff at our four regional homes for unweds know our stringent criteria. Selection of appropriate subjects, newborns with no familial ties whatsoever, is critical. Equally important, however, is selection of proper guardians for the control group. Not all officers are cut out for fatherhood, and we must avoid any household dramatics that could influence test results.
Project Lullaby archives, 1955

NOVEMBER 1988

After putting away the groceries, Willow unfolded the newspaper and skimmed the front page. Taking a seat at the table, she separated the paper's sections and flipped to the national page. A small photo in the lower right corner caught her eye.

Her father.

Capital Crash Claims Colonel

U.S. Army Colonel Theodore Finch, 63, died Thursday evening in a fiery Beltway wreck that closed a two-mile stretch of highway in the nation's capital. His vehicle struck a concrete abutment en route to an interview where he allegedly intended to expose a hidden military research program. The cause of the accident is under investigation.

Finch asserted in a letter to the *Washington Post*

that he spent decades involved in covert research into psychic phenomena. He wrote, "Even my own adopted daughter was part of it, without her consent." Army spokesperson Cassandra Peters called such allegations ridiculous.

Willow put the newspaper down on the table and wiped her eyes. She wanted to hug Fin, but he wouldn't be home from school for hours. Rocking in her chair, she rubbed her eyes again. She massaged her temples, staring at the dot pattern of the photo on the newsprint, knowing the dots made a picture of her father but not letting herself see him. Her eyes stung, and she tucked a stray wisp of hair behind her ear and it caught in her fingers that curled and clenched and clawed at her scalp and pulled her head down onto the table. A silent howl stole her breath and hot tears ran onto the paper.

She fought unsuccessfully for composure, unsure she even believed the story. Thirteen years of rejected remorse welled up at the image of her father in pain. All the suffering she created for him by running away arrived in a compact wad, expanding to blot out everything else. That she'd despised him for his part in the experiments, that he'd always been distant and authoritarian, all her justifications for running away, gave no shelter from her anguish. They flared like a grass fire before the gale, grievances now forever to remain unredressed. Willow clamped her teeth onto her sleeve to hold back her screams.

After twenty minutes Willow lifted her head. She rose unsteadily and shuffled to the sink to wash her face. The cool water soothed her flushed and sticky skin. She closed the tap and dried her face with a paper towel, which came away gray.

Although unsure the words wouldn't send her over the edge again, she crossed back to her chair to reread the story. A word in it contributed to her episode, and she needed to look for it again.

Adopted.

He never told me, but he wrote it in a letter to a fucking newspaper? This is all bullshit. He didn't write that letter, and this was no accident. They killed him. They killed my dad.

A shudder ran through her and fresh tears stung her eyes, but she wiped them away angrily.

He wasn't my dad at all, the lying bastard! No wonder he let them do those things, I was just some guinea pig.

Grinding her teeth, Willow pounded the paper with her fist.

If he didn't write the letter, she wondered, was he really her dad after all? Why would it say she was adopted, if she wasn't? How far did the lie go?

Willow rocked back and forth, tears flowing unhindered and spattering the newsprint.

He never told me. I was too stupid to know, and he never told me. He never told me.

Adopted.

With a long, ragged breath, Willow mastered her tears once more.

Who wrote the letter? She tried to figure it out. Someone else in the program, someone with enough influence to order a killing. Why mention the research itself so bluntly? Why mention it at all? Why even write a letter? All it would do was lend credibility to anyone who called it a cover-up. It would draw more attention to the accident and put the program at risk.

It would draw attention. It would guarantee the crash was reported nationally.

The letter had been sent to the *Post*, but the message was meant for Ester Finch.

She read the story again, looking for signs of what they expected her to do. It must be a crude attempt to lure her into the open. Perhaps they hoped she would try to attend her father's funeral, except the story didn't make mention of it. Maybe they went out of the way to mention the *Washington Post* so she might get in touch with the paper.

They went out of the way to tell me I was adopted.

Did she believe it? Knowing where it came from, knowing it was a trap, could she take the idea seriously? Facing her feelings about the question brought fresh tears. Learning of his death at the same time that she learned of his lifetime of deception felt like losing him twice. Pain and confusion swirled, but not the debilitating anguish that hit her the first time.

Someone intending to bait a trap might invent a confusing detail in order to pique the target's interest. Of course, a confusing detail wouldn't have to be untrue to serve such a function.

Why didn't he tell me?

If the letter was forged, if he wasn't about to blow the whistle, why kill him? To hurt her? To make her careless? Why not let her think he was her real father? Maybe they didn't know he never told her.

Her tears dried up, as her rage at her false father shrank and faded. So many things made sense now. He'd told her as much as duty demanded, but kept as much as he could to himself. He wanted to shield her from some pain, knowing he was responsible for too much already. Instead of as a monster turning over his own flesh and blood for experimentation, Willow saw him as a duty-bound man trying to show kindness to a stranger in his home.

Now he was dead, and his killers wanted her to know he hadn't been her biological father. That she might have a family, a real family. A mother. They wanted her to be careless, to show herself. To look for her mother.

Clearly it was a desperation tactic. They couldn't be sure she'd see the story, that she was even alive. They couldn't think she would be foolish enough to start asking around for adoption records in the name Ester Finch.

For that matter, why should she go looking for a woman she didn't know, who was quite likely dead, who gave her up as an infant? There was no reason to presume her mother would be interested in meeting her. They couldn't establish a normal parent-child relationship at this point. It offended Willow that her hunters thought she would be flushed out of hiding by something so cliché.

But the image of a reunion with her mother shimmered on the horizon of her thoughts. Ted Finch claimed to be a widower, that her mother died when Ester was born. If that were a lie, she might have a family somewhere. Fin might have grandparents, aunts, uncles, cousins. A family.

Willow drummed her fingers as she thought.

If she wasn't careless, there were investigative avenues open to her that didn't exist for normal people. If she was methodical and patient, she could search in mystical places without leaving any trail, without showing herself. Find her mother, and take something back from the people who took away her father.

*** *** ***

When the door opened, Brad presented the bottle of red with a flourish. Willow accepted his usual Tuesday night offering casually, her hand brushing his and sending a thrill of energy up his arm. Before she could move away, he pulled her in tight against his chest. Her fathomless jade eyes looked up into his face as he bent to kiss her, then slipped closed.

Every week it was the same, this blissful reunion.

"Honey, I'm home," he murmured into her warm, autumnal hair.

With the door closed and his heavy winter coat hanging on the coat tree, Brad followed Willow into the kitchen where he could smell chicken roasting. She put the wine in the refrigerator.

"The chicken needs a few more minutes," she said, her hands fitfully smoothing her splattered apron against her stomach.

Brad winked and said, "I don't mind waiting."

She smiled, but turned away and began wiping the counter with a dish towel.

Wasn't she happy to see him?

"Wil?"

She removed the apron, turned to him and set the towel down. Brad took her hands.

"Let's go to the living room," she said.

Brad trailed along, holding one warm hand. He sat in the corner of the sofa and pulled her onto his lap with his arm around her. She snuggled into him, a good sign, and she kissed the fingertips of his left hand.

"The chicken smells great," he said as she arranged his hands on her tummy, pressing the palms gently but firmly into place. Brad leaned forward to nuzzle her ear, but stopped when he felt a twitch of movement under his right thumb. Willow held still and he felt it again, a brief skimming against the base of his thumb. The tiny sensation took him back to the bungalow, right after fall midterms. To the happy months before his marriage, when Willow was pregnant with Fin.

"Do you still grade on a curve?" Willow whispered.

***

"I'm going to do it right this time."

"Do what right?"

"This. Us."

Willow looked at him hard, and he didn't look away.

"I'll be with you," he said. "Through this, and after too. I'll be with you."

"What about—"

"Please don't. I know what you're thinking, and all I can say is I'm certain." How could he explain to her what he felt? He'd made such a mess of things the first time and now had the opportunity to do it over. "I'm not even sure Mel and Kyle will notice I'm gone."

Willow looked away.

"You're right," said Brad. "It will be messy. But I just can't do it again. I should have made this choice years ago."

"Yes."

"I should have, but I couldn't. I didn't want either of you to be mad at me." Listening to the words coming out of his mouth made Brad realize what an ass he'd been. By not wanting to cause temporary emotional turbulence he had doomed them all to years of unfulfillment. If he had ever truly loved Melissa, that feeling had faded, but he didn't want to hurt her. Not wanting to hurt her was not the same thing as loving her. He loved Willow, of that he had no doubt. He shook his head. "How have you put up with me?"

"You never made me any promises. I never asked you for any. Not until now. Our entire relationship has been based on never expecting anything from each other. If you're telling me you're going to leave your wife and be with me, be a father for this baby and for Fin, you better mean it. I've never asked you to leave her. I've never asked you to choose. But if you are choosing, it has to be genuine."

"It is."

"This is too important for short answers. I want to wait. I want you to think about this. I want us both to think about it. When you come over next week, then you can make a promise. Or not."

Brad understood her reluctance, but his mind was made up. He would wait a week, then promise her the moon and stars, anything she wanted.

Willow saw his smile and added, "And don't think you can just reverse us. If you choose me, you're choosing me only. No little chippy on the side."

Brad kissed her.

*** *** ***

The pillowcase wasn't going to get any crisper. Already smooth and flat, it sported razor-sharp seams. Willow admitted to herself that she was stalling and unplugged the iron. She eyed the old ironing board warily. It merely stood there on its odd, scissor-like legs looking mundane. It could at least show some appreciation. After all, she had rescued it from mildewing in the basement.

Willow glanced at the basket full of freshly ironed clothes on the sofa. Fin probably wouldn't show any appreciation for his well-pressed undies either.

Still stalling.

One cup of coffee then on to business.

Willow shook her head and spread the pillowcase out to cover as much of the silvery surface of the ironing board as possible. It was from Fin's stone-age Underdog sheet set.

"There's no need to fear. Underdog is here," Willow assured herself and reached under the pillowcase.

Her hand encountered nothing but the worn ironing board cover. Willow sighed and pulled out her empty hand. Could she even be certain her earlier experience with conjuring items from nothingness hadn't been a trick engineered by Severin? At the time, her innate skepticism had been allayed, but was that just her own desire to believe?

Willow's fingers traced the jagged sunburst of yellow super-energy haloing Underdog as she counted and recounted its spikes. She counted by fives, then threes, then sevens, always trying to end on the spike directly above Underdog's big googly eyes. She tried it with twos and that didn't work either.

Brow furrowed, Willow picked up the hem in her right hand and hesitantly slipped her left hand underneath. A shiver of static stood her hairs on end. Probing a little deeper, her pinkie brushed something cool and glassy.

Sucking in her breath, Willow froze for a second. When she moved again, she curled her fingers around a small, cylindrical object. It fit in her palm.

What would it be? *What will it tell me about my mother?*

Study it. Don't jump to conclusions. Literal interpretations are usually incorrect.

Once her fist was clear of the pillowcase, Willow opened it.

Empty.

Willow blinked. Whatever it was had disappeared. Severin told her that all objects pulled from the Elsewhere returned to it, but she recalled them having a longer half-life.

She decided to try again, and not dawdle so much.

After five full minutes of fruitless groping which left her feeling like a teenage boy on his first date, Willow stared defiantly down at Underdog.

"Cerberus had three heads, you know."

The cartoon dog grinned back at her.

Feeling superstitious, Willow began her zen counting ceremony again.

Fives. Threes. Sevens. Twos.

Once again when she slid them under the cloth, her fingers found their way to a small, glassy object, this one a cube. She quickly pulled her hand out.

Empty again.

After glaring at Underdog, Willow went into the kitchen and poured herself a cup of coffee, but it was cold and too bitter. She dumped it down the sink and ran a glass of water instead. Leaning against the counter, she sipped and thought.

The objects were there, but she couldn't bring them through. There were three ways to interpret that. Well, four, really, but Willow wasn't willing to believe she was imagining it. That left three likely explanations. First, Severin's table was more powerful than her half-assed improvised one. Or, second, Severin's presence was necessary. Third, the very fact of the disappearance was her message.

"Stupid transitory extra-dimensional souvenirs."

Having Severin in the room was unthinkable, during this or any other activity. If he was the required catalyst, then the magic-table technique was simply not an option. But she owed it to herself to rule out the other explanations before giving up on the whole enterprise.

If the evaporation was her sign, what did it mean? How should she interpret this message?

It could mean her mother was missing. Vanished. Gone. But that wasn't news. Willow had always known that. Perhaps it was confirmation that her mother was dead, as she had always been told.

That didn't feel right.

Being unable to see the mystery objects, or to truly posses them, could mean there was nothing to be known. There simply was no information.

How could that be? Willow existed, after all. She came from somewhere. Or, in this case, someone.

Perhaps her mother was hiding from her. That would imply her mother knew about this sort of strangeness, which seemed unlikely. She could be hidden, though, by someone who did know. The military men, for instance.

They didn't really know about it, though. They only suspected. The program she grew up in had been attempting to learn about this kind of thing, but they never achieved results. If they had, they would have retrieved Ester Finch. If they lacked the knowledge to find Ester, they lacked the knowledge to effectively hide her mother in this way.

Could the Elsewhere be telling her she'd be better off not finding her mother? Or that she might find her, but nothing would come of it?

The scientific thing to do was repeat this experiment and try to replicate the results. If she used Severin's table and got the same handful of nothing, she would have her answer: there was no answer.

However, if, using Severin's table, she found a clue, she might find the woman who gave her life, and gave her up.

***   ***   ***

When Willow opened the door Brad showed her his duffle bag. Apparently he thought he'd move right in. She wasn't ready for that yet. She rose up on her tiptoes and kissed him. While returning the kiss, he scooted the duffle in with his foot.

"What's in the bag?" Willow shut the door.

"Some clothes. I'll go back this weekend and get the rest." He beamed at her.

A mixture of emotions careened through Willow. For the past 13 years she told herself she didn't deserve a real relationship with Brad, that she had to keep him at arm's length so leaving would be easier. Obviously she'd been invested all along, despite her efforts to the contrary, because the possibility of having him, really having him, thrilled her. The military's attempt to lure her out of hiding with her father's murder demonstrated that her trail had grown cold and her adversaries were out of ideas. Maybe it was time, at last, to allow herself some happiness. At the same time, she knew they had to take things slower. There was Fin to think about, if nothing else.

Brad failed to notice her unease and bounded to the kitchen. Willow trailed behind.

"Oh, I love fondue!" He poked the bubbling cheese with a skewer.

Smiling, Willow gestured to the plate of bread chunks and assorted vegetables.

"Pumpernickel!"

Once his mouth was full, Willow spoke, explaining her position. "I love you, Brad." He nodded and pointed at himself, then at her. She continued, "We need to take this slowly. If we rush, we'll regret it later."

Brad swallowed a painfully large chunk, but Willow kept talking. "We need to let Fin warm up to the idea for one thing. For another, you've got to be sensitive to Melissa and Kyle."

Whatever Brad had been about to say, he didn't. His shoulders sagged and he toyed with his skewer before stabbing another chunk of bread. "I want to do the right thing," he said and plunged the morsel into the fondue pot. "What does that mean in this case?"

Willow picked up her own skewer and watched the light reflect off it for a moment. She speared a small piece of broccoli. "I think it means, much as I would like for you to stay, you don't yet. You make some time in your schedule for Fin. And you decide how you're going to tell Melissa. You can't just walk out. That would be a horrible thing to do to someone, and you're going to have to deal with her in the future, at least in regards to Kyle."

Brad nodded.

Willow dunked her broccoli and blew on it before putting it in her mouth.

"Are you real, Willow Charm?" He looked intently at her. She shrugged one shoulder.

He went on, "You're the most amazing person I've ever met. Ever. After everything that's happened, you're looking out for Mel and Kyle? If you'll still have me after the way I've lived my life, I'm the luckiest person I've ever met." He took her hands. "Will you be mine?"

"Is this the promise?"

"Yes."

"Yes." Joy flooded through her, and she saw it reflected in Brad's eyes, and his smile.

While they ate they made plans for Brad to take Fin on an outing over the weekend. It would take time for their son to warm up to the idea of Brad being around all the time. Willow was guardedly optimistic that he would adjust before he was old enough to get his own apartment.

"I just remembered the Thanksgiving visit to the in-laws," Brad said.

"Two weeks again?"

He nodded and didn't make eye contact. "I can't bail on the trip."

"No," Willow agreed. She'd waited this long. What was two more weeks? "That would be cruel. It's going to be hard enough anyway." She blew out the candle under the nearly empty fondue pot.

"We're flying out next Friday, so I can see you next week."

Willow smiled. "That will make it like a fairy tale."

"How so?" Brad chased the last dollop of cheese around the pot with his finger.

"In fairy tales, everything happens three times, right?"

Brad shrugged.

"Three wishes. Three pigs. Three bears."

"Okay. And you're going to send me away three times?"

"You will come back to me three times. By following the fairy tale conventions, we'll earn our happy ending."

"Third time's my Willow Charm?"

Willow groaned.

*** *** ***

Willow had never before considered the upside of having a son who at age 13 was taller than her. Fortunately he wasn't much taller, though, otherwise his clothes would have looked ridiculous on her instead of merely weird. Surely most adult women weren't running around in ragged jeans and an old U2 tee. None of the new *Joshua Tree* 'crap' for her tender boy. Nope. Had to be *War*. "After that they kinda got lousy, Mom." Top the ensemble off with an army surplus parka and a wool cap suitable for a Himalayan expedition and she was virtually unrecognizable.

Even so, she felt exposed lingering on the corner with dry leaves gusting around her.

There wasn't much activity at Threshold House. The population looked lower than when she'd been associated with them. Which would make her mission easier, assuming Severin wasn't one of the ones to have moved on, taking his magic table with him.

Hoping Severin was still around felt uncomfortable, and Willow moved her mind along to planning her infiltration.

Around lunchtime there was a flurry of activity in the House. Willow caught a glimpse of Severin through the windows. He looked the same as ever, perhaps a bit grayer.

Willow's stomach knotted itself up. He was still there. That meant she had to go through with this. She wasn't getting what she needed from her ironing board, and Fin was starting to wonder why she suddenly spent so much time with it.

An hour later, Severin and a group of college-age boys came out of the House and piled into a small white van. Severin rode shotgun. As they drove past, Willow took a sudden interest in her shoes.

Once they were a few blocks away, she crossed the street, trying to look casual. She took a deep breath and climbed the front steps. The door wasn't locked and she walked right in. The rooms she passed were empty, of people and of the clutter of habitation. Such orderliness made her nervous. It said this was no longer a place she belonged. Wasting no time, she started up the stairs.

The attic smelled the same. Dusty and stale and somehow organic. It looked the same too.

Willow stared at the table for several seconds before crossing to it. The sheet glowed in the gloom. Suddenly too hot, she pulled off her cap. Her hair tumbled out and she felt a little better.

Willow tucked the hat into a pocket and ran her hand tentatively over the white fabric. Nothing suggested this was anything other than an ordinary sheet draped over an ordinary door. She hadn't expected to feel anything unusual — magical — but was disappointed anyway. What if this didn't work?

It would. *I'll find something to lead me to my mother.*

It was foolish to procrastinate. Severin could return at any moment. The fingers of both her hands drummed on the door's surface. The sheet barely muted the sound of her nails clicking against it.

Maybe it would be better if this didn't work. She'd lived this long without a mother. Did she need the added stress right now? With the baby on the way, and the situation with Brad and needing to explain all of that to Fin.

The sound of her fingers grew louder and Willow forced herself to stop them. In the ensuing silence she thought she could hear the House sigh and settle.

Her hands were sweaty with anxiety, and Willow rubbed them on Fin's jeans before lifting the edge of the sheet and reaching underneath with her left hand. The wooden door was warm and slick. Her fingers slid over it for a second before slipping right through. Willow gasped. This wasn't how it worked before. She groped in the warm nothingness, reluctant to reach deeper.

Something grabbed her hand.

Willow shrieked and jerked her arm back.

She was a few steps away from the table now, staring at it. The sheet settled back haphazardly.

Nothing moved.

Willow stared at her hand. Pink and cold. A fuzzy electric shock crept up her arm. Her hand was wet. Dripping. The air smelled of a rain shower.

Stumbling and unsteady, Willow fled.

*** *** ***

Severin sat in his hammock, needing to understand before he made a move.

Willow had snuck in and used his table. She had been rather careless, leaving one of her long red hairs, and not even bothering to straighten up. Did she want him to know?

More important, what had she been after? And did she get it?

The hair ran smoothly between his fingers. He wrapped it around his left thumb. It felt like her. Maybe he could use it.

Severin laced the hair around the fingers of his left hand and approached the table. He smoothed the sheet. It felt almost alive. With the slightest of smiles, Severin lifted the hem and reached under with his left hand. Willow's hair coursed with energy and he felt himself reaching through the surface of the table and into the recesses of the Elsewhere, into the abyss that birthed the powerful slab of rock in the basement. He reached deeper, his arm disappearing from the elbow down. Something brushed his fingertips and Severin reached deeper.

A hand gripped his, painfully.

Severin's smile grew and he pulled his arm back out, keeping an equally tight grip. Willow would not find him so easy to evade this time.

His hand emerged, grasping a pale, slender female hand. Energy writhed through and around him. His hair bristled and his ears rang. The smell of rain and ozone flooded the room. The sheet lifted as the owner of the hand rose beneath it. Finally a female form was clear. She lay on the table, breathing raggedly. Severin whipped the sheet away.

A soaking wet blond woman blinked up at him from the emerald-green painted door. She was petite, and completely nude. She swung her legs over the edge of the table and sat. Her grip on his hand relaxed.

Severin stared at her, his smile faltering.

*** *** ***

Gale pulled her hand away from the man. He let her go without a struggle, looking as surprised as she was.

He wasn't Brian.

When she felt the first pull, the first call, she had assumed it was Brian. He finally found her and was going to join with her again. She eagerly answered, her heart skipping. But the caller recoiled, violently. Sparks of green light numbed her, erased her mind, sent her tumbling to the floor.

As she drove her green Pinto across the Beck Street bridge, the call came again. She tried to ignore it, but it was much stronger and had a different flavor. It felt familiar.

Gale latched onto it with her entire being. The chartreuse light skittered over her skin. It lifted her and squeezed. It became her, or she became it, and she flew and crackled through an unknown dimension. When she could see again, everything was white.

Now she was in a new place, cold, wet, and naked.

Gale's hands, working on their own, pulled the sheet up to cover her nudity. Her eyes never left the man. He studied her as well, with eyes of an intense pale blue. He was not tall, fit, or well-groomed, but he commanded attention. Here was power. Here was the man she hadn't even known she'd been seeking. Here was the man who could control the green lightning.

For the first time in over 30 years, Gale felt the stirrings of sexual arousal.

"Who are you?" the man asked.

"Don't you know? Can't you feel it?"

He cocked his head, but didn't drop his gaze. He reached for her with his left hand, a thin, green line woven around his fingers, fading. He touched her cheek.

A brilliant flash of green-white filled Gale's vision, and she felt it fill his too.

Together they saw roiling clouds, ball lightning, colors dancing on the distant horizon. The heavy smell of ozone mingled with smoke and something cloyingly sweet. A hiss of steam accompanied muffled voices on loudspeakers. They shared a momentary surge of pain and a terrible feeling of separation.

Two tiny babies shimmered into being in a dim train car, sleeping with their thumbs in each other's mouths.

The man — her brother, Gale now knew — caressed her cheek. His smooth thumb brushed her lips, parted them and slipped between and into her mouth. Though it tasted sour, Gale sucked greedily. She slid her own thumb into his waiting mouth.

The circuit completed, their minds opened to each other and to some other place. A place her brother knew as the Elsewhere. For the first time in her life, Gale understood. This Elsewhere was her homeland, and more. It was her mother and her father. It was her brother. And it was her. She and this wonderful, powerful man who had brought her to him, finally, after so many years of separation and solitude, were one. She would never be alone again.

The Elsewhere reveled in their reunion as much as Gale did, and in its reverie they learned the story of their birth and all that came after.

*** *** ***

Rain pelted against the glass in angry bursts, and a constant low growl of thunder underlaid the steady clackety-clack of the train. I closed my eyes, but still saw the flashes of lightning punctuating the night sky. The train was already hours behind schedule and now slowed even further.

Weariness clung to me like a shroud and I envied my fellow passengers their ability to sleep. My insomnia was worse than ever since Malcolm enlisted, choosing an uncertain life in the navy over a certain life with me. Eloping was supposed to bring financial security, but instead led to a complete upheaval of my life. "I, Malcolm Tenpenny, take you, Delia Seagrave..." For better or worse. The next morning, after a night of crude motel sex, he left and tried to get an annulment. It wasn't until after I convinced the judge an annulment was inappropriate that I found out the fancy car he drove was stolen and he only owned the one suit. Still, I thought I better hang on to him for a while.

Malcolm Tenpenny proved to be a slippery bastard though, and ran off with a redhead in a convertible. The next I heard of him was eight months later when the redhead tracked me down and told me he was at boot camp in South Carolina. I planned to surprise my husband and make sure I got whatever part of his paycheck I could manage.

With a jerk, the train stopped. The porter entered the carriage and awakened the passengers. He announced that we were switching to a different line to finish the journey.

I shuffled my few belongings as the other passengers disembarked, wanting to be the last one off. Hopefully I would find a forgotten bag or wallet, something to help cover the cost of my ticket. I moved to the rear of the car and began a furtive search.

A deafening crack of thunder and an accompanying green flash of lightning exploded inside the train car.

My hair crackled with static and my skin twitched and crawled. Several seconds later, and still blinking away spots, I noticed something laying in the exact center of the aisle. Confirming myself to be alone, I walked closer.

Two babies. Naked. One boy, one girl, sucking each other's thumbs.

Again I looked around the train. Malcolm Tenpenny certainly needed a son.

I snatched the tiny boy child and, as he began to cry, wrapped him in a white flannel nightgown from my overnight bag. The girl on the floor wailed. I considered taking her too, but two babies would be unmanageable.

The first thing I had to do was get far away from this train before anyone discovered the other child, or raised an alarm about there being one missing.

Waiting inside the crowded depot, I took a seat in a corner and tried to quiet the baby. His eyes were squeezed shut, his tiny hands fists. The weight of what I had done began to settle on my shoulders. How could I make him be quiet?

People shot me dirty looks for disturbing their sleep. Wanting to look like a mother, like I knew what I was doing, I turned away toward the wall and unbuttoned my blouse partway. I put the frantic infant to my breast and he latched on. His eyes snapped open, a brilliant, blinding blue, and energy coursed through my body leading to a peculiar heaviness, a flooding ache in my breasts as they magically filled with milk. The baby suckled greedily and I felt myself drowning in his terrible gaze.

Tears slid down my cheeks. A momentary impulse brought this child to me and I would never be free of him.

He drained my left breast and began fussing again. I numbly moved him to my right side, unable to break eye contact. This was my son. His name was Severin. My ticket to a life with Malcolm.

"Severin Seagrave Tenpenny," I whispered, and touched his silky black hair.

Severin's presence helped me keep my husband for less than a year. Malcolm died at Pearl Harbor, leaving me to care for the uncanny child. Even before he could talk, Severin controlled my life. He took from me what he needed, compelling me with his icy eyes.

I wonder sometimes how different things might have been had I taken the girl instead.

*** *** ***

Gale surfaced from the vision, aware again of her surroundings and the solid, reassuring touch of her brother, before submerging with him once more in the cold ocean of collective memory.

*** *** ***

The Jennifer Kent Home for Orphans was a privately run orphanage. It consisted of a large Victorian house and a small carriage house. The orphans lived in the main house with four caregivers. I was given the carriage house. The downstairs I used as a makeshift chapel and Sunday-school classroom. Upstairs, under the slanting eaves, I had my living quarters.

I started at the home in September of 1954. I was 19. The posting was to be temporary. I would act as a counselor and tutor to the children, who ranged in age from infants to teens.

When the children got home from school on the first day, Miss Kent made a brief introduction. There were eight of them, five boys and three girls. The boys were all around 10 years old. Two of the girls were younger, and obviously sisters.

Then there was Gale.

Gale's features were fine, delicate. She looked frail. Her ash-blonde hair fell to the middle of her back, pulled back in a single, centered, green barrette. I found blondes fascinating, as everyone in my family had been brunette.

She sat in the middle of the group, but apart from it. She felt my gaze and looked up at me briefly, dismissively. Her vivid, green eyes left spots in my vision. She was old beyond her years and immediately captivated me.

I read her file that evening. Discovered as a newborn on December 21, 1940 in the aisle of a third-class car of a transcontinental train. It was in all the papers. An unusually grand display of the aurora borealis and numerous instances of ball-lightning coincided with a mishap at a switching station. The passengers were transferred to a different line and the conductor found the crying babe. Her parents could not be located.

By the time she was ten, she lived permanently in the Jennifer Kent Home for Orphans. She was now almost 14.

Even though our meeting was preordained, I knew the rest of society would not see it as such. We would need to be cautious.

Her birthday fell during the school's Christmas holiday. Gale appeared at my door midmorning and I knew the time had come. She looked at me with wide eyes. I invited her in.

She pliantly obeyed me as I sat her down and talked to her about the importance of keeping our relationship secret. I spoke soothingly, sonorously, getting quieter and quieter until there was no longer any need for words. I stared into her bright green eyes and impressed upon her that what we were to have was sacred, and not for the ears or eyes of any but us. We would not speak of it, even with each other. We would give no outward sign.

She understood, of course.

All that we needed was the blessing of God. We went downstairs into the chapel and there I performed a marriage ceremony. Gale squeezed my hand and smiled. The time had come to consummate our union. She led me to a small cave in a wooded area along the rear border of the orphanage's property.

I spent the afternoon heightening her energies. When it was time for the final release, I positioned my mouth above hers and breathed in her vitality.

Gale was a bottomless well of strength for me to draw from. We went to that cave many times over the next several months, and each time I drank deeply of her. My ability to intuit and influence grew exponentially with each visit.

My post at the home ended with school in early June and I was loath to leave, but excited as well. I arranged to come back in the fall and saw the summer as a chance to stretch my legs.

The summer of 1955 I spent with a traveling ministry, learning how to work with a crowd, bring them to a frenzy, and draw strength from them. It was not all that different from the technique I had already mastered.

In September when I returned to the orphanage, Gale was gone. The staff informed me she had gotten herself in a family way and been sent to a center for unwed mothers.

I got on with my job, expecting never to see Gale again. I prayed for a good outcome for her, and for her to keep her silence. I knew that when this school year was over, I would move on to other endeavors.

My plans changed on the night of November 12. It rained all day, a steady, chilly drizzle. There was a knock on my door. It was Gale, obviously exhausted, with a newborn babe in her arms. Her shapeless smock was drenched, and streaked with mud and blood. Her face was red and puffy from crying. Her hair had been cut short and was plastered against her scalp. I took the sleeping baby from her and welcomed her into my room.

As Gale dried herself, I examined the child. A girl, rosy and healthy-looking, if a little small. I put her in the center of my bed. Gale told me she wanted to call her Grace.

Gale explained that she needed to go back to the unwed mothers' center. She promised to return to me as soon as she could. She kissed me and left. It wasn't for many minutes that I realized she left the baby behind.

I don't know if Gale ever came back.

I hurriedly typed a letter to Miss Kent, explaining about a family emergency I needed to attend to. I packed my few belongings and altered my records in the Home's office, obscuring pertinent details and removing certain papers altogether.

Somewhere down the line, across several state borders, I dropped Grace at a police station, explaining I heard her crying behind a motel. I left before they thought to ask any questions.

When I found Gale, I found an angel. The strength I drew from her sustained me through the years, and made it possible for me to accomplish many great and holy works. Sadly, my next wife, Molly, lacked Gale's boundless wellspring of divine fire.

I wonder sometimes what purpose God had for taking Gale from me.

*** *** ***

The images faded and Gale blinked. Her brother gently pushed her thumb from his mouth with his tongue.

"We're the same," he said and pulled his thumb out of her mouth, but stroked her cheek again.

Gale nodded. "Twins," she said with wonder. She let the sheet drop.

Chapter Eleven

THE BASEMENT

Cletus and Merlene Tuttle were newlyweds in 1949 when the young man calling himself Brian Shaw first arrived in Blessed. Cletus recalls inviting him home for supper, and helping him get cleaned up. Merlene is still impressed.

"He had such a way about him," she says. "He was terribly bashful, and his words came kinda slow. You know, he had just the loveliest way of talking. Old-fashioned. Reminded me of my Grandpappy. I simply adored him." She stops, lost in reminiscence. "His eyes. They were... I don't know how to say it. His eyes were so full of something. Love, I reckon. I see the same thing now when I watch him on the television. I always feel like he's talking right to me."

from *Brainwashed*, by Julie Rome ©1998 Futhark Press

Severin came up the steps into the attic, marveling at how, in only a day, he had adjusted to another's constant presence in his domain. The fact that it was the twin he never knew of made it all the more amazing. It would soon be time to figure out just where she'd come from. Soon. For now he was enjoying getting to know her.

Topping the steps he spotted Gale, nude, her back to him, trailing her finger through the dust on a stack of boxes. He noticed the cant of her hips, and she swiveled them oh so slightly.

Severin licked his lips.

Gale looked over her shoulder and asked, "Did you find something?"

"Yes."

She pouted. "Do I have to be dressed all the time?"

"Only when you go downstairs." Gale's fear that she would disappear if she were covered was ridiculous; only the sheet on his table acted as a doorway to the Elsewhere. But it was an endearing fear and meant she would nearly always be naked and waiting for him.

Smirking, she walked to him. "Show me."

Severin held up the sweater, a pea green cardigan of generous proportions. Gale blinked.

"Marsh is quite tall," Severin explained. "He said he doesn't need this one anymore."

Gale took the sweater before Severin could open any of the buttons, slipping it over her head and shimmying as it fell about her body. It hung two-thirds down her thighs and the sleeves were a foot too long. She worked her hands free and smoothed the knit fabric against her torso.

"I like it. Thank you." She kissed Severin, who enfolded her in his arms. She reached down the front of his pants, and breathed, "Do you like it? I think you do."

Severin crushed her to him, raising her off the floor. She wrapped her legs around his waist, unfastening his fly before extricating her hand. When his pants lay heaped around his feet, she whispered, "Move away from the steps."

***

"Further explanation would be pointless. You have to try it."

Gale hung her head.

Severin frowned. "What's wrong?"

Gale hugged her knees, refused to make eye contact. Severin was about to repeat his question when she started speaking in a soft monotone.

"I felt a call, when you brought me here. I felt it, and I thought it was someone else. The man from our vision. Trying to pull me to him. Yours was the second time I felt it. Someone else, the someone else, tried to pull me in before. And I wanted to go, but it broke off. Now, I don't want to go. But I would." Her eyes were shut tight, her voice a harsh whisper. "Oh god! I would go. I would."

Severin massaged his left hand, recalling the tingle where the red hair had been wound. He imagined Willow's hasty departure, amused that she had scared herself witless. Gale too. The most delicious part only now came clear, that Gale was the very thing Willow sought. Her mother. Willow was the child Gale had lost. That connection allowed Willow to initiate the contact, to open the channel. If not for her actions, Severin would still be in the dark about his sister.

Abruptly he realized he was Willow's uncle.

Bemused chuckling seemed likely to further upset Gale, so he took his time replying to keep it under control. "I know who was looking for you."

Gale seized him with her eyes, wild panic and confusion spilling from her mind, flooding the room. Severin embraced her, saying, "No, no. Not like that. No." She trembled, and made staccato utterances that tried to be words.

As he held her, Severin saw indistinct images of a man. The someone else. The man whose memory he overheard when Gale first arrived, the shadowy father of her lost child. He could discern nothing more.

Severin said, "Not him." She quieted and her breathing stabilized.

He held her face, stared into her eyes. Her cheeks were wet. After a few seconds he said, "Trust me."

Tears ran down her face, but she smiled. He said, "Try it. You'll be fine."

Gale wiped her face on her forearm as she stood. "What do I do?"

"Lift the sheet, but don't look under it. Reach in and see what you find."

Severin knew Gale was better off for having missed her daughter's call. Gale surely was not what Willow envisioned as a mother, and just as surely Willow didn't fit Gale's juvenile daydreams of her little girl. Willow's disappointment was going to crush Gale, but her brother would be right there, and in her hurt his sister would do anything he asked.

Anything.

Gale hugged herself, shivering. Her tiny, halting steps carried her obliquely toward the table, and Severin knew he'd have to prompt her again, coax her the last few feet.

Her continued fear of the thing fascinated him. Like her physique, her complexion, it was another way his twin was his opposite. It was important that they were so unalike. It meant they covered more of the spectrum. She saw things from a different angle. Together, they wielded far more than the sum of their individual power.

He held his tongue, wanting to study her further, to let the struggle play itself out.

Gale stopped, huddling against whatever threat she felt from the table three feet away.

Willow also had seemed leery of the table, yet instantly mastered its use. Because Gale arrived by way of it, perhaps her trepidation was understandable. She feared that some force would pull her away again.

He knew it didn't work that way. The forces under that sheet were the very ones from which he and Gale sprang with a burst of ball lightning, as they'd both witnessed in the uncanny memory of their own birth. Nothing was more natural for them than to reach through the Threshold. Gale even passed entirely across the Elsewhere. Puzzling that it left her more fearful, rather than less.

Her right hand reached toward the edge of the sheet, flinching back repeatedly. Severin licked his lips. She caught the drooping edge and froze. Keeping her face averted, she snaked her left hand beneath the fabric and across the surface of the door. She yanked it back out again and scurried over to Severin's embrace.

"Good. Good. You did fine. See? I told you."

Gale held her left arm against her body like a broken wing, her fist quivering.

"Shall we see what it is?"

She nodded. Severin took her hand in both of his and worried at the white knuckles. He pried insistently until at last the slender fingers uncurled to reveal a crumpled piece of paper in her palm.

"Open it," Severin said.

Gale teased apart the wad, expanding it into an irregular sheet about six inches across with ragged edges all the way around. A single large capital letter took up most of the space.

"It's an M," she said, showing him.

"No," he replied, turning the paper 180 degrees. "It's a W."

*** *** ***

"Is this Willow?"

Willow hesitated before answering. The woman on the phone sounded frightened.

"Hmmm." She hoped that sounded noncommittal.

"This is so..." A sob. "So hard."

Klaxons sounded inside Willow's head. "Is it Fin?" she asked.

"I've been searching," the woman continued. "My darling Kelly—"

"Kelly?" Willow cut the woman off. "You have the wrong number." Adrenaline with no outlet coursed through her veins. A pungent metallic smell lurked. She did not want to talk to this stranger, but was unable to put the phone down.

"No! Please! Willow!" The woman sounded frantic.

Against her better judgment, Willow said, "Yes."

A muffled sound of nose-blowing and throat-clearing followed. "I'm sorry I'm such a wreck." More throat clearing. "I think I'm your mother."

The pale winter light refracted upward into sickly green, and Willow's hands tingled.

"Do you feel that?" asked the woman. Her mother?

Willow gulped.

"You do! We're connected. You are my baby."

"How—"

"Can we meet? I need to see you."

Willow nodded, her vision still emerald.

"Wonderful. Tomorrow is good. Tomorrow?"

More nodding. Willow felt like a bobble-head Chihuahua.

"Can I come to your house?"

"No!" Fin would be going hiking with Brad, but they might come back early. He couldn't know anything about this, not yet. "Where—"

A whispered consultation swirled across the phone line, a man's low voice joining her mother's, and the emerald was now shot with sapphire.

"You can come to my hotel."

"Who's with you? Who were you talking to?"

A pause. "My brother."

Willow's alarm returned in a rush.

"He won't be there tomorrow. It will just be us," the voice reassured. "Tomorrow at 10:00 at the Howard Johnson's."

Willow nodded again and the woman, her mother, hung up.

The tingling in her hands ceased abruptly, leaving a longing in its place. The weak sunlight filtering through her eyelids returned red warmth and clarity to Willow's thoughts. Her right hand crept onto her fluttering stomach and she felt movement beneath the skin. A fitting time to meet her mother.

Rapid, atonal beeping startled Willow, and she belatedly hung up the phone. A large glass of water cleared the taste of copper and seawater from her mouth.

There was no doubt that she shared a connection with the woman on the phone, Willow just wasn't sure she wanted to experience it again. It drained her. She curled up on the sofa under a quilt and fell asleep.

*** *** ***

"That air certainly is crisp!"

"It's cold. Must we be happy about it?"

Brad took off his blue watch cap, smoothed his hair, and put the hat back on. "Well, I am. It's invigorating."

Fin rolled his eyes as he trudged up the trail to where Brad waited. Fin wore a black hooded sweatshirt under his denim jacket. His bangs protruded from the hood, nearly masking his eyes. His jeans were worn through at the knees. He was taller than his mother, like Kyle. The boys were both slim, gangly teens who always seemed annoyed with Brad. Other than that, there was little indication they were brothers.

"It was warm the last time I came up here. I showed this place to your mother."

"Was she as excited as I am?"

Brad smirked. "At least. Does this mean you want to hear my story?"

"No. It means I'm not excited."

"Just as well," Brad replied. "You're too young for most of it anyway."

Hands in his pockets, Fin scuffed a stone loose with his foot and kicked it into the barren undergrowth. Brad surveyed the horizon, a panorama of leafless trees clawing at the leaden belly of the sky. Perhaps an indoor activity would have been more conducive to cheerful father-and-son bonding.

"Can we go now? I'm freezing."

"But you haven't seen the lake."

Fin glowered.

Brad looked at the ground. "I'm sorry this isn't turning out to be fun for you. I loved hiking when I was 13."

They stood silent for a few minutes in the tranquil November afternoon.

"Can we go — to the lake? Now? I'm still freezing."

"Yes," Brad sighed. He added, more brightly, "This time, see if you can keep up with an old man."

"An old man who smokes," Fin corrected.

Ten minutes later Brad leaned against a tree and waited for Fin, who lagged about 100 feet behind, taking his time and looking mostly at his feet.

This shouldn't be so hard.

Brad and Willow talked often about the need for he and Fin to spend time together, but it never seemed to happen. Brad knew his son only superficially. Strangely, the same was true of Kyle. Melissa was so possessive of him. Brad hoped that would make it easier for the two of them when he left. Right now he needed to put them out of his mind and pay attention to Fin, who was dawdling and kicking small rocks. Brad said, "If you want to get this over with, you should pick up the pace."

Fin gave him an impenetrable glance. "Why did you bring me here?"

"I don't know," Brad lied. He had been rehearsing his answer to this question ever since they'd resumed hiking. His planned answer was an explanation that all they had in common was Willow, and this place meant something to her. That he'd hoped to make up for lost time by trying to return to his own past. It would sound a little hokey, but that was part of the mission. Vulnerability. The idea was to open up a little, and start sharing something meaningful.

"Do you want some jerky?" Brad asked.

"Sure." Fin took one hand out of his pocket to accept the dried meat. He took a bite, then put his hand back in his pocket, jerky and all.

Five minutes later they cleared the ridge and could see the small lake below. Wind blew strong on the crest, coming off the lake in frigid gusts.

"Technically, I have seen the lake. Also, I have realized that I was merely cold earlier. Now I am freezing."

"Okay," Brad relented. "Let's move back down out of the wind and you can help me build a fire."

Fin blinked. "Why?"

"I'm cold, too. Fire is hot."

"Okay," Fin agreed reluctantly.

As they gathered twigs and branches, Brad said, "Even though it was warmer, we still needed a fire. Me and your mother. We went swimming—"

"This is probably that story I'm too young for," Fin interrupted.

"Not this part. We camped overnight, and in the morning the fire had gone out. So I went off by myself looking for more firewood. And I saw something."

Fin held an armload of gnarled gray branches, waiting for Brad to continue. Brad crouched near the heap of wood he had collected, watching for Fin's patience to expire. Fin walked over, let his armload tumble onto Brad's heap, and set off for more fuel.

"Don't you want to hear what it was?" Brad asked.

"Guess so," Fin replied without turning.

"A ghost."

Fin looked over his shoulder, smirking. "Really?"

"I think so. She's very strange."

"She?" Now Fin stopped pretending to scan for worthwhile firewood and leaned against a trunk, hands again in his pockets.

"It was just before dawn. I don't know if you realize how dark a forest can be before sunup, but I had gotten a bit lost. It was somewhere down the other side of the ridge, closer to the lake."

"What did she look like?"

Brad smiled. "She's a tiny little blonde thing. Soaking wet. She's about your age, but pregnant to beat the band. She's upset, trying to tell me something, but I can never hear her."

"And she's a ghost?"

"I don't know what she is. I thought she was real. I try to help her, but when I get too close she vanishes."

"Like, thin air?"

"Well, except for the blackberries. I picked those and your mother and I had them for breakfast."

"How often do you come out here?" Fin asked.

Brad blinked. "I don't think I've been back since that day, as a matter of fact. Why?"

"Then where else did you see the ghost?"

The cold air rushed down Brad's collar. Outwitted by a 13-year-old. Fin held him with a steady gaze.

Brad didn't like staring contests. He glanced to one side, looking at the horizon. A mischievous thought struck him and he had to work hard not to smile. He just stared at that distant point, silently counting to ten. "Right there," he said with a slight nod, indicating a point to Fin's left.

Fin sprang away from the tree, whirling around and almost toppling as loose branches tangled up his feet. He high-stepped, flapping his elbows, hands trapped in pockets. Once he had his balance, Fin glared at Brad, who slumped over with wheezing laugher.

"Are we going to actually make a fire?" Fin demanded. "Today?"

Brad sat up and took off his hat, rubbing his eyes. "Yeah, I think we are." He took a deep breath, stood up, brushed himself off, and replaced the hat. "I think we're ready."

Brad bent and arranged the wood, building a pyramid of several small branches with dead leaves, twigs, and tufts of dry grass tucked underneath. He selected a pair of reasonably straight sticks and presented them to Fin. "You want to do the honors?"

"I don't know which is worse, if you're joking or if you're not."

Brad took the disposable lighter from his jacket pocket and presented it. "Same question."

Fin smiled, momentarily, and took the lighter. He applied the flame to the kindling and handed it back to Brad. "Thanks," he said.

*** *** ***

When Willow arrived at the Howard Johnson's she realized she didn't know the woman's name or room number. Maybe she would be waiting in the lobby. If it really was her mother, they should recognize each other. Upon entering the building, though, Willow thought she knew which way to go. Trusting her instinct, she got on the elevator and pushed the button for the second floor.

The ride was short.

Her feet scuffed the green and brown carpet in the hallway, and when she reached out to knock on the door of room 222 an enormous spark flew from her fingers. She heard the crackle and saw the intense burst of green-white light, but felt only the merest tingle. The door opened and Willow beheld her mother.

They stared at each other for several minutes. Her mother was petite, quite thin, and surprisingly young-looking. Her feet were bare, as were her legs. She wore an oversized green sweater as a dress, with the sleeves bunched up to her elbows. The v-neck exposed her scrawny collarbones. Her features were delicate, her eyes a brilliant unnatural green, her hair short, wild and pale blond. Her fragile hands reached for Willow's, hesitated, then clasped on. A desperate longing poured through her icy fingers. Willow allowed herself to be led into the room, closing the door behind her. They sat on the edge of the bed.

Her mother sighed and dropped Willow's hands.

"I'm Gale," she said. "I'm so happy to have found you."

Willow nodded, not trusting her voice. Her left hand rotated the hemp bracelet on her right wrist around and around.

"You're beautiful. I knew you would be, but I could never picture you all grown up. To me you're still my little baby." She smiled wistfully and patted Willow's knee.

"How did you find me?"

Gale looked puzzled, her eyebrows furrowed. "I don't know, honestly. A feeling."

Willow nodded. "I tried to look for you, but it's very complicated."

"Oh, I know. I know just what you mean. But, we've found each other now," she hurried on, "so let's not worry about the technicalities."

They sat in silence.

"What do we do now?" Willow asked.

"I could brush your hair."

Willow was nonplussed. "Uh, no thanks. Not right now."

Gale's cheeks flushed. She shook her head. "I'm sorry." She shook her head again. "I imagine you have some questions for me."

"Yes, I guess I do." Willow considered. She'd never thought about what she wanted her mother for, just knew she wanted her. *Why is this so difficult?* "How old were you when you had me?"

"Fourteen."

Holy shit. "Who was my father?"

"My husband," Gale said after some hesitation.

Married at 14? What sort of Deliverance family did I come from, Willow wondered.

"What was his name?"

Gale opened her mouth and froze.

Willow waited, studying her mother. Even given the fact that she'd had Willow when she was 14, she looked young. Younger than 47 anyway. Must be good genes.

"It's your birthday today," Gale said.

Abrupt change of topic, then.

"Yes," Willow confirmed.

Gale reached out and stroked Willow's hair. "My beautiful Kelly."

"Es— Willow. It's Willow now."

"Of course. Kelly's the name I gave you before you were taken away."

"Why was I taken away if you were married?"

Gale looked down, wringing her hands in her lap.

"I understand that this is difficult for you," Willow said, "but it's hard for me too. And if you're not going to answer my questions, it's going to be impossible."

The haunted green eyes snapped back onto her. Perhaps there had been a good reason to take her baby away. Horrific scenarios bloomed and burst in Willow's mind. Maybe Gale had been in prison. Or a mental hospital. If she'd given birth in some government institution, that could explain how the baby wound up in military sponsored psychological tests. Willow stood.

"I love you," Gale said, her voice breaking with emotion.

It was so obvious now. She had recently been released from wherever — and which would be better? To have a mother who was a murderer? or one who was just crazy? — and didn't understand how the world worked. That explained the thrift-store clothes and the bad haircut. And this desperate clinging. Willow knew she had to leave before Gale became any more attached.

"I have to go," she stammered, and rushed out the door.

*** *** ***

Severin tried not to gloat, but the effort was too much. He enjoyed being right, and Willow had vindicated him admirably in her rebuke of Gale's neediness. He gloated quietly, so she wouldn't detect his presence in the connecting room.

He waited two minutes after he heard Willow leave before letting himself in. Gale lay on her side at the foot of the bed, gnawing on her fingers, her wide eyes blank.

"Are you okay?"

Gale didn't respond. Severin had expected hysterics, and catatonia instead was rather alarming.

He walked over and stood beside the bed, where he could stroke her hair for a moment. Straightening he said, "I heard the whole thing. For a daughter to show such disrespect is appalling." Gale drew her knees up to her chest and rolled over away from Severin, staying in a fetal ball. Severin went on, "I would have taken a firmer approach with her, were she mine."

"She deserted you already." Gale's voice seemed separate from her body, which showed no movement at all. "You couldn't have kept her here."

Severin felt like protesting that with the benefit of experience he could certainly manage. Instead he sat on the bed and said, "You're right. She won't listen."

"She's not my baby anymore." Gale's disembodied voice sounded on the verge of tears.

"That's not true, dear Sister. She'll always be your baby."

"Will she really?"

"Yes."

"And I can keep her?" The voice was steadier now.

"Absolutely."

"And you'll help me?" Gale uncurled on the bed, and held Severin's eyes with her own. They were clear and sharp, unmarred by tears.

"If I can," he replied, patting her knee.

"Promise."

"I promise."

She smiled.

Severin bent to kiss her, and she enfolded him in her arms. His hand slid up her thigh, under her sweater.

***

Driving home in the van, Severin listened while Gale vented her frustration with Willow — or Kelly, as Gale called her. Blindness and stupidity were recurring themes, and so long as Gale attributed them to Kelly, Severin nodded or muttered small affirmations. When Gale applied these traits to herself, Severin would interrupt to correct her, building her up. Kelly was the problem, which Severin promised to help her with. He kept Gale focused on Kelly, who couldn't possibly comprehend loss as Gale could, clearly had some growing up to do. Was still a baby, which was easier to establish while calling her by the name Gale had given her. Kelly needed a mother more than she knew, needed to be protected from herself. Kept under control.

Gale stared out the window for several blocks, and began speaking as if she'd forgotten Severin was there.

"I'll have my little baby-doll back soon. I'll brush her hair and sing to her, and I'll tuck her in at bedtime. I love the way her green eyes go closed when I lay her down. I had to look around to get the green eyes. Kelly has beautiful green eyes."

It was time to take Gale to the basement, to show her where to tuck her baby in.

Severin made the turn into the alley behind Threshold House, and said, "If we go in through the basement, no one will know we're here." Gale looked at him dubiously. "It will be fun, sneaking in. We could stay down in the basement for a while. I've never shown you my workshop."

Gale's mouth quirked and she shook her head. She said, "Okay."

After parking in the small gravel area beside the huge derelict garage, Severin got out and met Gale by her door. He pressed himself flat against the side of the van and shaded his eyes as he squinted through the gate at the back of the House.

"Come on," he said, holding the gate open. He stuck his hands in his pockets and strolled across the yard, with Gale tagging along. Rather than going to the back door, he veered right and descended the stairwell to the basement door, which he quickly unlocked. Severin ushered Gale into the dark space and closed the door behind them.

In the pitch blackness, he caught Gale up in a crushing embrace. She whimpered, and he shushed in her ear. As she melted against him, he reached unerringly to the pull-string and gave it a quick tug to turn on the single 100-watt bulb.

It was a large open space, with bare stone walls and an earth floor, slightly damp but clean. Ancient wooden posts stood in a regular grid, each as thick as a man, to support the large House overhead. Stairs ran up along the wall to the left. A few worktables, cabinets and shelves lurked along the perimeter.

What commanded attention was the rough-hewn stone slab in the center of the basement. It was like the prow of a fossil shipwreck, or the berg that did it in.

Severin let Gale go, and she drifted closer to the slab. "It looks like Stonehenge."

"That's what I wanted to show you. It's my major project at the moment, and why I don't let anyone else come down here."

Gale stalked the stone, gradually drawing near enough to lay her palm on it. She sighed. Severin walked up behind her, and reached around to undo the buttons on her sweater. Quivering, she let him disrobe her and slithered onto the inclined surface.

"It's cold, Severin." Gale rolled over and arched her back. She ground her knees together, moaning.

"You like my toy?" Severin asked, taking off his pants.

Gale looked him over, and said, "That's not a toy, little man. Be careful where you point it."

Severin climbed onto his contraption as Gale spread her legs. "I will be. Don't worry."

As Severin went inside her, Gale pawed at his face. Severin kissed her fingers, and when she put her thumb in his mouth he gave her his own to suck on.

***

"We can't sleep down here, it's too clammy."

"The attic's drafty, Brother dear. We'll probably get pneumonia either way. Let's stay down here this time." Gale trailed her fingers through Severin's chest hair, then laid her palm over his heart. He felt her warmth and his own pulse, synched perfectly with hers.

"There are a lot of stairs to contend with…" he said.

"So much exercise." She smirked. "And, so much going up and down the stairs."

Severin chuckled. "No, we can't sleep on this. That's not what it's meant for."

Gale straddled him and surveyed the stone structure beneath them. "What is it for?"

"I spent a great deal of time with my table finding the answer to that. It took many attempts merely to determine the right way to ask the question." Gale pouted and ground her hips. Severin smiled. "It collects and focuses energy, like a lens or an antenna. It can be tuned to receive different kinds of energy, magic on different wavelengths."

"What kind of energy is it tuned to right now?"

"It's not tuned yet, so all forms of energy are slightly affected. That's why we can get our exercise on it."

"What do you mean?"

"We're in the focus zone. There's a force that holds any power source fast in this spot, with a strength related to the quality of the source. Were it attuned to our particular signatures, we could not escape."

Gale's gyrations intensified. "What would happen to us? Would it drain all our energy? Would it kill us?"

Severin clutched her thighs and shook his head, momentarily at a loss for words. "No. The trapping force is a distortion of time. Suspended animation. All the energy that normally propels us about in the universe would get stored away in this apparatus, and that's why we wouldn't be able to move. An oversimplification, but it should give you the basic idea."

She lay against him, undulating. "I still think it sounds dangerous."

"Well, it could be, but I've been careful. I just haven't figured out what I might use it for yet."

Gale pushed herself up and looked Severin in the eye. "I think I have an idea, but I don't know if it would work."

Severin smiled. Having led her to it, he knew her idea would work. "Do tell."

"It's just a suggestion, I mean you should think about it and be sure it's safe."

"Of course."

Gale bit her lip. "Never mind. There's no way we could get her down here."

***

"I don't think she'll come again. She hates me."

Severin smiled slyly and shook his head. "No, Sister, she doesn't hate you. You're not quite what she expected, that's true. But that was not the source of her frustration."

"I drove her away."

"No, she never fully came to you to begin with. If you call her again, she will come."

Gale shook her head, staring into the corner.

Severin continued. "The only thing you have to tell her is that you're ready to answer all her questions."

Gale looked mournfully at Severin. "And I can't. Don't you think I want to?"

"All you need to do is tell her you will this time."

"She won't believe me."

Severin smiled again, but his thoughts darkened. His sister had a point. Willow was intelligent and perceptive, and would likely see through a blatant deception. Especially because Gale herself knew for certain she wouldn't be able to speak about her past. He said, "I know how to fix that."

Gale's eyes sparkled with hope, which was vital. If she withdrew completely there would be no way to carry out the plan.

"I will give you a history you can speak of. My own past is unknown to the child. You can tell her my story, or more precisely my so-called mother's. It will suit our aims perfectly. Your husband's name was Malcolm, and he was a soldier. He was killed in action before she was born."

"Malcolm... What was he like?"

"I don't know. I never met him." Severin stopped. Gale could hardly say that to Willow! "Kind, but he was taken away by war before you really got to know him. You were very young and in love, and he was a bit older."

"Kind..."

Severin thought a moment. "Korea. He was killed in Korea. The dates will line up well enough."

"Korea."

"But don't get into details unless it's absolutely necessary. It was a long time ago, and you were very young."

"Okay. Malcolm was kind, he was older than me, and he went off to the Korean War and got killed."

"Perfect."

"She'll wonder why I couldn't keep her."

Severin nodded. "I think this part can be the truth." Gale frantically shook her head, and Severin hastened to clarify. "Just that you were deemed too young. That Willow — Kelly — was taken away and they didn't tell you where or why."

Gale calmed, and nodded. "Okay. Malcolm died in Korea, and

because I was so young they took my baby, took away..." Gale trailed off, tears on her cheeks.

"Excellent! But tell me Malcolm was her father."

Gale glowered, tears still flowing. Severin nodded encouragingly.

After clearing her throat, Gale said, "Kelly, your father's name was Malcolm, and we were married when I was very young. You arrived while he was away in Korea, and he died there. So they, they said I was too young to raise you. And they took you away."

No tears this time. Well, superb delivery regardless.

"Yes, perfect."

Gale cleared her throat again. "Then what?"

Severin clasped his hands and stood up. "Right. Actually, before that. We have to backtrack to when she first arrives at the room. Offer her the tea before you start your conversation."

Chapter Twelve

Room 222

After those ten long years traveling the tent revival circuit, Brian Shaw was ready for a new challenge. Radio was giving way to television, and Shaw was one of the first to use the power of the cathode ray tube to beam his pulpit straight into the living rooms of the American South.
    from *Brainwashed*, by Julie Rome ©1998 Futhark Press

"We fly out on Friday morning and will be gone for two weeks. Are you sure you want me to go?"

Willow looked dejected, but nodded.

Brad didn't want to go. Ever since he'd made the decision to commit to Willow, his home life had become unbearable. Kyle had no respect for him, and Melissa treated him like an annoying piece of furniture. He saw now that these were not new developments.

Sure, his leaving would be hard. Feelings would be hurt, but it would be better for everyone in the long run.

The divorce would probably go pretty easily. Melissa didn't love him anymore, so she would have no reason to contest things once he made it clear he intended to be generous with alimony. She could keep the house. It was paid for. Kyle's college fund was already well-enough stocked to see him through four years as long as he didn't aspire to the Ivy League. The idea of Kyle in the Ivy League was laughable. Their football programs weren't up to his standards. Fin also had a college fund, in his own name, which would keep it out of the divorce settlement.

Work would be ticklish, but Melissa could transfer to a different branch if she felt it necessary. As Loan Director, he needed to stay in the main office. Maybe he could change his focus, perhaps manage a branch. Or even move to a different bank altogether. A whole range of possibilities stood before him now.

Where to live? They could stay here in Willow's apartment, but there was no reason to. She wouldn't need to work anymore if she didn't want to. This place only had two bedrooms. Once the baby came, it would be too small. Would she want to get married? They would have to wait, of course, until the divorce went through.

"Brad."

Willow waved her hand in front of his eyes and Brad snapped back into the present moment.

"Where'd you go?" she asked.

"I was picturing us married, living in a house with a white picket fence."

Willow looked startled.

"Well, it was more fun than thinking about spending two weeks with the soon-to-be-ex in-laws." He grimaced.

She blinked at him and he kissed her forehead. Placing his hand on her belly, he asked, "How are you feeling?"

"No morning sickness to speak of. I have been a bit blue..." she trailed off.

"I shouldn't go. I should be here in case you need me."

"No. It's really nothing. I've just been thinking."

"Thinking makes you sad?"

"Depends on what I'm thinking about."

"So, what were you thinking about that made you sad?"

"Little things sometimes get to me," she said after a pause. "An article in the paper about a car accident. A phone call from a stranger who thought my name was Kelly. Just these little things. I think it's hormonal." She stood and went to the kitchen.

Brad stayed on the sofa, and listened to her get a drink of water and move on to the bathroom. He was certain she and Melissa were twins, but over the years they had grown more dissimilar. He didn't think Willow had changed all that much, but Mel sure had. It would be weird to only have contact with one of them. He didn't think he would miss having sex with Mel — she'd made it into a chore — but it was sad to think about how far apart they'd grown. The more he considered it, the less he thought he would miss her.

"I love you," he called to Willow.

When she came back to the sofa some time later, her face looked flushed. Brad pulled her in close and rubbed her shoulders. "You're tense."

She nodded. "It's almost time to go pick Fin up. Will you come to bed with me first?"

"Well, it's quite an imposition, you understand."

"I need to feel connected to you."

She didn't realize he was joking. Brad stood and picked her up, carried her through the kitchen and down the hall to her bedroom.

"Soon this will be our room," he said.

*** *** ***

As she lay spent in Brad's embrace, Willow knew it would be nearly impossible to let him go, but she had to, this once more. He would be halfway across the country for two weeks. It would give them both time to be sure. The status quo wasn't great, but there was no reason to ditch it and make so many lives miserable if in the long run it wouldn't work.

Brad's luscious gray eyes held hers in the low light and she let her worries recede again and kissed him.

Later he gently broke away and slid out of the bed.

"I'll be right back."

Willow propped herself up on her elbow and watched him, admiring his still-trim physique. He found his pants and dug through the pockets, then returned to the bed.

"I wanted to get you a ring," he said and opened his hand. On the palm lay a simple silver band. "I know it's not fancy, but I liked it."

Reaching out one finger, Willow traced the circle. "I like it too."

He took her left hand and slid the ring onto her middle finger, as close as they dared come to an official engagement right now. It fit snugly, a reassuring embodiment of his love to sustain her while he was away. "With this ring I promise to spend the rest of my life with you, Willow Charm."

"Oh, Brad!" Tears welled, and she blinked through them. Her mind was made up, and it appeared his was too.

They would use the two-week hiatus to close out their old lives in preparation for the new. She determined to resolve all of her Mom issues, all of her Dad issues, all of her Ester 'Kelly' Finch life. When Brad came back, she would wholly be Willow Charm. There would be no prehistory to cause problems, and she would have Fin at least on the road to acceptance. Life would be complete.

After making love again, they dressed. Brad skipped his customary shower, saying he wanted to be reminded of her for a while longer. They drove together to pick up Fin from Beacon and Ember.

As usual, Fin was quiet, but Willow allowed herself to think he acted less hostile toward Brad. Perhaps their hike had started them on the path to a healthier relationship.

Brad dropped them off at home, ruffled Fin's hair and gave Willow a quick hug. He drove off into the dark. Willow watched him until he turned the corner.

***   ***   ***

Social Security numbers for Guam and American Samoa start with 586, and the hum of the aquarium filter listed them off in order, beginning with those assigned in 1976, bereft of any other information about the recipients.

Melissa gritted her teeth and pretended to read the book she held, which was blank. She brought the journal along in the hopes of providing herself with a haven of meaninglessness, but it wasn't working. She scheduled this appointment for first thing in the morning so the doctor wouldn't have time to fall behind, thus lengthening her term in hell.

Murray Robertson just became a Masonic Sovereign Grand Inspector-General of the 33rd and Last Degree, but secretly preferred the title of his last level better — Sublime Prince of the Royal Secret.

The tranquilizer she swallowed at the water fountain in the hall hadn't kicked in yet. Melissa closed her eyes and took deep breaths.

An armada of fire trucks, ambulances and other rescue vehicles flew past on the highway outside, providing an exhaustive accounting of the more mundane aspects of the bureaucracy of the Roman Catholic church. 'Bishops must retire at age 75,' the whoop of a police car said.

If only her insides weren't screwed up, this wouldn't be necessary. But they were, so here she was, visiting the gynecologist for the first time in six or seven years. Kyle, 13 now, greatly resented her clinginess. This misery was required if she ever wanted to have another baby, to ensure herself more years of sanity.

The heavyset young woman on the other side of the waiting room riffled through a copy of *People* magazine, the fluttering of the pages assuring Melissa that there are fewer than 33 super-colossal olives per pound.

"Mrs Tanner, you can come back now."

Melissa shoved the torrent of trivia aside enough to follow the nurse back to the exam room and robotically undress. Her composure cracked while the nurse took her medical history, and Melissa was relieved when she was left alone in the room.

Her exam gown was striped, white and pink. A parade of UPC codes marched through her head.

No matter how bad it got, Melissa was prepared to tough it out. She would endure any test, procedure, or treatment. If she could get through this day, she would earn a decade of quiet.

The antiseptic smell assaulting her nostrils told her the locations of each of the 10,513 McDonald's restaurants worldwide.

Someone scuffled past in the hallway and Melissa knew the names of all of the deer hunters who injured themselves by falling out of trees during Pennsylvania's 1985 doe season.

The doctor hurried into the room, smiling. His teeth were very white.

"It's been a long time since your last exam, so I'd like to start with that. We might find our answer right away," his voice said, while his paisley necktie said, 'A teenager in New Mexico has created over 1,000 variations of the same Dungeons and Dragons monster. Let me show them to you.'

Melissa scooted down to the end of the table and put her feet in the stirrups. She stared at the sign on the ceiling. It said 'relax.'

The stupid claymation raisins weren't going anywhere.

Blue corn and oat bran were going to be very popular.

The doctor inserted the speculum. It was cold and unnatural and treated Melissa to a list, arranged by student number, of female Buckminster University dropouts, and rafts of minutia about who they were having sex with. Melissa saw her own information, a novelty, partnered with Brad. Then Brad's name again, associated with someone else.

Melissa gasped. It was definitely her Brad. The American Express card number was his. She tried to glean more information, but as soon as she focused on it, it slipped away, replaced by a list of major league hockey teams, by division.

The doctor was saying something, but Melissa couldn't understand him. Fury and hurt and fear burst her fragile defenses.

Brad was probably with his mistress last night. Melissa shuddered. In two days they would fly to her parents' house for Thanksgiving. How would she ever endure the entire two weeks now that she knew? Brad was having an affair, and she couldn't stop him. If she even confronted him, she might lose him.

And drown forever.

*** *** ***

Room 222. Willow stared at the flat brown door, wishing for a sign, some indication she was doing the right thing. Fiddling with the belt of her coat, she wondered if this meeting would go better than their last one. When Gale called the second time, she promised to answer Willow's questions. More important, she sounded calm.

Still, memories of the first meeting made Willow nervous and she resolved that if it didn't work this time, there would be no next time.

Willow let her belt go and reached up to knock, but stopped her fist partway there. She stuffed her hands in her coat pockets, and thought some more.

Am I doing the right thing?

Inside her pocket, her thumb worried at the ring on her middle finger. There was so much going on right now, with the pregnancy, and Brad, and the inevitable difficulties of explaining those things to Fin. In the immediate aftermath of finding out about Ted Finch's lies it seemed very important to locate her roots, some connection to her past, but now might not be the best time.

Maybe the thing to do was leave a note at the front desk. Let Gale down easy. Tell her they could meet some other time. She could go pick Fin up from Beacon and Ember. She could talk to Ember about—

The door of room 222 opened.

Willow's hands flew to her hair, tucking stray locks away, making herself presentable.

Gale stood smiling in the doorway.

"I thought you were out here," she said, stepping back to allow Willow to enter.

Careful to avoid contact with Gale, Willow crossed to the small sitting area, but remained standing. The room was cold.

Gale wore the same sweater-dress as before, but today her hair was neater and she had on a pair of white socks.

"I'm glad you came," she said. "I'm sorry things went badly before. I allowed myself to become too emotional."

"I understand."

"Would you like some coffee? Or tea? There's a coffee maker in the bathroom."

"Tea would be good. Please."

Gale smiled. "I'll be right back."

She went into the bathroom and Willow heard water running. For a few awkward minutes Willow considered leaving, but she would have to pass the open bathroom door on her way out. A whistling hiss came from the boiler and moments later Gale was back. She handed Willow a steaming styrofoam cup with a tea bag in it, along with a plastic stirring stick.

"Why don't you ask me some of your questions. Just, please, go slowly. It's a painful time for me to talk about, but I'll do my best."

Willow nodded and sat in the chair. "Who was my father?"

Gale took a deep breath. "His name was Malcolm. He died in Korea."

"Why was I taken away?"

"I was too young to raise you." Gale stared into her brewing tea as if she hoped to find something in its depths. "My family hadn't approved of my marriage, and once Malcolm died they wouldn't take me back unless I gave you up."

"I see." This made sense. Willow plucked the tea bag out of her cup and dropped it into the waste basket. The tea smelled funny, probably the hot styrofoam. She took a tiny sip. It tasted like slightly disinfected tea.

"You said you named me Kelly."

"Yes. It's a lovely name. Not that there's anything wrong with Willow."

"They both have two Ls," Willow offered. Another few sips of tea afforded her the time to consider her next question. "Where was I born?"

"In the hospital."

"Yes, of course, but..." It was a reasonable answer, Willow knew that on one level, but on another level she found it confusing. The entire situation was suddenly confusing. "But..."

"Oh, Kelly, I'm sorry it had to come to this," Gale said.

Come to what? Willow tried to ask, but her mouth wouldn't obey.

She wanted Brad, but he wasn't even in the state. She wanted Fin. She wanted to leave. When she tried to stand, her knees buckled and she slumped to the carpet. Her thoughts were sluggish.

Horrible woman. Crazy.

As her eyes drooped, Willow saw Gale open the connecting door to the next room. A jolt of fear sent her heart racing. Her fingers scrabbled in the carpet as someone joined Gale in the room.

"Hello Willow," Severin said, bending over her. "You're going to join the TEF after all."

Everything went white, even the noise.

*** *** ***

Severin crouched beside the van and looked through the gate and across the yard to the rear of the House. No one at the windows, no one in the yard. A furtive glance confirmed that none of the neighbors were cleaning their gutters or raking their back yards.

Assured they were unobserved, he hurried over to Gale's door and motioned for her to get out as he slid the side door open. Willow lay across the back seat. Severin jumped in to lift her shoulders while Gale reached in for her knees, and they awkwardly transferred her out of the vehicle. Once he stepped back down to the gravel driveway, Severin adjusted his grip. Willow's slight form was easy for him to manage, carrying her like a child. He whispered at Gale to shut the door and started off for the House.

After about twenty strides he found Willow less easy to carry and quickened his pace. Gale darted past him and opened the basement door before he reached it. She stood aside until he ducked through, then closed it behind them and turned on the light.

Severin stooped to lay Willow on the dirt floor near the great stone slab. He stood and rubbed his back.

"She goes on it, right?"

"Shhh!" Severin pointed up to indicate that people upstairs might hear them. He said softly, "Yes. But we must make preparations."

Gale sat alongside Willow and stroked her hair.

Severin sighed, but Gale didn't notice. "The drug will wear off before long. We have to get to work." He stooped again and began unbuttoning Willow's top. Gale tried to push him away, her eyes flashing. He looked at her in surprise.

"This is part of the preparations. She has to be nude."

Gale glared. Severin held his ground, but he knew she'd create an unacceptably noisy protest if he tried to tamper further with Willow's clothes.

"Sister, will you please undress the child?" He stood back, and Gale looked from him to Willow, then back to him. "Time is short."

Gale closed her eyes for a moment, and her face relaxed. She blinked cheerfully, and gazed at Willow's slack features, cooing. "Mommy's baby Kelly has to go sleepy-time, now. Yes. Mommy undress her all over, get her ready for bed." Severin warily moved over to the slab, hoping Gale's murmuring wouldn't carry.

He watched as Willow's clothing came off. She wasn't anybody's baby anymore. Suggestions of her toned musculature showed, but she was smooth and feminine. He matched her contours to how he'd always imagined them, observed that she was aging gracefully. Her lower abdomen did protrude a bit. That didn't match.

"...so wonderful that Mommy's baby can stay here, now." Gale tweaked Willow's nose before lifting one unconscious shoulder to unclasp her bra. She rolled Willow's pink cotton panties down her thighs and slipped them the rest of the way off. Severin blinked and turned his attention to the stone.

Stooping, he ran his hands over the coarse, cold surface, making sure it was clean. He looked back over to the women, and nodded. He collected Willow and reverently laid her on her back on the slab. Straightening and adjusting her legs allowed him a moment to caress her smooth warm skin.

So much potential.

As he laid her arms at her sides, Severin noticed a plain silver ring on the middle finger of her left hand. He frowned. Optimally she would be completely nude. Tugging on the ring did no good. It fit tightly and resisted his efforts to remove it. Gale stood to one side and watched the whole operation, dabbing at her eyes.

Willow moaned and her brow furrowed. The ring would have to stay. He didn't have time to argue with it.

"Now," Severin announced, "I must go upstairs to complete the activation. To focus the lens."

"Can I stay with her?" Gale asked.

Severin nodded with a smile. Halfway over to the steps he turned back, thinking perhaps Gale wanted some reassurance. He walked back to her and held out his arms, and she hurled herself into his embrace. She shivered. Severin patted her head, nonplussed. Before he could decide what he was supposed to say, she wriggled free of him and sat on the edge of the stone next to Willow's head, resumed stroking Willow's hair.

"You can't be on the stone right now. Later it will be fine, but not while I'm activating it."

Gale looked at Willow searchingly. She repositioned herself off the stone so she'd have a clear view of Willow's face. Severin climbed the steps two at a time all the way to the attic.

Winded, he approached the white-sheeted table. He took a deep breath and held it, willing his fingers steady.

Exhaling, he raised the sheet and slid his left hand under. He encountered not the smooth wooden door, but the chill hardness of the slab. He caressed it, his palm in contact with the same point where Willow lay four stories below.

He drew another breath and twisted his hand. The rock surface slid and vibrated against his skin. It grew warm. He was panting now, as he applied more force. Such fine adjustments, against such enormous resistance.

Dust fell from the rafters, the windows rattled. The entire slab turned minutely, sending a groan through the timbers of the House.

Severin gritted his teeth. His hand felt crushed beneath the stone.

His heart raced and his head filled with inchoate buzzing. Now that he'd imparted some momentum, the slab continued to pivot with excruciating slowness. It would keep turning unless Severin could stop it. It had to be precisely aligned. For a few seconds Severin didn't have to exert, but merely endure the grinding weight. He could feel it coming into phase, the heat increasing on his palm.

Now!

Severin howled as he strained to slow the rotation. He thought the bones in his arm would splinter, his hand crumble into ashes. He kept pushing. He felt the motion slowing, felt the attunement growing stronger.

Not too much, not too much.

While the stone still moved almost imperceptibly he eased up, hoping he'd timed it right. The slab came to rest, and pure white light, cool and strong, flowed into Severin through his palm. He lingered, catching his breath and enjoying the radiance.

He yanked his hand out from beneath the sheet and looked at it. Unharmed, but throbbing.

Severin went back down the stairs at a relaxed pace, smirking at the few people he passed. They looked nervously at the ceilings, or out the windows. No one asked him any questions, but they all peered at him timidly as he went by.

In the basement, Gale cowered under a workbench. Severin clicked his tongue and walked over to the slab to inspect his handiwork and felt a surge of pride.

The stone's customary gray color had disappeared. It was now a sleek, crystalline greenish white, attuned to the frequency of the Elsewhere. He leaned close to Willow's face, and from so near he could discern an uncanny stillness to her features. She didn't appear to be breathing.

He stood and turned to Gale. "We've succeeded!" Gale showed no reaction, hadn't acknowledged Severin's arrival. "Sister, we're in business. How shall we celebrate?"

Gale edged out from under the workbench, shaking her head. Severin offered a hand to help her stand.

"I think I was too close. To it. The stone. I felt, things. Shaking. Twisting."

Severin frowned. "How do you feel now?"

Gale shrugged.

The frown faded and he put his arm around her. "I'd say you weren't too close. You had a great seat for the show, that's all." He gave her shoulder a gentle squeeze and steered her toward the steps.

"I'm tired." Gale's right foot dragged, and her face looked drained. "I hope I can make it up to the attic."

"You can rest. I have a few loose ends to tidy up. Why don't you take a nap until I finish?"

Gale nodded. They went up, all the way up. For the second half of the climb she took the steps one by one, placing both feet on each tread before advancing. It was slow, but Gale made the entire journey under her own power. Severin wrapped her in a blanket in the hammock, kissed her on the cheek, and went back downstairs.

He headed outdoors this time, to the van for Willow's purse. He went through it out there, searching for her keys. In addition to those, he discovered a small book and a prescription bottle. Prenatal vitamins. The book's cover promised 3,000 Names For Boy and Girl.

Of course. The tummy bulge. She was about two months, maybe three. It only made sense. Classic timing. He was always the last to know.

This time at least she was where he wanted her. It wasn't the pregnancy he'd intended for her, but it would serve his purposes all the same.

***

Willow's key turned in the lock and the door opened under a gentle push of Severin's gloved hand with not so much as a squeak, which wasn't surprising. It wouldn't do for the building superintendent to have squeaky hinges. He shut the door behind him and turned on the lights.

Severin studied the cluttered living room. Numerous books and magazines lay open, or formed uneasy stacks, on the coffee table, the battered sofa, much of the brown carpet. The far end of the narrow space held a small table and two dining chairs. He relaxed and moved farther into the room. So far there were no indications that would tell an investigator she'd been anticipating a major event.

He went to the right, into the tight galley kitchen. No dishes on the counter, no notes on the refrigerator. Through the kitchen lay a hallway running right and left. Severin chose right, and arrived at a bedroom. He turned on the light.

The concert posters on the walls and ceiling, and the dirty laundry scattered over the floor and the bed, told him this must be the boy's room. Heaps of tapes, a Walkman, more books, and an acoustic guitar filled the small space. He switched off the light and turned to explore the other end of the hall.

Past the bathroom and around a corner he located Willow's room. It was spare and neat, the bed made with military precision. A chair next to the small dresser allowed it to double as a desk, and its surface was the only part of this room that matched the rest of the apartment. Sheaves of yellow notes layered with technical journals and reference books.

Wedged between the wall and a coffee can full of pencils, a bundle of envelopes caught Severin's eye. Most bore the return address of a company called Industrial Harmonics, evidently a defense contractor. Shuffled among the check stubs and bland administrative correspondence lay diagrams and equations relating to specific engineering projects. How Willow put to use the education Severin financed.

One packet was devoted to her most recent project, enhancing the signal strength of extremely small transceivers. Each letter posed a new dilemma, and thanked Willow for offering an innovative solution to the one before. Nearly all of this was in the form of jargon and equations that meant nothing to Severin.

He surveyed the improvised desktop again, feeling that something was amiss.

No drawings.

The nearby wastebasket held nothing.

Notes and bound printed matter took up the whole work surface, so where had she actually worked? The notes themselves were all on legal paper, yet he saw no pad.

It was in the top drawer, with her underthings. A yellow legal pad containing dozens of Willow's drawings. Severin knew that he beheld the rough drafts, that the refined versions had been mailed off to her nefarious employer. He grinned. These rough, wild gems were far better than the tame, polished things she submitted for her paycheck. This new stockpile of drawings meant prospective TEF recruits could be evaluated for years to come.

Severin saw that the company had revealed only the absolute minimum information about the project's real goals, gave no hint of how any one component would add to the whole. How disappointing to be unable to envision the actual devices that would be built using Willow's contributions. Galling that someone of such singular gifts was taken for granted by an impersonal corporation. She would certainly be more appreciated in her new position.

Severin took a few of the letters and the sketchpad and worked his way back to the front door, turning off all the lights along the way.

*** *** ***

Saturday morning Brad rolled out of bed and went straight to the shower. He didn't want to smell like Melissa when he saw Willow.

Bad weather in Chicago had delayed their flight home. By the time they got the over-caffeinated Kyle into bed, it had been 2:00 a.m. Melissa was still sound asleep. Brad hoped to be out the door before she woke up and handed him a Honey-Do list.

He needed to see Willow, to reaffirm their decision. Then the only thing on his Honey-Do list would be to dissolve his marriage. The trip proved how easy that would be. Melissa was frosty the whole time, not even pestering him for sex. He thought she might be working up to asking him for a divorce.

After dressing in the hallway, Brad crept down the stairs, grabbed a bag of airline peanuts to eat in the car, and made his escape.

The large house on Clover Street was quiet. The tenants, all students, had probably been partying late. Brad stood in the vestibule, listening. No sounds came from her apartment, so Fin must also be sleeping.

Brad knocked lightly on the door, and waited. No response.

He knocked louder, but still received no reply.

After fruitlessly knocking a few more times, he decided to come back later. She must be sleeping.

A cup of coffee and a sticky bun at the Shamrock Diner filled him up better than the peanuts. Someone had left a copy of yesterday's paper in his booth and he read that to catch up on local news.

Back at Willow's door an hour later, Brad went through his knocking ritual again, and again got no reply.

He spent the rest of the day busying himself with imaginary errands and checking for her. She never did answer the door. Disappointed and a little concerned, Brad headed home at about four in the afternoon. She and Fin had probably gone somewhere.

Melissa was livid when he got home. Not unreasonably, he told himself. She didn't know he knew the marriage was over. It was a huge temptation to tell her he was leaving. He held off because he wanted to talk to Willow first.

He planned to check in at Willow's house again in the evening, but Melissa made that untenable. The next day she was up early, but he left after breakfast while she showered.

Willow's apartment was still apparently empty. Brad's concerns blossomed into worries. Several hours later he knew he had to take some sort of action. The only thing he could think of was to talk to Beacon and Ember. She would have told them if she was going somewhere.

If they even had a phone, Brad had no idea what the number was, or their last name for that matter, so he needed to drive out to their house on the organic farm. On the way he began to obsess over where Willow might be. His mind kept coming back to the thought that she sent him away. Not once, but three times.

Maybe she didn't really want to be with him. It was hard to believe because she seemed happy about the idea. But she hadn't let him stay. She sent him away three times. She knew this last time would be for two weeks. Could she have been planning to leave town? The idea was repellent and fascinating. Also extraordinarily painful. The only thing that had made his visit to Melissa's family bearable was the knowledge that he would be coming back to Willow.

If she were gone...

Beacon and Ember lived in two rooms above the farm's onsite produce market. Brad parked under an oak tree and hurried toward it. The shop was doing a brisk business in apples and squash. Through a clump of customers dressed in their church clothes, Brad spotted Fin working behind the cash register.

His heart soared.

To the left and up the stairs. He was knocking on their door. Beacon yelled out, "It's open," and Brad was in their jumbled living room. Willow wasn't there. Beacon looked surprised to see him. Ember too.

"Where's Wil?" Brad asked.

*** *** ***

Hours later, after the police finished searching Willow's apartment, Brad sat with Fin at the kitchen table. A miserable day was about to get worse.

Fin refused to make eye contact, but his shaking had subsided. Delaying the inevitable conversation, Brad just sat too. Being near Fin, her son, made him feel a connection to her. Where the hell could she be?

Beacon and Ember hadn't seen her for two weeks, not since she'd dropped Fin off on a Saturday at lunchtime. She only said she had a few things to do, something vague. They had expected her back that evening.

No one worried until sometime on Sunday. They decided Willow had most likely gone somewhere with Brad. The police were very interested in that supposition, but lost interest after confirming his trip with the airline.

Fin had continued going to school. Beacon and Ember took good care of him. Everything was fine. Then Brad showed up without Willow.

Ember was probably still crying. Brad wished he could be, too.

The police weren't concerned. They expressed compassion for Fin, and even a little for Brad, but they were convinced she left of her own accord. Beacon's information about Willow's past only strengthened their belief.

It turned out Willow wasn't her real name. That was her Threshold name. Her real name, according to Beacon, was Liz. Elizabeth? Brad had never heard anything about it before, and from his reaction, neither had Fin. What had she said, that Fin Chester was a family name? Could her real name be Elizabeth Chester?

The police seemed to think someone living under an alias was more likely than most to cut and run. They did promise to keep looking into things.

And that left Brad to take possession of Fin.

Melissa wasn't going to like this.

Truth be told, Brad wasn't going to like it either, but what other choice was there? If he moved in here with Fin, neither of them would be happy. He would be destroying his other family for nothing. Without Willow to run to, Brad found himself disinclined to run at all. It was one thing to leave his wife for another woman. It was something else entirely to leave his wife, period.

No matter what, things would never be the same. After tonight Melissa would know about Willow and Fin. Brad's gut clenched with cold dread.

He sighed. He was the one who set this bed on fire, now he'd have to lie in it.

Willow was gone, and he didn't know if she would ever come back. He squeezed his eyes shut and willed the tears away. Something terrible must have happened. It was simply impossible to think she'd voluntarily leave her son. If the worst had happened and she wouldn't be back, he owed it to Melissa and Kyle to try to make things work, to try to avoid turning one tragedy into two.

"Fin."

The boy didn't acknowledge him.

Brad took a deep breath. "Fin, I'm sure she'll come back. I don't know where she is, but I know she would never leave you. Don't let what the police said get to you. She will come back."

Fin sniffled.

"But in the meantime," Brad went on, "you'll need to come home with me."

Fin looked up sharply and glared at him.

"We'll leave a note here so she knows where to find you. There's not really any other choice."

"I want to stay with Ember and Beacon."

"I know. But they don't really have enough room. And they aren't your relatives. I'm your father."

Fin snorted.

Brad ignored it. "Has your mom ever mentioned Melissa? Or Kyle?"

Fin looked back at the table, but nodded.

"They'll be there." He paused. *Christ this is awkward.* "Kyle is my son. He's your age. Melissa is my wife."

"I know that."

"I hope you'll get along. But it will be difficult."

Fin said nothing.

"They don't know about you. Or your mom."

"You're a bastard." Fin's voice was cold and precise.

"I never wanted to be the bad guy."

"Well nice job, dickweed. You've fucked everything up. I hate you."

Chapter Thirteen

GELATINOUS DARKNESS

General, we regret the delays on the project, but unavoidable circumstances have hampered our progress. A key member of our engineering staff departed unexpectedly. Recruiting a replacement is our highest priority.
    Project Lullaby archives: letter from Industrial Harmonics, 1989

DECEMBER 4, 1988

Kyle Tanner leapt off the sofa and yelled at the referee on ESPN. "Offsides, you shithead!"

His mom clucked something disapproving, but he tuned her out. It wasn't like she understood the game or anything.

As commercials played, Kyle dashed to the kitchen for another can of Mountain Dew. He heard his dad pulling into the garage and felt happy. That would keep his mom occupied for a while and he could watch the game in peace.

"Dad's home," he yelled and dove back onto the sofa.

His mom sighed, said something about not abusing the furniture, and left the room. Kyle grabbed the remote and turned the volume up as the game came back on.

The slow-mo instant replays confirmed Kyle's opinion about the stupidity of the refs.

His dad called him, but Kyle ignored it. Green Bay was lining up. Fourth and twelve. They would be idiots to try running again.

"Kyle!"

His dad switched the TV off and stood there through Kyle's loud protests. Kyle turned to his mom for back-up, but she was crying.

Kyle stopped talking abruptly and sat down.

"Why's Mom crying?"

"Your mother and I need to talk, but first I want you to meet someone."

His mom blew her nose into a tissue and glared. This could be great. When they fought it meant a lot more free time for Kyle.

His dad went into the kitchen. Kyle waited on the sofa. When his dad came back he brought a kid with him. Some scruffy kid who looked like he went to the weirdo school. He kept staring at the floor. Kyle didn't know him.

"Kyle, this is Fin," his dad said.

What the hell kind of name was Fin? He must go to the weirdo school with a name like that.

"Kyle, say hello." His dad sounded serious, which didn't happen too often.

"Hi."

Fin didn't say anything.

"Fin," his dad prompted.

Fin mumbled something that could have been a greeting.

Kyle's mom sobbed.

"Why don't you guys watch the game together?" his dad said. "Melissa, let's talk in the other room."

Kyle turned the TV back on, but quieter. He wanted to hear a little of what his parents were talking about, see if the fight was anything good. Fin just stood there with his hands in his pockets and stared at the floor.

"We can't keep him here!" Kyle heard his mom say.

Kyle looked at Fin again as his dad said something he couldn't hear. His mom responded shrilly, "You can't ask me to live with him, Brad. It's bad enough that he exists. I will not live with a constant reminder of your mistakes!"

"He's my son, Melissa." Dad raised his voice. "His mother is missing. He will live here."

"Brad—"

"Whether or not you live here with him is your choice."

The game held no interest for Kyle any longer. This weird kid was Dad's son. No wonder Mom was pissed.

Fin's whole body was shaking. Kyle brushed past him and found his parents at the foot of the stairs.

"I'm not leaving," Kyle said. "All my stuff's here. I'm not leaving."

His dad smiled at him and ruffled his hair. His mom was shaking even harder than Fin. She turned and stomped up the stairs.

"Let's show your brother his new room."

Brother? Well, that made sense of course, if he was Dad's kid.

"I'm not sharing my room," Kyle stated.

His dad looked at him for a few seconds, then went back into the family room to get Fin. Kyle followed behind as his dad picked up an army surplus duffel bag and led Fin up the stairs and to the larger spare bedroom, the one where Grandma stayed when she visited from Indianapolis. They went inside and shut the door. Kyle stood in the hallway, guarding his turf until his dad came out about half an hour later.

"How you doin' Tiger?"

Kyle shrugged.

"Wanna talk?"

"No."

"Let me know if you change your mind."

Kyle nodded and watched his dad walk to his parents' bedroom. The door was locked, so his dad went into the smaller spare bedroom, the one with the day bed and the sewing machine.

Kyle smiled to himself and went into his room. This new state of affairs could definitely be used to his advantage.

*** *** ***

There simply was no good solution. Melissa glared at the rapidly cooling wedge of goopy cheese and too much sauce on her plate.

"More pizza, Fin? Kyle?" she heard Brad ask. "There's some sausage left."

Obviously Brad needed to be punished for bringing the horrid creature into the house, this bastard child he'd sired with another woman. His 'son.' Not only was it an insult to Melissa, and a complete ridicule of their marriage in a way that surpassed the affair itself, it was displacing Kyle. Unacceptable. They were both 13, depriving her son of his place as firstborn. The little monster even laid claim to Kyle's birthday, leaving Melissa no way to put her own son forward. The only thing in Kyle's favor was being a legitimate product of their marriage. Now the affair and this creature pretty much negated the whole idea of the marriage being worth anything.

Brad had to be punished.

Switching her glare from her dinner to her husband, Melissa flared her nostrils and fought to keep her temper in check as he blithely served up third helpings to both boys.

The thing to do of course, was move out, but that wasn't an option at all. Kyle made it clear he planned to stay, and without him along to dampen the visions, Melissa would lose her mind. Brad wasn't going anywhere. He thought they should all learn to love each other and live together in some platitude of universal brotherhood.

He would hear nothing of getting rid of the creature. Was absolutely deaf to the idea of foster homes. Or adoption. Or boarding school. Or sending him to live with his mother's relatives. Or just sending him back to the useless hippies who'd had him when the mother disappeared. He was so wrapped up in this idea of being a good father in a happy family he couldn't see the reality of the situation.

The creature sided with Melissa on the whole 'Creature not living in this house' thing. Brad wouldn't listen to him either.

The few bites of pizza she'd managed to swallow sat in her stomach like a fist. Melissa stood and carried her plate to the kitchen, dropping it in the sink where it clattered but didn't break.

Once Kyle discovered how much it bothered her to see him and the creature together he used it to push her buttons. Which shouldn't work since she knew he was doing it, but worked anyway. Better even.

Melissa shoved her uneaten dinner into the garbage disposal, turned the water on full blast, and switched the machine on. A satisfying grinding sound came from the sink. A tiny, tight smile stretched Melissa's mouth. Glancing around the kitchen, her eyes settled on the annual Christmas poinsettia from the bank. There was no way they would have a merry holiday this year anyway.

The tacky white flowers and gnarly roots made a very, very satisfying grinding sound.

She could of course express her displeasure with Brad by moving down to the room in the basement. It even had a bathroom. But that was more like punishing herself. Why should she give up the master bedroom and live in the basement like some second-class citizen? But if she sent Brad to live down there, she'd be stuck up on the second floor with the creature.

Surely they could move the creature down to the basement and pretend he wasn't there, right? Wrong. Brad didn't want him to feel 'isolated.'

So fucking infuriating.

The rancid cherry on top of her shit sundae? The bastard worked. He made the visions go away just like Kyle did. What a surprise that evening she'd come downstairs to discover Brad had taken Kyle to a sleep-over, and the only person in the house with her was the creature. The boys were completely equivalent, leaving her no way to ignore the fact that he was Brad's son.

The Christmas cookies from Piedmont's went quietly, but were satisfying anyway because they were Brad's favorites. Especially the macaroons.

Ending her marriage was out of the question. Not only would it leave her alone at home too much of the time, it would make work impossible. She couldn't divorce Brad and continue at the same bank.

Transferring to another branch would be pointless. She would be unable to function.

The arrangement they'd worked out in the days since the creature arrived didn't punish Brad enough. He was oblivious to her cold fury, even though she wouldn't let him sleep in the master bedroom. The spare bedroom suited him just fine. Whenever she tried to yell at him, he sat there and took it. His only concern was that the boys not be around. He would absorb everything she could throw at him and act like he agreed with all of it. Which made it not terribly cathartic.

By accepting all of the blame immediately, he cheated her. How could she get him to feel?

Besides putting him down the disposal?

The only answer she saw was unappealing. She would have to move out, at least for a little while.

That would get his attention. If she left him here alone with both boys, his world would quickly disintegrate.

It would get Kyle's attention, too. Without her there to act as referee, he would grow tired of his 'brother.'

Her return was inevitable, though they need not know it. Brad would feel true remorse. Kyle would no longer take her for granted. And the creature? Well, once Brad would listen to her, the creature wouldn't be around much longer.

How would she preserve her sanity? Pills were the only option. She would need to take a week off work, of course. Get a hotel room. Spend the whole time comatose.

It would be worth it if she could prove her point.

*** *** ***

Severin thought about the temperature of the oceans as he drummed his fingers on his sheet-shrouded table, quite pleased with how fluid and casual he had become. The types of unconscious mannerisms needed for his purposes didn't come naturally to him at all. Where Willow's fingers were restless, always seeking something to rap on, twist, tug, or worry, Severin favored calm, interlaced digits.

So, cooling the seas. Counteract a few decades' worth of humanity fouling the environment, why not? Not even expecting to get any recognition for it.

In ten seconds he felt too foolish to continue. Something was happening, he knew. But he had no way to determine what, and no means of controlling it. Willow did it effortlessly. No will, no awareness that she was fidgeting, or that by doing so she reshaped the universe. For Severin, it would have to be something he could work deliberately.

There was no way to attain that using what he could learn from Willow. Control was precisely what her power lacked, seemingly by design. Can't help you, the supernatural Teamster declared, that's someone else's department.

Severin stroked his beard slowly, smiling. Someone else... an opposite likeness, a double.

A twin.

Severin recalled the puzzle his table offered him on the subject of Willow when he first met her: the glove, the salt shaker, and the die. Now the clue was obvious, that all of those items belonged in sets of two. Appearing alone, they spoke of Willow's absent sibling. Someone out there held all the pieces missing from Willow, the yin to her yang. Antimatter to her matter.

Willow had never wanted to see how much alike she and Severin were, but here was proof. Both twins, and both separated from their siblings.

His smile progressed into hearty chuckling, as he pictured Gale's face when he asked her what she'd done with her other child.

***   ***   ***

Little bubbles of light surround her. Some are pinkish, some like golden sunlight, but mostly they are bright, pure white. They rise all around her, always drifting upward through the swirling gelatinous green darkness. When they touch her skin they tickle as they slide up and over her. For a fleeting second one will press against an eyeball, allowing her to peer inside at the kaleidoscopic rainbow.

The bubbles make music. An effervescent tinkling sound, like being inside a glass of champagne, only richer and more intoxicating. The pink ones hum, the golden ones chime. Once, a flock of bright luminous greens buzzed and beeped like telephone noises — dial tones, busy signals, and touch tones.

And underneath it all, an intricate double beat that Willow understands is her heartbeat and that of her baby.

Suspended in this thick green atmosphere she watches and listens to the lights. There is nothing else to do. If she twirls her fingers or wiggles her ears the lights will tell her things, sometimes.

They tell her she is warm, a furnace. They tell her she is safe.

The lights want peace and quiet. Mostly quiet.

*** *** ***

Melissa was back.

She had only been gone a week, and she still seemed really pissed, so why she came back was a mystery. If he had the option of not living with Brad and Kyle, Fin Tanner knew he would take it and never look back.

Fin was pretty sure she was on drugs. He knew people at school who were, and she had the same disconnected air about her. The same slightly slept-in smell. Some kind of pills. Valium, most likely.

He went back to reading his book and tried to ignore her.

"Hi Mom," Kyle said. "I moved down to the basement. It's really cool. Dad let me choose the paint and everything."

"The basement?"

"Yeah. That way I can have all my friends over and we can hang out down there and have privacy and stuff."

Melissa stalked over in front of Brad. "Brad?" she demanded. "Won't Kyle feel isolated in the basement?"

"No," Brad said cautiously, glancing at Fin, letting her know they weren't to discuss certain things in front of him, like he was an absolute moron or something. Like he didn't know she hated him.

Brad continued carefully, "Kyle won't feel isolated in the basement because this has always been his home. He knows he's welcome to move back upstairs anytime he wants."

Melissa suppressed some kind of noise. It sounded painful.

"I told Fin he could have my room," Kyle said, "but he didn't want it."

Fin felt Melissa's glare. Didn't she know Kyle was trying to tick her off? It was blatantly obvious. "My room's fine," he muttered, not looking up.

"Fin's feeling more at home now. We brought some more of his things over," Brad said.

"More?"

Fin is, in fact, not feeling more at home.

Seeing all his stuff in this alien environment made everything worse. It was Brad's way of saying he didn't think Mom was coming back. Fin knew she was, so he had to stay in this house so she could find him.

"So, are you back to stay, Mel?" Brad asked, leading her out of the family room.

Fin relaxed a little and tried to find his place in his book. He had to flip back a page. Kyle stood in front of him, bouncing on the balls of his feet. Fin pretended to read.

He longed for a place of his own, a place that felt comfortable. But he didn't want that place to be here, in this house. Unlike Brad, he wasn't ready to give up on Mom.

"If you take my room, it'll really piss her off," Kyle said.

"I know."

"So you'll do it? It'll be hilarious."

"No."

"Oh, come on. My room's great. It's, like, twice as big as Grandma's room. It's got cable, and a phone, and you can hear Mom and Dad through the wall when they do it. *That's* hilarious."

Fin looked at Kyle, disbelieving.

"Seriously." Kyle waited, certain he'd closed the deal.

"You should go into real estate," Fin said. He left Kyle looking confused and went upstairs. Revulsion swept him as he passed the door to the master bedroom. Brad and Melissa screwing was supposed to be a selling point? It made Grandma's room more appealing all the time.

*** *** ***

6 MONTHS LATER - JUNE 1, 1989

"Happy Birthday, Tiger." Brad handed Fin the envelope. Rather, he held it out toward the 14-year-old along with a smile he suspected looked rehearsed, and they sat frozen like that at the dining room table for ten tense seconds before the boy showed any reaction at all. At last Fin rolled his eyes and lifted his own hand to accept the card.

Fin stared at the envelope for a full minute. Brad glanced at the front door, just for a second.

"I'm sure Melissa took Kyle somewhere nice, Brad."

"Aren't you going to open your card, wise guy?"

"Wow. A card. You shouldn't have."

Brad smiled less self-consciously. "Just open it."

Fin's sulk receded half a step, and he tore the red paper and withdrew the preprinted warm sentiments. As he opened the card, a thin rounded triangle of plastic tumbled into his lap. Fin tossed the unread card onto the table and retrieved the guitar pick. His eyes sparked for a moment, and Brad started to mist up. That was the happiest his son had looked in almost a year.

"Wait right there," he said, glad of the excuse to dart out of the room and wipe his eyes. He took the gift-wrapped guitar case out of the coat closet and hurried back to lay it on the table with a flourish. "I was afraid you'd guess what it was. Happy birthday!"

Fin folded his arms and slouched. He wouldn't look at Brad, who felt tears threatening again, different ones. Brad swallowed, putting the water works on hold for later. He wanted to put his arm around Fin's shoulders, but he stayed on the opposite side of the table instead. He slid into a chair and said, "I miss her, too."

"Like hell you do!" Fin shouted, glaring at Brad. His face was red, his eyes dry. "You want to pretend this is all normal. You think this will help me forget!"

Brad blinked, and stared at his hands. "I hope it's the right one," he said softly. Fin looked baffled, which diminished the sense of hostility. "Your mother described the one you liked. But I don't know much about them, so..."

Fin sat up, and reached tentatively toward the gift. He ripped the paper and fumbled with the clasps that held the case closed. In a matter of seconds he lifted the lid and looked at the instrument, a red lacquered Ibanez with a whammy bar. Fin's eyes were moist now, which Brad took as a sign he had indeed bought the right guitar.

"Thank you," Fin croaked.

Brad nodded, remembering Willow. She'd wanted to finance this herself, but money had always been too tight for her to buy it. Brad's throat was too tight for him to speak.

*** *** ***

Severin descended the basement stairs slowly, listening to Gale prattle while she brushed Willow's hair. The usual childish Mommy fantasies, Gale playing with her doll. She recounted the events of the day, indistinguishable from the events of the previous day, and talked about what a big girl Kelly had become. The monotony, and the juvenile voice Gale affected, irritated Severin, but she seemed happy at these times, so he indulged it by giving her time down here alone.

He paused, not listening anymore but thinking. As soon as she noticed his presence, Gale would halt her conversation. Severin wanted to join in this time, to learn more about Gale's past, about which she was physically incapable of talking.

About her other child.

He cleared his throat and proceeded to the bottom of the stairs. Gale fell silent, but looked serene enough, perched beside Willow on the translucent slab. She continued to brush Willow's hair.

"Don't mind me," Severin said. "Pretend I'm not here."

Of course it wasn't that easy. Gale remained silent. Severin walked over to his workbench and shuffled some items around. He rearranged his tools, then returned them to their customary positions. After repeating the exercise, he admitted to himself that he had run out of pretexts for loitering. He would have to try to get her talking.

Severin turned to face Gale and said, "She is like a living doll, isn't she?"

Gale nodded, but her brow creased. This was dangerous ground. Severin almost opted to head back upstairs, but he stubbornly resisted retreat. Instead, he said, "I never played with dolls myself, of course. But I had cherished possessions." He'd planned to say he'd had toys, but realized as he spoke that it was untrue.

Gale nodded again, still guarded.

"I was especially fond of two toy boats," Severin lied, "but one day I left them beside the stream. When I returned, the green one was gone. It was never as much fun to use the yellow one by itself."

Gale gave him a stricken look, the hairbrush frozen mid-stroke.

"I was quite young. I've hardly even thought about that green boat in years."

Gale returned to tending Willow's hair, her motions listless and her head hung low.

Severin observed his sister for a few moments. This was as far as he felt he dared to press her tonight. He could build on this, though.

Gale began speaking again, to Willow or to him Severin couldn't be sure.

"Once there was a young maiden, all alone in the world. She was an orphan, abandoned on a passenger train when she was born, four days before Christmas." Severin knew this much already. He'd been on that train, too. But he didn't interrupt. "One day a handsome young man appeared."

Most of the next section Severin already knew as well, how the mysterious young man corrupted Gale and ran off. In the version he'd seen when he and Gale first touched, there had been only one infant. He kept his silence with some difficulty while Gale recounted, and obviously relived, torrid pleasures in the cave. Finally, she spoke of her pregnancy.

"The maiden escaped just before the child was born and was rewarded with not one baby, but two. Two perfect baby girls with bright green eyes." Severin held his breath. "The first baby, the one she would keep, she named Grace. The second baby she named Kelly. Kelly would be offered to the maiden's tormentors, in exchange for the maiden's freedom. The exhausted maiden hid Kelly, then went to her husband and gave him Grace. Their reunion was joyous, but brief. Little did the maiden know she would never see them again."

Gale lapsed into a long, melancholy silence. At last she gave a tiny sigh and said, "Upon the maiden's return to her captors, the nurses greedily took baby Kelly. The maiden never saw her again either."

Gale glanced at Severin, her eyes sparkling. "Until the maiden's brother reunited her with her lost baby."

Severin smiled, and held out his hand. Gale laid aside her brush and took his hand, and together they went up the stairs.

So Willow was the one Gale sacrificed. Little Baby Kelly, contraband to be confiscated as a smokescreen so she could hold onto Grace. But the second child vanished along with its father, leaving Gale with no one.

A sad tale, but also frustrating. Beyond confirmation that he'd been right to guess at the existence of another baby, it taught Severin nothing. As long as the identity of the man who deflowered Gale remained locked away, it seemed, none of Gale's other secrets would be of use.

*** *** ***

1 YEAR LATER - JULY 1990

Someone had been coming and going through the sliding door in the family room at night. One of the boys, but Brad didn't know which yet.

Once Melissa fell asleep, he got out of bed and set up camp by the railing overlooking the room in question. He suspected Kyle. Sneaking out to see friends, or sneaking a girl in. Or beer.

Deep shadows created pits of utter blackness in the family room. Out of one of those shadows crept a silent figure. The shaggy hair showed Brad he'd been wrong. It was Fin.

Carrying a paper grocery bag, Fin moved cautiously to the door and slid it open. Once outside he turned on a small flashlight.

What was he up to? Brad had been so sure it would be Kyle, he was at a loss.

The thin beam of light crossed the back yard and Brad repositioned to the window in order not to lose Fin as he entered the woods.

Fin stopped about ten yards into the trees. This boy remained such a mystery, even after living with them for two years. Maybe he was going out there to drink a few beers.

The light winked out.

The woods were one of the reasons Brad wanted to buy this house in the first place, to give Kyle a place to explore. Such a shame Melissa never permitted it. There were some great climbing trees, a couple of candidates for an awesome treehouse, even the bomb shelter. Kyle could have had wonderful adventures down there.

The bomb shelter.

Of course.

Brad never mentioned it to Mel because he'd known she wouldn't approve. He planned to let Kyle discover it, but Kyle never did.

Fin did. His troubled, lonely boy.

The flashlight reappeared and came back toward the house.

The bag must have contained supplies. Brad smiled. There was no reason to confront Fin. It would mean a lot to him to have a place all his own where he could escape the antagonism of Melissa and Kyle.

*** *** ***

The Freud text joined the other books in the stack beside the hammock. Severin studied the bearded face on the cover before turning his attention to his sleeping twin, nestled under his left arm with her head on his chest and her leg curled across his stomach. He never truly perceived himself before he had her. Inwardly he thanked Willow for showing him the way to this mirror of his origins.

They'd come from the Elsewhere, he and Gale. The Elsewhere was their mother and their father. And it was alive. More than alive, the sum of humanity's dreams and urges. The headwaters of every yearning. All the basest desires of the world clamoring in darkness, wanting pleasure upon pleasure and wanting it Now. But being all, it was all alone, incomplete.

Together he and his sister gestated in the womb of this Collective Id. The Id wanted instant gratification and Severin and Gale were its children, born to satisfy every carnal impulse. Making up for lost time was proving to be an enjoyable challenge.

According to the good Dr Freud, the id was present at birth but the next psychic aspect, the ego, arose in early childhood. The ego was pragmatic in contrast to the churning passions of the id. These forces were doomed to perpetual antagonism, the ego alternately resisting and appeasing the insatiable id.

Severin doubted much of a Collective Ego yet existed, if it ever would. The ego's formation was founded on the reality principle, on the discovery of one's limitations, and humanity's collective mind effectively had none. Being able to shape reality to suit its whims meant it might never progress beyond infancy.

It was the third psychic aspect that dominated Severin's interest, however. The superego. While the ego could only serve as a countering force for the id, the superego supplied meaning and purpose. Control.

No Collective Superego would ever form, however, because the collective had no society to impose a scheme of rewards and punishments. It was solitary by definition, and thus had no one to teach it how to behave.

The ultimate power vacuum.

If Severin could become that governing force, the entire world could be remade in his own image. He smiled at this vision of offspring overthrowing parent, and wondered what allowed Freud to so aptly describe the deeper reality, even if he had mislabeled it. Had he, too, been touched by the Elsewhere?

Willow, a second-generation descendant of the Collective Id, demonstrated a far stronger bond with it than either Severin or his sister. How to explain that? Something extra from her father, Gale's demon lover?

The question was academic, as Willow's captivity served his ends regardless. The slab that held her would soak up her energy and store it, building until he chose to release it. His original plan, to employ her power personally, disintegrated when he learned that he lacked the vital tool for shaping and manipulating it.

Severin's smile widened. He still had the power, crude though it was. He would turn that power against the Id, disorienting it, creating his opportunity to vault into the Collective Superego role.

But not tonight.

Severin gripped Gale tightly and slipped out of the hammock with her. As she was half asleep, he laid her on his table and mounted her, pulling the pristine white sheet over their hips to transport their pleasure across the Threshold and into the Elsewhere. Give the Id a thrill it had never experienced directly before.

*** *** ***

"Hello, Brad," Beacon said somewhat coldly. Apparently he had yet to forgive Brad for being married to someone who wasn't Willow.

"Hi, Beacon. Come on in." Brad opened the door fully and stepped back to make room. "Have you heard from Wil?"

"I have some things for Fin." Beacon held up a cardboard box.

"He's not home. I think he's at the arcade."

"Shit, Brad. This is hard. Em and I are going to California. Not just me and Em. All of us. Jeffrey got an offer from a developer that was too good to pass up. It's quite an opportunity for us."

Brad knew what Beacon was talking about. TealCorp had just financed the purchase of 85 acres to the west of Webster, near the new highway interchange. They paid above market price, but would make a mint anyway.

"Well, you wouldn't have wanted to be next door to the overpass anyway. Right?"

Beacon smiled halfheartedly. "When we packed up, we found some things of Wil's. We thought Fin should have them." He reluctantly offered the box to Brad.

Brad accepted the box and set it in the hallway. "You wanna come in and wait for Fin?"

Beacon shook his head. "I'd like to, but I can't. Tell him to call us tonight."

While Melissa had Kyle at the pool, Brad took the box downstairs to the den. Tears stung his eyes as he opened it.

Her things.

A brown sweater. A white mug. A couple of cheap paperbacks and an electrical engineering text. The stub of a yellow candle. The lava lamp. A photo from a Following picnic showing Ember, Willow, himself, and a toddler Fin, along with three other people whose names he couldn't remember.

Brad sobbed and stroked the image of Willow. He longed to keep the picture, but knew Fin needed it even more than he did.

There was nothing else in the box, and Brad felt that Fin deserved more. He was so sullen these days, more than the typical teenager bit. Brad wished he could reach out to him, but Fin resisted. Brad knew that he shouldn't be surprised, and that he most certainly should take it personally. Despite whatever mistakes he'd made, and would undoubtedly continue to make, he did it all in an attempt to do the right thing.

In the closet down here, on the top shelf, in a box labeled 'college papers' Brad kept his own mementos of Willow. Now would be a good time to pass them on to Fin. If Fin knew they came from Brad, he wouldn't accept them, but things would be different if he thought they all came from Beacon and Ember. It might help him find some peace.

To the pathetic collection from Beacon, Brad added a braided leather belt, four cassette tapes, a sketch book, and Fin's old stuffed monkey.

He wallowed in misery for fifteen minutes before cleaning himself up and putting the box of treasure in Fin's room.

Chapter Fourteen

HENGE CONTRAPTION

*All I can say is, it makes me sick to see this blot upon the proud
tradition of the Green and Gray. In my day a hero was someone
you looked up to, not some drunken quarterback who got away
with murder. The thick-headed among today's Buck-U Broncos
fans will scream that it wasn't murder, but that was just blind
luck. He was blind drunk when he got behind the wheel. Any
normal citizen, guilty of the same deeds, would rot in prison. I'm
just saying what everybody's thinking.*
         Webster Daily Press letter to the editor, 3-20-1995

SPRING 1995

Severin set the milk crate on his basement workbench. It contained
a dozen printed circuit boards he'd bought at the university's surplus
outlet, and a plastic grocery bag.

He had to work quickly.

Severin plugged in his soldering iron and laid out three of the
boards side by side, a network card and two internal modems. Next he
removed the bag to a clear space further down the table and untwisted
it. He lifted out the contents and arranged them on the bare plywood.

A female barbarian carved from jade, several small metal fish, and
an earring shaped like a globe, all from his table in the attic. He selected
the figurine and the 28.8 modem, then licked his index finger and
checked to see if his iron was hot. Nearly ready. The solder and flux
were poised for use, as were the snips and the fine steel wire.

Sometimes the batteries were easy to assemble. If the curio from the
table happened to have a metal surface, he could solder it directly to the

electronics. In cases like the jade carving, however, he had to construct an armature to hold the item in contact with the circuitry. Severin worked quickly to secure the figurine, ensnaring her with strands of steel. These more complex batteries didn't always work out. Sometimes they took too long and the curio vanished. They were worth the trouble though, those that succeeded being among the most effective for storing Willow's energy.

Working with the earring next, he attached it to the network card with two lengths of wire.

Within the first few months he had Willow down here, he'd detected a leak. Her energies were not all being captured. The slab possessed an innate capacitance, but too feeble for the one it held. Severin experimented, and interrogated his table. Made some inspired guesses. He understood that his solution would have to resonate with both Willow and the Elsewhere, and through trial and error he learned that her affinity for technology brought results.

By the end of the year, he'd discovered how to make these batteries to take up the overflow, and how to set them up in an array. Each completed battery was balanced on end, standing in snaky rows like so many surreal dominoes all over the basement. They formed an elaborate pattern, splitting into four branches that met the sides of the opalescent stone wedge in pairs.

Someday it would be time to set them off. They really were dominoes in a way, for toppling them was the means of discharging their energy. As each was spent, the power would cascade into the next, and the next, all the way down the line until those four columns hit the slab simultaneously. Feeding the energy back into it, sending a surge into Willow.

She would serve as a conduit, channeling this power directly into the Elsewhere, stunning it, and allowing Severin to ascend into control.

Severin could be patient. Energy would continue pooling throughout Willow's prolonged gestation, and more power was definitely better when picking a fight with someone so much bigger.

Too light a touch, and the Elsewhere might not even feel it. Or, far worse, it might become annoyed. Hitting it too hard didn't seem possible.

To make sure, after this child left Willow's womb, Severin would place another within it. He looked over his shoulder at his prisoner. He lingered, knowing he was wasting time, that the objects from the table would begin to expire soon. Gale wasn't down here tonight to get jealous if he looked. He let his eyes caress Willow's paralyzed body until his neck grew stiff.

*** *** ***

Rain-slicked pavement at night presented an especial challenge for Melissa. Streaky red, white and amber reflections from traffic and streetlights wove an aurora of trivia. The van ahead of her hit its brakes, and she knew how much lead paint was considered permissible in school lunches.

She ran her wipers for a pass to clear the spray and wiped her cheeks with the back of her hand. The van inched ahead, and she could see the dark lightning of police lights, amid pulsing red from the ambulance. Melissa shook her head in a futile attempt to rid it of Amazonian butterfly classifications and swerved over to the curb. Still crying, she slammed the Audi into park and ran past the barricade toward the scene.

The phone call from Kyle's football buddy was short on details and compelled her to rush to Kyle's aid, leaving Brad behind, asleep and unaware.

Her tears became heavier, but her thoughts cleared as she drew nearer to the crumpled Camaro and the toppled utility pole. An officer tried to ward her off at the row of red flares hissing on the damp street, but she hissed at him, "It's my son!" and flew to the back of the ambulance.

"Kyle!" she shrieked. He lay propped on a stretcher, with one pant leg sheared away and a bloodied brace fitted around his right knee. Clear plastic bags drained into him through an IV in his left arm. He held an oxygen mask to his face, and waved weakly when he spotted his mother.

Melissa nearly toppled to the sidewalk when a paramedic blocked her attempt to climb in, but Kyle mumbled and tried to sit up. She took advantage of the distraction to get inside. Clasping his hand, she said, "Kyle, baby, are you okay? What happened?" Kyle almost smiled, but seemed too drowsy. His eyes rolled for a moment and settled on Melissa.

"We gave him some strong medication, Ma'am," said a female EMT. "Are you his mother?"

"Yes, I'm his mother." Melissa gave Kyle's hand a squeeze and beamed a proud smile at the woman, who stared back.

"Well, you should know his leg is broken at the knee, and there could be other injuries. We're about to get underway to the hospital."

"I'm riding with him."

This time the lady paramedic blinked. "Then hang on, and stay out of our way."

Melissa nodded and turned back to Kyle. "How did this happen? Kyle, tell Mother what happened."

"He can't talk right now," another EMT explained, "but look for yourself." He gestured out at the scene, and up the block.

Melissa looked at the wreckage, and shuddered. Pictures of cars in that state usually accompanied newspaper reports of fatal accidents.

Traffic had been shunted onto a side street, leaving only flares and police cruisers on the one-way thoroughfare. Police officers clustered in a parking space along the left, in front of a bar. One of the policemen pointed, and she saw the tire marks.

A pair of serpentine black stripes undulated over both lanes, leading half a block from that parking space to the ruins of Kyle's car.

The ambulance's rear doors shut, and the vehicle lurched into motion. Melissa looked at Kyle, and he tried once again to smile at her. The realization that pain killers were not the only thing impairing him struck her full in the face, and she dropped his hand.

How could he be so stupid!

Rage flashed red, but cooled rapidly. No. He would not throw it all away.

She wouldn't allow his misjudgment to take her source of pride away from her. Why should she be punished for the rashness of a 19-year-old?

The rest of the ride, Melissa thought furiously. People to be called, connections to be worked. Ugliness to be kept out of the papers. Buckminster's lawyers would scramble to protect the up-and-coming quarterback from a scandal, to protect the university. She had to make her phone time count. She wouldn't be allowed to remain with Kyle if he went into surgery, which appeared certain. The leg was bad. Her endurance had been exceeded just driving downtown, and how was she going to get her car back?

Focus!

When the rear doors opened again, Melissa bolted up the corridor to the pay phones near the admitting desk. It was on the route to the surgical ward, and she gambled that Kyle would be trundled past and his proximity would be enough to allow her to recruit allies for him.

She phoned the coach, or rather his wife, who knew the drill. The woman had the university's legal counsel and the paper's editor on speed-dial. It would be handled. Melissa pointed out the wet roads, offering to relay an entire eyewitness rendition of the unfortunate accident, in which no one was killed Thank God and luckily nobody but the driver was involved. The coach's wife 'mm-hmmed' several times, as if taking notes. As the stretcher rolled by, Melissa concluded the call.

At the drinking fountain she discreetly took a small bottle from her purse. She swallowed six pills as the ceiling grid became a code for winning lottery numbers of the past ten years. Melissa walked to a seat in the waiting area, where she passed out.

*** *** ***

The clatter of two movie projectors filled the small, metal-lined room. Brad looked around, fascinated. He'd never been in a projection booth before. Tom Bishop, the man he'd come to see, smiled easily as he tried to finish up his phone conversation. He gestured for Brad to sit on a rickety chair in front of his desk and Brad experienced a sudden surreal moment of knowing how his clients felt when they came to see him about a loan.

"No, we can't do that many matinees," this side of the conversation went. "We need to have at least half an hour between showings to clear everyone out and clean the theatre."

A poster from *Star Wars* hung beside one for *The Rocky Horror Picture Show* on the wall behind the desk. The giant platters of film turned slowly in the middle of the room, feeding into the two noisy projectors. How was it possible the sound didn't carry to the audience?

"But sometimes people do stay for all the credits. Look, I'll take another look at the schedule and call you back." He hung up the phone and turned his attention to Brad, shaking his hand.

"I'm Tom Bishop. Everyone calls me Bishop."

"Brad Tanner. Brad."

Brad liked Bishop right away. He should have been imposing, being about six and a half feet tall, long-haired, and fully bearded, but his demeanor was gentle.

"So, you're Fin's dad?"

Brad nodded. "I hope you didn't tell him about our meeting."

Bishop shook his head, but looked curious.

"Unfortunately my son doesn't like me much." *Christ, this is awkward.* "Fin won't allow me to be a part of his life. He has what he thinks are good reasons. Sometimes I think they're good reasons, too, but he's still my son."

Bishop sat back in his chair and watched Brad, waiting for him to continue.

"I wanted to talk to you, since you're his landlord now."

Bishop shook his head. "No, I'm not the landlord." He smiled. "But, I guess I'm the den mother. I gather the rent checks and make sure the utilities get paid, that sort of thing. The house manager, if you will."

"I'm not sure how well you've gotten to know Fin," Brad said.

"He's a good chess player."

"I suppose he is. That would be his mother's influence. Well, as you get to know more about him, you'll notice that he's a, uh, free spirit."

"He's irresponsible, you mean."

Brad sighed. "I don't want him to get evicted from this apartment. I would like to have an arrangement with you. If Fin loses his job, or seems like he's getting into something too deep, I'd like you to let me know."

Bishop didn't look entirely comfortable.

"I'm not asking you to be his babysitter. I know he gets up to all kinds of stuff I wouldn't approve of. What I'm saying is, he wouldn't call me to bail him out of jail even if he had no other options. He'd stay in jail. He wouldn't ask me for money. He'd get evicted again, or get his kneecaps busted by loan sharks, or whatever. What I would like from you is a head's up if he's getting into that sort of trouble. I'll pay his rent if necessary. I'll do what I can to help him, as long as he doesn't know about it. If he knows, he'll refuse." Which was completely unlike Kyle. Even with his hefty college account, Kyle wasn't shy about asking his parents for money. Fin never asked, or touched his account. The statements showed it still contained a little over $100,000.

"You want to be his safety net."

"I want to be his father. He's not interested. I'd like to make sure he lives long enough to reconsider."

*** *** ***

Her second heartbeat has grown stronger.

She thinks about the baby growing inside her, safe and warm, serenaded by the bubbles of light. She thinks about family. The lights tell her they are her family, that she comes from them. Minuscule pinpoints of slippery pale emerald eerily caress the length of her body.

Their soporific song tells her of her mother and her mother's brother. Cloudy notions of kinship, uniformity, ancestry, and genetics seep into her mind and wait to be unraveled and understood. Willow thinks they will be waiting a long time. There is so much she doesn't know, and the lights do not like to be questioned.

The lights embrace her as family, but their song has become disorganized and atonal.

Willow closes her ears to the noise.

*** *** ***

"Sleep, baby, sleep," Gale sang. "The large stars are the sheep."

Kelly's soft hair shone in the dim light as Gale ran the brush through it. There were never any tangles. Gale always kept it smooth and neat. The deep red color was beginning to grow out and Gale could finally see the blond roots that were her gift to her baby, along with her lovely green eyes.

Her eyes had even been green at birth. That was unusual.

"The small stars are the lambs I guess.

"The bright moon is the shepherdess."

Another ten strokes and she would be done for tonight.

Gale returned the silver brush to the toiletry kit and sat gazing at her daughter. Kelly looked peaceful on her crystal bed. The henge contraption reminded Gale of a wave that was trapped in time along with her baby.

Occasional pangs reminded her she had never found Grace, but she tried not to dwell on that. It made her sad, and everything else in her life was perfect. Or would be, once she and Severin made a baby together. She looked much younger than her 54 years, and had yet to reach menopause. Gale knew it would be unusual for a woman of her advanced age to conceive, but it wasn't unheard of, and she was special. They both were. She ached to carry Severin's baby. A child they made together would unquestionably be remarkable. No one else shared their connection to the Elsewhere. They were practically royalty. Severin was always so focused. He would make a devoted father. What better way to show her love than to give him a child to carry on his legacy?

For all the years of her isolation Gale wanted nothing more than to be reunited with her Kelly and her Grace, but she had to admit now, six years after finding Kelly, that the reality had been somewhat disappointing. Certainly it was better than all the years of desperate loneliness, but Gale longed for a real baby, not a grown woman who would reject her if given the chance.

Severin stood at his workbench, soldering another domino battery out of objects he'd coaxed Gale into pulling from the Elsewhere. Her brother, so wise, instinctively knew what each item needed in order to remain in the here and now. Without his intervention they would disappear and be of no use.

The floor of the basement was a maze of Severin's handiwork. The intricate, mysterious innards of many computers stood in snaky lines, all leading to Kelly. Gale smiled, knowing the goal he worked toward was for her. He was modifying his henge contraption so they could keep Kelly safe longer. Safe and home.

Once she made a baby with Severin, Gale didn't think she'd have time to worry so much about Kelly. A real, precious, tiny baby would need her so much more. It would complete their family.

Singing the lullaby quietly again, she ran the damp cloth over Kelly's face. After making sure Severin wasn't peeking, Gale quickly washed Kelly's torso. Her belly was rather prominent now. She looked almost six months along, and Gale could sometimes see the baby moving inside, if she watched very carefully. The movements were excruciatingly slow because of the stasis field.

Tonight the angle of a tiny knee or elbow bulged on the left side. Gale placed her hand over the bump and felt its warmth and solidity. With eyes closed, Gale placed her other hand on her own stomach, under her green sweater, and remembered her own pregnancy.

Gradually the child inside Kelly shifted, and Gale imagined the movement inside her own body. Such completeness! Then it was over. The baby sank back into the darkness where it floated, waiting, and Gale felt empty.

It was good that Severin worked so hard to slow Kelly's time down even more. Otherwise, she would deliver in a few short years.

Gale kissed Kelly's forehead. She longed to tuck her baby in, but couldn't shake her fears that Kelly would disappear if covered up, like the things on Severin's table.

"Goodnight, baby," she whispered.

Treading carefully to avoid Severin's dominoes, Gale approached her brother and slid her arms around him.

"Not now, Sister. I'm at a critical point," he rebuffed.

She peered around him but could make no sense of the clutter on the table.

"How much longer?"

"I don't know."

Gale waited for more, and when none came she sat on the edge of the workbench to wait.

Severin's fingers nimbly manipulated the fine wires and bits of base metals. Gale imagined herself under his touch. A shiver of pleasure ran through her in anticipation of their coupling. She undid the top two buttons of her sweater, leaving it open to her navel.

Concentration etched her brother's stern face. Gale smiled and slipped her hand under her sweater to caress herself, imagining it his hand. He made faces like that sometimes while they made love. So focused!

A few minutes later, Gale's sweater lay behind her on the workbench and her right hand was buried between her legs. As she fingered herself, she stared at Severin, drinking him in. She never grew tired of him.

A moan slipped out and Severin glanced at her. His eyebrows lifted, but he continued working. Shortly after that he set his tools down and finally directed his full attention on Gale. She came instantly.

He chuckled.

"Dear Sister, you are a sight."

Gale panted and smiled at him.

Her pulse slowed as he placed his newest creation in its designated spot and made a few adjustments to the overall design, but quickened again when he turned back to her.

The workbench was sturdy enough to hold them, but they ended up on the floor, Gale driven over and over to the brink of climax. Severin drank deeply from her for a blissful eternity. He finally allowed her release mere moments before his own orgasm, and they swam through the surge of energy together.

***   ***   ***

1 YEAR LATER - FALL 1996

Glancing at the CV of the potential recruit he would be meeting soon, Marsh was amused to see that her name was Rain. That would make Severin's job easier, assuming she joined.

Rain Beauregard, age 17, computer savant, in an accelerated degree program that would see her with a doctorate by 22. Assuming she stayed in school. If Marsh and his colleagues could convince her to abandon her formal studies, she would be a valuable asset to the TEF.

Marsh read through her research into quantum tunneling in semiconductors until Vine poked his head through the door and announced her arrival.

"Rain, this is Marsh," said Vine. "Marsh: Rain Beauregard." He pulled the door shut as he left the office.

"Pleased to meet you," said Rain as she slung her canvas messenger bag over the back of a chair. They shook hands across the desk and she met his eye. Her self-confidence impressed Marsh. Most of the young recruits were a bit withdrawn.

"I'd like to ask you a few questions about your research before the tour, if that's okay with you," said Marsh, gesturing for her to sit.

"No problem." She sat comfortably, as if she belonged there.

"So. Quantum tunneling, huh?" Marsh began.

"It's a fascinating field."

"I hear those semiconductor things are going to be big."

Rain smiled, like a seashore breeze. "It's not mentioned there, but I'm also pursuing inquiry into superconductor phenomena."

"As a sideline?"

"Not at all. I see a great deal of synergy between semi and super. I hope to unify them, in an applied sense."

Marsh cocked his head. "Shouldn't the theoretical sense get sorted out first?"

"If you want to be old-fashioned about it."

While their conversation grew ever more geeky, Marsh studied her. She kept her light blond hair pulled back in a thick ponytail so it wouldn't be a distraction. Her hazel eyes displayed her intelligence, which Marsh suspected dwarfed his own. The no-nonsense job interview suit she wore showed that she took this seriously.

When they exhausted his quantum tunneling talking points, Marsh brought the formal interview to a close.

"With qualifications like yours, why did you choose Buckminster University over someplace like MIT?"

She smiled. "I learned of Threshold Electronics Fabrication through some patent research. After a lot of digging I discovered that your organization has a very progressive R&D philosophy, and an impressive budget, and that Buckminster is where you recruit from exclusively."

Marsh sat back in his chair, contemplative. He asked, "Are you still interested in us?"

"Give me the tour and I'll let you know."

After a quick look at the media room, offices, and dining hall on the ground floor, Marsh led Rain upstairs.

"This floor and the third have dormitories. Most new recruits share, but you'd get your own room." He considered telling her that was because she'd be their first female member, but decided maybe that wasn't a selling point.

They poked their heads into an empty single room. Rain seemed neither impressed nor disappointed. Marsh led her around the large open staircase toward the computer labs.

"How long have you been a member?" she asked.

Marsh smiled. "Eight years. I joined when I was 19 and struggling with tuition at Buck U."

"And you're happy here? Challenged?"

"Every day. Currently I'm working on a project involving neural-net impulse modulation."

Rain's entire countenance perked up with interest.

Trying not to blush Marsh said, "I can show you later, if you're interested. Here's the computer lab."

Looking into the room, Rain gasped. "You have a Cray!"

She sat down at the nearest unoccupied workstation.

"It's about 90% off-the-shelf, something NASA ordered and didn't want. The rest is enhancements we've made. Doubled the speed." Marsh hoped he didn't sound too boastful.

Rain was by this time setting up an array of complicated equations. All other work stopped as everyone else gathered around to see what she was up to. One by one, the terminal screens around the room flooded with psychedelic colors: Mandelbrot and Julia sets, Lorenz Attractors, and patterns Marsh had never seen before. They were beautiful, some like smoldering eclipses and others throbbing with writhing bands.

After about fifteen minutes, Marsh cleared his throat. Rain put all the screens back to their previous modes and made to get up, but Marsh lightly touched her shoulder to tell her to stay put. The momentary contact made him blush hotly, and he was thankful for the low light level.

With a few keystrokes he called up a scan of a notebook page covered in mad schematics. A brief text file also appeared, with sparse instructions for the recruit. Since his own initiation the folder and graph paper had been replaced with digital representations. Marsh scanned in the whole collection himself, but didn't know where the drawings had come from. Like everyone else, he originally believed them to be Severin's handiwork but had since come to be sure that wasn't true.

He felt foolish subjecting Rain to this ritual, as she was obviously the smartest person in the building. For that very reason, though, it should be worthwhile seeing what she would produce, and skipping it would make Severin cross. She had half an hour to complete the test, so Marsh absented himself to the kitchen and watched the clock.

Half an hour in the kitchen passed like two years in jail. Finally, Marsh skipped back up the stairs and fetched her to complete the tour.

He showed her the third-floor server room and more sleeping quarters. On the way out toward the converted garage, he explained that most of the hardware projects were based there, including the neural-net modulator prototype his team was building.

Marsh felt pretty good about the chances of her joining.

"Would I get my own sweater?" she asked.

"Yes."

"Are they provided? Or do I need to go on a quest to find one, or kill someone and assume their mantle?"

"They're provided," Marsh reassured quickly, not wanting to be the one she killed in her excitement.

"Okay," she said. "When would I get my name?"

"That's up to Severin."

"Severin? Why doesn't he have a theme name?"

"Because he's Severin. He's the one with the money."

Rain nodded, accepting the logic of this. "And I'm the only girl?"

"We've tried recruiting other women, they just weren't interested." It would suck if this was the reason she turned them down. Out of desperation, Marsh decided to mention Gale. "Severin's girlfriend lives here, so you wouldn't be the only woman in the house."

"I'd join anyway," she said. "This place is everything I dreamed it would be. The pure research I can do here will be so much more satisfying without constantly worrying about funding the way I would at a university. Now, show me this project of yours."

Chapter Fifteen

MAIL CALL

*Pentagon unlikely to pay up without further progress, and,
lacking the input of Miss Charm, further progress not anticipated,
so time to cut losses. Dissolve Ind Harm shell corp and find a
buyer for the devices in their current form.*
        IOTA internal memorandum, 1999

FEBRUARY 2000

Severin flipped through the day's mail without interest until he
opened a plain white envelope.

```
Dear TEF,
We have recently acquired some intriguing
merchandise that we are offering for sale to the
highest bidder. You have demonstrated an interest
in similar items in the past. If you are
interested, please respond through the usual
channels and we will provide details.
                    IOTA
```

Severin personally selected the card to send in response. At Olaf's he
located a nice shot of the Emerald City.

A week later, another letter arrived at the House.

```
Dear TEF,
The merchandise we are dealing with was developed
under a secret contract with the United States
Army. It takes the form of listening devices hidden
inside body jewelry, nipple rings, etc., for use in
assorted wetworks.
We are offering one semi-trailer of these
devices, as well as the equipment needed to receive
their signals. This is a one time only offer. The
bidding starts at $10 million.
We will schedule demonstrations for interested
parties.
                    IOTA
```

Severin took the letter to the attic and ferreted a bundle of old envelopes out of a box. He compared IOTA's letter to the ones he'd stolen from Willow's apartment years before.

What was he expecting? That they'd call themselves IOTA in one of the letters, or mention which agencies funded the project? The letters to Willow were vague, evasive even, just as he remembered. Familiar touches appeared in the text, but nothing conclusive.

It has to be the same thing! This was where the components she designed ended up.

Severin stowed all the letters back in the box while he thought things through. If there was even a slight chance these devices contained Willow's handiwork, he must look into it. Willow-authored technology would be ideal for battery creation. No more scrounging for scraps in the Elsewhere and rushing to make them permanent, and the results would be astronomically more potent.

He had to move quickly, write a check before some other bidder became interested.

But spending the money sight-unseen was irrational. The demonstration would be a wise thing. It would prove these IOTA jokers had what they claimed.

He went downstairs to talk to Cliff about their revenue outlook. It had been months since he inquired about their patent-licensing contracts, although he knew the mutual funds were healthy. If this strange proposition led somewhere, he'd need the cash on short notice.

***   ***   ***

Brad stared across his desk at the two young men in his office, who seemed to have stepped out of one of the hygiene films he remembered from elementary school. Colorful pages of their business plan covered the desk.

"What you're looking for is more of a venture-capital arrangement," Brad said. "The bank can't release such a large sum without collateral."

The men looked at one another, and both smoothed their green cardigans before the one on the right, David Clifford, spoke.

"That kind of financing takes months, if you're lucky. We need to wrap up this project right away, and we're a little overextended."

"The bank can't release such a large sum without collateral."

"It's only a couple million."

Brad raised one eyebrow.

The tall one on the left, Jay Marshall, chimed in. "Why don't you come look over our operation. It's just a few blocks from here."

Brad nodded. "Tell me about this place. What do you have there that could offset the loan?"

"Well, there's the House, the building. The building. Over 5000 square feet."

"That's a start."

"It's a beautiful place."

"What else?"

"Computers," said Mr Clifford. "We have tons of equipment—"

"Anything else? Depreciation is a major problem with computers."

The men exchanged another glance.

"This project is very important, critical, for us." Mr Marshall had taken the wheel again. "If there's anything in the business plan that wasn't clear, I'd be more than happy to go into more detail. The projections of royalties on our patents can seem confusing, for example."

"Ah," Brad said. "You could put up your rights in those patents themselves as collateral."

The two young men exchanged horrified grimaces. They shook their heads in unison.

Brad rolled his eyes.

Mr Clifford tried again. "Perhaps a quick stroll to the facility. Come in for a quick look around, and I'm sure you'll start to understand."

"I don't need to understand your lavishly illustrated plans for world domination. You need to understand about collateral. Say it with me. The bank can't release such a large sum..."

"Fine. It's clear we don't have access to anything that matters to you." He stood and began collecting their papers.

Mr Marshall stood, too, and held out a business card. "In case anything changes."

Brad rose to accept the card and show them out. There was only the company name and a phone number.

Threshold Electronics Fabrication.

***   ***   ***

5 MONTHS LATER - JULY 2000

Severin glided into the dark and deserted media room with Gale trailing behind. The huge television threw dim illumination. A young female newscaster mouthed the day's events, muted by the last ones to leave the room.

Severin tried to get a dose of breaking news every few days, almost always in the dead of night when the others had all turned in. Gale accompanied him in this, as in everything, although she rarely paid attention to the broadcasts. Careful to keep the volume low, Severin unmuted the television and settled onto the leather sofa. Gale curled up beside him.

It had been longer than usual, two or three weeks, since Severin last took any notice of world events. Bidding for Willow's crucial devices had preoccupied him, especially when it became clear another party was highly interested. Time ran out to present a larger offer, Cliff and Marsh having failed to secure a loan.

At the demonstration, Severin had become convinced he could feel a faint echo of Willow's power in the ingenious micro-transceivers hidden inside the tiny silver hoops and barbells. The conviction that Willow masterminded their design compounded both his desire to possess them and the furious sense of unfairness at their loss. No one else would fully appreciate or utilize them. No one else could be allowed to own them. Severin's efforts to learn the identity of the winning bidder had so far led nowhere. Frustration replaced all colors, all textures.

Severin rubbed his temples. However bleak the search, he would track down his rival eventually. Now he needed to pause and allow himself to be distracted for a few moments, to refresh his wits and find out what had happened while he'd been consumed.

After a few minutes of murder investigations and train derailments, the announcer told them to "Stay tuned, for financials and sports results, and the latest development in televangelist Brian Shaw's personal income tax scandal."

Gale sat up shivering as the commercials started. Severin looked at her in the low light, and she rubbed her eyes.

"Bad dream?"

She shook her head. "I don't think I was sleeping. I just got a chill all the sudden."

Severin gathered her to his side. She shivered.

The block of commercials ended, and the newscaster spoke over footage of the dapper television preacher leaving a courthouse. "You could say he never had a prayer."

With a guttural sound, Gale stood and nearly toppled.

The voiceover continued. "Popular religious broadcaster Brian Shaw testified today about his tax returns, or at least that's what he was supposed to do. Appearing without an attorney, and without any written notes, Shaw was repeatedly directed to get to the point. He attempted to launch monologues about everything from the separation of church and state to the place of Creationism in public education. Circuit Court Judge Roland Bellafranca asked flat-out if the reverend intended to produce any income records and, when Shaw instead began another unrelated speech, assessed the maximum fine on top of eleven million dollars in back taxes, plus interest. Pass the collection plate!"

Severin smirked at the televised image of Reverend Shaw with his flock of reporters, then noticed Gale crouched on the floor, one hand covering her face while the other reached for the screen. She hopped back and forth in the same bent posture, scrambled up onto the sofa where she stood on the cushions and pointed at the television. Her eyes were wild, and she kept putting one hand over her mouth. Lunging off the sofa, she wrapped her arms around her head and crawled on her knees up to the television.

"Sister!" Severin hissed, but she didn't respond. "Gale?" he tried in a softer tone.

The next segment came on, stocks and exchange rates, and Gale yelped and seized the surface of the screen.

"No!" she exclaimed, and Severin moved up behind her and put his hand on her shoulder.

"Hush, Sister. What is it?"

Gale dissolved into tears and slumped over on the rug.

Severin resumed his seat on the sofa, staring at the financial reports but thinking about the previous segment and its impact on Gale. Was she a fan of Shaw's program? That didn't track. She never mentioned the man. It wasn't the reverend's legal troubles that triggered the episode. It was his name, his image even more so.

She knew him.

The mysterious dark influence in Gale's youth. Kelly's father, and her twin's. A common, horny minister.

More correctly a rich, horny minister.

Gale's sobs slowed, interspersed with moaning.

Severin weighed this new information about Gale. Although he resisted admitting it, he could see certain parallels between himself and her erstwhile abuser. Apparently spiritual leaders were Gale's type. He wondered what else he and Shaw might have in common.

Muting the television, he stood and went to Gale. She sniffled. He scooped her up off the floor and cradled her in his arms, starting for the stairs. She burrowed into his chest, her tears spent.

Walking up the steps, Severin continued to ponder. The coincidence vexed him. Her past contained this other, and not a faceless, random stranger but a famous preacher, a TV star. What was Severin to do with this knowledge? What did Shaw signify and why wasn't his chapter over?

By the time he laid Gale in the hammock, he'd made up his mind to do some digging into Shaw's off-camera activities.

*** *** ***

Marsh paused to check the dry-erase message board on the second floor.

1. are the episodes simultaneous as well as identical?
2. what role do the devices play?
3. why does everyone agree that it's a spaceship?

The agenda for that afternoon's discussion group about the dream. The second question was always somewhere on the list, probably should be first. The third question most tempted Marsh to join this particular session.

While tracing the body jewelry since the auction ended, the TEF learned that everyone who got pierced with it began to experience the same recurring dream. TEF volunteers got pierced, and they had the same dream, too. Marsh twice taped one of the devices to his earlobe, and even that was enough to trigger it both times.

All the subjects described unmistakably the same dream Marsh had. This could be accounted for by the power of suggestion (one of yesterday's discussion topics), at least partially. Even so, it seemed odd and significant that although everyone who recounted the dream used words suggesting an undersea setting, they unanimously described the menacing vehicle descending at the end as a spaceship.

Several of the people in the House attributed the phenomenon to aliens, pointing out that maybe the dreamers all called it a spaceship simply because it was one. This faction's nominal leader was Leaf, one of the youngest members, whose guesswork/triangulation would place the extraterrestrials within the bounds of our solar system.

Fortunately, there were a few TEF members who hadn't heard any details about the dream, and didn't socialize with Leaf. One of these, Free, would soon be awake. Marsh quietly continued around to the fourth door and opened it. He ducked into the dimness within and pulled the door shut.

A bed had been moved into this storeroom, along with monitoring equipment. Oscilloscopes and computer screens provided most of the light, the windows being heavily draped. Free was a champion napper, having dropped off just past lunchtime despite the dozen electrodes attached to his forehead, arms, and chest.

"REM stage is tapering off," Rainbow whispered.

Marsh nodded, and moved around to the opposite side of the bed where Free lay wired up. Marsh picked up a small metal box from the stand beside the bed and opened it, waiting. Shortly, Rainbow gave the okay sign, and Marsh gently peeled back the tape holding the silver hoop against the side of Free's neck. By the time Free yawned and opened his eyes, the device was safely caged.

"Tell us about any dreams you can remember," Marsh said.

Free rubbed his eyes. "It was this dark, sandy place. The air felt heavy. The sky was black. I was scared. Then there were lights, a circle of weird green lights, right above me. I got more afraid. The spaceship came down out of the circle, and one of its legs held out a key for me."

Rainbow and Marsh looked at each other across the bed.

"Why would a spaceship have legs?" Rainbow asked.

Free shrugged and sat up. "I didn't think about that. I just knew it was a spaceship. It was this round, kind of lumpy, greenish thing, with legs growing out of the top and curving down. Real long legs, like a spider. And the way it came down, it was like it was hanging by a thread."

"Thank you," Marsh said. "Go get some coffee."

Once Free removed all the electrodes, pulled on his green sweater, and left, Marsh came back around to Rainbow's side of the bed. "How did the recording come out?" he inquired. The neural-net modulator was still a prototype. Not all of the sources of interference were fully understood, so getting a clear signal involved as much art as science.

"Looks crisp. I'm loading the reference waveforms." Software would perform a comparison, hunting through all the overlapping peaks and valleys in the recording of Free's dream to see if it held the same distinctive signature that appeared in the reference recordings. To create the references, three different people called up their most intense recollections of the dream. Marsh's machine, and Rainbow's software, spotted the one common thread in the tangles of neural activity.

Now they found it again in Free's recording.

"So much for the power of suggestion," Marsh muttered.

"This is so fantastic. The recording we got of the dream — Free's session was the first time we recorded the dream in real-time, instead of from memory. We should make it one of the reference waveforms. Of course, the match is so close anyway they're all pretty much interchangeable."

"Rainbow..."

"But we'll get to understand things even better in the next couple of months, and probably start to find important, subtle differences from one recording to another. We should wire up some other subjects to catch the dream again."

"Rainbow?"

"Yes?"

"Breathe. All the recording does is back up the verbal description. It's the fact that Free had no advance information about the dream that makes this a landmark."

Rainbow had been bouncing on her knees on the bed, and now sagged and pouted.

"It's still fantastic, though," Marsh added.

"The waveforms rule out interpretive bias," Rainbow asserted. "Maybe we hear what we want to hear, but pictures don't lie."

"I agree with you. Unfortunately, we're a long way from reconstructing an actual picture. It's only a squiggly line, which is only convincing to the few of us who can interpret it — and we come right back to the same credibility issue as with the verbal interview. Skeptics can say we see what we want to see. We need much more bandwidth."

"Well, like I said, another couple of months."

"Probably more like six," Marsh muttered.

"I feel optimistic."

"I am being optimistic. I have a new project…"

"Oh, no. You don't dilute your focus now, not now of all times."

"This project found me, and it has Severin all over it. I can't shrug it off."

"Maybe I can help accelerate it," Rainbow suggested.

"Quite possibly. The basic analogy is audio recording. You make a tape, and you can play it back for someone else. Only instead of sound, it's thoughts and images."

"That's ambitious. But, if we just agreed the bandwidth for image reconstruction isn't there yet, isn't it a bit too ambitious?"

"It's Severin's pet, so I think a high ambition-to-logic ratio is to be expected. However in this case, he is aware that we will not soon be able to put pictures into other people's heads. We've run some simulations and it looks like there could be tactical application nonetheless."

"'Tactical'?"

"We theorize it will be a bad-acid-trip projector. We call it the Perceptual Disruption Field. Still want to help?"

"I think I'll stay on the image reconstruction side."

"I look forward to rejoining you."

"Oh, don't be so upset." Rainbow patted the mattress, and Marsh shifted from his chair to the side of the bed. She started kneading his shoulders. "It's non-lethal, your karma's not as bad as it could be."

Marsh chuckled. "It's the dictatorial aspect. If I wanted to be told what to work on, I could be out in the regular world."

"I know how to cheer you up. Close your eyes."

Marsh's inner drive-in cued up the first reel, slightly out of focus. He felt cheered up already. Having a brilliant younger woman pursue him would do that to a guy. They'd been pretty serious for a year now and he still couldn't believe his luck. The bed moved as Rainbow hopped down. The door opened.

"No peeking!" Rainbow admonished without slowing down, and Marsh was alone at the end of the line for popcorn where he couldn't see the movie screen. He sat, eyes shut, for two minutes. He was about to go looking for her when Rainbow returned.

"Hang on a sec," she said. "Okay, open your eyes."

She held a length of monofilament fishing line, from which hung a detailed model of the spaceship from the dream. It was fashioned from a deflated basketball and the ribs of an old umbrella, the whole thing sprayed with the glow-in-the-dark paint they had in the garage workshop.

Marsh said, "I guess some of us can put pictures in other people's heads."

∗∗∗   ∗∗∗   ∗∗∗

Tom Bishop settled his imposing frame into the brown leather chair opposite Brad's desk as Brad tried to keep panic at bay. Bishop didn't look upset, so there was no reason to assume the worst. Maybe he just needed a mortgage.

They shook hands as Brad crossed the office to close the door. He tried on his VP of Lending smile but thought it wasn't at peak wattage, and so let it drop.

"What can I do for you Bishop? Is there a problem with Fin?"

Bishop exhaled loudly and said, "You never mentioned that Fin has a brother, Brad."

Brad sat behind his desk and laced his fingers together on his blotter. "Kyle? Is that important?"

With a rueful smile Bishop continued, "Omar — one of the other tenants — graduated at the end of summer semester. We had an empty room."

"Oh no." Brad recalled Melissa telling him Kyle had moved into a new apartment.

"Of course, Fin never attends house meetings, so I didn't find out who Kyle was until too late. It never occurred to me that they'd be brothers. They're utterly unalike."

Brad snorted a laugh. "That they are. Has Fin moved out?"

"No. He's adamant about that. Keeps grumbling about how Kyle won't force him out of this house, too. What's he mean by that?"

Brad sighed. "It's a long story. Let's just say Fin was never made to feel welcome by Kyle or my wife."

Bishop nodded, considering. Brad hoped he wouldn't press for details.

The worry Brad felt in the aftermath of Kyle's car accident had taken a long time to dissipate. Luckily Kyle suffered no permanent damage beyond his knee. He didn't even have a limp after the third surgery and the physical therapy, but it killed his football career. That left Kyle adrift in life and angry with the world. He dropped out of school a year before graduation and spent much of his trust fund on 'entertainment.' Brad had never seen him so vulnerable, or so similar to Fin.

Fin too dropped out of college, but only after he'd taken a full-time job doing computer graphics for *Sycamore*, a local magazine. He had never touched the money in his trust fund. Brad once snuck into Nero's, the dank basement bar he frequented in grad school, to hear Fin's band Nicotine play. The music was loud and angry, but Brad had never seen Fin happier.

Brad felt proud of his son the musician, even though he didn't care for the actual music, just as he'd felt proud of his son the athlete even though he didn't especially care about sports. But Kyle could no longer be the athlete.

For a period of two years, Brad found himself in the novel position of worrying more about Kyle than about Fin.

Then three months ago, Kyle regained his footing. His partying lessened and he started getting back in shape. At dinner on Brad's birthday came the news that he'd gotten a job working for a private security firm, something secretive he wouldn't say much about except to assure his mother he wasn't a rent-a-cop.

With both of his sons finally straightened out, living the lives that made them happy, Brad began to feel a sense of accomplishment. As difficult as life had been, they'd made it through. The only loose end was Willow, and Brad long ago learned to live without a resolution to her story, though he never stopped hoping for one.

Now came the news that all was not well with his sons after all. What should he do?

"I don't expect you to do anything about it," said Bishop. "I just thought you'd want to know, and hoped you might shed a little light."

Brad nodded. "My advice would be to keep them separated as much as possible. They'll mostly go their own ways, but they will go out of their way to antagonize each other if given the opportunity. Hopefully Kyle will move out soon. If he talks about it, don't make a big deal about the rent. I'll cover anything he owes. I'd like to see this resolved without bloodshed, if possible."

Bishop whistled quietly. "It's as bad as that, is it?"

"I'm afraid so." Brad sighed. "I never mentioned Kyle because I honestly never even considered the possibility he'd turn up at your house. He played football for Buckminster. Lived in a townhouse with a couple other athletes." Brad looked directly at Bishop. "My sons' worlds do not overlap."

"They do now," said Bishop cheerfully.

*** *** ***

An afternoon in Buckminster's immense library told Severin a lot about Reverend Brian Shaw, but little of what he saw in the periodicals deviated from the topics of the man's ministry and philanthropic activities. A near-total whitewash. Most of it written by Shaw's publicists.

The lone exception, a biography entitled *Brainwashed*, contained a detailed reconstruction of Brian Shaw's origins. He came from a mysterious, remote town in the deepest Ozarks, some fundamentalist enclave. There was a gap during Shaw's late teens, but Severin had heard all the important details of that era from Gale.

The newsworthiness of Shaw's tax difficulties appeared to be a matter of some debate, with the print journalists turning up their noses while their television colleagues dug in with gusto. It wasn't very illuminating in any case.

Now Severin stood in the attic, preparing to poll the Elsewhere about the goodly reverend in hopes of learning something useful. Previous attempts to get anything about Gale's history from the table, over the 11 years since her arrival, had been fruitless, but now Severin knew who to ask about, and would have a much straighter line of interpretation.

He lifted the corner of the sheet with his right hand, and reached in with his left.

Withdrawing his hand, he turned it over to see a tacky little gold pendant in the shape of an angel on his palm. "I know that," Severin grumbled, and began to return the unsightly thing when he noted a small detail that stopped him. He drew his hand back, raised it for closer inspection. The insipid golden creature's halo didn't match the rest of it. He knotted his brow, staring at the place where the small hoop of silver attached to the rest of the item. It was strangely constructed.

The halo was an earring.

Severin closed his fist around the angel, and felt it vanish. The earring! The jewelry! It took him several deep breaths to overcome the sense of loss over the device that had just returned to the Elsewhere. He told himself it probably hadn't been functional, merely representational. He opened his empty hand.

Shaw's tax troubles were a smokescreen to hide the diversion of ministry funds to outbid the TEF on the jewelry.

Severin paced the attic. His new adversary and Gale's old tormentor, the same person. Clearly not a person to be underestimated, but Severin had the critical advantage now. Shaw surely forgot about Gale years ago, and didn't know of the TEF as the other bidder for the devices. He certainly didn't realize his own daughter had designed the jewelry's miraculous insides.

What was his interest in Willow's masterpiece?

Severin needed more information, fresh intelligence about the shape of Shaw's plans and the scope of his operation. He had to get inside.

He'd need to send someone inside.

Severin marched down the stairs to find Marsh.

Chapter Sixteen

Listening Post

*Reverend Brian Shaw, father of Shaw Ministries, was found dead
in his home yesterday of an apparent heart attack at the age of
sixty-five. His body was discovered after he failed to appear as
scheduled for the Sunday morning broadcast. He had been dead
for several days. The future of the Ministries' works is unclear and
a successor is yet to be named.*
Webster Daily Press, 10-2-2000

FALL 2000

"At this point, we have no idea where the cache is. We know only
that it's no longer at Shaw's compound in Donner." Marsh didn't add
that it would still be there if Severin had listened to him three weeks ago
when Truth first expressed his concerns about Shaw. Or that Truth
would be safely home.

Three months ago, Severin insisted someone from the TEF be
insinuated into Shaw Ministries, because he was convinced that was
where the secret technology ended up. Getting Truth in had not been
difficult, which made it all the more surprising when he confirmed
Severin's assertion. Marsh kept expecting Severin to come to his senses,
and get their man out of there, but that never happened.

A button camera Truth planted outdoors during his second week at
Shaw Ministries showed a fleet of trucks departing late the previous
night. Truth had not been heard from in four days, which wasn't all that
abnormal, but taken with the sudden mobilization under cover of
darkness, and the business wire stories about a rash of firings from
Shaw's personal staff, it fit into a distressing pattern.

Severin nodded impassively. "He'll keep leaking them into the supply chain, he needs the test data. We can still obtain samples at the point of sale."

Marsh felt his hands clench into fists. He turned to leave.

"Your team will have a new focus," Severin announced, as if to an enthralled audience and not one person's departing back. "We must learn where Shaw has taken the devices, and what steps he has taken to protect them. He'll be on his guard now."

*** *** ***

"The lamb is sleeping on the green," Gale crooned softly as she ran the silver brush through Kelly's hair. This at least was still a pleasure. Severin was always so preoccupied. "With wool so soft and warm and clean. Sleep baby sl—"

A surge of energy like a wave of gelatinous air rocked Gale back and almost toppled her off the slab of seasick-white stone and onto the trailing lines of domino batteries. A gentle popping sound accompanied the surge.

Gale dropped the hairbrush which was vibrating like a tuning fork, and looked at Severin. Half a moment later the wave hit him and he turned from his workbench, a look of surprise on his face.

The wave emanated from Kelly. Nothing like that had ever happened before. Gale was suddenly terrified, shaking. What if Severin's latest modification went wrong?

Severin looked concerned too. He set his tools down, and took one hesitant step toward the slab. Behind him, the domino he'd been working to stabilize vanished.

Gale stood and leaned on Severin for support. He didn't ask her if she was okay. He only stared at Kelly. Gale stared too.

Between Kelly's legs a trickle of fluid sluggishly pooled. Gale leaned closer and recognized the sweet, earthy smell immediately. Amniotic fluid.

"Is it urine?" Severin asked.

Gale relished her secret knowledge for a moment, but knew she had to share it quickly or he would figure it out for himself.

"No. Her water broke."

Severin said nothing.

"She's going into labor."

"Damn." He glanced at his workbench and swore again when he saw that his domino was gone.

The baby would be here soon. Gale reached out and laid her right hand on Kelly's distended abdomen.

Severin never talked about the baby. He only ever seemed concerned about Kelly and his infernal henge contraption. Always wanting to perfect her stasis. The burst of energy that accompanied the bursting of her water demonstrated how imperfect the stasis was. Who knew what effect the contractions would have. She might even wake up.

And Gale would be forgotten.

Nauseated, Gale turned away from Kelly.

Her dream of a perfect family life with Severin collapsed like a sandcastle in the encroaching tide. What was she going to do?

Kelly will ruin everything if she wakes up.

***   ***   ***

Marsh sat on the wooden porch swing, slowly arcing forward and back as he watched the pedestrian traffic down at the intersection. It had now been over a week since they'd heard from Truth, which caused Marsh untold guilt and worry, some of which spilled over into his personal life. There was no reason to think Shaw would cause trouble at the piercing parlor in Webster, in fact he had every reason to avoid drawing attention to any of his distribution sites, but Marsh fretted anyway.

Pale autumn sunlight struggled through the low bank of clouds. Right on cue, there she was, rounding the corner. His own personal Rainbow. Marsh smiled and waved. She waved back, her blond hair and green cardigan a stark contrast to the gray day.

He met her at the sidewalk with a hug and silently escorted her up the porch stairs and through the front door. Neither of them spoke, but

Rainbow lifted her sweater and blouse to reveal her navel, red and bandaged from a recent piercing.

Marsh blew it a kiss before they walked into the kitchen. The quiet murmur of those lingering over coffee ceased upon their entrance. Everyone gathered around to get a look at Rainbow's navel, and Branch joined Marsh and Rainbow as they left through the back door.

In silence, the threesome crossed the expansive back yard to the garage. Marsh unlocked the door, and relocked it once they were all inside. Rainbow unlocked the next door, and Branch raised the trapdoor to the stairs. Down in the basement beneath the garage they were finally free to speak.

"Did she have it?" Branch asked.

Rainbow's answer needed to wait as she reached into her mouth and pulled the tiny silver barbell out of her tongue. She handed it to Marsh, who placed it in a small metal box.

"Yes! Talisman Tattoo had our backs. It's probably the only silver-and-turquoise left in town. I was lucky." As she finished speaking, Rainbow took a second, smaller barbell from Marsh and stuck it in her tongue in place of the first.

"I really admire the lengths you're willing to go to for the organization, Rainbow," Branch said. Marsh was damn proud of her, too, but knew she was tired of hearing it.

"Yeah, well, the whole physical pain part is easy. It's the ditz routine I need to affect that bothers me. 'Like, wow, y'know?'"

Marsh gave her a peck on the cheek and moved over to the workbench.

Rainbow took her sweater off and tossed it onto a stool. She pulled up the ridiculous hippie blouse and prodded at the bandage on her belly.

"This part sucks."

She gingerly pulled the bandage off with one hand while holding her blouse out of the way with the other, staring at the silver ornament in her navel with consternation.

"I'll help," Marsh said.

While Rainbow grimaced and swore, Marsh deftly removed the ring and replaced it with the dummy Branch prepared earlier. He handed the new jewelry off to Branch, re-sterilized Rainbow's navel, and put a fresh bandage on it.

Branch was already on the intercom, calling for his cohorts to come look at his new prize.

"The broadcast was disappointing," Marsh said. "It's hard to get a good signal off a tongue piercing."

Rainbow put her cardigan back on and leaned against him, while he stroked her blond hair. "I think the piercer's had the dream, even though she wouldn't say anything about it. It freaked her out."

*** *** ***

In the downtown listening post, Marsh sat at his desk, headset clamped to his ear. Rainbow, Shale, and Free sat at their own desks, similarly occupied.

The TEF thought it best to keep surveillance activity related to the jewelry and Reverend Shaw offsite to protect the organization. They rented a place in the basement of a building that housed a used record store called Dogstar, an art supply shop called Olaf's, and the offices of *Sycamore*, the Buckminster University alumni magazine. The small room was perfect: cheap, nondescript and relatively inaccessible. The entrance was located behind a ramshackle chain link fence off an alley with no other business entrances.

Three days ago a stranger walked into this hidden office. Consensus was that it was a random occurrence, but to be on the safe side the team had been monitoring the intruder constantly. Now it was Marsh's turn.

The report from the night before lay in front of him and he read through it again. Buck's usual meticulousness was in evidence. Their boy got lucky. Ten pages detailed flirtations that led quickly to sex. Lots of sex. Buck had gotten quite creative in his description of the noises they made.

Listening to the two of them eating breakfast now, Marsh wondered how different the sex could have sounded.

The only interesting thing was that the mark's new lady friend happened to be the body piercer at Talisman Tattoo, the shop where Rainbow got their samples. Could that be a coincidence? Marsh thought of Rainbow in potential danger and concentrated on his work again.

Slurping coffee. Clinking silverware. A second order of French toast. Would this breakfast never end?

The man with the unlikely name Fin Tanner said, "Speaking of cults, I saw something strange… three days ago."

He's going to tell her about us!

But the topic was immediately dropped.

Marsh made a careful entry in the logbook and noted the time.

A short while later the couple began talking about dreams. Specifically *the* dream. The piercer was a reporter, investigating said dream. How could the TEF not have known she was a reporter?

While the pair rambled on about the Buckminster University budget, Marsh made a quick decision.

"Rainbow, take Shale and Free in the van. Your body piercer friend is at the Shamrock right now with her new boyfriend. We need to bring her in."

Rainbow and the two men stood, pulling off their headsets.

"Rainbow drives. Do it like we practiced. Scenario 2."

All three nodded, pulled on their sweaters, and left.

Marsh called Threshold House and alerted them to the incoming package before bending back to his listening post.

The girl was poking her nose in all the wrong places. So far she wasn't onto anything that would harm his organization. Just enough, he hoped, to draw the attention of their main rival. With any luck at all, she would be abducted by them and taken to their new headquarters. The TEF would use the tracking device they were about to plant in her jewelry to find that headquarters. Then they could take possession of the entire cache of covert jewelry and Rainbow would no longer need to sacrifice herself to gather stray samples.

Marsh was feeling smug until over the headset he heard Fin Tanner say, "The other day, I was trying to avoid a coworker and I ended up in this weird basement office below Dogstar."

How fast could a person abandon the outpost, working alone? Marsh knew he needed to find out.

*** *** ***

Brad paced along the yellow police tape, watching the fire department's bombardment dampen the smoldering ruins of the block that once contained Fin's workplace. Crews were exploring the wreckage in search of remains or trapped survivors, and so far had not found any of either.

He'd been talking to an important client at the bank when the blast occurred. The building lurched, giving all his office furniture a moment of fidgety life. The vault alarm tripped. Brad hurried downstairs expecting to see the lobby filled with debris and gun-toting robbers, but everything seemed normal apart from the alarm ringing on the wall, and the alarm on all the faces. Several minutes after it happened, someone coming in from the street informed them of the explosion's location.

Brad didn't remember leaving the bank. He did recall the emergency vehicles howling past him along the way. Most of the *Sycamore* staff had congregated in a nearby parking lot, but Fin wasn't among them. None of them recalled Fin showing up for work in the first place.

Brad punched the boarding house's number into his cellphone, hoping Fin or Kyle would pick up. Or Bishop. That might even be better, assuming Fin was asleep in his bed and knew nothing of this and Kyle would be pissy over being asked about Fin, and wouldn't know or care about his brother's whereabouts anyway.

Nobody answered.

***

As helicopter footage of the collapsed buildings played on the evening news, Brad called the hospital. They claimed no one named Fin Tanner had been admitted, and wouldn't tell him much else. The hospital desk echoed the televised accounts in stating there had been no critical injuries in the incident.

Brad hung up and his phone rang.

"Fin?"

"Brad, this is Bishop."

An icicle rammed through Brad's gut.

Bishop continued, "Fin's fine. He got checked over, and they thought maybe there's a chance of a concussion, so they kept him in the emergency ward for a while. That's all. He's supposed to call me for a lift when they say he can go."

The icicle melted, sloshing warm relief over Brad. "Thanks for calling, Tom. I got the run-around when I called. And nobody had seen Fin. I know how it is with him, but still, under the circumstances..."

"He's fine."

"Possible concussion, you said?"

"They're just being careful. You know, lawsuits. Do you want him to call you when he gets home?"

Yes.

"Brad? Do you want me to ask Fin to call you?"

Brad drew a deep breath. "Just let him know I called."

✳✳✳   ✳✳✳   ✳✳✳

Marsh smoothed his green sweater and picked a small bit of lint off the waistband. He knocked on the basement door. Nausea lurked as he waited for a reply. It was well-known in the House that when Severin was in the basement he was not to be disturbed. Marsh hoped his news warranted the interruption.

He was about to knock again when the door opened a crack and a bright green eye peered up at him.

"Hello, Gale. Sorry to interrupt." Marsh tried to convey gravity in his tone. "Could you please tell Severin I urgently need to speak with him. Urgently."

The green eye stared at him and he stared back. Finally she closed the door and Marsh could hear her start down the steps. He leaned on the edge of one of the large tables and waited.

When Marsh heard Severin's stomping tread on the stairs he steeled himself and straightened to his full height, wanting to be less easily intimidated.

Severin came through the door and closed it behind himself. He glared at Marsh. "Well?"

"Earlier today we planted a trace on our pet body piercer. She has since been taken to the reverend's new headquarters. We know where they are."

As he spoke, Marsh watched Severin's expression change from supreme irritation to feverish excitement. He even smiled a little.

"How's the PDF working?"

"Vine is loading the primary unit into van number three right now. His team is preparing the broadcast dishes in the other vans. They expect to be ready within two hours."

Severin rubbed his hands together. "Leave as soon as everything is ready. I need all that jewelry."

Marsh nodded. "There is some bad news."

Severin looked at him, waiting.

"The outpost has been destroyed. The entire block exploded. Gas leak."

"Gas leak?" Severin asked, incredulous.

"They found us," Marsh confirmed, "but we had enough heads-up to get everything out. I think they blew it up out of spite."

*** *** ***

Three vans pulled into the detached garage along the alley, arriving singly a few minutes apart. They took separate routes on their return from the factory, to draw less attention and confuse potential pursuers. None had been followed.

After observing the third van's arrival, Severin went downstairs to meet the team leader in the dining room. He paced until Marsh came through the back door.

"Yes," Marsh said immediately, raising his hand to forestall

Severin's rush of questions. Impudent, but as it appeared the raid had been successful Severin abided. Marsh pulled out a chair and sat wearily. Severin loomed, impatient.

"We got it all. It's being unloaded now. No pursuit, and we've followed signal containment procedures the whole way. We weren't tracked."

"You're absolutely certain that no one tailed you?"

"No one was in any condition to give chase. The PDF was highly effective."

"Any casualties?"

Marsh raised his eyebrows, and took a long moment to answer this simple question. "Buck will need stitches, and probably has a concussion."

"Mercenaries?" Severin asked.

Marsh grinned. "No, in fact. It was the petite body piercer we tagged to find the factory. She escaped during the confusion, shielded from the PDF just as we intended." The grin dropped. "But on her way out, she beat up Buck pretty badly. She's not someone to treat lightly."

"Buck was the only injury to your team?"

"Affirmative. We saw some self-inflicted damage among the reverend's mercenaries, and there was one fatality."

Now Severin raised his eyebrows. Marsh again took a long time to speak.

"Shaw."

Severin pulled out a chair for himself. This could get serious. Plus, on a certain level he admired Shaw, thought him a worthy opponent.

"How?"

Marsh shook his head. "He was in his office, alone, not a mark on him. It could have been his own people, or some other faction. Additional people were seen departing, besides the piercer. She had two men with her — they stole a truck from Shaw's motor pool. A black car also left, number of occupants unknown."

Severin was suddenly angry. "So someone was in a condition to follow!"

"They all left ahead of us," Marsh protested feebly. He firmed up. "We were very careful. No one tailed us."

Severin paced, unsure when he had stood up. "It's critical that no forensic evidence points back to the TEF. Shaw's death will be investigated thoroughly."

Marsh nodded. "No prints, I'm sure of that. I'll have Vine and Rainbow keep tabs on the police, so we'll know if there's any reason for concern. I don't think we need to worry."

Severin folded his arms. "Why not?"

Marsh yawned. "Shaw had a lot of secrets. I don't think whoever takes over for him will want it all exposed."

Secrets, Severin mused. Marsh was probably right. *Secrets prefer to stay hidden.*

Chapter Seventeen

Y<small>AHOO</small> S<small>EARCH</small>

*We have a lead on the theft of the jewelry. I cross-referenced the
lease on that basement office in Webster with some of the late
reverend's notes, and one outfit came up — Technological
Evolution Front. Reconnaissance has been initiated. You will
have the tactical report by tomorrow.*
Samaritan Security Agency internal briefing #AB3829

Brad gazed uneasily at the computer monitor. His wife had done a
Yahoo search for untraceable poisons.

That can't be good.

Following the same links she had, he discovered how infeasible such
poisons were. This failed to reassure him.

Brad had long suspected Melissa was unhappy with him. Or maybe
disappointed. Frustrated? Disgruntled. That had the right feel to it.
Disgruntled workers carried guns, or torched their workplaces. They
harbored underlying, undiagnosed grievances.

His wife was disgruntled.

He didn't know why. Of course they'd had their ups and downs
during their 25 years together, but now with the boys out of the house
and no other distractions, he devoted most of his time to her. Things
should be better than ever. Instead his wife was no longer gruntled.

Brad wondered how long he'd last.

Melissa wasn't the only disgruntled one. Fin fit that category too,
but might change his tune if he knew he was in concordance with
Melissa. More likely he would choose a synonym, an uglier way of
saying it, something messier than Mel would admit to. That left Kyle. As

far as Brad knew, Kyle was completely gruntled. He had no respect for Brad, but that wasn't the same thing. It didn't lead to homicide.

In all honesty, Brad couldn't claim a whole helluva lot of gruntlement for himself either. This discovery about Melissa's secret feelings suggested a chicken-and-egg argument. Which one of them wandered out of gruntlehood first? Who led whom? Or was it pushing? A furtive shove every now and then.

"Brad."

His femme fatale stood in the doorway. He smiled at her, using his best high-wattage, you'll-love-making-the-payments-every-month smile from the bank.

"Hi, babe."

"What are you doing to my computer?"

He tried to decide if her annoyance was anything out of the ordinary, and couldn't.

"My printer's out of ink," he said and started printing a batch of spreadsheets, relegating the browser to the background.

Was she studying him, trying to figure out if he knew? Brad turned the smile down several notches and studied her in return.

She kept her glossy hair short now, but it was still the same rich honey color. He avoided her vivid green eyes and concentrated on her mouth, the lips turned down in a slight frown.

"Don't get too wrapped up in work stuff right now. Dinner's nearly ready."

Brad kept his smile steady, trying not to show any notice of the chill trickle of sweat running down his temple. "Okay. I'll be right down."

Melissa sketched a tight grin and withdrew.

Dinner. Brad's smile ran off to hide.

He brought those web pages back up and rechecked the information, now finding it even less reassuring. A poison wouldn't have to be untraceable to kill him. Even to serve as a murder weapon, it could be perfectly detectable so long as its effects mimicked a coronary, or if the body were damaged or arranged in a misleading manner.

So, already I'm 'the body.'

Brad closed up all the files and shut down Melissa's computer. He snatched the printouts as an afterthought and scrawled some notes in the margins, crossed out a few figures, and fanned them on his own desk.

The roast smelled delicious. Melissa must have it out by now, resting before she sliced it. The carrots, potatoes and onions might already be dished.

To be in character, he should stay up here absorbed in 'work stuff' until she called him. To deviate might arouse her suspicions. What the hell. The game aroused Brad.

Brad hurried down to the kitchen where two empty plates sat on the counter, and the roasting pan, laden with the full complement of root vegetables and beef, sat on top of the stove. His wife stood at the island, dishing salad. She looked up shrewdly at his approach.

"Smells fantastic!" Brad proclaimed, striding past the speechless Melissa to inhale the steam coming off the main course. "Shall I carve?"

She turned to follow his progress and now stood with her back to the island, tossing an invisible salad and blinking. Brad flashed the good smile and picked up the carving utensils.

"Yes. Sure." She glanced around for a moment as if to relocate the wily salad.

Brad worked quickly, releasing thin slabs of pink beef. He moved them to the plates individually, alternating until each plate held four identical slices.

"Looks like leftovers for a month." He paused for another hearty sniff. "But I don't mind."

He selected the vegetables from random locations in the pan, again alternating in their placement on the plates. Melissa stared at him over her shoulder, the salads all but ignored. Brad bobbed his eyebrows and winked.

"I'll help carry." Before Melissa gave a response, Brad sidestepped her, snatched both salad bowls, and twirled into the dining room. He had the bowls placed before Melissa appeared in the doorway holding the plates. Brad stood behind her chair, waiting to push it in.

"Get the wine." Melissa set the plates down but made no move to sit.

Brad nodded, still beaming, and hurried back into the kitchen. He mopped his brow on his sleeve before picking up the bottle. Then he needed the corkscrew and two glasses, meaning Melissa was alone with the food for about ten seconds.

She stood at the corner of the dark cherry table, equidistant from both ladder-back chairs, not looking at him. Brad set the wine glasses on the table and fumbled with the corkscrew. On the wall opposite him hung Melissa's only concessions to art. Most art annoyed her, but Brad had won her over once and spent a great deal of money on these two rather large, rather ugly originals by an allegedly well-known American post-modernist. The purple one was called *letitia - i grow weary* and the yellow one *9 views of kilimanjaro - #2 subaqueous* for unknown reasons. Each was three feet square, framed in clear acrylic, and a glossy solid color. In all honesty, they looked like the allegedly well-known American post-modernist did them with spray paint.

Generally they hung there on the wall, behind Melissa so she wouldn't have to look at them, and mocked Brad. Tonight they earned their keep. Or at least *letitia* did. Reflected in the glassy purple surface, Brad had a clear view of Melissa. He was careful not to meet her eyes, but instead watched her hands as his own took up the corkscrew and opened the wine bottle with practiced ease.

The poison could be in the wine.

Keeping his eye furtively on Melissa, Brad raised the bottle and sniffed. Heady and piquant, with a hint of mellow oaky insouciance.

Maybe she coated one of the glasses with something. Brad had to glance away from her in order to pour, so he made it worth his while, filling both glasses to the rim.

"Brad. You'll spill it on the rug!"

Pleased at getting a reaction from her, if not a confession, Brad re-corked the bottle and slid the glasses to the table settings. Melissa shook her head, and lit the candles with a wooden match. Maybe it was some sort of airborne poison, but then she would get a dose too. Maybe she didn't care.

While she shook out the match, Brad sat down in her usual chair. She glared at him. "I don't know what's gotten into you tonight."

"Nothing has, so far. I'm starved." He stabbed a large chunk of potato, saluted her with it, got no reaction, and stuck the whole thing in his mouth. A little mealy, but otherwise okay. Brad chewed carefully before swallowing. No need to choke to death and end the game so quickly.

Melissa sat in his chair and took a hefty gulp of wine. She began to daintily cut up and eat her roast. Brad watched her, but she wasn't hesitant about any of the food. He relaxed a little.

Their dinner conversation amounted to chit chat about the office and a halfhearted attempt on Brad's part to find out how his wife felt about her life. He asked her if she would like her own car, maybe something sporty, or an SUV. She declined. Did she want to go back to school? Or maybe look for a more rewarding job than the one she held at the bank? No and emphatically no, thank you very much, please stop talking now Brad, I have a headache.

Once the plates were cleared, Brad thought he was safe, at least for tonight, but Melissa surprised him with coffee and a platter of macaroons from Piedmont's.

He loved Piedmont's coconut macaroons.

While Melissa stood at the counter, pouring coffee, Brad put his arms around her from behind and nuzzled her neck.

"Brad! I'll spill."

"I love you, Mel."

She set the coffee pot down and looked at him suspiciously. When was the last time he'd said those words to her? It was something he felt he ought to say, perhaps to mollify her, but he didn't mean it. Not anymore. Not for a long time.

Mustering his courage, Brad took a bite of cookie, chewed

thoroughly, and swallowed. He washed it down with a sip of coffee and utterly failed to keel over. In a way it was a shame. Piedmont's coconut macaroons would have been a helluva way to go.

*** *** ***

Tightening.

It's as if the darkness is becoming thicker, less flexible. But only around her belly. Its constriction takes her breath. The lights surrounding her seethe in angry, virulent greens, their music deep and dangerous.

The lights are frightened. The pressure is nothing they've experienced before. Their voices, confused and slight, are quickly dampened by the solidifying darkness. Willow cannot understand them.

Her heartbeats keep time, but she forgets to count them. She thinks she might be descending, slowly sinking through a denser, warmer layer of darkness. She wonders what the bottom will feel like when she finally reaches it.

Tighter and tighter, and then release. Willow watches the lights grow paler, and then white, tinking and plinking.

Her toes don't touch anything yet. She's still not at the bottom.

*** *** ***

"Banker's hours they say. They obviously aren't bankers."

Brad gave Melissa a sly glance, but she had her head turned away. Staring out the passenger-side window, or regarding her own dim, distorted reflection. Outside was full dark between chill puddles of sickly streetlight.

He swallowed as he returned his attention to the road. "Should I take the left at Myrtle? Get Chinese?"

"I was going to heat up the casserole from Sunday," Melissa replied to the window.

Sunday's casserole. *Casserole? Wasn't it meatloaf?* Well, he'd survived eating it, regardless. Of course, if she wanted to get his guard down it wouldn't be too hard to taint the dish on the second pass. If she was trying to trick him it would mean she noticed his reluctance to eat her cooking. It wouldn't make sense for her to pass up an opportunity like Sunday. She had no guarantee he'd ever accept food from her again.

If she meant to poison him, though, it would be pointless to base any decisions on what made sense. Why had he let that so-called casserole happen? His own actions weren't making sense.

"But if you're in the mood for Chinese, go ahead."

∗∗∗   ∗∗∗   ∗∗∗

Melissa pushed the remains of her lo mein around the plate with her fork and eyed the two fortune cookies on the tray with the bill. Which one would Brad take? Meaning, which fate would he foist onto her?

Not a rational way of looking at things, she realized. They were just fortune cookies, not even authentically Chinese. No ancient wisdom for her. Besides, ever since she'd overheard Kyle and his football buddies talking about them, back when he was in high school, she couldn't ever read one without mentally adding 'in bed' at the end.

Many friends make good times *in bed*.

Be open to new experiences *in bed*.

It is better to give than to receive *in bed*.

Kyle and his friends found this hilarious, and Melissa had to admit it could occasionally be amusing. But not lately, because lately in bed she wasn't doing much of anything besides sleeping. Brad was so insufferably present all the time. By the time they got to bed she wanted nothing to do with him, but when she thought about spending time away from him, she felt like she was drowning.

Her life had become impossible. With Brad and without him.

Brad scooped up the dregs of his pork fried rice and sat back with his miniature tea cup. At this rate it would take him forever to pick a cookie. This time she would get to do the fortune foisting.

Melissa chose the cookie closer to Brad and cracked it open.

"It's blank."

"You get to write your own future," Brad said. He pried the remaining cookie open. "Hey, I got two!"

Bastard.

"A mysterious stranger will soon enter your life."

In bed.

Melissa fumed in silence and waited to hear the other one, but Brad started eating his cookie.

"What's the other one say?" she asked in a falsely cheerful voice.

"Mmmf glumf," Brad mumbled. He swallowed a gulp of tea and started again. "Your wife is beautiful and you are the envy of others." He smiled.

"What? It doesn't say that." Melissa took the slip of paper from him and read it. "A mysterious stranger will soon enter your life."

"Doubles." Brad shrugged. "I guess some people I've never met will come to me and ask me to lend them large sums of money. Good thing I've got the training to handle just that sort of situation."

He obviously thought he was being funny, so Melissa chuckled. Nothing like Loan Department humor. Thank god.

"Maybe the strangers will be at the party Friday."

Brad looked frantic. "Are we having a party?"

Melissa sighed. "No, Brad. Cocktails and hors d'oeuvres at the Shiny Octopus."

He stared at her, slowly tilting his head to the left in the apparent hopes that the marbles inside would roll into the proper holes. She watched for several seconds, wondering how far he could physically go, but decided she didn't want to know. His head might pop right off, and then what would she do? Plunk it in the freezer? She wasn't ready for that yet, had more research to do. She'd better help him out.

"The awards dinner for the small business incubator."

All the marbles found their homes and his face lit up. "Oh, yeah. That should be a lot of fun."

He didn't sound sarcastic. Melissa shook her head.

"Tomorrow night let's grab a quick dinner out," said Brad, "then we can go shopping."

"Shopping?" This was unprecedented.

"I think I need new dress shoes. Maybe a new belt. And you're always saying I need to update my ties."

Melissa stared.

"You can look at dresses if you want. I'll even hold your purse."

If they went to the mall, she could get a break from him, without being too far away.

Melissa smiled for real.

*** *** ***

One superfluous pair of glossy black, size 12 dress shoes later, Brad wandered around the men's department of Whitman & Partridge. The fussy salesman was keeping his purchases at the counter. Besides the shoes, Brad chose a belt, undershirts, black dress socks, and five colorful silk ties. Nothing he actually needed, but he was killing time until Melissa came to get him. This excursion was a convenient excuse to avoid eating her cooking again, but now he had to make good and buy stuff.

They would be here until the mall closed. That's how it was when Melissa got to trying things on. Brad wondered if he could catch part of a movie. The theatre was right next door to Whitman & Partridge, down on the first floor. He checked his watch. Already 8:30. Maybe he should browse the suits and sport jackets, or look for a new overcoat.

My life is so damn boring.

Except it wasn't anymore. His wife was plotting to poison him. That wasn't boring at all. If his life was going to be exciting, he might as well spice up his wardrobe, too.

Brad surreptitiously crossed the invisible border between the stodgy old guy department and the hip Gen-X department.

Whitman & Partridge weren't known for their cutting-edge fashions, but Brad felt quite rebellious anyway. Maybe next time he'd be really daring and go to the Gap.

He chose a black leather jacket, a pair of motorcycle boots, sunglasses, three pairs of cargo pants, a dozen assorted bulky sweaters and long-sleeve pullovers, and a shiny, monochromatic shirt-and-tie combo.

Feeling reckless, and vowing not to get his hair cut for the foreseeable future, Brad went back to the loafer department to pay for everything and wait for his murderess.

Beside his chair stood a sale table overflowing with cardigans. Blue ones, gray ones, green ones, red ones. Buy one get one free. Brad counted them like sheep until Melissa arrived, carrying a single shopping bag.

"Brad?" She looked bewildered, scanning his small mountain of packages.

"Ready to go?" he asked. As he stood, he bumped the sale table, sending an avalanche of sweaters to the ground.

Melissa rolled her eyes and crossed her arms.

Brad scooped the sweaters up and dumped them back onto the table. One of the green ones had landed in the bag with his leather jacket. The thought of shoplifting gave Brad an unaccustomed thrill, but he dutifully pulled the cardigan out and tossed it with the others. It didn't go with his new, midlife-crisis look.

If Mel had her way, it would be more like a dead-man-walking look. Midlife would have been when he met her.

Shaking her head, Melissa led him toward the escalator. "What in the world did you buy? You said you needed shoes."

***   ***   ***

Severin held the fine silvery loop between his thumb and forefinger, calling up an image of the schematics Willow drew for its elaborate innards. He placed it back on the dark gray bed of foam rubber alongside dozens of others like it, nodded to the two sweater-clad technicians, and climbed the ladder to street level.

Most of the liberated jewelry waited up here in the main part of the garage because the hidden lab below wasn't ready to handle volume. Stacks of foil-wrapped cartons covered most of the work areas and crowded the already tight aisles. Severin closed the hatch and rolled the rug back over it.

Three technicians wearing lightweight headsets sat on tall stools, poring over oscilloscopes. They pretended not to notice Severin's reappearance, probably due to the way he growled at them earlier to keep their minds on their work. He surveyed the narrow, overcrowded room and cursed under his breath. He'd have to shift a mound of cartons to reach a position where he could see any of the readouts, or else interrupt someone to get a progress report. He tried to decide which was less undignified.

Two sets of headlights played over the windows, followed by the sounds of gunning engines and tires skidding on the alley's loose gravel outside. Everyone looked up, then at each other.

The door burst inward with a rush of armed men wearing black ski masks and black fatigues. The first one in pointed his gun at the technician nearest the door, shouting "Over there! Move! Up against the wall!" The next two gunmen filed in and took positions beside the first, each with his gun leveled at a different technician. Two more, also brandishing guns, brought up the rear and seized stacks of boxes and dashed back outside, returning quickly for more.

The three sweaters had their hands up, unable to get to the wall where the aggressors wanted them, although a path would soon be cleared. No one had yet addressed Severin, or aimed a firearm at him, so he stood still on top of the hatchway and watched the robbery unfold. These were certainly the preacher's mercenaries coming to take back their treasure.

After the first minute, with more than half the cartons left inside, the gunmen showed anxiety. They shifted their feet and shot glances at each other. One of the three on guard duty joined in carrying the booty outside, and the one who'd entered first grunted at a technician to help them load. Pale and sweating, the tech looked at Severin.

Severin gave a tiny nod, wanting to keep attention off himself. The sweater stumbled toward a stack of boxes, hands still up, eyes riveted to Severin. The sentries tilted their heads, and both slowly shifted their aim to Severin.

For ten long seconds Severin stared at the space between the guards, while the rest of the attackers and one of his Followers scurried in and out and the piles of Willow's electronics shrank. As long as the underground lab remained secret, they wouldn't get it all. The plundering continued as the guards turned back to the cowering technicians.

Another minute passed, and with all the most grabbable boxes already grabbed, the four men unloading the garage often impeded one another, especially at the doorway. Tension showed in the armed men's movements. Every moment made it worse, and added to the chance for someone downstairs to reveal their presence.

"Horn," Severin said to the technician who'd been pressed into enemy service. The sentries tensed and locked back onto Severin. Horn froze, agony in his eyes.

Severin spoke softly but firmly. "Shift the stacks toward the door. You stay inside and organize the boxes so they can be loaded more efficiently. Teamwork."

Horn looked at the sentries, one of whom shrugged.

With Horn acting in this new role, the raid's efficiency increased. Another thirty seconds and the whole of the upstairs cache was depleted.

The tallest of the hooded men strode in and aimed his weapon at each of the Green Sweaters in turn, then at Severin. Turning his head he asked, "Is that all of it?"

Horn blanched even paler, which scarcely seemed possible, and his eyes darted over to Severin. Severin met his stare, willing the perspiring man to keep silent.

One of the other mercenaries answered, though, saying, "Yeah, that's it. Let's move."

The tall one let out a barking laugh as he angled his gun upward, raking the ceiling with a stream of bullets. Within the confined space, the gun's report and muzzle flash were devastating. All the men in black looked at the one who'd fired, as his laughter diminished to a childish giggle. Two of the others released celebratory salvos through the ceiling as well, knocking out one fluorescent fixture in a shower of glass and sparks, before all five hastened out the door and sped off.

Severin's technicians crouched behind their workbenches. Someone was sobbing. An acrid blue haze permeated the room. Severin stood on the hatch for another minute before he stepped to the side and opened it. Peering down, he saw two terrified faces.

"Gentlemen," Severin said, "the devices in your lab have gone up inestimably in value."

***   ***   ***

Melissa sat on the foot of the bed, listening to Brad's gentle snoring in absolute blackness. Lately he'd become so much more attentive. He helped out in the kitchen, when he even allowed her to cook. He talked to her, asked about her day. Agreed with her opinions.

Obviously, he suspected something.

Brad had been messing with her computer, so she could guess what he suspected. Poison was old news. Now, it could serve as a decoy.

Melissa stood and walked quietly to the dresser. She placed her hand on the pull of her underwear drawer, and took a deep breath.

If Brad paid any attention to her credit card bill, if Brad paid her credit card bill, he might have more current cause for alarm. She opened the drawer.

Finding a source had been the tough part. Webster's criminal element was elusive, and for the most part quite tame. Lots of people would sell her pot, but apparently none of them were armed. No street gangs, no Mafiosi. She ended up getting the damn thing at Walmart.

Melissa reached to the back of the drawer and pulled out a box, which she set atop the dresser. She opened the box and took out a small revolver.

Working by touch, she loaded one chamber. She spun the cylinder and closed the weapon with a flick of her wrist. She pivoted on her heel and aimed at the snores. She cocked the hammer.

I guess this would be Polish Roulette, she thought, and almost let a hoot of laughter escape. The hammer clicked and she gasped.

Shaking and tingling, she unloaded the gun, stowed it, and crawled under the covers.

Chapter Eighteen

Viridian Bank

The financial health of the organization is superb, thanks to your labors. Remuneration of this kind serves to show that our work is valued by the broader society. It's good to feel wanted, but we must never lose sight of our greater calling. Profits in the short term mean little next to our true purpose of midwifing the next stage of the human condition.
from TEF annual report by Severin Tenpenny

"Mel, I'm going to walk Mr Balencourt downstairs to go over some forms with Walt. I might be a while." Brad rolled his eyes so that Melissa could see his exasperation but Balencourt couldn't.

Melissa nodded.

Escorting the elderly Mr Balencourt to the elevator, Brad glanced back at his wife. She sat there, not smiling, but not looking upset either. She didn't look like she wanted to kill him. Maybe she had decided to hire a hit man instead of doing it herself. Maybe it was Balencourt. His cluelessness could be a front.

Brad suppressed a smile.

Two floors down and they were in the lobby. Walt sat at his desk, talking on the phone. Brad directed Balencourt to a comfy chair and walked away before the old guy could ask another rambling question.

There was a short line at the tellers which would get longer at lunchtime, a few minutes from now. Last in line stood a tiny blonde woman in a green sweater-dress and oversized flip-flops.

The combination looked so unusual, especially for November weather, that Brad decided to keep an eye on her. He'd worked in the bank for 25 years and they'd never been robbed. A great record, but somewhat dull. Maybe this waif would liven things up.

She turned to check the clock above the vault and Brad blinked. *Ghost Girl!*

He hadn't seen her in years. What was she doing in the bank? He'd always seen her before in secluded places, never in crowds. It warmed Brad to see her again. Their last meeting, if you could call it that, left him unsettled and he'd always wondered what happened to her and her ghost baby. She wasn't pregnant now, and looked older.

Can ghosts age?

A teller window opened up and the woman moved to the counter. Brad felt his mouth drop open and hastily closed it. Wouldn't do for the VP of Lending to be drooling all over the lobby. Sheryl, the teller, took Ghost Girl's deposit slip and envelope, all the while smiling and chatting like this was an ordinary transaction. Brad stared at Ghost Girl, trying to convince himself it was someone else, someone who bore Ghost Girl a striking resemblance, but only became more sure it was her.

He caught a look at her eerie green eyes when she glanced at the clock again and knew he was right.

When she left the bank, he followed.

*** *** ***

In the supply closet, Melissa searched for a box of staples. She shifted a stack of sticky notes and by the resulting slight noise she knew how many errors various players made in the 1992 Little League World Series.

Melissa sucked in a breath and backed away from the shelf. Absolutely no freshmen at UCLA declared xylophone performance as their major this year. She staggered into the door and it swung shut with a thump that revealed the names of every staff member at the Finnish consulate in London from 1960 to April 1972.

Where the hell is Brad?

Orange was by far the most popular sherbet flavor among United States senators.

*** *** ***

The non-ghostly Ghost Girl meticulously obeyed pedestrian laws, so Brad could keep her in sight without getting too close. Her right flip-flop slapped harshly with each step. They crossed out of downtown Webster proper, into an older residential neighborhood where many of the large houses had been converted into student apartments and second-tier fraternities. Brad knew Kyle thought of them as loser frats, but they were actually academic or service-oriented organizations. Brad helped many of them obtain mortgages over the years.

If Ghost Girl wasn't a ghost, what the hell was she? Why had he seen her all those times over so many years? What became of her baby? If she were alive, the child might be as well.

Two blocks later Ghost Girl turned left onto the street where Willow once lived with Ember and Beacon. The bungalow was long gone, torn down and replaced by a small apartment building. Nostalgia plucked at Brad and he hurried his pace.

She crossed to the other side of the street, but Brad stayed on his side in hopes of being less conspicuous in the thinning crowd. He followed her at a distance for another four blocks.

At the next corner Ghost Girl crossed the side-street and headed away from Brad. After finding a hole in traffic, he darted across the street and caught sight of her approaching the biggest house on the block, a hulking green-shingled behemoth. It stood three stories tall, with a dormered attic above that, and Brad recalled the first time Willow brought him here for dinner with her commune friends. This was Severin's house.

Or had been.

Brad loitered at the corner and kept his eye on the House. His Ghost Girl — whom he'd first seen when he was with Willow — stopped on the front porch of the Threshold Elsewhere Following House — where he'd been with Willow — to exchange a few words with several men in sweaters matching her green dress, and matching the cardigans worn by the representatives of Threshold Electronics Fabrication who, mere months ago, asked him for a large loan. Without collateral.

The attempt to fit these pieces together strained Brad's brain.

The front door of Threshold House opened and Severin stepped out. He wasn't wearing a green sweater, just the same simple black clothes Brad remembered. Severin pulled Ghost Girl to him and kissed her. He led her into the House with his hand on her ass. Brad found the gesture unsettling.

He stared at the house for many minutes without seeing it. Instead he saw Willow, and he saw how he gradually stopped thinking about her. The stab of loss came again, and Brad wallowed in it. He detested himself for giving up on Willow, for shrinking back from the happy memories along with the memory of pain. It all flooded back, and he felt closer to her than he had since that day he'd left twelve years ago.

Distantly he heard the bells of the University's clock announce the half hour and he checked his watch. 12:30. Melissa would be wondering where he was. If he hurried he could get some sandwiches on the way back and they could have a quick lunch together in his office before his afternoon meetings.

*** *** ***

Rows of tiny blue boxes crowded to the edge of a shelf at eye level, neatly placed for the convenience of the next person who needed paperclips. An average 40-year-old woman in the United States has owned 63 toothbrushes. Melissa shut her eyes and pawed the wall for the light switch. Warm darkness enshrouded her mind, as she leaned back against the door.

A woman's heels clicked past out in the corridor, unwelcome trivia delivered in strict cadence with each step. The most popular colors for souvenir concert tees: (click) black, (click) white , (click) red , (click) blue , and (click) purple , (click) in that order , (click) as of 1989.

Melissa bit her fist to keep from screaming and sank to the floor.

*** *** ***

Brad knew lines at sandwich shops got longer during lunch hour, too. Of course there wasn't much to be done about that now, now that he'd hurried and had to stand in line anyway. It took ten minutes to reach the counter, minutes Brad had earmarked for eating with his wife.

Finally, his turn. The college-aged girl behind the counter looked up at him impatiently, and Brad glanced at the menu board for the first time.

"Two twelve-inch turkey subs." *Nice save.*

He ran halfway back to the bank, slowing down to allow for a little airing-out and a chance to catch his breath before planting himself behind a desk for the afternoon. In the elevator he checked his watch again. 12:50. He'd kept his murderess waiting.

***   ***   ***

Melissa huddled in the dark closet, eyes clenched tight against any possible glimmer revealed by the crack under the door. Even with her hands over her ears, an insidious murmur seeped through.

A ringing phone recited par for each hole at the least popular golf course in Illinois.

Footsteps, openings and closings of office doors, the businesslike chortling of the president's sycophants, a dropped pen, a file drawer slamming shut, more phones, photocopiers, and a shrill, distant sneeze all confided drab facts to Melissa, cobwebbing her own thoughts.

The elevator shaft adjoined the supply closet, making the tiny room a perfect resonator for every mechanical grunt and wheeze. She heard the car descend, the drone of the motor debating seventh-century Siamese court etiquette with the thrum of the cables. She heard the doors open, a hollow scrape whispering how many poppy seeds per square inch adorn an average supermarket bagel.

She heard the doors scrape closed.

She heard the car coming back up.

Melissa cringed, listening to the elevator's ascent. Shelves rattled in her closet when it stopped. This floor.

The doors opened. She heard footfalls turn the corner in the hall and pass right by the door she hunched against. A man in leather shoes, hurrying. That this was the only picture suggested by the rhythmic sound brought happy tears to Melissa's eyes.

Brad came back. That must be him out there, hurrying.

She wiped her cheeks as she stood up, adjusted her skirt, and drew a deep breath before turning and opening the closet door.

He better be hurrying.

***   ***   ***

Severin surveyed the winding courses of domino batteries that now occupied most of the basement floor. In twelve years, he'd built and placed 6,201 of them. As the array grew, as it could store a greater quantity of Willow's energies, her stasis deepened and the progress of her pregnancy slowed.

It was her pregnancy that made her a wellspring of otherworldly power. The more of her gestational energies he could intercept, the more he could slow her down, and thus the more he could prolong the profitable arrangement. With enough batteries, Severin had believed he could halt her temporal momentum altogether.

He thought he'd keep her from ever going into labor.

The next contraction began to build, stretching the Elsewhere tight all around Willow. Pulling it taut altered its frequency, shifting it out of Severin's key. During a contraction, with his perceptions confined to his ordinary senses, he felt like he had a sack over his head.

The slow-motion implosion would expand over the next hour or two, the tension increasing as it grew to cover the whole town. Possibly the whole state. When at last it relaxed there would be a sudden wave as the fabric of the Elsewhere snapped back into shape. The wave's turbulence and swift current always swamped Severin's awareness, an overload he had to recuperate from before he could properly connect again across the Threshold.

Building enough dominoes had seemed feasible, at first. Severin had even set himself a target of a thousand, thinking with that he'd have a surplus. But the more of them he created, the less effect each new domino had on the stasis holding Willow in place. The first thousand had done only half the job he expected, so he resigned himself to building a thousand more.

That batch accounted for even less headway, about half what the first lot had earned him.

There was nothing to do but build more, and try to grow the array faster than the diminishing of its returns. By the time he hit 4,000 and Willow hadn't been slowed appreciably, he faced the futility of trying to bring her to a complete stop. He still needed to build more batteries, though, because the ones already in place were mostly full.

So was the basement.

An enormous quantity of power had been stored up in his dominoes over the years, poised for release back into its source. Severin tugged his beard in frustration. It wasn't as much as he'd hoped for. How pitifully naive he'd been to imagine perpetuating the process via a second pregnancy for Willow. There simply wasn't room enough or time enough to set up the number of dominoes that would require.

He gritted his teeth as the contraction intensified. It didn't hurt, but he detested the washed-out feeling as it pulled the Elsewhere away from him.

***   ***   ***

The Canadian music charts, featuring the top 20 songs for each of the past 416 weeks, washed through Melissa, leaving tide pools of Barenaked Ladies, Rush, I Mother Earth, The Tea Party and Alanis Morisette. The tide pools proved fertile breeding ground for minutiae regarding each act's discography, contract negotiations, love life, and preferred brand of laundry detergent, which spiraled into industrial recipes for major and minor cleaning products and their global market share and distribution, which in turn led to a comparative analysis of soil acidity levels in southeast Asia.

Melissa stuffed five or six yellow pills into her mouth and fumbled for her glass.

The water rushing out of the faucet told her the history of British sewage pipes and the part played in their development by Mr John Doulton who went on to great fame as a maker of fine porcelain, followed by the April 1995 price estimates of Royal Doulton figurines at auction.

Sloshing water on herself, Melissa gulped and swallowed. She dropped the glass, which shattered in the marble sink to the tune of all the rejected names for paint colors at the Dutch Boy company last year. Avocado Fog tainted her vision a sickening green as she opened the door and lurched into the bedroom, aiming herself at the bed.

Peace crept in at the edges of her perceptions and Melissa began to relax.

After 25 years, Brad was now losing his effectiveness. At first it was only slight, like maybe he was getting to the edge of his range, but it began happening when he was in the room with her, eerie surges of pressure carrying away Brad's usefulness like waves eroding a beach. So far it was temporary, but it was getting worse. The tide encroached farther each time. Now she couldn't count on him at all. He could be in the room, or beside her on the sofa like tonight, and the visions would come at her in a headlong rush. Blinding and numbing only her ability to cope, they left her totally aware of every insignificant detail.

They'd been watching *Titanic* on HBO. Brad still was.

Just as things finally started happening on screen, Melissa felt a wave pass over her. She thought she was really getting into the movie, but the sound effects of the ship breaking apart started telling her the snapping strengths of various types of twine and wire. It was as if the strange wave washed off Brad's protective layer, and let her demons in.

Brad had also begun sneaking out of the house at night, and out of the office during the day. Most likely he had a new mistress. *Bastard.*

If she hoped to get any good out of Brad's corpse, she would need to act soon. The longer she waited, the more he would wear out. It was a gamble whether he would work at all dead, but he certainly wouldn't if he no longer did alive.

Since he wasn't working reliably anymore, she had no time to plan her actions. She was too often plagued by the onslaught of trivia. Suicide remained an option, but she didn't want to resort to it out of confusion.

She needed to use her lucid time productively, so that meant no more wasting time watching TV or reading. If all went well and she found a solution, she could catch up on current events and prime time soap operas.

Maybe Kyle would still work. He wasn't returning her calls, which wasn't unusual, but she needed to know. Was Brad wearing out, or was she herself getting worse? If she could get near Kyle she could gather information.

If Brad's carcass didn't work, would she kill herself right away? Or would she perhaps bring Kyle home and keep him there?

Melissa drifted off into drugged slumber with a smile on her lips.

*** *** ***

The periodic tightening comes more often, she thinks. She also thinks it is lasting longer, but she always forgets to count and so can't be sure.

Layers, like those of the atmosphere, or of the Earth. She is passing through strata of darkness, sinking toward the center.

She hears voices sometimes, voices that don't come from the bubbles of light. These voices come from outside. The new voices caress her belly. They are measuring, taking stock. Willow doesn't like the proprietary air of the new voices, or the way they shoo away the bubbles. Without the lights there is nothing to look at. She has no way of gauging her progress.

Her toes stretch downward, groping. How many more layers will there be?

*** *** ***

Threshold House rarely seemed quiet, which made it a challenge to decide what time of day to infiltrate. Brad had been spying on the place at all hours, sneaking off whenever he could, even in the dead of night. It was all he could think about. Work was slipping. He hadn't brought in the paper or turned on the news in days. Willow could be in that building, waiting for rescue, but first he had to get inside. He decided on mid-afternoon Sunday, while one shift slept and another sweater-clad herd worked out back in the garage. Severin himself went out there most days.

Brad parked around the corner, pulled on his new green cardigan, and walked to where he had an oblique vantage point on the back yard. After about twenty-five minutes, he spotted Severin striding toward the garage, an island of black in a sea of green sweaters. Brad casually hurried around the block and opened the front door. A small, tasteful sign beside it read 'Consultation by Appointment.'

He'd been here before, years ago, with Willow. The layout looked the same, but the decor was decidedly less squalid. Ahead of him the central staircase ran up to the second floor before doubling back on itself and continuing up to the third. Quick glances into the rooms on the ground floor revealed a library and conference room at the front of the House, with an office and living room opening off from them. He knew the kitchen and communal dining hall took up the entire rear of this floor.

At the top of the stairs were two bathrooms side by side. To his right the stairs continued up. The center of the House was a cavernous hallway with a railing encircling the open staircase in the center. Besides the bathrooms, Brad counted ten doors arrayed at regular intervals around the perimeter. Ten rooms to search on this floor alone. He'd better move fast.

On a certain level Brad knew it was irrational to assume Willow was being held somewhere in this house, but on another level it felt perfectly rational. Severin was a creepy motherfucker, and back in the day he fostered an interest in Willow. Plus there was the whole supernatural connection. Severin had kissed Ghost Girl, uniting two previously separate parts of Brad's past. That must mean something.

Moving clockwise, Brad found an empty room with a set of bunk beds. Next along was a stuffy room crammed with racks of computer equipment. Miles of neatly bundled multicolored cables ran through holes in the floor, ceiling and right-hand wall. Brad checked the room to the right and discovered a computer lab staffed by three green-sweaters with their backs to him. An unoccupied room with two single beds was followed by two smaller rooms, each with a sleeping occupant. Voices came from the last room along the front of the House. The next two rooms were empty singles. The final room on this floor held occupied bunk beds. Brad scurried up the stairs to the third floor.

The layout here looked the same as below, except the stairs didn't continue up. Willow always referred to Severin hanging out in his attic lair, so there must be another set of stairs, possibly in one of the bedrooms. But which one? The corner rooms were the doubles, the ones in between were singles. At least downstairs.

Up here there was an extra door.

Brad hurried to it and found it unlocked. He knew Severin was out, so he opened the door and smiled. The attic stairs. Pulling the door shut behind him, Brad noticed a hook and eye but decided not to lock the door. It wouldn't do him any good to be trapped up here. It would be better to be quick, find Willow, and get the hell out.

Taking the stairs two at a time, Brad emerged into the attic and was disappointed. A hammock hung between the corners of two dormers, and large stacks of dusty crates and boxes lined the outer walls, with a few pieces of sheet-draped furniture mixed in. The four large dormer windows let in enough light to see there was no one up here.

Had he expected to find Willow just sitting up here? Maybe there were crawl spaces behind the knee-walls.

Brad looked around and spotted a half-sized door on the other side of the attic, behind a sheet-shrouded table. He approached it and was about to shove the table aside when he was stopped by a voice coming from the stairs. Willow's voice.

"Don't touch it."

*** *** ***

The green-sweater whirled around and Gale gasped. It wasn't anyone she knew. He was fairly tall, taller than Severin certainly, with conservative hair and intense gray eyes. Gale blinked.

The man straightened and glared at her. Who was he?

"It's you," he said with a mixture of disdain and satisfaction. "I expected Severin to catch me."

"Did you come through the table?"

He threw a puzzled glance at the table, but quickly looked back to her.

"I see you're not pregnant anymore. Congratulations. Was it a boy or girl?"

Gale was baffled. "My... my..." This stranger was making her confused. He looked at her more intently, catching her eyes and holding them. He barked an unamused laugh and shook his head.

"It was twin girls, wasn't it?"

Gale felt like she'd been gut-punched. Her eyes went wide, apparently all the answer the man needed.

"You're their mother. All those years I never made the connection. Well," he took several long, quick strides and seized her by the arm, "I want her back."

"Who?" Gale managed to whisper.

His gray eyes cut into her. "Willow."

This man wanted Kelly! Whoever he was, wherever he came from, he knew about her past and he wanted to take her baby away.

Shaking overtook Gale and she sagged.

This could solve everything!

"You need to leave before my brother catches you here. You'll never save her if he knows you're after her."

"I'm not leaving without her."

"You have to. She's safe for now. I take good care of her. I don't let him touch her. She's safe until she has the baby. After that, he'll want to use her."

The man looked angry and confused.

"She's only been in labor for a few weeks. She won't deliver for at least two more. We've been monitoring her."

"What? Labor doesn't—"

"Nothing about this is normal. She's been pregnant for twelve years.

She was pregnant when we brought her here. She's still pregnant. And if Severin has his way, she'll be pregnant again. I don't want that."

"Severin's your brother?"

Gale nodded.

"Why should I trust you?"

"I want her out of here. I see the way he looks at her. He should only look that way at me. The baby should be mine."

The man's grip tightened. "Where is she?"

Gale looked up into his handsome face. She needed him to trust her. This was the opportunity she'd been waiting for. With his help Kelly would be safe and not a threat. "She's in the basement." She went on before the man could react. "The door's in the kitchen, but it's locked. And the henge contraption is complicated. We'll have to come up with a plan."

She could tell the man wanted to bolt down the stairs.

"What's your name? I'm Gale."

"Brad."

"Brad. We need to work together. Right now you have to leave so Severin doesn't find you. You go and let me think of a plan. We'll get together and arrange it. Then we'll save Kelly." The desperation in her voice convinced him.

"When?"

"Mondays I go to the bank. Tomorrow."

Brad nodded.

"We'll meet at the clock in front of Viridian Bank on Alder Street. 11:30."

"11:30 tomorrow." His grip tightened again and his eyes flashed. "And believe me when I say you'd better be there."

Gale nodded.

*** *** ***

The wait was interminable. Brad was no good to anyone all morning. He canceled all his appointments, foisting his duties onto underlings, and spent the time brooding.

In front of him lay a portfolio of Gale Napier Tenpenny's holdings with Viridian Bank. Fucking enormous holdings they were. She must be in charge of the finances, at least in name, for the entire organization. She opened the accounts in late 1988. When Willow disappeared.

The woman was as mysterious as ever. Maybe more so. He saw her ghost repeatedly over the years, but she wasn't dead. She was Severin's sister, but also in love with him. She was Willow's mother, and Melissa's, but she looked scarcely older than himself. When he'd seen her as a spirit, she'd always been terribly young, true. But still.

Of course this shed some unwelcome light on Willow. Who's real name was Liz, or maybe Kelly. Had she known Severin was her uncle?

Could she possibly still be pregnant? If Gale was to be believed, which was a stretch, Willow had been pregnant for twelve years. That would make it his baby. The child they were going to have together. *Our second chance.* He wanted to believe he might still get that second chance, but it was too fantastical to credit.

Gale also mentioned some sort of contraption. Was it a life support machine?

He shut the folder and stood. Pacing his office didn't make the time go by any faster. He glanced at his watch. 11:00.

Close enough.

Trying to look like he had some place to be, Brad passed the wrathful Melissa and went to the men's room. After killing a few minutes attempting to make himself look less like a banker he snuck down the fire stairs to the ground floor.

Small talk with Murray ate up a few more minutes. Brad exited through the back door. He didn't want Gale to know he worked at Viridian.

Hurrying down the alley to the connecting street brought him to the corner by the clock at 11:15. He stayed back so his coworkers wouldn't see him through the window, and waited impatiently, wishing he still smoked.

Fourteen minutes later he spotted Gale approaching from the other end of the block. He waved to her before she got to the bank door and she changed course to meet him. She wore the same sweater dress.

Her electric green eyes looked haunted.

"I'll need you to distract him," she said.

"Severin?"

She nodded. "Tonight. Come to the front door and make a disturbance. While he's dealing with you, I'll go to the basement and unhook her."

"Is she okay?"

"Of course." Gale took a moment to find her place again before continuing. "I'll take her out the back door and through the gate. I'll need at least five minutes. Ten would be better. We'll go someplace safe until she has the baby. After that, you and she can go wherever you want, away from here. Away from my brother. I'll take the baby. That will appease him. We'll be a family." She drifted at the end and her eyes looked a little glassy.

She wanted to take the baby? Not fucking likely. He and Willow had earned this second chance. No way this loony woman would rob them of that. Once Willow was... what? Awake? Back? Coherent? Once Willow was Willow, they would send Gale away.

He couldn't tell her that.

"All right."

Gale smiled tightly. "This will be best for all of us."

"But I don't think I understand. How can she be pregnant for so long?"

"The henge contraption holds her in stasis."

Well of course. "Henge contraption?"

"My brother is a most brilliant man, Brad. He only needs to realize he doesn't need Willow or her power. He is capable of so much, even without her. He'll see."

With that she turned and entered the bank.

Chapter Nineteen

Front Porch

Respected colleagues,
    An opportunity has arisen in my personal life, something I
must follow. I look back with pride at my years and my
accomplishments here at Viridian. My only regret is the
abruptness of my departure. I want my friends here to know this
new chapter in my life will be a happy one.
    from Brad Tanner's letter of resignation

Brad half-carried Melissa to the car after their early dinner. They'd gone straight to Marinello's from the bank, so they were wearing their work clothes. It was a good thing she hadn't changed into dressy heels, or he would have to carry her outright. He suspected her rubbery legs and unfocused eyes resulted more from the alcohol in the five drinks she ordered and less from the four pills he slipped into them over the course of the meal. She used the pills so heavily these days, her tolerance had reached rock-star levels.

He'd told her he wanted to go out and enjoy themselves, just for the hell of it, but even so he was startled at how eagerly she ordered whiskey sours. Public drinking offended Melissa, almost as deeply as overt demonstrations of affection.

After buckling her seat belt, Brad circled to his side of the silver Lexus and got in. He glanced at his watch. 7:04. Melissa pawed at the clasp of her purse, pouting.

"Do you need something out of that?"

Melissa let her hands slump into her lap and concentrated on aiming both of her eyes in Brad's direction. "Rememmer when we met?" She paused to moisten her lips. "Do you remember," now she pointed at Brad's knee, "where we first met?"

"Yes. It was up in my office."

"No, it was in yer office. That was later. Wait, you said 'office,' din you?"

Brad started the car and buckled himself in, but made no move to pull out. "Why do you ask?"

Melissa shook her head and fell silent. In the dark Brad couldn't tell for certain, but he suspected she was crying. He shrugged and put the car in motion.

Less than five minutes later he pulled into a space on Oak Avenue, half a block past Threshold House.

"Not our street," Melissa said icily.

Brad froze with his hand on the key, the car still running. Sweat ran down the back of his neck. She had to cooperate enough to get her up on the porch or she wouldn't be much of a distraction.

"Shabby. Ours's nicer."

Releasing a gust of breath, Brad switched off the engine and looked at Melissa, but she hadn't stirred. He got out and went around to her door, helped her stand, steadied her with a hand on her elbow. He tossed her oddly heavy purse onto her seat and was about to shut the door when Melissa pulled away and lunged back into the car. Clutching her pocketbook, she swayed into a standing position and shut the door herself, brushing futilely at a few flyaway strands of her unkempt hair and offering her elbow back to Brad.

He walked her up the block, helping her stay on the sidewalk. She said nothing as they mounted the front steps of the House, and leaned drowsily against Brad's shoulder as they waited after he rang the bell.

Long moments later a young woman in jeans and a green sweater opened the heavy inner door and looked out through the storm door. Brad now had a view of the main stairs inside.

"Please tell Severin someone is here to see him. We'll wait here." Brad tried for pokerfaced menace, wondering how he came across. The young lady went up the stairs, presumably to fetch Severin, so something was working.

Melissa lifted her head, attempted to stand up straight. Brad watched peripherally as she looked up at him several times. She still didn't say anything.

Shortly, Severin descended the stairs and strode to the door. He regarded his visitors through the glass darkly, hands clasped behind his back.

"You don't remember me, do you, Severin?"

"Should I?" Severin's pokerface was very good.

"It's been a long time. I suppose I never made much of an impression."

"I suppose not. Is that all?"

"Take a closer look at my companion. You and I have business to discuss."

Severin sneered, but he appraised Melissa. After staring at her for too long, he shrugged.

Brad nodded. "Give it a minute to sink in. Even I figured it out, eventually. Of course, I was sleeping with both of them at the time."

Color drained from Severin's face, and he reached for the latch.

"Not so fast." Brad placed his arm around Melissa's shoulders and drew her back a step, supporting her weight until her slowed reflexes could adjust to the sudden movement. He said, "Let's be clear on the terms."

Severin said, "Absolutely. You have my attention." His eyes hadn't left Melissa since Brad prompted him to study her.

Brad wondered if Severin could be lured down the street if he kept backing up and dragging Melissa along. "You know what I have. By your reaction, I know you have what I want. How do I know you're dealing in good faith?" As he spoke, Brad saw Gale padding down the big staircase behind Severin. She glanced his way as she turned toward the kitchen. Then she whirled and stared at Melissa, transfixed as her brother.

Melissa twisted to shake off Brad's arm. "Take me home, now! Said we were goin' out to havva good time, not talk business."

Brad tried to regain his hold on Melissa, but she flailed and pushed him away. Severin was on the porch in a flash, holding her in a headlock. Brad reached for her again, but Severin shot him a warning look and clamped his arm tight across her throat, cutting off her air. Brad raised his hands and stepped back, while Melissa rattled and coughed. He felt his hands close into fists at the sight of Melissa's distress.

Save it, he told himself. Not for her.

"Yes, let's be clear on terms," Severin said. "You have ten seconds to vanish and never come back." His eyes gleamed with eerie green light, which then washed over the rest of his face. It grew stronger, flooding the porch, and Brad squinted at the storm door to try to understand the source of the unnatural glow.

But there was no storm door.

The flash ceased, revealing Gale in the opening where the door had been, limned in emerald light. Her palms faced outward, as if to press on the glass that wasn't there. Green St Elmo's fire writhed in her hair and traced the door frame in fading wisps.

Brad goggled.

Severin laughed. "Sister, darling, whatever do you think you're doing?"

Melissa's eyes snapped open and she rammed her right elbow into Severin's ribs. She tore loose from him and stood glaring at Brad. Severin gasped and cradled his side, and Gale sobbed.

"Grace! Oh Mommy's here now!" Gale lunged from the doorway, arms outstretched, and Melissa tensed for the embrace wearing an expression of horrified dismay.

With a strangled roar, Severin hauled the two women apart. Gale shrieked, and he backhanded her. He twisted Melissa's arm up behind her back. Keeping an eye on Gale, he said to Brad, "I estimate you have five seconds left."

Brad stood rooted to the porch. The plan went to hell when Gale came outside. Now she was glowing, and Severin had issued an ultimatum. The green radiance appeared again, standing Gale's hair straight out. Strange buzzing numbness washed over Brad, and he stumbled farther away from Gale as she stalked after Severin and Melissa. Perhaps the plan had only gone to heck. If Gale kept Severin busy, Brad could go inside for Willow.

Gale swiped at Severin. He used Melissa as a shield, levering her around by her arm. Gale screamed in frustration, pulling back rather than risk harming her daughter with the spooky green fire.

The action moved away from the door, and Brad cast a glance inside. Just down that hall and into the kitchen would get him to the basement steps. Severin was distracted, but not so much that he wouldn't work out where Brad was going if he spotted Brad entering his House.

Melissa grimaced in pain from Severin wrenching her arm. She tried to pull away. Severin heaved her back, drawing them both off balance. At the edge of the porch, Melissa stomped on Severin's foot. He bellowed and they both toppled to the lawn.

Severin wouldn't see if Brad dashed inside right now. Before he could take a step, Severin rose, holding Melissa's wrist.

Brad turned and fled the porch. He sprinted down the sidewalk until he reached the corner. Slowing to a jog, he looked back at the battle scene. It looked like Melissa was on her feet, with Severin and Gale using her in a tug-of-war.

*** *** ***

Blackness constricted Melissa's sight to a tiny round area of confusion, with Brad right at the center. He seemed to be very small and far away, then he turned and stepped out of the fuzzy circle and he wasn't there at all.

He'd been right here a second ago, almost knocked her over. Then these other people started yelling and pushing, and where the hell was Brad going?

Melissa felt her knees leave the ground, simultaneous with a wrenching jolt all down her arm. The blackness withdrew a bit, letting more of the world show through. She looked to her right and saw the strange, dumpy little man Brad had been talking to. He looked like he'd retired from the Grateful Dead or something, and he had her arm. Didn't want to let go, either.

On her left Melissa found the weird lady with the scary eyes, the one with the 'Mommy' delusions, hauling on her other arm and screaming. They jerked her back and forth as she tried to tell them to knock it off, but either her voice wasn't working or they were too absorbed in their Springer moment to pay any attention to her.

Melissa gave up trying to talk and concentrated on locating Brad. He'd better get this under control, and soon. Her eyesight was close to normal now, and she could identify the spot where she'd last seen her husband's image. A street corner, about 100 yards away. He wasn't there now.

Ditched! That slimy son of a bitch!

She got both of her feet under her and obtained enough leverage to yank herself loose from the weirdoes. For a moment everything went quiet.

"Look," Melissa said shakily, "I'm leaving."

She had to catch up with Brad before she started falling to pieces. A snowflake glided to the ground beside her. *Fabulous.* Air filled with snow, the millions of random intersecting trajectories. She'd have a seizure.

"Grace, my beautiful baby," the lady said. "You must come with me. All these years... Look at you!"

Melissa spotted her purse on the porch. Mommy Dearest was in the way, and Melissa didn't want to have her back turned to either one of these people. Gotta keep the crazy lady talking. "I'm not your baby. I've never seen you in my life." She edged between them and spun around to keep them both in view as she backed up onto the porch.

The woman cried out as if struck, clawing at her hair. "They took you away from me, Grace!"

"Stop calling me that!" Melissa threw a look at the man, who hadn't moved. He wore a smirk, and looked at her with uncanny blue eyes. An echo of the visions rang remotely in her mind as their eyes met. He smiled more warmly.

"I can teach you what it means, how to use your gift. To control it, rather than being controlled."

Melissa's hands and knees quaked. She shut her eyes tight and shook her head, trying to drive this stranger out of it. She snatched up her purse and twisted the clasp. Both the man and the woman stepped closer. Melissa's hands steadied as she raised her gun and aimed it at the man's face. He stopped, and when Melissa flashed a snarl at the woman, she did too.

***   ***   ***

Brad cut into the back yard of the first house on the street, running across the lawns rather than going all the way to the alley. An eight-foot, solid wooden fence surrounded Threshold House's lot. Brad leaned against it to catch his breath. He hadn't climbed an eight-foot fence in decades.

The snow that had been threatening all day drifted down around Brad and began to sheath the grass in large, wet flakes. His panting breaths hung white in the air.

A chilling scream came from out front. Brad couldn't count on the fighting to go on indefinitely. He had to keep moving, leave enough time to get back out with Willow.

Grabbing the upper edge of the wall, he pulled himself up. Once his chin cleared the top, he flung one elbow over and started trying to bring a leg up. His feet scuffed uselessly on the smooth boards, and he thought he'd have to let go and get his breath again for another try.

Awareness of how little time he had fed his determination, and with a grunt of pain he levered himself up another few inches, enough to hook his heel over the top. Using that foothold, he twisted across the top of the fence and tumbled into an unpruned mass of winter-dead climbing roses on the other side.

Struggling for a proper lungful of air, he crawled out of the thorny hedge and stood up. He moved toward the back of the House, the motion helping to loosen his cramped solar plexus. Scratches stung on his arms, back, and face. He kept moving, thinking only of Willow.

***   ***   ***

"Grace—"

"No! Quiet, you. Both of you. Neither of you knows anything about me. You're trying to confuse me."

"I just want to help you," the man said. He remained still as stone, showing no fear of the weapon but respecting it enough to hang back.

"Gra—" the woman choked the name off. "Can't you see?"

Melissa's face grew warm. Her jaw hurt, and flecks of spittle flew as she replied, "You're not my mother!"

"She is."

He was smirking again. Melissa felt dizzy. She backed away, not wanting to be within their reach. The woman nodded and smiled hopefully.

"No," Melissa protested, feeling the flush in her cheeks and the unacceptable sting of oncoming tears. "How? Brad doesn't know anything."

"Yes, he does," the woman said. "He found me, but he didn't tell me about you. He kept things from both of us. But he brought you here! He brought Mommy's lovely Grace home."

This was eating up too much time. Brad could be miles away. This was his game all along, ditch her with these wackos and run off. *He knew!* He knew she planned to shoot him tonight. Where had he dug up this sideshow?

Melissa sidestepped toward the edge of the porch.

"I can't allow you to leave," the man said.

Melissa sneered and waggled the gun at him.

He shook his head. "You can't go."

"Fuck you," Melissa muttered, searching out the first step with her foot while keeping her attention on the two maniacs. The man folded his arms across his chest and glared. He closed his eyes and drew in a deep breath. Melissa thought he seemed resigned to the obvious, but the lady howled and leapt on him.

"Not Grace! You won't!"

The man threw her off like a wet towel, and she struck green sparks from the wooden porch when she landed.

"Get back in place, Sister! I have enjoyed your company oh so very much, but if you expect to remain with me you will not interfere with what you cannot understand."

"I understand perfectly, Brother!" The lady got up as if she hadn't even felt the body slam. "I sat back and watched what you did to Kelly, and it won't happen again!" She began to glow, green like a chemical flame.

Melissa stumbled leaving the porch. The green aurora was a new form for her visions.

I'm getting worse! What will this be like? Will I be able to find Brad and finish things?

Melissa floated above the concrete walkway, frantic at her mind's further deterioration. The green glow around the woman flung itself at the man, who caught it in one hand.

Every hair on Melissa's body chimed, and the walkway pounded the back of her head.

Cursing, Melissa scrambled to her feet and immediately collapsed. Her hand found warm stickiness seeping through her hair, and more pain kept trying to get into her skull even though it was full. She rolled onto all fours, tried to look around her.

She didn't know where her gun was, couldn't make sense of the shouting.

***   ***   ***

There was no one in the kitchen. The basement door was locked. Brad threw himself against it a few times, without progress other than a throbbing in his shoulder.

He stepped away and tried to calculate where to kick it to break the lock, but doubted his luck would be any better with that approach. He looked around the expansive mess hall for some kind of implement. Maybe they'd have a fire axe.

He settled for a stand mixer. Setting the bowl aside and disconnecting the cord, he hefted the appliance. He grasped it by the neck and aimed the base at the door, letting his arms pivot at the shoulders as he got a feel for the movement. One, two, three practice swings, then he slammed the mixer against the door, striking right beside the knob.

With a loud crack, the door crashed open. A piece about ten inches across, with the knob protruding, dropped belatedly from the frame and clunked on the stairs.

Cringing at the extent of the noise, Brad dropped the mixer and entered the dark stairway. He ran his hand over the wall, looking for a light switch, but didn't locate one. He blundered down in the dark, feeling for a switch along the wall the whole time.

At the bottom, he paused to get his bearings. At least let his eyes adjust. Indirect light came from upstairs, and now that he had reached the bottom of them he could see the steps. Nothing at all in the room lay near enough to the stairs to share in the pitiful light from above.

After several deep breaths Brad struck out, probing ahead with his toes and trailing the fingers of his right hand along the wall. "Willow?" he called. With the next step his foot encountered something that resisted only faintly, and an odd clattering sound began.

Brad froze. The noise moved off into the darkness. He took another tentative step and felt something brush across his face. With a yelp he batted it away. A light came on and he saw its pull string snagged on one of his sleeve buttons.

He stood next to an exterior door, near one corner of a vast murky room spanning the entire footprint of the House. In the center of this chamber hulked a huge block of milky green stone with a naked, pregnant woman laying on it.

"Willow!"

Between Brad and Willow, the dirt floor was nearly covered with what looked like the guts of a thousand obsolete computers, standing on end in long serpentine rows. Like dominoes.

Brad identified the source of the strange noise as he watched the cascade move along the distant edge of the room. Glancing down to where he'd bumped the first one, Brad was startled to be unable to find it. Next to his footprints in the dusty floor, a row of neatly spaced marks suggested dominoes had been there at one time. He looked across the room, and saw that with each collision the last domino in the line vanished.

Taking care not to bump any others, Brad started toward the center of the room. The falling dominoes split into two cascades. Two rows of them dead-ended on his side of the big white stone.

That, Brad thought, must be a henge contraption.

The twin streams each split again. The dominoes were now vanishing four times as fast, and all converging on Willow.

*** *** ***

With an enormous labor, Melissa opened her eyes. The man was staring at her, while he fended off his sister's attempts to reach her. They were shouting.

Melissa sat up, and the madwoman got around her brother and swooped down on her.

"Frightened me! Can't lose you, not again."

"Let me check her pupils," the man demanded, crouching next to the woman. Melissa tried to push them both away, without success. The woman moved aside, keeping hold of Melissa's hand, and the man leaned in close. His spooky blue eyes became all Melissa could see, and the pain in her head diminished a fraction.

"She's fine," he announced. The woman helped her stand.

Melissa's head throbbed. She thought she could walk, but not run. She looked around, seeking to avoid eye contact with the woman, whose green eyes sought something that had been misplaced deep inside

Melissa's own.

The snow had picked up since Brad's departure. Flakes the size of quarters and nickels plummeted heavily around her, plastering the landscape in a damp shroud. No air moved. There was no breeze to stir the crumpled brown leaves on the sidewalk.

But if they did stir, Melissa saw the way their meaning could change. If that little one were turned the other way, the snow would be lighter. Flip that same leaf over, and the precipitation changes to sleet. It was a previously unknown level to her visions, this inkling of relevance. She'd known all her life that her accursed cacophony of trivia comprised accurate information, but never before felt a means of directing it. The insight momentarily soothed a latent itch in her mind. To be able to call that up at will would be infinitely better than depending on Brad or anyone else for shelter.

"I told you," Severin said, "I can teach you what it means. You don't have to be at its mercy. You can feel the difference already, can't you? Imagine being the master instead of the slave. Imagine being free."

"Don't listen to him," the woman admonished. "You don't know what he did to your sister. We'll be okay now that we're together. Mommy will protect you."

Melissa looked the woman straight in the eye, and knew that this was her biological mother.

"Did you feel that?" the woman asked. "Kelly felt it, too."

"You really are my mother."

"Yes! Yes, baby, I am."

Melissa laughed hoarsely, which brought a pile driver into motion in her skull. She kept chuckling anyway and shook her head.

"What?"

"You're the last person I ever wanted to see. You made me like this. You abandoned me."

Her mother's face darkened. "I looked so hard for you. I never wanted to be away from you for a second."

"Tell me how it happened. How did you lose me?"

The woman looked down, squeezing Melissa's hands as she muttered, "I gave you to, to someone. To look after you, just for a little bit. When I came back he was gone. You were gone."

"You left me with 'someone'? Who? Did you even know him?"

Her mother looked up again, defiant. "Your father. I left you with your father."

Melissa's outrage grew. "Dare I ask what pressing errand drew you away, that required you to entrust me to his tender care?"

The woman swallowed. She stared imploringly at Melissa, but gave no other answer. Melissa pulled her hands free and looked over at the man, seated on the edge of the porch.

"You!" the woman exclaimed. "I did it for you, don't you understand? You were the one I wanted to keep, and Kelly made that possible. I could give them Kelly, and they would never know about you!"

Melissa spotted her revolver in the grass, and collected it. She placed it back in her purse. She walked over to the man and extended her hand. He kissed the back of it.

She suspected he was full of shit about being able to help her, wouldn't let herself believe anyone could. On the other hand, she'd been prepared to go through with murder-suicide tonight. What did she have to lose?

"You are apparently my uncle, and you know of me as Grace. I prefer to be called Melissa."

"Welcome, Melissa. I am Severin. There is much I hope to teach you, and much I'm sure you can teach me along the way."

*** *** ***

Brad hopped over several rows of dominoes, hurrying to the altar slab. Its unearthly color, and the darker lichen scabbing its sides like alien graffiti, gave him the willies. He wanted to remove a few dominoes from each line near the end, so the cascade couldn't reach Willow, but was afraid to touch them. Partly out of concern that he'd knock more of them down, but mainly because of the way they stopped existing when disturbed.

He looked at Willow, laying so still on her back. A black strip of velcro encircled her enormous round belly that held their future together. Wires from a small box on the belt led to a tiny screen sitting on the floor nearby, some kind of monitor.

Brad undid the belt and lifted Willow off the stone. He carefully stepped back across the nearby dominoes, finding much of the room now cleared of them. He carried Willow to the outside door, and gently laid her down. He stripped off his suede jacket and wrapped it around her. Crying, he patted her cheek and said her name.

He bent and kissed her lips, and she stirred.

"Willow! Oh, Willow!" Brad kissed her forehead, weeping with joy now. Her brow creased. Brad smiled and stroked her cheek.

Her eyes flashed open, and she gasped. An animal howl came from her, and she struggled in the bulky suede covering. Brad held her, whimpering, fearing that he'd caused her agony by moving her. She relaxed after several seconds, and Brad sought her eyes. She looked pale, and perspiration speckled her face, but her green eyes were clear as she looked back at him.

A contraction. He should have anticipated this.

"Arms," she muttered. Brad began to rearrange the jacket, when a surge of heat bathed his back.

He looked over his shoulder at the block of stone. Its previous unhealthy color, like milk from a bowl of Lucky Charms, was now a vibrant, radioactive green, ramping quickly into white-hot incandescence. His face baked in the brief moment it was turned that way. Creaking and popping sounds came from the wooden structure overhead.

"We have to get out of here," Brad told Willow. She nodded. Brad stood to unlock the outside door and pull it open. He stooped to gather up Willow again, and chanced one parting look at the glowing hunk of rock.

It had sunk partway into the floor, and as Brad stared it slipped lower still. In another second the heat abated, as only the tip of the stone showed above the dirt floor.

It dipped away, leaving the floor unmarked. No hole, nowhere the slab could have gone.

Brad ran across the back yard with Willow in his arms, leaving a clear trail in the fresh snow. When he reached the gate, he set her down and helped her with the sleeves. The jacket covered her almost to her knees, but she must be freezing. She hugged her belly.

"I'm in labor."

"Yes, I'm going to take you to the hospital now."

Willow nodded, and reached out to him. She put one arm over his shoulder as he lifted her again and they moved through the gate into the alley. Halfway to their first turn, about a quarter of the way to the car, she started to tense.

"It's another contraction," Brad tried to say soothingly. Willow's hand clutched the hair near the base of his skull. "That's good, Wil. Hang in there," he said through his teeth.

By the time Brad could see the car, Willow relaxed again. Her breathing was rapid and shallow. Brad thought that wasn't how she should be doing it, but he didn't know what to tell her that would help. His arms were sagging. He increased his pace.

Reaching Oak Avenue, he looked down to Threshold House. No one out front.

At the car, Brad supported Willow with one arm while he got the door open for her, and pirouetted around the door to place her in the seat. She smiled distantly for a moment, then her face went slack. She blinked in slow motion.

Brad hurried over to his side and got in. His tires squealed as he pulled out.

***   ***   ***

Melissa immediately disliked the old house. Too many stairs. Her newfound uncle kept up a steady stream of hooey about destiny and complementary forces and power games, but Melissa was preoccupied with the endless ascent and the grinding agony in her skull.

Numerous oddball people wearing silly cardigans stared from assorted doorways, but none had the temerity to question Severin.

When they reached the third floor, Severin turned to face her and said, "Wait here." He returned soon with a small damp towel, which he positioned on the back of her head. It felt good, more so than Melissa expected, so even when the door he opened led only to more stairs she didn't protest.

One more flight and they reached a drafty attic. Severin made a vague gesture which Melissa interpreted as an invitation to sit on the hassock. He took a bottle down from a crossbeam and presented her with a glass of red wine.

"Is this a good idea?" Melissa asked. Her head throbbed and she had trouble concentrating. Severin smiled, and Melissa did not feel reassured.

"So, what happens now?" she asked while swirling the wine in her glass. A deep, overpowering fatigue stalked her.

"As I said outside, teaching. The Elsewhere has asked much of you, too much, and never provided an explanation. A cruel quirk of fate ripped you from the balancing force you were meant to accompany. Tonight, fate is kind in bringing us together. For I can provide that balance. I can help."

"Uh huh. What exactly are we discussing here, old man? I'm not some naive coed."

Severin rubbed his chin, pouting. At length he shrugged "Sex. Your body and mine must entwine. We will explore the Threshold, and you will see the pieces of the picture that have been concealed from you."

Melissa set aside her unsipped wine and said, "That's where I thought this was going, 'Uncle.' Find another May for your December." She stood shakily. "I'm leaving."

Severin shrugged again, and the faintest smile haunted his eyes.

Melissa reached the top of the stairs and paused to survey them before taking the first step. She still felt the seductive drowsiness, and needed to plan her moves. She focused on the shadowy staircase.

In its dwindling parallel treads, she saw specific gravities of the principal rock strata of the Carolinas. Melissa clutched the railing, and its cool firmness under her grip whispered the contents of Jacqueline Donohue's handbag.

Severin chuckled, and said, "Perhaps I've misread you. Maybe you like coping with your enriched perceptions on your own." Melissa stepped back to shoot him a glare without tumbling headlong down the steps.

"You know the way out, Melissa. You're free to leave right now."

"Fuck you."

"To put it crudely." Severin reclined in a hammock, and wore a devilish smile.

All the way up the interminable staircase, with her uncle at her side, the visions had been silent. The moment she tried to leave, they returned.

Melissa sighed. She trudged toward the hammock and the visions were chased away once more.

She was at a loss to get aboard the swinging bed with her limbs so heavy.

Severin slid off the opposite side with surprising agility and said, "Not here."

Melissa allowed Severin to lead her by the hand to a makeshift table draped in a pristine white sheet. He embraced her, running his hands over her back and gently kissing her neck. He was warm and strong, and he gave off a subtle musky smell, appealing in its way and better than Melissa would have predicted. Melissa felt cradled like a child as he laid her on her back on the table.

Before she passed out, Melissa slid her panties out from under her skirt.

*** *** ***

Gale's anger paralyzed her as Grace turned away and approached Severin. They spoke, but all she heard was a roar. They entered the

House together without giving her so much as a backward glance, and she stood in the snow staring after them for long moments.

Remembering the baby and the original mission that brought her downstairs, she stormed inside and toward the kitchen. While Severin and Grace got up to whatever unspeakable mischief upstairs, she would have plenty of time to release Kelly. Once she had the baby, she wouldn't need anybody else. Severin's rejection didn't matter, and losing Grace was nothing. She and the baby would be a family.

Wiping her cheeks and sniffling, Gale entered the kitchen and saw the cellar entrance ajar, the mixer on the floor nearby. Another few steps showed her the damaged door, and the light on below.

She plunged down the steps, heedless of Severin's silly toys.

But there were none.

Nothing important remained, not the dominoes, not the huge rock in the center of the room. Not Kelly.

Not the baby.

A dizzy minute of wild grief left Gale on her knees, weeping and laughing at the same time.

She noticed the open door to the outside.

Comprehension leaked in through her despair, dripping hints of the truth that evaporated before she could piece it together. Gradually the shape of her betrayal soaked in.

Catch him! Chase him! Burn him! Break him! The mantra cycled endlessly as she dashed to the garage, as she snatched up keys and opened the door, as she backed the van into the alley, as she roared out onto the main road and spotted a lone set of tire tracks in the fresh white blanket on the street.

Chapter Twenty

SNOW STORM

I want to be the hero of your story, even if that makes me somebody else's villain.
from Brad Tanner's love note to Willow Charm

Brad cranked the heater and hit the wipers. The snow was falling thicker now. Willow would be freezing. He glanced over at her, huddled on the passenger side, and turned on the seat warmers.

"Hey, Wil, we'll be there soon."

She looked at him blankly. "I'm naked."

"Yeah, but the jacket should warm you up." He reached over and stroked her damp red hair, overwhelmed to have found her.

"Where's Fin?"

"He's fine. We'll see him after the baby's born."

She nodded slowly. "That was Threshold House."

"I don't think they call it that anymore."

"What did Severin do to me?"

"I'm not sure." Brad slid his warm hand down to clutch her icy one as he made the turn onto Evergreen Street, noticing for the first time that she still wore the silver ring he gave her on their last night together. He smiled and squeezed her hand to reassure her. "You were in the basement on a rock."

She nodded and stared at her belly. "It's been a long time."

"Wil, you have no idea."

She looked at him.

"It's been twelve years."

No other cars were out, but Brad slowed anyway. Snow was

accumulating quickly.

"I thought you looked older," she said. "And this car..."

"It's new," he confirmed.

"It's from the Jetsons. Does it actually have a computer?"

"That's the navigation system. See the map?"

Her hand clenched his and she sucked in her breath. Another contraction.

Brad looked out the window. They were driving through a remote stretch of the Buckminster campus, surrounded by vast parking lots and athletic fields. A cluster of dorms squatted a couple hundred yards away. The hospital was several miles off.

"You can watch the map and see how close we're getting to the hospital."

Willow made a choked sort of sound and her grip loosened. Brad whipped his head around to look at her. Her eyes were wide and teary, her right hand crept from her stomach to her chest. Her left hand lay limp in Brad's.

"Wil! What's wrong?"

She made no reply, only dropped her right hand.

Brad swerved to the curb and threw the car into park.

"Wil!"

Reaching across, he shook her. Her terrified eyes latched on to him.

"Wil!"

He felt for her pulse in her neck. It was racing. What should he do? He should get her to the hospital. They would take care of her. Her pulse still raced, but erratically now. Her skin glazed over with cold sweat. Her belly felt rigid as stone.

"Willow!"

She exhaled a luminous white cloud. He shouldn't be able to see her breath in the warm car.

Ages later she dragged in a ragged lungful of air and shuddered. The shuddering overtook her and her entire body shook violently.

The next thing Brad knew, he was outside the car, yanking her door open. He unbuckled her and scooped her up with the idea of carrying her to the closest dorm for help. She bucked in his arms, gasping for breath.

"Down," she said.

"Down? Put you down?"

She nodded once, jerkily.

Not wanting to, Brad planted her on her bare feet in the snow, staying at the ready to steady her or pick her up again. His coat hung open on her tiny frame and snowflakes landed on her torso. They didn't melt.

Iron fear gripped Brad. Whatever terrible thing was happening to her, the hospital wouldn't help.

Brushing him off, Willow went to her hands and knees. She wretched and brought forth a semi-coagulated lump of luminescent green jelly. It lay steaming in the snow before losing its shape. Willow heaved again. Brad held her hair back, but she seemed to be done. Maybe now she would be okay. He tried to help her back to her feet, but she collapsed.

Panicking, Brad rolled her onto her back and bent to lift her when a pair of headlights pulled in behind the Lexus.

Thank god. Help.

He bent to Willow again. Her eyes rolled wildly, only occasionally meeting his.

"It's okay, Wil," he sobbed.

The good samaritan driver approached. Brad looked up. "Do you have a cell—"

Gale.

She threw herself at him, fists flying, and knocked him to the ground.

"Ruined everything!" she shrieked, pummeling him with surprising strength.

"Gale, stop!"

"He doesn't want me!" She punched him. "*She* doesn't want me!"

Brad tried to grab her hands and she screamed.

"You can't take her! I can't be alone!"

Brad levered her off of him and scrambled to his feet. He had to keep her away from Willow, but couldn't abandon Willow unconscious in the snow.

"My Grace doesn't want me!"

Gale lunged, but Brad sidestepped. She whirled, her green eyes as bright as the moon.

"Severin doesn't want me!"

Charging again, she slipped and landed hard on the pavement. Brad pounced and tried to pin her. An intolerable wailing came from her.

"Even B—" she choked and started over. "Even Bri—" A guttural, feral cry worked its way out of her like dull razors through burlap. "Brian!" she screamed in triumph. "Even Brian didn't want me!"

She threw Brad off and leapt to her feet. Blood trickled from her right nostril. She spat more blood into the snow, along with green static sparks.

She caught Brad in her electric gaze. A pool of green light formed at her feet and she sank to her knees, staring at him. The green energy climbed Gale in a web of miniature lightning. It collected around her head, and she thrust out both fists toward Brad. The power arced along her arms, laddering outward until it leapt from one hand to the other. She flared her nostrils and the writhing bolt lashed out.

"Mommy."

Willow's nearly inaudible plea saved Brad. Gale jerked away and the chartreuse bolt missed him by inches, raising every hair on his body. It arched and grounded itself at the edge of the parking lot, throwing up clods of frozen earth.

"Kelly." With greenish-white sparks dancing over the skin of her bare legs and through her elf locks of ashen hair, Gale rushed to where Willow lay. The streetlights turned her sweater a flat gray. Steam rose all around her as the snow melted without even touching her.

Brad swallowed a mouthful of metallic spit and rushed after Gale.

She would kill Willow.

Gale fell to her knees again, reaching for Willow. Before Brad could get to them, Willow lifted her hand and touched Gale.

"No!" Brad yelled.

Their fingers intertwined.

A blinding flare of phosphorescence rocked Brad. His vision swam with afterimages. When he could see again, Willow was clutching Gale's hand in both of hers. All the white-hot energy crackled along Gale's arm and into Willow.

Willow took a deep breath.

Brad stood in shock.

Gale stroked Willow's hair with her free hand. She looked up at Brad. "My baby needs me. Severin took too much of her. She needs me." She smiled down at Willow, stroking her hair and singing a lullaby.

Willow stared up at her mother, clutching her hand. A small smile lit her face.

Willow's hands dropped and she gave a small cry of surprise. Brad approached cautiously. Gale looked at him and her mouth moved, but no sound came. Her dress had become a gray smock.

She stood, sopping wet, and he saw that her abdomen was swollen in pregnancy like when he first saw her all those years ago in the woods. Smiling and cradling her stomach, she took a step backward and dissolved into the wind-driven snow.

Brad stared after her for a second, then looked down at Willow.

"The baby's coming," she said.

He kissed her forehead and lifted her into his arms.

"There's no time to get to the hospital," she said.

Brad placed her in the back seat of the car.

"I don't know what to do."

She laughed lightly. "I've got the hard part. All you need to do is be here."

"Always, Willow. Always."

*** *** ***

"It's a girl. She's a girl," Brad said.

"Is she okay?"

A tiny cry answered her question and Willow relaxed.

"She's beautiful," Brad said. He showed her their tiny daughter. "You'd better hold her," he said, handing her over. A perfect joy flooded through Willow. She cuddled the baby while Brad cleaned things up between her legs as best he could. The leather upholstery would never be the same. Climbing in with them, he shut the door to keep out the cold.

"I love you Willow."

"I love you too."

The baby looked out at them with smoky gray eyes, Brad's eyes. She was nearly bald.

"What's her name?" Brad asked, drying her with a black cashmere scarf.

Willow thought about that. A twelve-year pregnancy, and she hadn't thought of a name.

How zen.

She grinned. "Zen. Her name's Zen Tanner."

About the Author

Rune Skelley lives in a northeastern college town, and works as a web developer and small business owner. Two jobs, marriage, and raising two sons did not quite account for every waking moment, so Rune took up fiction writing to fill the hole where a social life should be.

Fun fact: Rune Skelley has 20 fingers and 20 toes, but doesn't type any faster than you do.

For a sneak peek at new novels, free stories, and other goodies, join the email list at: runeskelley.com/shrugging-lessons

Rune strives to set aside time every day to answer messages from readers. Say hey at heyrune@runeskelley.com

Free Short Story

Vesuvius Has Many Questions...

Being the only one who can hear him, Fin is his only source of answers.

Learn about a key event that bridges *Tenpenny Zen* and *Miss Brandymoon's Device*, in *Shrugging Lessons*, a story told from Vesuvius's point of view.

Available exclusively to my readers group, free for a limited time.

Sign up for the author's readers group and receive a free copy of the short story, *Shrugging Lessons*.

Visit runeskelley.com/shrugging-lessons

www.ingramcontent.com/pod-product-compliance
Lightning Source LLC
Chambersburg PA
CBHW072126250626
47159CB00007B/2582